NONE of US
the SAME

NONE of US the SAME

Book One of the
Sweet Wine of Youth Trilogy

Jeffrey K. Walker

Ballybur

This is a work of fiction. Names, characters, businesses, places, events and incidents are either the products of the author's imagination or used in a fictitious manner. Any resemblance to actual persons, living or dead, or actual events is purely coincidental.

Printed in the United States of America
First Printing, 2017

ISBN 978-1-947108-00-4

Published by Ballybur Publishing

Cover and book design © John H. Matthews
www.BookConnectors.com

Edited by Kathy A. Walker

Author photograph by Paul Harrison

Poem by Siegfried Sassoon and
cover photographs in public domain

For Kathy

The Bishop tells us: "When the boys come back
They will not be the same; for they'll have fought
In a just cause: they lead the last attack
On Anti-Christ; their comrade's blood has bought
New right to breed an honourable race.
They have challenged Death and dared him face to face."

"We're none of us the same!" the boys reply.
"For George lost both his legs; and Bill's stone blind;
Poor Jim's shot through the lungs and like to die;
And Bert's gone syphilitic: you'll not find
A chap who's served that hasn't found some change."
And the Bishop said; "The ways of God are strange!"

"They" by Siegfried Sassoon (1918)

CHAPTER ONE

Deirdre

The old one in the last bed had riled them again. One of the trainees, impossibly young in a stiff white pinafore, stood pleading and wide-eyed. "I can't bathe Mr. Duffy again, Sister! He...he... *touches* his...his...*nether parts* when he sees me comin' with the towel and basin," said the girl, struggling out her careful words in unconcealed mortification. Only the good Lord Himself knew what the Daughters of Charity would make of this poor girl's conundrum. But Deirdre Brannigan was a lay nurse, not that it eased the suffering of the trainee standing before her burning with embarrassment.

"Fetch a friend or two who can hold his arms while you bathe him. 'Tis hard enough keeping everyone and everything clean without your delicate sensibilities aggravating the situation," Deirdre said with mild scolding, calm in the fretting storm.

"I've... I've tried that," the trainee said, two others vouching the truth of her timid protest with vigorous nods. "His... *manhood* still becomes... quite... *tall*... anyways. And he likewise leers at me in a most distressin' manner." An unsettling murmur rippled across the clustered trainees, tinged with an edge of mutiny. Deirdre knew she must nip this.

"Ladies," she began with deliberate sternness, as if she were not just a few years clear of training herself, "let us be mindful this is a charity hospital with a mission to care for the least fortunate of our Lord's children with kindness and understanding." She sucked at her cheeks a little, checking a smile that rose from her unintentional imitation of Sister Mary Evangeline. Deirdre soldiered on, channeling the formidable matron. "If our Blessed Mother could bear the pain and sorrow of kneeling by the cross of her precious Son, I would hope and pray you can muster the strength to endure the sight of an addled old man's... *nether part*. Regardless of its height." She stared down each trainee, ending with the complainant, who burst into loud sobs.

"Bridget, you're made of sterner stuff. Dry your eyes and blow your nose now." She handed her an immaculate handkerchief, speaking quietly and taking the poor girl aside. "Come along. I'd a few tricks from the sisters when I was a trainee myself. I'll entrust them to you, for use with present and future Mr. Duffys." She turned and gave a backward nod and scowl, signaling the stricken girl should follow and stop her sniffling.

As the two women approached Mr. Duffy's bedside, he was gleaming with lurid anticipation. Running a purple tongue over cracked lips, he reached under the bedclothes and rubbed himself with surprising vigor given his decrepitude. Deirdre, terse and businesslike, pulled his arms over the blanket. "These will remain in plain sight, Mr. Duffy, or I'll have the porters bathe you with lye and the dandy brush from the horses." He fell into an offended silence, shocked by her unexpected bluntness.

After pulling the nightshirt over his head, Deirdre commenced bathing the spent old man, his mind half gone from decades of drink, running a soapy sponge over the yellowed skin of his sunken chest and spindle arms. She handed over the sponge to Bridget for washing his other side. Half done, they pulled the sheet back over his chest, then folded it back from his lower body, leaving him exposed upon the bed. A crooked grin crept across the old man's toothless gob, his withered penis rising from the greasy grey pubic hair. Bridget gave a short gasp and began a turn that Deirdre froze with an icy glance. Drawing a wooden tongue depressor from the pocket of her apron, Deirdre bent it back and thwacked the old man's withered scrotum.

"Aggghhh! Y'are a right demon bitch, y'are! Damn ya to hell, woman!" the old man yelped. He curled on his side, both arms shoved between his legs.

Deirdre turned to Bridget and said, clear and even, "You can finish bathing Mr. Duffy now. He'll be giving no more trouble this day." Not taking her eyes from the old man, she handed the tongue depressor with dignified ceremony to Bridget and said, "I recommend liberal use until such time as he learns to act proper at bath time."

Bridget would share her secret with the others before the hour was out, so Deirdre hoped. She walked back down the double line of beds filled by broken men with a litany of illnesses. Some would soon be back to their poverty and filth. Others would pass to their reward here—perhaps tonight, maybe in a week or a month.

As she reached the day room, the door flew open and trainees flushed out in their identical uniforms, like schoolgirls off to summer holiday. Deirdre halted one by the arm and asked, "What's all the caterwaulin' here? You'll disturb the patients with your silliness."

"'Tis war! Have you not heard, Sister? We're to fight the Germans!" The girl's eyes were wide and wild with anticipation of parades and dances and handsome young soldiers in fine uniforms. She knew the girl had every reason to be thrilled, young as she was. She released her, the girl scampering down the corridor to join with her friends in their jubilation.

In the now deserted room, Deirdre could hear the bells of Dublin—Catholic, Protestant, no matter—commencing to sound. First just the one, probably St. Patrick's, this side of the Liffey, a few blocks away. Then another, more distant than the first. Likely the Pro Cathedral off Sackville Street, the Catholics joining from the other side. Soon enough, every church in the city added its peal. Above the din, she could make out cheering, a crowd already gathering on St. Stephen's Green. Deirdre stared down from her window, scowling at the burgeoning celebration on the Green below. Speaking to no one, maybe everyone, she muttered into the antiseptic air, under the crescendo of bells.

"Those stupid, stupid old men. What have they gone and done to us now?"

Breakfast at the Brannigan's might be unpleasant to one not accustomed to the general raucousness of the household. The younger children, well into their school holiday, skittered about for diversion. Deirdre and her mother saw to the growling stomachs of Daniel and the second-born, Frank, who awaited another day at the brewery cooperage. Bacon and black pudding in the skillet, strong tea on the hob, and brown bread cooling from the oven provided the accompaniment to the chaos of this and every morning.

"You'll need to be quick about it," said Eda, sliding plates before the two men. "The trams aren't runnin', so you'll be walkin' to your work."

Daniel slid an arm about his wife's waist, landing his hand with a pat on her backside. Eda gave him a little slap and smile, then turned back to the stove. She set about making up smaller plates for herself, Deirdre and the children.

"You couldn't know that, Mam! You haven't left this kitchen since you woke," Deirdre said, shaking her head for the thousandth time.

"Mind your tongue, Deirdre, and don't be questionin' your mother's powers," said her father with the faintest smile, followed by an imperceptible wink. Dee replied in kind—no one else noticed—the exchange freighted with long usage between father and first-born.

"Holy Mother of God, no powers have I," said Eda, waving the back of her free hand at Daniel while she turned more rashers in the skillet. "*Ach* Deirdre, 'twas my mother, God rest her soul, had the true sight, not me."

Eda returned to the table with a huge pot of tea, refilling Daniel and Frank's mugs, both her strong hands needed to steady it. Daniel gave her another pat and received a second slap for his trouble. "Tis yer father with the powers, if any are to be had under this roof," Eda declared. "By all the Holy Saints I swear, each and every time he was about hangin' his trousers on a peg near the bed, one of ye popped out nine months later."

"Those be only powers the good Lord gives to any strappin' Dublin man," Daniel said with pantomime humility, another curl at the corner of his mouth and a tiny wink to Dee.

"Was there much talk of the war at the hospital, Dee?" Frank asked. "You'd think they'd be needing doctors and nurses and the like for the soldiers at the fighting."

Deirdre spun from the pantry cupboard where she'd been cutting thick slices of bread for the younger children. Brandishing the breadknife, she said to Frank, "Tis all the silly trainees could natter on about." Her knife flashed again. "And I'll not be hearing about the medical needs of those fools who take a soldier's coat to get themselves shot over Serbia. Of all the God-forsaken places on this green earth."

"What of Belgium?" Frank said. "Sure, if one small nation can be done over altogether without reply, what's to keep the Kaiser from marching through Dublin?"

"The Kaiser, you say? The King's wee cousin Willy?" Dee said with a taunt. "Why in the name of the Blessed Virgin should we give a fig about the King's family squabbles?" She turned with a dismissive wave at Frank.

Daniel listened without a word, but Eda's worried eyes caught his. He replied with a slight shake of his head to keep clear of this argument for now.

Wolfing the last of his breakfast, Frank said, "We best be on our way, Da, what with the walk ahead. 'Twouldn't do for the foreman to arrive late," Frank said with pretentious gravity.

"And an apprentice as well," Eda said with a raised brow and admonishing look. "Although that particular fact hasn't made it through your thick skull, *mo bhuchaill*, with the carousin' and the carryin' on 'til the pubs close of an evenin'."

With a half-hearted swat at Frank's gingery head that belied any genuine anger, Dee said, "Off with the both of you now. There's precious little time for your messing about this day." In a flurry of jackets and caps and children hugging legs, the two men, father and son, spilled out the door and into the morning hurly-burly of the Liberties. They called farewells to young Sean, already out on the street with his band of friends after nicking a bit of bacon and buttered bread from his mother's kitchen.

With the younger children quieted by mouthfuls of bread and jam, Dee and her mother sat together at the lovingly worn table, as they had done for as long as Dee could recall, even before moving to this house after Da was made foreman.

"Mam, why do you fill their heads," she motioned to the children, "with this Donegal nonsense about seeing the future and the like?"

Eda, her patient eyes full of love for her daughter, washed down a mouthful of bread and said, "There's no harm in't, sure? Just a bit of tradition from the old place. Your Da and me have got you and Frank and now the young ones as fine an education as the Christian Brothers and the Mercy Sisters can give." She patted Dee's hand and held it in her rougher palm. "That doesn't mean there aren't things above and below can't be explained in books."

"But how could you know the trams weren't running this mornin', Mam? The stop's more than three streets away," Dee said.

Eda wiped her hands in her apron and thought for a moment. "Listen close round you now," she said and took another slow drink of tea. The two sat in silence for a long minute, the children chewing their breakfast.

"I hear the callin' and shoutin' and cloppin' you'd expect of a Wednesday morn in the Liberties," Dee said.

"Do you then, *stóirín*? Do you indeed?" asked her mother with a wry smile just visible above the rim of her mug. "Now, tell me what *don't* you hear?"

"Jesus, Mary and Joseph, Mam! I *don't* hear a thousand things," Dee said in exasperation.

"Ahhh, now there's the thing, isn't it? What I don't hear are tram bells."

Dee listened for another moment or more. A broad admiring smile crept across her face. "I wouldn't have took notice in ten thousand years."

Eda studied Dee for a moment with an unspoken look of concern, reaching over to smooth back some of her daughter's unruly hair. "I'm not so sure of that, Deirdre. There may be more of your grandmam in you than you credit."

"Of that I have great doubt, Mam," Dee said with a short laugh. "I'm lucky to get through a day of disasters at St. Vincent's, let alone foresee anything."

"You've come along right quick with your nursin'. Haven't the Sisters already gave you that ward full o' poor souls, and supervising the young nurses to boot?" said Eda with unconcealed pride.

"I wouldn't put much stock in that, Mam," Dee said. "Most days I suspect their confessor made me the penance for all their sins." Eda shook her head with a soft laugh as Dee added, "Although 'tis not clear to me when the Daughters of Charity would have the chance for much grievous sinning."

"Now don't be takin' your fun at the expense of the nuns, Deirdre," Eda said. "I remember well that Sister Mary Evangeline herself came to see if you might have a vocation for the order."

Dee choked out an involuntary laugh. "Oh, that'd been a disastrous thing. Like visitin' the ten plagues of Egypt upon them all at once." Dee smiled across the table at her mother. "Nursing's a deep enough vocation. And I do have a bit of a way with it." She studied her mother's calm and content face, lined more by laughter than sadness. "But I'd not want to miss a life like you and Da have."

The two youngest Brannigans tried to scamper off. Dee caught them and wiped the red currant from their cheeks and fingers. She kissed each in turn, nodding them out the door to their play.

Eda sat gazing with the deepest affection, leavened by a little wonder, at her eldest daughter. "You've grown to a woman of great strength, Deirdre. That fills the heart of your father and me each and every day."

Dee broke away from her mother's intense look with an uncharacteristic blush. "I'm naught but what you and Da have made me, Mam. And I'll love and honour you both 'til the end of my days."

"That's all we'd ever ask or want," Eda said. She rose to clear the table. "You best be on your way to St. Vincent's. No telling what foolishness will be goin' on in the streets with all manner of eejits over the moon with this war."

CHAPTER TWO

Jack

27th day of July, 1914
201 Gower Street
St. John's

My Dearest Johnny,

I'm happy each and every summer to know I'll be putting a letter into the hand of our Jackie for him to take you personal. What a fine thing it was when first you asked me to send Jackie to you. He's come up a bit much in the City and a month at the light each summer has done him more good than you can know. Who'd have known when Jackie first came up to you, just he and Will, these seven year gone, that he'd finagle his whole band o' brigands into your laps, too? Geordie and Sandy are good and decent lads who've been loyal friends, in school and out, and like sons to me so underfoot they always be, especially when there's a meal to be had. And poor young Toby, with his father gone these 10 year now and just him and his ma! The boys took him in—such good hearts—when he grew so fast all the other younger lads made terrible sport of him. Will's a quiet and sometimes quare type, *but he's the one looked after poor Toby, timid as a hare, and brought him along to the Church Lads' Brigade and other such things.*

I hope the crate of provisions made it safe to Rosie, being as how those lads feed like a herd of caribou. There's some sweetmeats for your little ones. I also sent along a dozen or so books. The bookseller found a good Catullus with both the english and the latin and a few of Walter Scott for young Teddy. Rick sends along tobacco, some tins of virginia cavendish and one of something called perique he says comes from Lousiane and has a good spice to it.

I'll have to end now, as Jackie and the lads will be leaving for the quay soon and I want to put this in his hand before he goes. I often think on our younger days at the light and the long walks at the shore with scarce a word needed between us. Maybe 'twas right for our parents to send me away before you became over dear to me, my lovely Johnny. But you have my own boy with you now, and that'll be enough for me.

With all the love that's in my heart,
Your dearest sister, Viola

Squinting into the morning sun, Jack and Will studied the cove, hands close around their eyes. "I'll be damned. What's she doing there?" Jack said, breaking their puzzled silence. Will pursed his lips as he peered out at the iceberg. "Does seem odd for high summer. I'd call that well out of season."

Down the rough grass that ran away from the lighthouse door to the edge of the sea cliff, they could see Jack's uncle silhouetted against the blue-grey water, familiar from the smoke that wreathed his head. Uncle Johnny would have something to say about this. As they approached, the keeper said, loud enough to carry back on the wind, "What think ye that might signify, b'ys?" Jack had long marveled at the prodigious volume of smoke Uncle Johnny could produce from a single bowl of flake cut.

"Do you recall any bergs so late in summer, Mr. Barlow?"

Uncle Johnny put a hand to his yellowed horn pipe and thumbed the smooth bowl, the carving long worn away. He exhaled another great burst of blue smoke and said, "Not in my time, that's a certainty." Pointing seaward with his pipestem, he continued, "I recollect Jackie's granddad speaking o' such a berg arrivin' in August his first—may chance his second—year as keeper. That was before me or Jackie's ma was born. Makes it '61 or '62, if I cipher justly."

"What do you think brought this big one down so late, Uncle?"

"That nor'easter that started up late yestere'en. Must ha' blown her right down and grounded her inside the point. All the fog and mist these past days, we'd not ha' seen her approachin'. That's twenty fathom to the bottom, so she's a biggun right enough, me dear b'ys."

"Seemed just a freshening breeze at suppertime, Uncle. Must have picked up greatly then?"

"She blew hard all night. Stronger each time I was up the light to wind the weight. You bucks wouldn't have noticed, sleepin' like the dead."

Will let a half smile escape. "I never sleep better than at the light, Mr. Barlow. Even through Geordie's snoring."

"… and that could wake the dead in Labrador," Jack added.

"Ayeh, enjoy the untroubled dreams o' youth while you can. They'll flee betimes, young Will'am." Uncle Johnny gave Will a sharp pat on the shoulder, accompanied by a sigh that leaked around his pipe stem. The keeper, after so many summers, had near as much affection for Will as he did for his own nephew.

"We've rather invaded you over the years, haven't we?" Will said.

Uncle Johnny tapped his pipe against the heel of his palm, then blew out some lingering ash. "Bah, you lads—'specially you, Will— you've been dear to our Jackie since you was in short pants at school. 'Tis a joy to have the lot of youse. Does a mite of good for our young ones, too." He began refilling the pipe from a worn-shiny leather pouch drawn from his trouser pocket. "Can be a lonely life for children."

As is the way with bergs, the longer they studied her, the more personality she revealed. At first, she was a uniform blinding white. As the sun arced through the crystalline sky, she became every kind of white—and every shade of grey as well—belying her craggy surface. She was shot through with streaks of blue, one near her middle perpendicular to the sea. A fine-lined fissure near her waterline showed burnt red. Her top sloped left to right, bowing down to the sea.

"You manage to conjure a berg in August? Not sure that's a skill I'd brag along the quays back home."

They turned together to see Geordie's substantial bulk ambling down the slope, riffling his hair and stretching like a bear just woke from winter. Behind him straggled two more figures, striking in their differing proportions, pulling jumpers over their heads against the sea breeze that carried the last of the nor'easter's chill. One was of a very average height and build, but suffered by comparison to his very tall and rail-thin companion. The three late risers joined up at the cliff's edge, adding to the quantum of surprise at the appearance of the strange iceberg.

"We have to row out to her," said the average-sized Sandy with immediate resolve. "No one will believe it back home."

Uncle Johnny let out another great billow, and said, "That sea's still chopped from last night's blow, 'specially for our skiff. 'Twill be hard pullin' all the way out to the point and back."

"I've rowed dories in worse, Mr. Barlow. Don't mind about that," Geordie said with a swagger that had expanded, commensurate with the width of his shoulders, over these last few years.

"You've grown a mighty lad, that you have. My Rosie trembles at the thought o' feedin' you each summer you've come up with our Jackie," Uncle Johnny said, poking an elbow in Geordie's expansive rib cage. "But mind you now, have a good look but stay well back o' her. In summer heat and warm seas, she's like to founder any moment. And when she splits, she'll pull you right down and there'd be no savin' ye."

"Will there be room for everyone… in the skiff? It seems small for all of us," asked Toby in his quiet halting way, as incongruous with his notable height as it was appropriate to his younger years.

Will reached up to put a hand on his shoulder. "We've not grown that large yet. Besides, we can push you through an oarlock if you make a nuisance." Will gave him an affectionate smile which Toby returned with a crooked reddening grin.

"Pa! Pa! There's a coastal boat—I think the *Lizzy Lindsay*. She's showin' a signal." Following after the shout came the Barlow's eldest with an old brass and leather spyglass under his arm.

Intent as they were on the strange berg, no one had noticed a schooner, her sails well-filled by the steady breeze, nosing out from behind the point on her way down to Bonavista. Uncle Johnny trained his glass at the colored swatches spanking off a foremast halyard. He read out the characters in the array of flags.

"M-B-M, then O-M-K." He slapped the barrel of the glass against his palm once, twice as he puzzled over the message. "Not a usual signal. Teddy, run up to my office and look in the Lloyds book, would you, b'y?"

"Already done so, Pa. Copied it out here." Teddy took a crumpled paper from his pocket, advertisements on one side and the signal copied out in Teddy's careful printing in a little white space on the other.

"Clever lad. You'll make a fine keeper one day." Uncle Johnny hugged the blushing lad to his hip while he read out the message.

"Declaration of war. Germany."

The group of men gathered at the edge of the cliff on this fine summer morning stood gazing out to the east over the sea. Toward Europe, where the lights would soon be going out. Holding his son a little tighter to his side, the keeper drew on his pipe.

Prudy had made her way down to see what the excitement was about. She slipped her tiny hand into Jack's and he lifted her, light as could be, perching her in the crook of his elbow. She threw her arms around his neck and nuzzled into his chest, rubbing her wind-chapped cheek against his rough jumper. Her head emerged, flaxy strands of hair clinging to the knit, just long enough for a quick whisper before burrowing back into the scratchy wool.

"After we come back from the berg," Jack whispered back to her. At the news of this delay, she gave a tiny shrug into his sweater. Seeing her disappointment, Jack said, "What kind of tale shall it be then?" Prudy raised her head and peeped at the others with one cornflower eye, then buried her face back into Jack's arm.

"Shall it be of a princess? And… an evil sea serpent… who keeps her prisoner on his… lonely iceberg?" Jack improvised. This brought a vigorous nod of agreement from the tiny girl, accompanied by a most innocent smile, as well as bemused looks from the gathered friends. Jack bounced her once and said, "Now back to the house with you, my lovely maid, and we'll get underway when I'm back from the point."

She squeezed Jack's neck as hard as a three-year-old might and landed a firm kiss on his unshaven cheek. He lowered her to the ground and she gamboled away up the grass like a rag doll, all loose arms and legs.

"If you could beguile the females a bit north of six and south of sixty the way you do that sweet child, you might have more luck with the ladies of St. John's," Sandy said, shouldering Jack sidewise.

Jack, eyebrows up, said over his shoulder, "No use in that, Sandy. You've torn through most of 'em already."

"And with little regard for—ahem—quality, one might add," said Geordie in the languid tones of their old Latin master. Toby stood near Geordie in a crimson blush over this talk of women. As to what it might imply he was still somewhat unsure, being a full two years younger than the others.

"Easy on now, lad. Jealousy is unbecoming a man of your... *stature*," Sandy said, squaring his shoulders and spreading his elbows in imitation of Geordie's broad chest and big arms.

"I must agree with Sandy," Will said. "There's something to be said for *quantitas* over *qualitas*"—Sandy nodding smugly at Geordie—"at least with baitfish and squid."

With Jack and Geordie swallowing chuckles, Will paused and with a dramatic stroking of his chin added, "Come to think, perhaps that doesn't apply quite as well to the ladies. Unless of course you're the gallant *Alexander* Hiscock." Will tossed an ingenuous look to Sandy—who loathed being addressed by his proper first name— inviting a reply. Sandy worked his mouth, eyes darting from face to face, struggling for a retort. Outmatched whenever Will entered the fray, he feigned renewed interest in the iceberg as a form of honorable retreat.

The others erupted, Toby now adding in his nervous laughter. They had long ago granted mutual license to take the piss. Without realizing, this had contributed much to their self-assuredness, with the exception of the younger Toby. However, Will had assured them when taking Toby along to the Church Lads' Brigade that first time over four years ago that he'd grow in confidence to match his prodigious height.

"Gentlemen, enough diversion at poor Sandy's expense, deserved as it may be. We must to sea for an ogle of this unseasonable ice."

With that, Geordie hefted the oars anew and strode off at the double-march to the rough stairs cut into the contours of the sea cliff, leading down to the small jetty.

The deep blue-green water of the cove, cool to the skin even in August, lapped against the skiff until they cleared the jetty. From there, the hefty swells from the previous night's nor'easter rolled the boat almost to the gunwales. Yet even pulling against an incoming tide, Geordie made good headway to the iceberg and they could soon make out long plumes of melting water cascading down her side. Even at some distance, the smell coming off her was a cold and otherworldly breath, ancient and subterranean. Her fissures were now distinguishable, jagged bolts of cobalt disappearing under the water's surface. The sun had been hidden behind a bank of cotton-wool clouds sliding across the sky. As the skiff floated broadside to the berg, the clouds slipped onward and the sun radiated down bright and unfiltered. In the pure light, the iceberg began to shine with an iridescent turquoise all along her waterline, sitting atop a lustrous bed of bright green.

"She's a wonder," said Toby. "Look at her glow!"

Jack said, matter-of-fact as his own awe would allow, "That's the sun down through the water, reflecting off the white ice. The green seawater gives the color."

"Either that or the Lady of the Lake is about to give me a bloody great sword," said Sandy, intent on the berg like the rest.

They bobbed and rolled in the swells, held by the power of the phosphorescent berg, until another bank of clouds moved in and the icy corona faded. With a cleansing sigh to pull himself from his trance, Geordie stowed the oars along the gunwales. "Gentlemen, we've a war now." He looked with purpose from face to face. "The King will rally the Empire, including this fair Dominion of Newfoundland. How shall we answer, b'ys?"

Jack rubbed a hand across his mouth, turning this over in his thoughts. "We're small, just 200,000 souls. Can we even raise our own regiment?"

"We'll surely find out when we return to St. John's," said Will. "If the rest of the important men are like my father, they'll consider it a point of honour to send our own regiment. The *pater* has always been a stalwart King-and-Empire man, after all." Will paused at what he just said, pondered a moment with annoyed brows, then added, "And won't a war be good for business."

"No difference to me, I'm away regardless. Halifax or Montreal. I'll join a Canadian regiment, needs be," said Sandy. Looking unsmiling back to shore, he murmured, "I'll not miss the chance to get off this rock."

"For once, Alexander may be right. They'll need strapping young men like us," Geordie said, fingering the handle of an oar.

They sat in silence for a few minutes, each to his own, as they drifted shoreward with the incoming tide. The wind had swung around to south-southeast and the warmer breeze cleared off whatever chill remained. Imperceptibly, the south wind and the flowing tide combined to lift the iceberg from the sea floor.

Coming back into the conversation, something occurred to Jack. "Will, you've done a year at Dalhousie and are due back soon. Wouldn't they make an officer of you?"

Will turned seaward, drawing the sharp saltiness deep into his lungs while mulling Jack's question. A random splash slapped his arms and chest, snapping him back. "I suppose you're right," he said. Taking another long breath to clear his thoughts, a puckish smile emerged. "But wouldn't I have to *want* to be an officer?"

"Enlist as a private soldier? Like the rest of us have no choice but to do?" asked Sandy with equal amusement and incredulity.

"I suppose that's exactly what I mean," said Will. "I don't have any military experience, outside the bits of riflery and first aid we had in the Church Lads' Brigade. Besides, it'll be over in a few months and I'd miss the whole show in some officer training course."

Geordie gave a great clap and rubbed his big hands in unabashed glee. "Ho-ho, won't the *paterfamilias* howl, my sweet William! I should very much like to be a fly on the wall when you tell him."

"You'd be quite a fly, Geordie. A horse-stinger at least," said Jack. "But you're getting well ahead of us. We've none of us, save Sandy, even agreed we'd enlist."

"Well, I'll have to look after you miscreants. Like as not get yourselves killed without me," Geordie said with nonchalant finality. "So that makes two. And now you, Naught-Lieutenant William Parsons?"

"A matter of honour, of that I'm sure," Will replied. "So yes, I suppose you can count me in."

"And me as well," Toby declared, adding more meekly, "if they'll overlook my age."

"Why Master Tobias Halfpenny, I expected no less from such an upstanding—and I daresay *upright*—young Newfoundlander," Geordie said, triggering another deep blush. "You're a credit to your father's memory," he added with more sincerity. This elicited a halting smile, a bit sad at the corners, from Toby.

Will caught Jack's uneasy wandering eyes. "That leaves you the last man standing, Jack. Or rather sitting, this being a smallish boat. What say you?"

Jack was uneasy with the cascading rush of the conversation. He was desperate to speak with Uncle Johnny. "I'm not altogether sure you aren't the finest gathering of damned fools I've ever seen, but if you four are determined to take the King's shilling, then I suppose…"

He was cut off by a deep rumble and crack. They spun as one toward the point, surprised by the much larger gap between the berg and the shoreline now. They sat suspended as the great massif split along its downward-running blue fissure, the smaller side sliding away into the sea. Freed of this enormous weight, the remaining section rolled around an axis well below the waterline. They watched the slow rotation as the larger berg capsized itself, replacing its sloping top with jagged double peaks, shedding water and sandy slurry from the sea floor. A second later, the sound of crashing surf surrounded them, followed by a fetid burst of wind that smelled of the grave. The surge from the foundering slammed the skiff and pushed it up and sideways. The friends grabbed at arms and legs and clothing, keeping all aboard. Geordie lunged to retrieve a dislodged oar from the water. As the boat settled, they all faced Jack.

"Seems I don't have much choice, b'ys. All for one and God help us," Jack said with forced bravado.

"That's my good lad, Jackie! And should we meet our final morn, we shall forever live in glorious memory," said Geordie, throwing his head back with a wide smile and unaffected laugh. "What was it the Romans said, Will, about dying for the *patria*? You were the only one awake in old Barnsley's class."

"*Dulce et decorum est pro patria more*," Will said, reciting with the diction of the Latin prize winner he had been not so very long ago.

Geordie began his strong and steady stroke, hauling them shoreward. "That's it"— *stroke*—"Sweet and becoming"—*stroke*—"to die for one's country."

All the young Barlows gathered around the bench under the gable in their big shared bedroom—save for Prudy, who perched on his lap— as Jack meandered his way through another tale. Uncle Johnny had come to hear from his office down the hall where he had been polishing chimneys for the light's six lamps. Occasional squeaks from his rag on the red chimney's glass punctuated the story as the keeper leaned against the doorframe of his children's room.

"Just as Paddy the little fisher thought he'd never see his family again, the wise old salmon he'd freed from his net just the day before leapt out of the water and pointed his way home through the terrible fog with his shimmerin' flipper..."

The sweet bite of Johnny's pipe filled the room, the afternoon sunlight falling in rays along the floor, refracted through the smoke. Johnny studied his nephew as Jack enthralled the children scattered around the floor. His young cousins adored his stories and started in asking as soon as the weather broke in May when Jack would return with a fresh trove for them. Truth be told, Rosie and Johnny enjoyed listening near as much as the young ones.

"Did he become King of the Fishers and marry a princess?" Prudy asked, her voice small as a cricket's.

"I hear tell he did, my sweet little maid. But that might just be a story for another day," said Jack, dodging promises since they were departing tomorrow.

"Jackie, can you lend me a hand in the office?" asked Uncle Johnny, with a look that carried more meaning than his words. "I've any number of chimneys to polish."

"Of course, Uncle," Jack said, giving Prudy a squeeze before sending her out the door and down the stairs after the rest. Uncle Johnny's office was at the top of the stairs on the second floor. The house was built right around the base of the whitewashed stone tower, plastered walls within and thick pit-sawn weatherboards without. The office was above the assistant keeper's room where the friends always slept in a jumble on the bed and the floor. There had been no assistant as far back as Jack could recall.

A white-painted cabinet with pigeon holes for the light's signal flags, the edges of slots for the more useful ones worn to bare wood, sat under the window. The large *Lloyd's Signal Book* lay atop the cabinet. A gouged and dented mahogany desk with the weather log sat just beside. The other walls were lined to the ceiling with overflowing bookshelves.

Johnny handed his nephew a rag and they took turns dabbing into a small wooden pail filled with jeweler's rouge in the middle of the table. The fine red powder polished soot from the chimneys without scratching the glass. They sat working in silence for some time, the only sound their soft rubbing and squeaks as the glass came clean. Finally, after a luxuriant puff on his pipe, Uncle Johnny spoke. "Jackie, I know you to be a young man of good sense and not inclined to rashness." Jack saw no need for a reply, so polished on in silence with a slight nod. "I've also seen o'er these past six or seven years how fierce loyal you are to your mates."

"And they to me, Uncle," Jack interjected.

"Ehya, to be sure, b'y. 'Tis sure, that," said Uncle Johnny. He rubbed and smoked for a few moments, pausing to choose his words with care. "I wonder if you've pondered all the import of what you've decided, regardin' this war."

"I've given it some mighty thought," said Jack, "and it seems there's no escaping that it's a matter of duty." He stared for a moment into the crimson-stained rag in his hand, then reached for another chimney.

"True, Jackie, all true. But none of you've seen what war looks like, I mean lookin' it in the face. There's a pernicious kind of evil comes with war," Uncle Johnny said, the words darkening his face. He stopped and studied his pipe for a moment.

"Ma said you saw some fighting in China, during your time in the Navy?" Jack watched his uncle's face move through a jumble of expressions, some he had never seen before.

"In my time before the mast, I saw the viciousness Christian men can bring upon others, enough to know I wanted no more part and came home to this light. And that was only a short fight against simple heathens with old weapons." Uncle Johnny's eyes followed his thoughts out the window. "There's precious little glory comes from war, far as I'd know, Jackie," Uncle Johnny said with a slow shake of his head. "Precious little."

"Surely this is different, Uncle?"

"There's always some will find words to make their choice a righteous one. And 'tis certain some German lad and his uncle are havin' this self-same conversation, sure as we're sitting here." They both paused to dip into the pail for more rouge. This uneasiness between them was something new and disturbing. Giving out a long sigh, Johnny said, "But I expect it's ever been so, that young men will go off to seek the bubble reputation." He placed his rag in the pail, relit his pipe, and gazed out over the sea again, lost in his own reverie.

Jack rose without a word and made his way down the stairs, passing Aunt Rosie peeling potatoes in the kitchen. Just then, the red door flew open and in ran two of the young Barlows, with Geordie, growling like a giant, in pursuit. Rosie gave a start, jumping in her seat. She placed a hand over her thumping heart and shouted, smiling, "Outside with the lot of youse, and shut that door!"

"I hear and obey, my Lady Rosamund," Geordie said with utmost gallantry as he scooped a small Barlow under each arm and shifted them out the door. Jack trailed along behind, into the warm summer afternoon.

As Geordie strode out with the two youngsters slung like sacks of meal across each hip, Sandy called from his sunny seat next to the door, "You might want to loosen your grip, Geordie. Young Samuel there is looking a bit blue in the face." Rolling his giggling bundles onto the grass, Geordie turned back to join Sandy and Jack on the bench, just as Will and Toby emerged from the door, too. They leaned against the warmed clapboards of the house as Jack rose and rounded to address them.

"We're off tomorrow, lads, so there's only one thing left for us here," Jack said. The others squinted back with clueless expressions. Jack motioned to the bog meadow stretching behind the lighthouse all the way to the tree line half a mile landward. It was the source of every manner of berries for Aunt Rosie's jams and pies, a different variety each fortnight right through the summer.

Geordie groaned and slid to a slouch, "No, Jackie, not that blasted juniper again."

"Aye, to the juniper. We've not ended a summer here without a footrace to the old tree in the bog," Jack said, heading off around the lighthouse. "Hurry on now!"

The others followed with little enthusiasm, jogging to catch up. "You don't think we're a bit old for this now?" said Will in his reasonable voice, always maddening to Jack on occasions like this.

"Not a whit, Will," Jack said, keeping up his stride.

"You always win," Sandy said, resigned to the race and his loss.

"Exactly why we'll never be too old," said Jack.

They stood along the edge of the bog, studying the lone gnarled tree standing at the center. The old tamarack leaned at an impossible angle away from the prevailing sou'westers. The four hundred yards to the tree were thick with hummocks of grass and small pools of clear peat-filtered water that reflected back snatches of sky and clouds.

"Ready, b'ys?" Jack said, eyeing down the line with competitive zeal. The others gathered themselves, rising to his challenge as any adolescents just crossed into manhood would, of course, do.

"Right," Jack said, lowering himself to a half-crouch. "We're away, lads!"

19th of August 1914

My dearest Vi,

I finish this letter early Sunday morning, awake between windings, when there's quiet time to think on matters. So between the jigs and the reels, I should be able to finish this for Jackie to put into your hand. The lads depart this morning, if the supply boat arrives as we expect. 'Tis a sorrow to see the boys' visit cut short, so much excitement they bring to the house. Our little Prudence is bursting into sobs at the thought of losing her cousin Jackie early. But a day is a year and a week is forever to a child like her. We fear she's been burnt to a scrunchion by all Jackie's attention and there'll be no living with her over the weeks ahead.

As you've heard by now, the boys are determined to enlist together and join in this war. Or should we be calling them men, by rights? It's a wonder how fast time has passed, grown as they are. Yet in some ways they're too green to burn, in particular poor young Toby. That sweet boy may be a long one but he's so thin you could shoot a gull through him. And so meek I swear he's aft times afraid of his own shadow. Sure, Sandy sees the five of them knocking round in strange lands and Geordie is so filled to the gills with King and Empire he's like to burst if he doesn't get a uniform on him. And good luck to His Majesty feeding that lad. He's not finished with one meal than he's on the baker's list again, ready for the next. Like the others, Jackie's set his mind on joining the fight, although I allow his heart mightn't be following close to his words. But he'd not dream of deserting his mates in such a circumstance. Of course, with Will going, there'd be no holding him back. Young Will can be deep as running water, no more so than now. I haven't puzzled out his thoughts, him being so accustomed to keeping his own counsel, save with our Jackie. He seems to have a mixed catch of reasons, but I'd wager his father's shadow falls over all of them. You'd know the better, since you took work at his family's premises these twenty-five years gone, back before you met your Rick.

I've no desire to worry you, Vi, but I sense the lads may be sailing too close to the wind in their haste to join up. What's to come when these big armies take the field against each other? Young men would seem weak things in the face of that. Pray God I'm wrong and it'll all be over in a few months. Well, let's you and me just hope all our darling boys will come home safe and sound when this foolishness is done. Maybe they'll come to the lighthouse again and we can hear their great tales of glory.

I thank you for the parcel of books. You know well how much they mean to me and what good they'll do the children. I fear I'd be lost had I not the fine library Pa began and, with your help, I've continued. Give my thanks to your Rick as well, and my affection to all your fine children.

> *With all my love to you, dearest Vi,*
> *Johnny*

CHAPTER THREE

Deirdre

The layered smells of oak wood—dry oak, sawn oak, wet oak, burnt oak—cloyed at her throat and stomach. She remembered how he brought this smell home in his hair and clothes, of how she had once made finger rings from the curly wood shavings that fell to the floor when he reached into his pockets.

Da must have a head near thick as an oak, right enough, she thought.

The young apprentice knew to a certainty the woman in the dark blue nurse's cloak standing in the entryway was not to be denied. He hurried off to fetch his foreman. Dee carefully banked her anger, ready to blow it to full flame as soon as her father made his way to the entrance of the cooperage. She saw him emerge from the shadows with the rattled apprentice walking sideways beside him, gesturing at her. When Daniel recognized her silhouette against the bright opening of the entry doors, he smiled and called out, "My darlin' daughter Deirdre! What brings you down here?" Daniel removed his cap and wiped his sweaty brow with a pale blue kerchief.

"Don't you 'darlin' daughter' me, Daniel Brannigan, you stupid ox of a man!" Dee threw his words back with more venom than the apprentice could imagine directing at a foreman. He couldn't think of anyone more important, not that he'd ever met, except maybe the pastor.

"Are you dotty? Or have you taken to the drink in your declinin' years?" Her anger blazed higher with each word she spat at him.

"Deirdre Ann Brannigan, you'll not address me so in my place of work," her father scolded, casting a quick side glance at the apprentice. Seeing that she was gathering herself for a renewed burst, he signaled with a terse jerk of his head to the young man to clear away to his duties. Daniel's expression softened with the apprentice's exit, never able to keep his anger going with his first born. "Now, calm yourself and tell me what's got you blowin' a gale," Daniel said, leading her toward a bench near the open doors.

"How could you do it?" she asked, swallowing a sob and squinting through burgeoning tears. "Frank joining up is nightmare enough. I'd expect that from a headstrong fool like him."

A rush of understanding burned red over Daniel's face, the lines of his forehead and around his mouth etching deeper. "So word's out then," he said, studying a calloused palm.

She sprang to her feet, rage flaring again, and shoved hard against her father's broad chest. "But why in the name of Patrick and Brigid and Columcille would you let yourself be dragged back in as well?" Even her prodigious will could no longer stanch the sobs. She collapsed to the bench, shoulders heaving. He handed her his kerchief, awkward in his embarrassment. Daniel blew out a long and pained sigh, turning half away from his daughter. A flicker ran through his thoughts. Just a quick image of a much smaller Dee, standing before a window in their tiny old flat, face contorted as she fought back tears over one of a thousand childish hurts, determined not to cry. *So much and so little changes*, he thought.

"I'd hoped to tell you myself tonight, when we were all round the table," Daniel said as he turned back to Dee. As ever when he witnessed her cry, darts of pain shot through him.

"Mam sent Molly to the hospital to fetch me home. And didn't Sister Mary Evangeline have a fit of apoplexy at me leaving the ward midday and all. Imagine Mam being so beside herself that she sent poor Molly," Deirdre said, calming her gasps, wiping once again at her nose. "The child must have been terrified every step o' the way." Dee then looked her father square in the eyes, her piercing stare dripping with accusation. "Bridie Fallon from up the street told Mam the awful truth. Her Brian had been down to the recruiting himself and the sergeant was wooing all the excitable fools there by droppin' your name as a new sergeant-major, just signed up," she said. "And with your own son, too."

Daniel went ashen, imagining the hurt he had caused his Eda. He would carry the burden of this particular stumble for many a year to come, that was as certain as the sunrise.

Dee pinched up her face as she felt hot tears again. "Mam was sitting at the table, rocking herself like 'twere a death in the family." She wiped the back of a hand against her cheek, concealing her deep emotion at the thought of her mother. "You'll have much to answer for this dark day, Daniel Brannigan. And for many a day hereafter," said Dee, doling out the penance to her miserable father.

They sat motionless as if frozen in amber, the bright daylight spilling through the entry, cleaving the deep shadows inside the corridor. The red brick walls breathed out a musty, turned-earth damp that chilled them both, though the day was fine. Dee's face played in and out of the shadows as she turned her head, bent, wiped, blew. Finally, after an eternity of silence had passed between them, Daniel slid toward her, his supplicant hands spread wide. They were both stripped bare, each hung to their own cross.

"Deirdre, there's such a great need of men… and they're raisin' so many new battalions here and everywhere," Daniel said, slow and quiet. "There's nowheres near enough sergeants to train and look after the young ones joining up in their thousands, including your brother and his mates."

Daniel sat next to her with surprising lightness for so solid a man carrying such a heavy burden. He took her hand in his much larger one, strong and hard from so many years of staves and hoops and mallets. They sat like that, Dee sobbing and sniffling, softer than before, at the thought of her mother.

He spoke again, a bit steadier. "I left my old regiment a lance corporal after South Africa, when you were just a wee girl. I never thought that would amount to much," he said with a forced smile. "It seems good enough to make me a company sergeant-major in this time of dire necessity."

"A far sight older sergeant-major as well," she added. "And I was just big enough to remember how hard 'twas on Mammy, with me and

Frankie to care for without you." Daniel studied his hands while she reminded him of the struggles he had left for Eda with the young ones.

"And you were wounded, weren't you?" Dee felt herself winding up again, so she calmed her voice with a great effort. "I remember you coming home leaning on a cane."

"Aye, that I was, but others had it worse," Daniel said, his thoughts running back to hard days long ago. He ran his tongue across his upper lip, the thirst and dust of the veldt still a phantom burning. He sat up taller, a newfound resolve stiffening his back. "But what's done is done. I've given my word to the commander of the new battalion," Daniel said, then let slide an impish look to Dee. "But I pressed him for one condition."

Dee pulled the kerchief back from her father's hand, wiping her eyes and nose again. "It better be a powerful important condition," she said with an indignant sniff.

"'Tis indeed," Daniel said. "He promised me your brother and his reckless friends will be assigned to my company." Dee sat up and faced him now. "So I might just be able to keep them clear of o'er much foolhardiness," Daniel said, convincing himself with as little success as he had his daughter.

Headquarters Royal Dublin Fusiliers
Naas, County Kildare

Ref: Urgent Need for Noncommissioned Officers   28th August, 1914

Dear L/Cpl Brannigan,

As you must be aware, your country faces the gravest peril at this time. In response to His Majesty calling all able-bodied loyal men to the colours, our Regiment is forming up several new battalions to join the fighting in France and Belgium. It is with humble pride that I have accepted command of one of these newly-formed battalions. Although hundreds of stalwart volunteers have come forward to enlist, we face a critical need for mature men of military experience to serve as noncommissioned officers, for our immediate training needs, as well as to accompany these selfsame troops to the field. This need is particularly acute, as the 1st Battalion will not return from Madras until early winter.

I well recall the steadfastness you exhibited under fire, even after receiving wounds, as a soldier of my company in the vicious fighting at Pieters Hill, during the relief of Ladysmith. We share memories both bitter and sweet, of the honour with which we acquitted ourselves that day and of the comrades who now sleep beneath the African dust. I am confident we can rely upon your same steadfastness in this current hour of need. I have been informed that your son, Francis, has enlisted in the battalion. Surely there is the greatest honour to be found in serving together, father and son, for King and Empire?

It is within my authority as Officer Commanding to offer you immediate appointment to the rank of Company Sergeant-Major when you consent to joining the new battalion, as I am confident you will. Please confirm soonest, either in person or by return evening post, your decision again to render service to your country and your King.

> *I remain, sir,*
> *Proudly your past and future comrade in arms,*
> *Arthur G. Lawless, Lieut.-Col.*

Eda wiped the sideboard for the third or the thirtieth time, avoiding discussion of the upcoming departures. "Mam, you'll rub the shellac right off if you don't settle yourself," Dee finally said, exasperated with the unceasing motion.

"Don't be visitin' your own sour disposition upon your mother, Deirdre," said Daniel, baiting her into conversing with him.

"Oh, to be sure, *Sergeant-Major* Brannigan! Don't let my sourness interfere with your inhaling that great pile o' rashers on your plate. You'd think the two of you were off for a day of the football at Croke Park, not to kill or be killed by Germans."

Eda returned to her wiping, all the harder from Dee's words. Not interrupting her polishing, she said to her husband, "Mind the clock. Your train might well leave early today."

"There's time yet, *stóirín,*" Daniel said. What little of the Irish he knew, he had from Eda. He seldom spoke a word of it within the children's hearing.

"We're doing our duty as all men of this land must and should do, sister," Frank said with all the condescending certainty of a recent convert. "And if we're to have the Home Rule, we need to show we're worthy of it."

"Oh, that small nations might be free, is't?" Dee said, mocking her brother's superciliousness. "'Tis just a squabble between the King and his naughty cousin." Frank reeled under his sister's terrible glare and turned his attention back to his food. "And you'll pay a terrible price for this King's folly, mark my words, Francis Brannigan."

Daniel rose as his oldest children squabbled, walking over to his wife. Turning her by the shoulders from her fervent polishing, he wrapped her in his arms. After a few slow and deep breaths freighted with unspoken feeling, he pulled back, looking down at her with pained tenderness. "I thought we'd not face these sorrows again, my sweet wife," he said to Eda, the back of his big hand gentle against her cheek. "The world's a cruel and unfair place, more often than not."

"Aye, husband, 'tis often cruel indeed." Eda sniffed against his woolen uniform, then lifted her head and smoothed the khaki worsted. Daniel kissed her on each cheek. Eda closed her eyes, not able to bear the sight of him so close. Daniel separated from his wife with great care, then moved with tentative steps toward his daughter.

"The young ones are outside at play. I told them to stay close so they can give their farewells as you leave," Eda said to her husband and son, sniffing against the back of her hand. Frank rose from the table and snatched his peaked hat from a peg by the door. He hugged his mother, who kissed his cheek and smoothed his unruly ruddy hair.

"Mind your father and your officers, Francis. And come home to me safe and sound, *mo bhuachaillín daor,*" Eda said with a shaky smile as she stroked the rougher sleeves of her son's soldier's tunic, looking him up and down a last time, pressing his image into her mind's eye like a summertime flower within an old book.

Daniel drew near his seething daughter. "I hope you'll see a way past the hurt, Deirdre." She scowled at him in reply. "You're our first born and so very dear to me." She looked away to the window, trying to block the sound of his voice from her mind. "I have such hopes that once we've seen this through, I'll see you settled and happy with a good man, bouncing your own first born on me rickety old knee." Daniel placed his arm around her shoulders and gave her a little smile with the secret wink they had shared for years.

Nothing was surer to reignite her anger. She shoved the arm away, his hand smacking against the window frame. "Don't be giving me all this soft-soap, talking of grandchildren and the like. You'll not get round me with your sentimentality." Through her rage, Dee could see nothing of her mother's horrified face. Nor of her brother standing at the door, gaping at her tirade. Certainly not her father, shrinking inside his new khaki as his heart broke beneath the shiny brass buttons.

"'Tis your choice to shatter this family, your choice entirely," she hissed at him between her teeth. "I'll never forgive you for this, no matter what you conjure to say on your way out the door." She pointed a finger close to her father's nose and shouted, "Shame on you and your foolishness! Shame!"

Daniel's legs weakened under the weight of her bitter accusations. Without words that could have any meaning now, he turned to the door, shoulders sloped, and slid from sight into the bright morning light. The excited shouting of the children bidding their father and brother goodbye failed to penetrate the gloomy pall filling the room. After the latch clicked as loud as she'd ever heard and her husband of twenty years and more disappeared from the home they had made together, Eda walked toward Deirdre with small, pained steps. She searched her daughter's face for a familiar look, some recognition of the child she had carried. Dee spun away from her mother's confused stare as Eda choked on fresh tears.

"*Ach, mo chailín*! My own dear girl!" Eda gasped through her sobs. "Since the day you first drew breath, that man has loved you more than was good for him. And surely more than you now deserve!" Eda grabbed Dee by both shoulders and gave her a tiny shake. She had strength for no more. "I'll pray to the Blessed Virgin you don't live to regret those bitter words of partin' you just visited upon your own father's head, Deirdre Ann Brannigan."

Dee pulled away and pounded up the stairs, ending the wretched scene with the slam of a door.

CHAPTER FOUR

Will

"The station master tells me there's a public meeting starting within the hour, so let's make haste, my hardy lads," Geordie said with a broad grin, excitement radiating from every inch of him.

"Where's the meeting to be then?" asked Will, lifting his knapsack from the train platform.

"The Church Lads' Armoury. I suggest we make our way toward the Cathedral, so we can stow our kit at Jack's house on Gower or Will's up Garrison Hill. We don't want to be carrying all this into a crowded meeting."

"Best stop at Jack's," Will said without explanation.

When they arrived at the Oakley's house, Jack set his satchel on the stoop and burst in through the door. He was greeted by shouts and a clamor of small feet, his youngest siblings running to him with ecstatic faces. With widespread arms, they engulfed his legs and waist. Behind the vanguard of smaller Oakley's, Viola strode down the hallway in her white apron, without which the others would hardly recognize her, pushing away flyaway hairs with the back of her hand as she grinned up at her eldest.

"You're more'n a week early, darlin' Jackie! We've just finished supper but I can find something for you b'ys in the larder," Viola said, kissing Jack and then smiling with a word of genuine pleasure to each of the others in turn.

"No time for that, Ma. We're just about dropping our bags, then we're off to the big meeting at the Armoury."

Viola's smile never wavered, but her eyes flashed concern as she said, "Of course, of course that's where you should be headed. Like the rest of the young bucks." She shooed the children out of the hall. "Just drop everything in the parlor and you can sort it after you come back," she said, leading the way to the front room.

"Ma, here's Uncle Johnny's letter," Jack said as he fished it from inside his coat. Viola squeezed it to her breast, then caught herself and hid it away in a pocket of her apron. Jack kissed his mother's greying hair and said, "We're off now, Ma. No tellin' when we'll be back, so don't fuss over anything to eat for us." With a chorus of goodbyes, the five were gone again, down the street and trotting up the hill toward the Armoury.

The meeting passed in a blur, tired as they were from their travels. The assembly hall was overflowing and stifling hot from the packed bodies and steaming emotions. The raucous cheers and shouted affirmations made it impossible to hear the speakers most of the time. As the crowd rose and sat, waved and clapped, Will caught a few glimpses of his father among the distinguished gentlemen of the stage party. Finally, an announcement was made that enlistments would be open after the meeting. With "God Save the King" and "Rule Britannia," the meeting collapsed under its own jingoistic weight, the great crowd spilling back onto Harvey Street and flowing downhill to awaiting pubs.

Men gathered at the entrance to the Armoury, perhaps two hundred, awaiting the reopening of the doors. A few were weaving their way to the front of the fluid queue, determined to have their names first on the regimental roll. Jack and Will stood together in the milling crowd, near their friends but a little apart, able to track the others' whereabouts by the guidon of Toby's tousled brown hair floating above the boaters and caps of the crowd. They noticed around them familiar faces of old friends from school and mates from the CLB. Others they knew from their neighborhoods or from sports days with the Methodist Guards, the Catholic Cadets, and the Presbyterian Highlanders.

They exchanged hellos and handshakes. Short conversations echoed the platitudes just heard from the stage, garnished with a bellicose bravado more strongly proclaimed than deeply felt. The heady mix of excitement and anxiety, in near equal measure, was thick and palpable. The long wait to reach the recruiting table added a dash of petulance to the mix. Thus was the great balloon of excitement deflated, giving the volunteers their first exposure to the tedious routines of military life. By the time Jack and Will, the last of the friends, had answered the recruiter's questions and signed their names to the roll, it was late summer twilight. The five regathered in front of the Armoury, exhausted by their long day of train travel and ricocheting emotions.

"*Alea iacta est*, brave legionnaires! The die is cast! Let us cross the Rubicon and find some blessed supper," Geordie said, patting his stomach with both hands. "I may be forced to eat the next passing nag otherwise."

"In the interest of sparing the horses, I wager Ma has something on the stove or in the larder," Jack said. Geordie, long a devotee of Viola Oakley's kitchen, brightened and led them away.

Will turned up Garrison Hill, as the bells tolled ten o'clock. From the Oakley's, it was a short walk to his family's house, dominating the street in its looming Queen Anne splendor. He could see it on the corner, white clapboards fading to a bluish grey in the growing darkness. The lights in the front parlor still burned bright, strange for this late hour. As he reached the short flight of stairs running up to the entry, the door opened and a sudden racket—all basses and baritones—rolled down to the pavement.

"We'll gather again at Davis's offices tomorrow at ten," Walter Parsons said in a voice accustomed to being heeded. "We've much to do, gentlemen, and in precious short time."

As the half-dozen men, some more familiar to Will than others, stepped off the stairs, they greeted him by name with hearty handshakes. Most had been on the platform at the meeting. "Quite a momentous day… makes all of us proud… young men from good families… put us on the map of the Empire…" Will murmured pleasantries in reply, none of the older men's words distinct or memorable.

"Ah, an early return. Well you should have, William," Walter boomed out, disregarding the sleeping neighborhood. "Your mother was anxious the Germans would shell the lighthouses, though God knows what gave her such an idea. Women get so blasted emotional at the mention of war. We must get accustomed to it, I suppose."

Will shifted the rucksack on his shoulder and lifted his small valise from the sidewalk. "We heard of the declaration by signal from a passing coastal ship, but had to wait until the Lighthouse Service boat came," Will said by way of both explanation and apology.

"Those lighthouse keepers live like Eskimos. Half their lives in the middle of nowhere with no company but their own dull thoughts," Walter said with undisguised distaste. "Do a great service when some canny Scotchman devises a machine to replace them all."

"The Barlows were as gracious as ever, Father, and Jack's Uncle Johnny did all he could to speed us on our way. The supply ship arrived on schedule but was running north. The nearest train depot was Lewisporte."

"God, what a jumbled mess—north to get south," Walter said, his scorn for the outports manifest. The Parsons were not so many generations removed from hauling cod themselves, not that Will had the temerity to point this out to his father. "Well, get yourself inside. We've important matters to discuss, you and I." Walter turned back into the house, certain of his son following. Will hefted his bags and trudged up the steps, watching his father disappear down the hall into his library.

As he set his load next to the hatstand, Will's mother appeared from the parlor, giving quiet directions to the maid, an exhausted and desultory young Ulster girl who was carrying a large tray of half-smoked cigars, empty brandy glasses, and a few sandwich corners— the remains of the still unexplained gathering of men.

"William darling, such a welcome surprise. When did you depart the lighthouse?" his mother asked, her preternatural calm unwavering as always.

"Three days ago, Mother," Will said, kissing her offered cheek. "We slept rough a few nights on the deck of the Lighthouse Service steamer, but managed to clean ourselves up a bit on the train," Will said, trying to smooth the indelible wrinkles from his sleeves. "We were sorry to cut short our visit, but given the circumstances..." he trailed off, stating what he believed to be the obvious.

"I was worried to death for your safety, William, and am utterly relieved you are home," his mother said with her usual detached tone, undermining the professed intensity of her anxieties.

"William, I need you here! You may get mollycoddling from your mother later!" his father bawled through the open doors of the library.

Will kissed his mother's cheek again and motioned down the hall with his eyes. "Better see what the *pater* is about."

"Good night, William. We can speak again after breakfast," said his mother, turning to float up the stairs, not a hair out of place, after what had turned into a rather long day.

Will made his way down the hall, a reflexive knot growing in his stomach as it had since boyhood. He slid the library doors closed behind him and settled into the chair to which his father had motioned him. Walter Parsons sat in all his imperium behind a large and heavily carved mahogany desk, contemplating the evening's final brandy in his right hand. He did not offer his son a drink. Will glanced around the familiar room, all leather spines and wood panels and brass fittings, a vague nautical air reflecting the source of the family's prosperity.

"My boy, that group of distinguished gentlemen is the Executive Committee of the Patriotic Association," Walter said, "appointed by the Governor to ensure the efficient raising and support of the Newfoundland Regiment for the duration of hostilities." Taking a long sip, he added off-handedly, "Not that the fighting will last long."

Will was unsurprised. St. John's was stuffed to the gills with fraternal organizations, paramilitary groups like the CLB, businessmen's associations, *ad hoc* committees of all colors and stripes, boosting the town and its trade. His father was involved in each, it often seemed, except the Catholic and Methodist ones.

"Yes, I know about the Regiment. We went directly to the Armoury from the station, as soon as we heard of the public meeting," said Will.

Walter was surprised. "Strange I didn't see you there. I was among the stage party," he said. "Why didn't you greet me after?"

"We arrived late and the crowd was so dense, you'd departed before I could make my way to the front," Will said, choosing a small lie to avoid a lecture on filial duty and whatever else Walter's irritation might light upon.

"No matter, no matter. You're here now and we have an important matter to discuss," Walter said, pushing the conversation along. "You will of course not be returning to Dalhousie next term."

A statement not a question, Will nodded his agreement and said, "I should think few will."

"Yes, one would hope. Indeed," said Walter, raising his eyebrows in disapproval of any unnamed students who might shirk their duty at this time of peril to the Empire. "You of course will join the Regiment," Walter continued without looking at Will. "Your year at university will overcome any objection to your age in receiving a commission. That and my position on the Executive Committee and place in the community." Walter rose and walked to the window and took a slow draught of brandy, well satisfied with the events of the day. "The Regiment will need steady young gentlemen as officers. Certainly if they're to lead some of the rabble we're likely to get from the outports, even from Labrador. Although the fighting should be finished before many of them slouch their way to St. John's."

Will steeled himself at this opening and said, "That's just it, Father, about the fighting being over quickly."

Walter turned and looked at Will. "What about it?"

"With Jack and Geordie and the others, we discussed the war and joining up, either here or with the Canadians, after we heard of the declaration," Will said, gathering momentum if little confidence. "We came to the same conclusion about the war being over quickly and don't want to miss out."

"You had substantial leisure to jaw over the matter," Walter said, suspicious of where Will was leading the conversation.

"Yes, we did," Will said. With an awkward attempt at casualness, he added, "And we decided to enlist together." Will's artifice of nonchalance was met with a thunderous silence while Walter stared at his son trying to make sense of what he was saying. Will continued, "After all, if I were to accept a commission, I'd likely not finish officer's training before the whole thing was settled."

Then the penny dropped. Walter's face went crimson as he stormed about the library, spilling his brandy on carpet, couch, desktop. "Do you sit here and tell me you intend to enlist in the Newfoundland Regiment as a *private soldier?*" Walter's chest heaved with angry exhalations. "Our only chance... my only son... a *private soldier?*"

Walter drilled an angry stare deep into his son. Will shifted with horrible discomfort in his chair, creaking the leather beneath him. There was no turning back. "Actually father, we already did enlist, the five of us, tonight after the meeting." His feigned easiness was betrayed by beads of sweat forming at his temples.

"Then you will withdraw your enlistment tomorrow, as early as possible!" Walter thundered across the room at his son, the denseness of the laden bookshelves absorbing his voice, giving it an uncomfortable intimacy. "Do you understand me, William? You will not humiliate me and stain this family's reputation with such abominable foolishness." Walter gave full head to his anger now. "Do you not comprehend how hard your grandfather and great-grandfather... and of course myself... struggled to make this a respected, prosperous family? One that is welcomed into the best homes, here and in England? What would your mother's family think, the daughter of a Church of England bishop, for God's sake?" Walter looked daggers at his son as he bellowed, "Are you completely mad, boy?"

This was the moment Will had known for the last three days was inevitable. As nausea pulsed through him, he feared he would vomit. Studying the arabesques in the silk carpet under his feet, his father's angry respirations shrieked in his ears. Jolts of fear ran down both legs, as he lifted his eyes to his father's purple face.

"I gave my word as a gentleman to my oldest and dearest friends," Will said in a shaky but regular cadence. "I will not break my word, as no gentleman would countenance for a moment," he said, not averting his gaze, fearing even to blink. There was an unnatural stillness in the tense room.

His father looked away first.

Walter barged to the window, glaring into the clear summer night. It seemed to Will the silence would last until dawn. Finally, Walter spoke without turning, calm, but in a voice as cold and dead as the air off the curious iceberg they had seen at the lighthouse a few days before. "You're quite correct, William, that a gentleman honours his word, even if that word is… intemperately given," intoned Walter. "However, you will have nothing from me. Not a word of support. No intercession on your behalf. Not a penny."

"You wish to play soldier with your friends, then live like a soldier. Including on a soldier's pay," Walter said, spitting the last words. He heaved a great sigh of dramatic resignation and drained what little was left in his glass before continuing. "I know it would be a fool's errand to keep your sisters or your mother, who has always been too sentimental where you're concerned, from communicating with you," Walter said without emotion, as if reading from a warehouse inventory. "But you will hear nothing from me after you leave this house and join the ranks. Do you understand now that there are consequences to your little gentleman's agreement?"

"Yes, Father," Will replied, wrung out by this horrible scene and the long eventful day.

"Now leave this room. I shall not see you again before you depart for training, which should be within the fortnight."

"And I suggest you find temporary lodging with one of your comrades," said Walter with gratuitous pettiness. "I'll not have you under my roof in these humiliating circumstances."

7 Garrison Hill
Early Wednesday morning

My dearest William,

I leave this note on your bed, knowing your father would be distressed if he knew I had written so soon after the unpleasantness *he endured last night. And I shan't see you today before you depart, since your father has forbidden even the servants from intercourse with you. I am confident this will not last, but best to honour his wishes for now. I could not let you go without a word from your loving mother however.*

William, you have all my heart and I fear I have little else to give. I shall pray for you every evening and morning, which is a gift my purse can sustain and is more precious than gold. May God protect you, as I know He will, in this righteous struggle.

I am told it is likely the Regiment will be posted to England for training. It would be best that you not visit my family there. I am sure your father will soften toward you, but until that time, I think it best not to involve your uncles and aunts in what is a matter best kept to us. Should circumstances change, I shall write to arrange a visit, your military obligations permitting. Are private soldiers allowed leave, I wonder?

Your friends have long been of utmost importance to you. Perhaps had I been able to give you a brother, you might have needed them a little less. Maybe it was never a good idea to allow you to accompany Jack to the lighthouse. Had you been here, you could not have made such a rash promise.

William, you will always be my precious boy. I shall fear for your safety every moment until you return to us. Your sisters, especially Augusta, are beside themselves with grief over this horrid rupture with your father and your imminent departure for foreign fields. We shall keep you close in our hearts until your return.

Your most loving and devoted,
Mother

CHAPTER FIVE

Deirdre

Dublin had fallen into an anxious routine in the eight months since the war began. There were plenty of Irishmen fighting and dying in France and Belgium over towns no one knew existed a year ago. The Munster Fusiliers and the Irish Guards had suffered huge losses early on and a battalion of the Dublin Fusiliers was dug into the sucking mud of Ypres. Now everyone was on tenterhooks for news of the landings in the Dardanelles, of which the Brannigans, father and son, were taking part with their battalion of the Dubs.

Deirdre continued her routine at St. Vincent's, although the group of trainees she had supervised in August was nearly gone, picked over by the military nursing services and the Volunteer Aid Detachments the Red Cross was recruiting. The absence of her father and brother left a gaping hole at home, mealtimes in particular. Her relationship with her mother had changed from the day the men left and Dee knew it was her fault. They were cordial enough, she and her mother, but Eda concentrated on the younger children. The easy laughter between mother and daughter had ceased. Most days, Dee ached from the quiet. She had regretted the ugly parting with her father from almost the moment he left, but could still not bring herself to write him. Foolish pride, she knew. She missed him desperately.

A novice nun, so fresh at the hospital Dee could not recall her name, moved down the ward, feet invisible beneath her long white habit. "Sister Mary Evangeline wishes to speak with you, Sister Brannigan. In her office."

"Please tell her I'll be down as soon as I finish with Mr. Corcoran." Dee turned back to changing a dressing on a septic leg sore. After finishing with the patient, Dee made her way to the broad staircase that consumed half the second floor landing and took the two flights to the Matron's Office with brisk steps. She touched the door a few times with her knuckles, pushing it open after a quiet "Come" from the nun within.

Sister Mary Evangeline sat at the desk in her sparse office from which she had administered St. Vincent's Hospital for over a decade. She had accepted Deirdre as a trainee at the age of sixteen, upon the unanimous recommendation of her teachers at the Mercy Sisters' school. Although Deirdre was a handful in her early days, full of stubbornness and overconfidence, the matron had never regretted this decision.

"Deirdre, please come with me," said Sister Mary Evangeline, rising from her desk. "Your mother is here to see you."

Her mother had never visited her at the hospital before. "That's a curious thing, Sister. I hope the young ones are alright."

"The youngsters are fine," she said, offering nothing more. "I asked Sister Louise to take your mother to my private rooms." They walked together through the courtyard, over to the convent wing. Sister Mary Evangeline's rooms were near the entrance. The nun eased open the door onto her sitting room. Eda sat in an armchair before the window that framed a dappled backdrop of lush foliage pocked with pink blossoms. She was sobbing against the waist of the young nun standing beside her.

Heart in her throat, Dee ran to her mother and dropped to her knees on the floor. She grabbed her mother's forearms. "Mam, what grieves you so?" she said, knowing what was to come. The only question was which one.

"*Ach*, Holy Mother of God, Deirdre! What're we to do? What now?" her mother shrieked, rocking back and forth. Sister Louise's lips moved in silent prayer beside her. Dee felt Sister Mary Evangeline's hands, light on her shoulders.

"Mam, is it Frank? What's happened to Frank?" Dee pleaded in her inexcusable desire to offer up her brother rather than the unthinkable alternative.

"'Tis your dear father! Your only father!" wailed Eda, dissolving into a flood of sobbing grief. "*Sé do bheatha, a Mhuire, tá an Tiarna leat…*" Eda gasped out her prayer to the Virgin as she clung with whitening knuckles to the rosary in her right hand.

Dee saw the crumpled paper clutched tight in her mother's left hand, the unmistakable pale yellow of a Post Office telegram. At the sight of it, any guttering hope of a mistake was snuffed. Dee collapsed onto the floor at Sister Mary Evangeline's feet, her mouth gaping in a silent wail. Her eyes darted about, wild and unfocused, arms flailing to find purchase on something, anything. She grabbed the nun's ankles through her habit, hugging them tight to her shoulder, as scalding tears flowed into the spotless white fabric.

"*Anois agus ar uair ár mbáis…*" Dee heard her mother's prayers waft away, soft and distant.

POST OFFICE TELEGRAPHS

Office: Dublin Main
Rec'd: 14th May, 1915

Office of Origin and   WAR OFFICE LONDON
Service Instructions: Handed to: addressee

TO: Brannigan, Ethna Mrs., in New Row, Dublin

Deeply regret to inform you that Sergeant-Major Daniel Brannigan, Royal Dublin Fusiliers, was killed in action on 26th April. Lord Kitchener expresses his sympathy.

Secretary, War Office

CHAPTER SIX

Jack

Undeterred by the coal fire stoked day and night, the dampness crept in through the thick stone walls of their barracks. The rain and fog came steady and unrelenting, like the Scots themselves. Will (Parsons, No. 274) entered the guard room. The others huddled around a battered wood table playing bored hands of cards.

"Smells like a schooner belowdecks in here," he said, shrugging off his great coat and removing his cap. The guard room bottled all the smells of camp life, a blend of fried bully beef, musty wool, and unwashed men, with occasional whiffs of brass and boot polish. Not that polishing anything was much use in the unending mud and muck of the Scottish Borders.

Jack (Oakley, No. 273) looked up from his cards. "My granddad's schooner smelled like spring flowers belowdecks, William." Sandy (Hiscock, No. 271) stood from his seat at the table and wandered about the room, halting with a poker before the fire. For diversion, he stirred the coals and tossed on a few more. He stood back from the grate and smoothed his uniform, having found a fastidious appearance made quite an impression upon the local lasses.

Will put a muddy foot up on a bench, unwinding a puttee from his calf. "I'm soaked to the bone just walking to the command hut," he said, hanging the drenched legging toward the fire, then starting on the second. Someone of importance back home had decided they would eschew the khaki puttees worn by the Brits and Canadians, opting for a distinguishing dark blue. Heckling from the Tommies began as soon as they stepped ashore and they had thereafter adopted the standard issue in short order. Months later, the taunt followed them still. They would remain 'Blue Puttees' for the duration, no doubt. There would be worse nicknames yet to come, soldiers being soldiers.

"So Toby's due with the new draft, eh?" Sandy asked the room.

"Yes, his name's on the movement order," Will said.

Geordie chuckled at the mention of Toby. "He was so worried about his tender age, then they struck him for his weight. Guess they'll grant you a few extra years in exchange for surplus height, but begrudge you a few pounds."

"A few pounds? He was thin as a rasher in the wind," said Jack. "No doctor with a conscience would've let him pass. He was a sight out of his shirt."

Will joined Jack at the table and said, "But between his mother's fishcakes and the sports master's kettle weights…"

"…Our brisk sodger laddie returns to the bosom o' the Regiment." Sandy had also found it useful with the ladies to affect a Scottish accent, as required.

A door opened and slammed in the main barracks room, followed by a flurry of footfalls. One of the platoon ducked his head in the guard room and hissed, "You better get yourselves on parade, b'ys. The new sergeant-major's here." The men threw on their tunics, rushing into the barracks where the others had already fallen into line. A slender-built man in a well-tailored uniform, steaming like a dreadnought, was scrutinizing each man from head to toe. His sleeves were lined above with sergeant-major's rank and below with service stripes. He had yet to speak a word.

The sergeant-major moved down the line of men, then did a facing turn in front of Geordie. For the first time since entering, he spoke.

"Your tunic is not buttoned," he said, low and calm. "I would recommend you do so now, soldier." Geordie looked down and saw he had missed a button in his haste and fumbled at them with his big hands.

"What is your name?" said the placid sergeant-major.

"King, No. 272."

The sergeant-major raised an eyebrow with mild surprise. "There are other Kings in this very company, are there not?"

"Yes, Sergeant-Major, three more."

"Four Kings altogether then?" He surveyed Geordie through deep-hooded eyes, dead as a salmon's, then continued in a quiet voice that dripped menace. "Three Kings were sufficient for our Lord Jesus Christ." He studied the floor, feigning deep thought. "Why am I blessed with such a surfeit of Kings, soldier?" Geordie's eyebrows knitted. The sergeant-major noticed. He was noticing everything.

"How am I to tell you apart, me not being the divine fucking Saviour of the world?" the sergeant-major inquired, calm as you please. "What's your first name, you great pile of shite, King, No. 272?"

"George, Sergeant-Major. George King."

"Why there are other George Kings in this battalion, I believe," said the sergeant-major, all treacle and cream again.

"Yes, Sergeant-Major," Geordie said, letting out his breath with the greatest care. "Funny thing is there are three George Kings in the battalion," he added with a tentative smile.

"Are you grinning at my consternation, King-fucking-272?" the sergeant-major said, screwing up his face. "As you're the only one I've encountered thus far, would it not be simpler for me to call you King-comma-George-comma-the-First?" he asked in quartermaster's English. A slight titter ran along the rank, but not a sound from Geordie. "Any objection to that, King fucking George the First?"

"No, Sergeant-Major," Geordie said, his voice raspy with nervousness.

The sergeant-major stepped back, still looking gimlet-eyed at Geordie. "Not that it should matter to an ignorant shite like you or your simpleton mates gathered here round, but my name is Sergeant-Major Pilmore."

He moved on to Sandy, next in the rank. Not finding fault with Sandy's immaculate uniform, Pilmore glared at him. "What pray tell would be your name then, soldier? And by Christ's fucking wounds, it better not be King."

"Hiscock, Sergeant-Major Pilmore, No. 271."

"Did you say His-Cock, soldier?" said Pilmore with bluff astonishment. "His-Cock?"

"Yes, Sergeant-Major."

"Do you not have a cock of your own?"

Sandy answered without hesitation, "Yes, Sergeant-Major, I have a cock."

"But you said it was *his* cock," said Pilmore, motioning with his head at Geordie. "So do you have his cock or your cock?"

"My cock, Sergeant-Major, mine and mine alone," said Sandy with gusto.

"Shouldn't your name by My-Cock then? What are you doing with His-Cock?" He nodded again at Geordie. "You're not a buggerer are you, what with all these other men's cocks?"

"That's my family name, Sergeant-Major. 'Twas my father's and my grandfather's before me," said Sandy with unaffected brio.

"All those His-Cocks then? So you come from a long line of sodomites? It's a wonder you've reproduced at all, what with all that buggery in the family."

"No buggery, Sergeant-Major Pilmore. It's our name," said Sandy, not at all perturbed.

"Then best I call you My-Cock, No. 271. Is that agreeable to you, since you claim to have only a cock of your own?"

"Yes, Sergeant-Major, anything for the good of the company. My-Cock it is," said Sandy with enthusiasm.

"I do appreciate a soldier who's so bloody agreeable, My-Cock. I don't trust a soldier with opinions."

Moving on to Will, Sergeant-Major Pilmore pulled a melodramatic look of surprise at his missing puttees. "Do you object to our standard puttees, soldier? I'm told you New-Found-Landers are particularly fond of blue ones." He paused and stepped forward, nose to nose with Will. "And what might your name be, bare shanks?"

"Parsons, Lance Corporal, No. 274, Sergeant-Major."

"So a monarch, a buggerer, and now a churchman?" said Pilmore with affected amusement. "What have they done to my beloved Royal Army?" Squaring up again to Will, the sergeant-major continued. "I'm the son of a parson myself, of the nonconformist Methodist variety. Do you have Methodists in that heathen wilderness you've abandoned? In your New-Found-Land?"

"Yes, Sergeant-Major, quite a few."

"Well, not to put too fine a point on it, I hate fucking Methodists. I am the youngest of eleven Methodist children of a bloody Methodist preacher. And each of them is now a Methodist preacher or the wife of a bloody Methodist preacher, getting routinely shagged in a good Methodist manner so they can keep dropping proper fucking Methodists out of their cunnies."

Will stood rigid with fear, staring a hole through the opposite wall.

"As a young man of little thought and prodigious appetites, I put a half-Methodist in the belly of our papist Irish chambermaid and was sent to wander the wilderness for my sins by my goddamned Methodist parents. Which is why I took the Queen's shilling these twenty-five years past and found a fucking fine home in the Army of Her Royal Highness, Victoria Regina, of blessed memory."

Pilmore moved on to Jack. "Which is how I ended up before this shimmering pile of sheep shite in glen-bugger-all Scotland, of all the barbarous places in this shite-eating veil of tears."

"Now what might your name be, son?" Pilmore asked Jack, in full confidence the soldier before him was cowed by all that had gone before.

"Oakley, No. 273, Sergeant-Major," he said, returning Pilmore's unblinking glare in kind.

Sergeant-Major Pilmore stood for a long while, staring him down. Jack neither flinched nor averted his eyes. With all the others near soiling themselves with fear, Pilmore leaned in and murmured so only Jack could hear, "You think you're not afraid of me. I can see that, son."

Jack held the sergeant-major's withering gaze.

"Nor anyone or anything," said Pilmore. "I've known your kind. They end up dead, the only question being how many they take with them." With a last lingering look, he added, "And that we shall determine apace, Oakley, No. 273."

The sergeant-major stepped back to the center of the room with sharp heel-clicking strides and addressed all the men again. "Am I misguided in assuming you shite-headed colonials are full of wonder as to why you've been blessed with a fine free-born Englishman as your new company sergeant-major?" During the rhetorical pause, he glanced along the rank of men.

"It seems the War Office has determined you aboriginals from the ragged edge of His Majesty's Empire are in need of some English stiffening to raise you from the wretched lot I see before me. And it is my singular fucking misfortune to be the beneficiary of Lord Kitchener's cock-eyed idea you might somehow be kept from besmirching the honour of the Royal Army." Sergeant-Major Pilmore took a few strides to his left for effect, then returned to the center of the line before continuing. "You fancy yourselves bloody brave heroes with icy water in your veins? Well, we're about to see how true that might be, my gallants."

Switching to a voice brisk with efficiency, the sergeant-major barked, "All ranks are restricted to post, pending movement. As soon as the new drafts arrive, it's off to Egypt for training. Then on to Gallipoli to join the 29th Division." Sergeant-Major Pilmore paused to savor the line of startled faces, then turned to Will. "Corporal Parsons, I expect you to instill some order in this rabble or I'll have those stripes for my fucking garters."

The sergeant-major then said with a satisfied smile, "We'll see who has the brass of a real soldier when you face Johnny Turk, who is mightily enjoying his heathen self shooting the bullocks off your fellow colonials from the underside of the world. And the fucking Irish, too."

CHAPTER SEVEN

Deirdre

As she pushed through the front door into the sitting room, she could make out Frank in the dim light of a small sideboard lamp. He was sitting alone at the old family table with an uncorked bottle and a single glass. The sharp smell of whisky wicked from the bottle into the room, wrinkling Deirdre's nose as it reached her. "So this is how you intend to spend your pension, Francis? While Mam tries to make ends meet with my pay and her widow's benefit, now that the parcels from the brewery have stopped." She swung the dark blue cloak from off her shoulders, shaking off a little misty rain before hanging it on a peg by the door.

Frank looked up at her with glassy eyes. He motioned for her to sit with him. "Bring a glass, Deirdre. We can toast the memory of our dear departed father, just the two of us here together." She wished she could be more angry, but the pitiful look of him and the sharp pang from the mention of their father cut off any sterner rebuke. She unpinned her white veil, extracted a few more pins from underneath, then ran weary fingers through her tumbling auburn hair. The deep mossy green of her eyes—her father's eyes, not the brown of her mother's—flashed at Frank in the weak lamplight as she turned back to the table.

Although she enjoyed the odd glass of cider, she was not fond of spirits. Nevertheless, she poured a small dram and slid onto the bench next to her brother. She raised her glass to him and said, "*Sláinte.*" They sat in silence, neither wishing to stir up trouble with an untoward word. There had been enough of those the last few weeks. She could see through the gloomy shadows Frank's artificial leg propped against the wall behind him.

"Do you miss him?" he said, in a husky whisper.

"Every moment of every day." They both drank their whiskies—Dee in sips, Frank in gulps—and returned to their prior silence.

"You didn't part well, that's certain," Frank said, uneasy with the prolonged quiet.

"That I surely did not." She took a longer swallow.

Eda padded down the stairs, surprised to see Dee sitting with Frank. "I didn't hear you come in the door, Deirdre. I was just putting the young ones to bed." Eda sat in her chair at the end of the table. "They've had trouble with their sleepin'." Brother and sister knew their mother would never touch strong drink, so neither offered. Eda reached down into her sewing basket and fished out some mending she had left off while seeing the children to bed. She began her small and certain stitches again, comforted by the familiar repetition.

Deirdre sighed and leaned back from the table, signaling the start of some new business, and turned to her brother. "Francis, you've been home a few weeks and I haven't yet had the nerve to bring this up. I've had a letter from Lieutenant Colonel Lawless, one he'd written just days after Da was lost." She smoothed her nurse's apron to calm herself before she could go on. "No telling how wild a route brought it here. I've read it out to Mam already." Eda looked up at her name and nodded in confirmation. "But we'd both like to hear what you know about Da's death, too."

Frank downed the remaining whisky and poured another generous portion. He took a long drink, then twiddled the glass in his hand while he spoke. "I saw him go down. Our company was split between two boats and I was in the other," Frank said, his mind detached a little from where he now sat. "I tried to get to him soon as we beached, but most of us were hit when the Turks laid a shell just landward. Jaysus, near everyone got it that day."

"Could he have been saved, do you think? I mean, had he gotten to a hospital ship?"

"The medical boat was lost a hundred yards from shore. Took a near direct hit. The surgeon and stretcher bearers never made it ashore. I mightn't have lost the leg had I not been left on the beach half the night."

Eda looked to her son, yet more tears in her eyes. "Did the men love your father, like the colonel said in his fine letter, Francis?"

Frank's heart was like to break from the hopefulness in her voice. "He was loved more than you could imagine. The men would've followed him to the fiery gates o' hell, Mam."

"*Ach,* isn't that a fine thing now, Deirdre?" Dee nodded and wiped a single tear from her own cheek. "'Tis a comfort for me to hear it from your own lips, Francis."

"Da was a grand fella, Mam. All the men were the better for knowin' him. We all grieved his loss." He drained his whisky in one and stared at the empty bottom of the glass.

"At least them that weren't killed by the Turks or the disease."

Sister Mary Evangeline sat at her desk without interrupting. After Dee had talked herself out, the nun spoke in a calming voice. "Deirdre, it's understandable you carry such guilt after your father's death. You admit yourself that you wronged him at your parting. It would be a daughter with a heart of stone not to feel the sharpest pangs of guilt under these circumstances."

"I've given myself more penance than any priest would, Sister, of that you can be sure." She was young enough still to have not lost all her freckles and they stood out stark against her reddening nose and cheeks as she spoke. The nun examined Deirdre with care. She saw signs of the burden the young nurse was carrying—the darkness under her eyes, the hair losing its luster, the boniness in her hands. She had seen these in others and knew Deirdre had a difficult way ahead. Many never found it, with drink their only relief. She would assist as she was able, but this was a road Deirdre must travel in her own way.

"My daughter, God has already forgiven you, whether you can reconcile yourself to that or not." Dee found the matron's steady voice so very reassuring. Likewise, she was comforted by the familiarity of St. Vincent's, as much her home these last five years as her parents' house. The rhythms of each work day, the piquant clean smell waiting just behind the front doors, the smooth finish of clean bedsheets under her palm—she had grown from girl to woman here.

"I don't know if I'll ever forgive myself, not all together," said Dee, chewing her lower lip to keep herself composed before the matron. She was wrung out of tears after so many months but the nun could see her agony plain as day.

"Then you must find your own way to self-forgiveness. From the weight of this burden you have placed upon yourself, Deirdre, it will require some great recompense." The matron's steady gaze urged her to continue.

"I've racked my brain many a night, Sister. Many more than 'twas good for me, sure. Since my brother Francis returned a few weeks past, I believe it's become plain." Since she had not yet said the words aloud, not even to her mother, she hesitated. Sister Mary Evangeline smiled to assure her this was a safe place to speak such weighty thoughts. Dee felt the breath go out of her as her chest constricted with affection for this fine woman who had chosen such a life of denial.

"'Tis no secret to you nor anyone how I feel about this awful war." The matron gave a knowing nod. "It took my Da entire and my brother by pieces. But my father chose to fight and I called down such horrible wrath upon him for that choice." Her voice caught and she swallowed hard before continuing. "He died with none to help him, at least none who might have saved him." Sister Mary Evangeline could see Deirdre was about to make a fateful leap, her calm turning to sadness, but she did not interrupt.

"I can't do a thing about my Da but there are others in their tens of thousands who made the same choice," she said with finality, "and I'll do what I'm able to save a few."

The nun closed her eyes and sat in quiet thought over the acute sense of loss she felt in letting this particular young woman go. So many others had left for the war already but there was something different about Deirdre. To be sure, she was bold and stubborn and held some not-quite Catholic opinions. Along with that baggage, however, she possessed a true intuition for healing that Sister Mary Evangeline had seldom seen in four decades of nursing. The matron herself lacked it, she knew, and had sought forgiveness from her confessor for occasional pangs of jealousy in this regard.

"We have good relations with all the nursing services, as you know. Although my heart aches with the thought of your leaving us, Deirdre, I will do what I can to see you brought into service as quickly as possible."

"Thank you, Sister, for this and all your kindnesses," Dee said, her eyes shining with affection for the matron.

"I shall pray for you daily, Deirdre, and ask Our Lady to preserve you through this purgatory you have set before yourself." With the tenderest pity, Sister Mary Evangeline added, "And I shall also pray that this war will be penance enough for you."

CHAPTER EIGHT

Will

Sergeant-Major Pilmore was everywhere. The soldiers of his company began to believe he had a twin in the battalion. Surely he must never sleep or eat or shave or shite. He was on one of his ceaseless strolls along their company's section of trench when Sandy spotted him rounding the traverse. "Good morning, Sergeant-Major," Sandy chirped. For reasons known to him alone, Sandy was ever pleased to see Sergeant-Major Pilmore, always greeting him with a most hearty welcome and sincere smile. The others were less pleased.

Pilmore stopped to observe the small knot of men, stripped to the waist and dripping sweat in the oppressive dust. Tomorrow they were just as likely to be slogging through sticky mud after another drenching rain. They were filling and stacking sandbags to repair the parapet and fire step in this section, shelled by the Turks the night before. Jack and Will stood to acknowledge the sergeant-major's presence with nods, while Toby continued shoveling loose dirt and small stones into a burlap sack.

"Tuppence! Stop your digging for a moment, would you? You're not a goddamned mole," Pilmore said in his characteristic even tone. This never varied, even at his most blasphemous. It was unnerving to all, with the notable exception of Sandy Hiscock.

"Tuppence!"

Will nudged Toby with the handle of his entrenching tool. Sergeant-Major Pilmore, in his peculiar way, had determined that anyone as tall as Toby could not be a mere Halfpenny. After weighing several denominations of coin—a shilling, half a crown—he had settled on two pennies. Hence, Tuppence, No. 842. Lost in his faraway thoughts of cleaner and cooler places, Toby startled, then snapped to his full lean height. "Yes, Sergeant-Major!" he said, eyes wide with surprise and trepidation. He was still unaccustomed to his new surname.

"Pack up your kit, my lucky little sausage, and report to battalion headquarters post haste," the sergeant-major said. "You're detailed to messenger duty until further notice." Pilmore and Sandy exchanged the smallest glance, passing without notice by the others.

Toby paused, mouth agape, but abandoned questioning the order in the face of Pilmore's steely stare. He pulled his grey flannel shirt over his angular shoulders and edged past the others to the dugout they shared when forward. He glanced back, still too cowed to speak, holding up a hand in meek farewell.

"Get along with yourself, Tuppence, *imshi*," the sergeant-major said, pushing along with his hands. "You're a man of leisure now, so don't strain my philanthropic impulse or you'll be liming shite-houses until we depart this heathen hell," said Pilmore, sounding as if he were ordering a half-pint of shandy. As Toby trotted down the trench, disappearing behind the angled traverse, the sergeant-major turned to Sandy with an annoyed stare. "And it is my fondest wish, My-Cock, not to see your vacant rictus anywhere near my dugout again." With that, he motioned to the others to carry on.

While hefting a sandbag to the top of the parapet, Sandy said, "Sergeant-Major, if you don't mind my asking, what news have you of King, No. 272?"

Pilmore raised a bushy eyebrow and sighed with showy petulance. "Perhaps it would be an efficient use of manpower, My-Cock you scion of buggery, if we appointed you battalion intelligence officer? Might that satisfy your endless curiosity about all the comings and goings of this bloody battalion of cod haulers?"

Sandy said with undisturbed ingenuousness, "No thank you, Sergeant-Major. I don't believe I'd be qualified for that." Pilmore's color began to rise, as was the regular result from his exchanges with Sandy. "It's just that he's a boyhood friend and we haven't had word of him since he was taken to the hospital ship."

Pilmore determined the quickest ending to another exchange with My-Cock was to answer. "His Highness King George the First, was, as of this morning's returns, still indisposed from a dose of enteric fever, shitting out his lovely royal insides."

"Do you suppose he'll make it through, Sergeant-Major?" asked Sandy, his smile dropping. The battalion had already lost significant strength to a variety of illnesses, a greater threat thus far than the Turks.

"My-Cock, the Almighty and I parted company over a stinking pile of dead dervishes at Omdurman in '98, so how could I bloody well know if George the First will survive?" He peered at Sandy, from all appearances expecting a reply.

"No Sergeant-Major, it would seem you wouldn't know, given your circumstances with the Almighty," Sandy said. He climbed down from the fire step to fetch another sand bag.

"I'm pleased you concur, My-Cock, as to the effects of my exclusion from the Covenant of Grace. Now if it would not inconvenience you to shut your gob and finish this sodding work before Abdul and his friends come to poke a bayonet up your arse?" And with that, Sergeant-Major Pilmore vanished around the next traverse.

"Have a care now, Sandy. Why do you insist on baiting him so?" Jack asked with genuine concern.

"That Englishman could make sure you never leave this place with your bollocks still attached," added Will, "of which you might have need once we return to St. John's."

Sandy hefted another bag, just filled by Will and tied off by Jack. "You're envious because I'm his favorite. Not very becoming, I must say," his accustomed grin returning. "Must be unpleasant for you, Will, being the master's favorite for so many years at school."

Will blushed, still vulnerable to schoolboy needling. "His favoritism seems to show in odd ways, Sandy, seeing as you found out nothing we didn't already know about Geordie. Does you no good at all, as far as I can see."

"Really, Corporal William Parsons? No good at all?" He returned to sandbagging, nearly bursting with his secret.

"You look like the cat that swallowed a bloody canary, so spit it out."

"Why do you think Toby got packed off to headquarters?" asked Sandy, with great self-satisfaction.

"You asked Pilmore to take Toby off the line?"

"I simply made the case that Tuppence,"—Will winced at one of their own using Pilmore's nickname—"being of an extraordinary height, was susceptible to snipers. We'd therefore need to raise the parapet along our entire section to protect him from the Turks."

Jack began to chuckle, leaning on his shovel handle. "You're a right sneaky bastard, my sweet b'y. Sneaky to the core." Sandy beamed at this backhand compliment.

"But a godsend to our side," said Will. "Thank you for looking after Toby. He's not taking well to this trench business."

All three glanced one to the other with concerned nods of agreement.

The flies and the lice were the same, front or rear. Bathing was quite sporting, given the Turks' habit of lobbing shells along the shoreline whenever a naked soldier went near the water. Most didn't risk it, adding to the filthiness and smell. Jack, Will and Sandy sat smoking and waving away flies just outside their assigned dugout near the beach, engaged as every morning with the endless cleaning of rifles necessitated by the peninsula's alternating dust and mud. Sandy paused to take a long drag from his cigarette, looking out over the water.

"I'll be damned if it isn't Banquo's Ghost!"

Jack and Will followed Sandy's surprised stare. Moving up the hillside from a makeshift pier was a large soldier who looked very much like Geordie. They all stood waving and shouting to their returning friend. As Geordie approached the dugout, they were to a man shocked by the look of him, his face gaunt and eyes sunk.

"Look who they finally turfed out of his malingering bed," said Will, trying to lighten their thoughts. "Welcome back to our mole's hole."

Geordie dropped his pack and rifle and plopped down on the makeshift bench, exhausted by the short climb up the slope. "The Sergeant-Major still in his usual form then?"

"He's in the finest fettle, is our Sergeant-Major," said Jack. "The man's immune to the flies and the dirt. He always looks like he just stepped off church parade."

"I don't believe he sweats," said Sandy. "I've examined him close as I dare and he does not sweat. Not a drop."

The three let Geordie catch his breath. Random rat-a-tats could be heard from the trenches in the hillside above them. In the distance, a few explosions rumbled farther up the line, friendly or Turk. Couldn't tell.

"So where's young Toby then?" said Geordie, ready to continue the conversation now that he had gotten his wind back.

"We've managed to keep him at battalion HQ on messenger duty," said Will. "Sandy's great friend, the Sergeant-Major, detailed him there." Will stubbed his cigarette and field dressed the butt, shaking the remnants of tobacco back into his pouch and sticking the bit of paper in his pocket. "I fear he may be getting wise to us."

"You know we can't keep him out of harm's way forever, yeh?" Geordie said, looking at Will alone. "He's a soldier, like us."

Jack noticed Will's discomfort at being called out on the subject of Toby. "Well, we can keep him from the line for a while longer at least."

Sandy gave Geordie a long appraising look. "You look like shite, b'y. How did you end up back here so soon? Shouldn't you convalesce in a Malta hospital or back in Blighty?"

Geordie looked out on the bay where his transport ship from Mudros was still anchored. "Too many worse than me, and bodies buried at sea and on land, ten and twenty a day. Truth is the disease and the Turks are taking a frightful toll, with replacements slow to come if at all." He wiped the back of his hand across his wet forehead. "We need men for duty now." Examining his scuffed boots, he added almost as an afterthought, "Things don't seem to be going so well with our division. Or the Anzacs. Or the French for that…"

A loud shriek interrupted and all four leapt into the dugout. A shell from a Turkish field gun exploded fifty yards up the beach, followed by a second shriek and bang.

"Good thing they don't have ammunition for more," said Jack as they emerged back into the daylight. "But they do get in lucky shots now and again."

A familiar voice called from the path winding along the hill from battalion HQ. The long and lanky soldier picking his way through the rocks could only be Toby. In his tunic and cap, unlike the others who had shed layers in the daytime heat, he looked the part of a headquarters runner.

"Keeping up appearances for the brass hats, are we young Toby?" said Geordie, turning to face him.

Toby grinned wide and gamboled the last few yards down the path. "Geordie! You're back! How do you feel?"

"Fit as an out-of-tune fiddle, my sweet b'y, and glad to be among familiar faces. Even one as ugly as Alexander's."

"What did they say was ailing you in the end anyways?" asked Toby, sincere in his interest.

Geordie stroked his chin in contemplation. "Depends which of the great medical minds you ask, Tobias. There was one school of thought pointing to either enteric fever or typhoid fever—which as it turns out is exactly the same thing, as far as one's arsehole is concerned."

Sandy offered Geordie a rolled cigarette and said, "Would you care for a seegar, Your Highness?"

"Why thank you, Alexander, how very kind," said Geordie, as he bent to light the fag from Will's match. "Now as I was saying, Master Halfpenny, there were two schools of thought," he said through exhaled smoke, then spit a shred of tobacco from his tongue. "The other theory, and the one which I favor, held it was the bad water that felled me." All were familiar with the deplorable water, most arriving in used petrol cans, few having been scrubbed out before refilling. Geordie took another drag, spit another shred or two. "As you, my boon companions, are well aware, I have had a long and sometimes troubled relationship with water." The others burst into laughter at their shared memories of Geordie's episodes of violent seasickness.

"Delightfully ironic, Geordie, but most fitting and proper," said Will.

"Then bad water shall be the story from here forward. Agreed, gentlemen?"

"Agreed," responded the others, more or less in unison. Geordie leaned back against the dugout door frame, exhausted from the effort of bantering. It did not go unnoticed.

As corporal of the section, Will realized Toby must be down from HQ for some reason. "What brings you to our side of town?"

"Yes… yes, it's official business." He fished a folded message from his tunic.

Will took the paper and read it with care, turning it over to see if there were additional instructions on the reverse. He refolded the paper and placed it under his leg.

"It seems we have some work tonight."

Morning and afternoon crawled on, the section relieved from other duties because of the raiding party that night. Most cleaned their rifles again, the one thing they could do that might help them later. Some wrote or reread letters from home. Others played cards or retold stories for the fiftieth time. At 1745, having checked equipment a last time, the section meandered single file up the twisting path to the headquarters dugout. There, immaculate as ever, waited Sergeant-Major Pilmore. The only addition to his uniform was a holstered Webley revolver attached to a lanyard.

The sergeant-major was all business. He stepped forward toward the men aligned in a rank. "Stand at ease," he said, showing unaccustomed consideration. "We've been given a bit of nasty business tonight, lads. Our job is to see the Turks get the nastier bit. We're not just trench raiding, we're to take out that noisome machine gun above the left flank of our sector that's been peppering us."

The men looked straight ahead, the evening's stakes having just been raised.

"We'll make our way up the line as soon as it's dark. When in place, we'll cut the wire on our parapet," he said, brandishing two pair of cutters. Noticing Geordie in formation, the sergeant-major handed him one. "Pleased to see you'll be joining us tonight, King. Strength enough to cut a bit of wire?"

Pilmore handed the second wire cutter to Palmer, a fisher from Twillingate almost as large as Geordie. "You two will remain behind and provide covering fire if things go to shite. Pass your cutters to Oakley and My-Cock when you're back. Corporal Parsons, you and the others will be with me. We'll make our way at a crouch until clear of our wire, then on our bellies the rest of the way."

Turning to Will, he said, "Parsons, fetch two satchels of Mills bombs and a Very light bandolier from the dugout. You take the flares and one satchel of grenades and choose your best arm for the other." Will exchanged a purposeful glance with Sandy, who nodded in acknowledgement.

"Once Oakley and My-Cock cut the Turk wire, we'll bomb our way up to the emplacement, pip the crew and destroy that gun. Then we'll send up a Very flare and hold until battalion pushes up relief. Like eating pie, eh lads?" And with that, Pilmore reentered the HQ dugout. The soldiers sat on the ground for a last cigarette. No smoking past here.

At 1845, the sergeant-major rejoined them and they set out for the front line. Their movement was quick, the battlefront compressed to a few hundred yards uphill from the sea. They squatted in a position opposite the machine gun emplacement, waiting to see if the Turks had noticed their movement. Ten minutes later, Sergeant-Major Pilmore motioned for Geordie and Palmer to cut their wire. The big men scrambled over the parapet on their chests. After a minute or two, they landed back in the trench with muffled grunts. Jack collected the wire cutters, handing one to Sandy.

"Good work, lads." Turning to Will and the others, the sergeant-major whispered a little louder, "We'll hold for five minutes to make sure those heathen bastards weren't tipped by the cutting. Then we'll jump the bags and get on with this sack of shite we've been handed. No lights or noise now."

Each one huddled in the trench, a sweaty grip on his rifle, trying not to count minutes. Finally, Sergeant-Major Pilmore moved up and down the line of men, patting each shoulder to stiffen them. Returning to the fire step where Will and Sandy waited with the palm-sized Mills bombs, he said, "Stay close to me through the wire, closer once we drop to a crawl. One way home to that bloody rock of yours, and that's through Johnny Turk yonder. Quiet as you please, lads." Pilmore was over the parapet with Sandy struggling behind. Just as Will mounted the step, he heard a loud rattle, accompanied by a sputtering of bullets burrowing into the sandbags.

When the machine gun fire passed, low moaning could be heard just beyond the parapet. The wounded man was struggling to keep from crying out, his pain finding release in tortured groans that rolled back down into the trench. The deadening effect of the sandbag walls rendered the excruciating sound chilling and close. Under the pale starlight, the silhouette of a head and shoulders appeared over the edge, pushed with grunts of effort from behind. Will grabbed the cloth of the man's uniform and heaved. Sergeant-Major Pilmore flopped onto the floor of the trench. The others rushed to attend him.

"No lights 'til we get Sandy! Do what you can, then we'll get him back to the beach soon as Sandy's in safe."

"No need to hurry, Corporal," said a shaky, faceless voice from below. "He's gone west."

Will could hear Sandy struggling. He whispered loud as he dared, "Sandy! Get yourself back in here!"

"Tangled up in some of our wire. Can't get my leg free. Have to feel along and use the cutters." All the men of the section were tensed, some standing, some kneeling around the body of the sergeant-major. Then they heard shuffling and scraping again.

Sandy's head appeared above the parapet. "Let me hand down this satchel of Mills. Don't want them scattering in the dark." Rising to his knees, he swung the dirty tan bag from his shoulder. The flash of light canvas was enough for the Turk gunner. The rattle sounded again. Just a few short bursts, no use wasting ammunition. The silhouette above the parapet crumpled, landing in the trench.

"Sandy, my sweet b'y!" Geordie shoved through the other men. Will unclipped an electric torch from his belt. No need for care now. He jumped down from the fire step, bending over Geordie's back.

The yellow circle of light fell on two motionless men, lying face up, Sandy's head resting limp on Sergeant-Major Pilmore's chest, both staring with dull eyes up at the night sky.

CHAPTER NINE

Deirdre

"Sister Brannigan, I simply cannot understand what could be wrong with passing some friendly words with a patient," protested the volunteer, looking very much as if she might stamp her foot.

Giving the young woman a sharp-eyed appraisal, Deirdre replied, "Miss Bannerman, your verbal ministrations look very much like flirting with the wounded officers. I'll ask you to busy yourself tending these men's medical needs, not assessing their matrimonial potential." The girl from the Volunteer Aid Detachment went crimson, more in anger at this Irishwoman's impertinence than from any well-deserved embarrassment.

Bold as brass this one, Dee thought. "Now report to Sister Campbell in Ward C. You'll be pleased to learn it's filled with other ranks"— Miss Bannerman was blotchy with indignation—"which will aid in restraining your verbal tendencies." The volunteer glared daggers, turned on her heels, and stomped out of the Officers Ward with a great show of hands and elbows.

Her Dublin trainees had been from respectable working folk. These Red Cross volunteers—the VADs—came from middle class and professional families, with a smattering of the upper crust thrown in.

Dee pegged Miss Bannerman as the daughter of a baronet, some Sir Ivor Humpity-Thrump or other, volunteering like many of the others to find an appropriate officer to marry while doing their patriotic duty. She did not begrudge the volunteers their dreams of handsome husbands, as long as they pulled their weight and gave an honest day's work. To be sure, she was not immune to a handsome face and a fine figure herself, though her experience with men back in Dublin had not been extensive. She attracted her share of attention from schoolmates of Frank's and some of the young men from Da's work she had met at brewery socials. She even kissed a few, furtive clinches in dark cloak rooms or benches on the Green, even letting one or two get a little familiar with his hands. And there was Tommy Kehoe with the fine wavy hair and the fetching white smile. She'd let things go a bit too far one night, him having too much of the drink taken. It was always pleasantly electric kissing him, but that night he had jammed her hand into the front of his trousers before she knew what was happening and rubbed it all along his hardness. He had earned a knee in the bullocks for his efforts. She last saw him in the doorway of a shuttered greengrocer's shop, vomiting six or seven pints of stout onto his best shoes.

Dr. Macintosh was working his way down the ward on evening rounds when Deirdre spotted him. With no prolonged fighting in the sector at present, doctors and nurses alike could spend more time attending each patient. This was a luxury the ebb and flow of battle could change in an instant.

"Good afternoon, Major Macintosh."

The doctor looked up from his examination of a lieutenant with a severe leg wound. "Ach, Sister Brannigan! And what sort of afternoon is it for you, this leisurely day?" Dr. Macintosh was a favorite of staff and patients alike. An exceptional Edinburgh-trained surgeon, he was surely the most affable and unflappable officer in the Royal Army Medical Corps.

"Nothing worth the mention, Doctor, and 'tis a blessing. And how was your visit with the French?"

"Well, the food 'twas better than our usual skilly, I'll admit," he said with a rub of the chin below his easy smile. Patting the patient on the arm, Macintosh said, "You're healing nicely, Lieutenant. We'll pack you back to Blighty as soon as we can arrange transport." Switching to purest Inverness-shire, as he was able to do at a gallop for effect, he added, "You'll be wantin' a guid bit o' mendin' afore ye'll be birlin' on tha' shank agin, laddie." He finished with a deliberate wink and the lieutenant returned a shaky smile and whispered his gratitude. The doctor turned and took Dee by the elbow, walking her away from the line of beds. "Sister Brannigan, would you care for a mug of tea and a little conversation? I've some matters from my visit with *les Français* I'd like to mull over with you, if you've the time."

"Of course, Major. I'd be interested to hear how the allies are getting on."

They turned toward the door and crossed the compound to a small cook tent. Inside, they were given tea and a few hard biscuits, finding seats at one of the small tables. After taking a long draw from his mug and ignoring the biscuits, Dr. Macintosh began. "Have you heard the term *triage*, Deirdre?" he asked, switching to first names away from the ears of the patients and the VADs.

"Aye, I have. The battalion aid stations use it to decide who should be treated in place and who sent back to us."

"That's the gist. A French field hospital I visited was flooded with four hundred patients in little more than an hour. To sort the deluge, they enforced most rigorous triage standards. They'd a ward for the dying to keep them away from those with some hope. Although it tugs at the heart, it was a most humane way of husbanding their resources."

"We'd be stretched for nursing staff, since I'm not sure how many of the VADs could handle work in a ward meant just for the dying."

"Aye, I imagine that would be too much for many. The other thing the French did, much to my surprise, was let the nurses handle triage. This freed doctors for surgery."

Now that's something, thought Dee, *something indeed*.

"I'd like you to take this on, Deirdre." Tending to his tea again, with a biscuit this time, he allowed Dee to mull his proposal. After sitting in silence for several moments, he pressed her, gentle as he could. "Deirdre lass, I've worked close with you for several months now. I've not seen in my twenty-odd years of doctorin' any could ken as fast as ye what's truly amiss wi' an ailin' sodger."

Dee gave the doctor, as good a man as she had known, a broad and disarming smile. "You needn't go all highland laddie with your flattery, Dr. Ferquhar Macintosh. I'm only puzzling over how to cover my surgical duties."

"I'd expect you back in surgery as soon as the intake of patients was cleared, Nurse Brannigan." He gave her an exaggerated wide-eyed look by way of emphasis. "You'll not get away from me as easy as that." With another long swallow of his now-cold tea, he sighed while a sober look came over him, whispering across the tiny table, "We need to be ready for the worst. I hear rumblings of something big afoot."

He glanced at the door of the cook tent as two male orderlies ambled out, then back to Deirdre with deep concern. "Bigger than anything we've yet seen."

29th of May, 1916
Dublin City

My dearest Daughter,

'Tis most sorry I am for not writing sooner, but Dublin City has been in a fearsome uproar since Eastertide. I'm sure you heard some of what's passed. It beggars belief, that much I'll say, with half Sackville Street a smoking rubble and Stephen's Green turned up like they was digging lazy beds for planting tatties. St. Vincent's kept tending the poor right through the fighting and you'd have been right proud, Deirdre.

Most thought the rebels a mad band o' troublemakers, tearing up buildings and frightening the whole city. Since those terrible executions at Kilmainham, I sense things are changing. Many say the English were over harsh on the leaders, mad as they were for rising in the first place. But they was brave men, right enough. Some say Mr. Pearse went a-whistling to his fate. Can you imagine such a thing? Your brother Francis is spitting angry, saying they was all traitors and they stabbed the Irish lads off at the fighting square in the back. Your brother Sean went missing for days during the troubles and I was frantic with the thought of losing him. He turned up Wednesday, tired and dirty and hungry but safe. Him and Francis have been bickering ever since. I scarce get a moment's peace, cepting when Sean is out with his lads, which is as often as not now days.

We're getting by well here, Deirdre, saints be praised. With my widow's pension and the children's allowance and Francis's invalid pay, we have plenty for a roof above and food in our mouths. With the death gratuity from the Crown, as well as the money from the Benevolent Society your Da paid into regular, I've bought up Shanahan's, just round the corner on the Coombe. I can hear you laughing at the thought of me a publican, but we needed something to keep meself and your brother busy. Francis didn't think much of the idea at first, but after I renamed the pub The Gallant Fusilier he warmed to it. He needs some honest work to take him from his woes. And if he's to be round the drink anyways, we might as well make a few bob from it. The pub has a fine flat, so we've let the house in New Row and moved above the pub. There's but the two bedrooms, so the men are in one, and we ladies in t'other. We'll make a place for you with me and Molly when you return safe, for which we pray to the Sacred and Perpetual Hearts each and every night.

With all your father's old friends from the cooperage and men from the regiment who've been sent home like Francis, we've a lovely group down the pub of an evening, telling the stories and singing the songs from the war and making the till ring. So you're not to worry over us and you needn't send money home. I'd be pleased to know you'd a bit to give you comfort where you are, hard as it must be.

My dearest girl, I love you with all that's in my heart, as your father did also. Come home to us safe and sound, when your duty to those poor men is done.

May the Holy Mother and all the
angels and saints be with you,

Your loving Mam

"Sister Brannigan, that'll be enough for tonight. You'll be no good to anyone if you're dead upon your feet," said Dr. Macintosh, his voice heavy with exhaustion.

"Aye, Major. Just want one last turn through the heads ward before retiring for the night."

"If you don't mind, Sister, I'll accompany you for a wee look as well." The two set off across the pea-gravel path that separated the head injuries from the general wards. The heads ward was kept as quiet as possible at night, the worst time for these poor men, with only a shaded desk lamp at each end. After Deirdre and Dr. Macintosh entered, a woman in a VAD uniform strode over to greet them.

"Good evening, Major Macintosh, Sister Brannigan," said the young woman. The activities preparing for the big operation—trench raiding, barrages and counter-barrages, mining and counter-mining—provided a steady flow of wounded to the Casualty Clearing Station, including terrible head injuries. The quiet of the ward was pierced from time to time by unintelligible jabbering from a patient in a bed along the right side.

Dr. Macintosh said to the VAD, "Bannerman, isn't it?" She nodded with a wan smile. "Has Private Connor been worse this evening?"

"He was much worse in the afternoon." Looking down the line of beds, they noted the restlessness of the Royal Inniskilling who had been injured by a splintering wooden beam when a German shell hit the roof of his dugout. He was the only survivor of the six occupants. "We gave him three-eighths of a grain of morphia two hours ago, but he's still agitated. He's suffering greatly, I fear."

"If he's still like this or worse in two hours' time, give him another half grain," said Macintosh.

"Yes, Doctor." The VAD walked off to make an annotation in the soldier's chart.

Deirdre waited until the volunteer was out of earshot and said to Dr. Macintosh, "That'll be enough morphia to sedate a horse, Major."

He heard her, but took a long moment gazing over the ward before answering. "Aye, Deirdre, 'tis a right good portion." With a lingering exhalation, he turned to her. "That poor lad will not long be with us. That you well know." Dee acknowledged this common and simple truth, although it was seldom spoken aloud. "'Tis perhaps a kindness either way, if a half grain of morphia puts him in a senseless sleep or slips him down the faerie road." He half-smiled with exhaustion and regret. "Now, off to bed with you, lass. And myself as well." With a brisk turn, Macintosh was out the door. Deirdre took a last look over the ward. Bannerman sat scribbling at her small desk.

"'Tis perhaps a kindness indeed," repeated Dee. Then she turned and headed off to her narrow bed and a few hours of sleep.

CHAPTER TEN

Will

The owner's daughter set a refilled bottle of wine and three glasses on the rickety square table. The wine's vinegary smell mingled with the stench of unwashed men and the cloying sweetness from long-ago manure inside the cramped and smokey shack. The *estaminet* was no more than a tarted-up cowshed, with a shaky counter of rough planks resting on two decaying barrels of unknown origin. From behind this moral barrier—it wouldn't have stopped a determined child—the owner never ventured. An empty right sleeve testified to the wounds that invalided him after the Marne. He viewed the British as annoyances from which a living could be extracted as long as the war continued along its meat-grinder course. The tables and chairs were a jumble of odd lots recovered from bombed-out homes. Some had legs wired in place, others had seats patched with odd bits of lumber. But it was near at hand whenever the battalion was out of the trenches and, within the owner's erratic opening hours, you could find a drink and an omelette. His sulky daughter provided a little feminine diversion, if little else.

"*Soixante centième*," mumbled the girl, bored to death by the soldiers and the weather and the war. Jack tossed a franc on the table and waved off her desultory move to make change.

Geordie half-filled the glasses and raised his, "To Sandy." The others echoed the sentiment.

"Wish I'd known your Sandy, seeing how I've toasted him a dozen times," said the third man in a broad Boston accent.

"You'd be a better man for knowing him, Ned," said Jack. It was getting easier to speak of Sandy. They had laid him in the stony dirt of a hill above Suvla Bay, next to Sergeant-Major Pilmore. Jack let slip a smile at the thought of the personal hell the sergeant-major must now be enduring, lying until Judgment Day next to My-Cock, No. 271.

"That you would, Neddie, that you would," said Geordie. He had recovered much of his vigor after his bout with bad water, bad microbes, bad place, bad time. But to Jack and the others, there were reminders of his illness in the fine lines creasing his forehead and the darkness under his eyes he could not seem to sleep away. They drained the mismatched glasses and Geordie refilled them, proposing another toast. "And to Jack's return from sniper school, a better man than he left, I'm sure."

"Still need to choose my spotter, Geordie. Best watch your tongue," said Jack. "Company commander says I can have my pick, so long as it's not his soldier servant Jennings." The three sat drinking and smoking, enjoying the small respite this hovel afforded from the mud and wet of soldiering.

"Ran into Will yesterday, over near the engineer's dump," said Jack. "He does brush up well in his officer's kit."

"*Mademoiselle!*" Geordie called across the shed. "*La même chose.*" The girl slouched off behind the counter for another refilled bottle. Returning to the table, she set it down with a thunk, sticking out an open palm without a word.

Geordie looked at Ned Tobin with expectant eyebrows. The American fished a franc from his pocket and placed it in her palm, saying with a smile and execrable accent, "*Garde la* money, *ma* damsel."

At this display of ostentation, grumbles drifted over from a nearby table of four Lancashires. One of them rose and approached, a bit unsteady on his bandy legs but full of Dutch courage not commensurate with his minuscule height and breadth. He wore the same garnet-red division patch as the Newfoundlanders, his battalion part of a sister brigade.

"We'd take it kindly if you five-bob fuckers wouldn't throw your pay round so free and easy like," the soldier said. "There's those of us don't need expectations risin' as to what can be charged for this shite wine 'n other such." Once word had got around that the Newfoundlanders and Canadians and Aussies were paid five shillings a day, the Brits, scraping by on one, had developed a roiling grudge that erupted whenever there was both alcohol and a colonial near at hand.

Geordie stood from the table, overshadowing the tiny Englishman, and said, "Now Tommy, we were just toasting our good fortune at having such a generous government, doling out the largesse like they do." The smaller man looked Geordie over with wavering resolve, but had painted himself into a corner. He could feel his mates' eyes burning through the back of his tunic.

"You fuckers are na better'n we be, even with all your fine kit an' five bleedin' bob a day," said the Lancastrian. He followed this with a wide and ill-aimed swing. Geordie caught the man's fist in his much larger palm.

"My friends and I were just saying we should share our good fortune with our English brethren," Geordie said with a tight smile and menacing look only the drunk soldier could see. With his free hand, he waved over the owner's daughter and held up his thumb and index finger. "*Deux, pour mes amis.*"

The girl scurried away and returned with two bottles, setting them before the seated Lancs. "*Merci, monsieur,*" she mumbled with an upraised look of relief as she brushed past Geordie.

One of the Lancs called out, "Steady on now, Billy! These blokes is alright by us." Geordie released his grip. "And he's a might big for a little shite like you anyways."

Geordie returned to his seat, not a feather ruffled. Ned offered him a cigarette from his pack of Navy Cuts. "Care for a gasper, Geordie?"

"Why thank you, Ned." He ran a lucifer match along the ridges of a cracked striker, most of '*Appolinaris*' chipped off the base. Geordie glanced over at the Lancs, now quite content with their fags, wine and laughter, even the impetuous Billy.

"There's another county heard from, eh?" said Geordie, slapping Jack on the shoulder.

"Fair dinkum, b'y. Much less untidy than I'd expected."

The Lancs now commenced with random songs in varying degrees of vulgarity, well into the wine stood them by Geordie. The friends watched in detached amusement, enjoying the Tommies' sloppy camaraderie. They were snapped from these revels when the creaky door of the *estaminet* opened and, stooping to clear the splintered lintel, in stepped Toby Halfpenny.

"Toby b'y, come sit yourself down," Jack shouted over a song verse from across the cramped and smoky room. "What brings you down here with the hoi polloi?"

Three German soldiers crossed the Rhine, parlez-vous...

Toby sat on a rickety stool and beamed at Geordie and Jack. "Running a message for Lieutenant Parsons to the engineer's depot."

"Is our Lieutenant Will a terror to work for then?" asked Geordie. "He can be mighty particular about things."

Three German soldiers crossed the Rhine, parlez-vous...

"Oh no, he's better than most of the officers. Just as long as his kit's clean, he's happy. And he eats whatever the men are having, each and every day."

"At least the food's better than we had in dear ol' Mesopolonica," said Geordie, answered by moans from Jack and Toby.

"Although I do miss the serving of black flies we had with every meal," quipped Jack, with another moan from Geordie and Toby.

Three German soldiers crossed the Rhine...

Ned, having joined the regiment after their return from Gallipoli, asked, "You had a fair rough time of it there, eh boys?"

"That we did, Ned, although I spent a pleasant portion of that tour of duty shitting blue stars in a hospital on Mudros. The bad water did me in—tasted of petrol and seawater."

To shag the women and drink the wine...

"Well, since neither of these barbarians have the manners to do so, I'll introduce myself," said the American. "Having heard tell of a long one named Toby who ran with them in the home port, I'll wager that's you."

Ned stuck out his hand and Toby shook it with animation. "Tobias Halfpenny."

"And Ned Tobin of Boston."

Inky dinky parlez-vous.

"A Yank? What would Sergeant-Major Pilmore have made with that?" said Toby.

"Steady on there, b'y. Let's not mock the memory of the Sergeant-Major, prickly as he was to all and sundry," said Jack.

"He did fancy Sandy though, didn't he?" Geordie said.

"So Sandy thought," said Toby.

Jack raised a glass again, "To Sergeant-Major Pilmore, proud heathen of a free-born Englishman, long may his memory endure."

"We'll not soon be forgetting our Sergeant-Major," said Geordie.

"Not in a year of Sundays," added Toby.

With that, they drained their glasses and Jack filled them again, emptying the second bottle. "So what do you hear round HQ these days, Toby? With all the message running Lieutenant Will has you doing, you must have heard somewhat of interest."

Oh, Kaiser Bill is feeling ill...

"There's always talk, not that much comes of it," said Toby, studying the floor for a diversion. "Lieutenant Parsons would know more about such things."

"Well, we've known since they shipped us back from Egypt we were to be part of some big show," said Jack. "We've had plenty of training here walking toward trenches. Course, not many other choices in France, seeing as the Germans are to be found that way."

The Crown Prince, he's gone barmy...

"Come now, Toby, why the secrecy?" said Geordie, drawing him out. "Don't forget two of us here know all your secrets."

We don't give a fuck for old von Kluck...

Toby studied another splintered floorboard, then looked up at the others. He paused, turning over in his thoughts just what he could say. "There's soon to be something big, b'ys, and we're to be a part of it. Something very big indeed."

And all his bleeding army...

7 Garrison Hill
12th of April, 1916

My Dear William,

It was with great pleasure I learned you were offered a commission after the losses at Gallipoli. Everyone now asks after our Lieutenant, which thrills your mother and sisters. We were pained to hear of the death of Alexander Hiscock at Gallipoli. Knowing he was a childhood friend, his ultimate sacrifice must have filled you with bursting pride. You will, of course, give his family the details of his glorious end upon your return.

Although I was angered by your decision to enlist as a private soldier, I must admit I may have reacted in haste. Since your commissioning became public in the Daily Star *(enclosed herein), there has been a general sense among gentlemen of influence that our family set a fine example by showing we Parsons weren't above doing the work expected from the lower sorts in defending the Empire. It seems a new age of egalitarianism has overtaken us and you stumbled into making the most of it.*

I have instructed Beasley & Atherton, our London agents, to establish a generous overdraft for you at Cox & Co, in Craig's Court. Atherton informed me this is where most officers have personal accounts. You may feel free to call at their offices in Fenchurch Street, near the station, should you require any other financial arrangements. I have given them a carte blanche to assist you. They have established accounts for you at Edward Smith tailors in Saville Row and Bates hat makers in Jermyn Street. I'll not have a son of this family looking anything less than a smart gentleman. Have them make you a few quality suits of mufti for wear while on leave, since you will be visiting your mother's relations.

Your father,
Walter Parsons

There were lulls when the heavies reduced their fire, but the smaller guns kept up the pounding around the clock. Couldn't let Fritz have his sleep, after all. Of course, the Germans had the same thought and kept up their insomniac's counter-fire, too. It had divided their world into those who shelled and those who were shelled, the roles reversing from barrage to counter-barrage. With Newtonian certainty, friendly fire brought hostile counter-fire. It had not ceased, day or night, back and forth, five days into the bombardment. They kept at their reconnaissance and trench raiding, shells be damned. The handful of prisoners they snatched were meant to be valuable to someone somewhere. All they saw were frightened Saxons or Württembergers in dirty grey-green uniforms.

Jack and Geordie sat either side of an upended grenade crate, picking through a pile of bullets in the parsimonious light of a smudgy paraffin lantern. Ned Tobin shared their underground shelter but not the tedious bullet picking. "It'd save your eyesight if you used a Lee-Enfield for your sniping."

"How else would we wile away the hours," Geordie replied, "having heard every tale of your kith and kin down to Brian Boru himself."

"And I yours, Geordie boy." Ned leaned back against the musty dugout wall, the side of his face lit by a sputtering candle stuck in a discarded beef tin. He inhaled a long drag of his cigarette, squinting at his leg in the dim light. He used the cherry end to burn a few lice along a seam in his breeches. At least they had plenty of tobacco.

Jack held two rounds close to the lantern and studied them. He tossed one and it clattered across the wooden bottom of an empty ammunition box at his feet. He slid the other into a clip and handed it over to Geordie, who tucked it in a leather bandolier draped across his thigh.

"My Ross is a finer weapon for sniping, Ned." He compared two more rounds, tossing both in the box. "Lot of bother it took getting one back from the Canadians. I'll not abandon her because she's a bit particular what gets shoved up her spout."

Geordie gave a breathy laugh while peering over two more bullets. "Unlike the ladies once preferred by our sweet b'y, Sandy Hiscock." He tossed the two rounds in the crate and exchanged a glance with Jack. The loss still ached, even these many months past. All three stopped and, with the instincts of every soldier, turned their eyes upward as deep thuds imbedded in the steady background rumble of explosions. Dirt and small stones sifted down between the rough-sawn planks of the dugout's ceiling.

Jack turned back to picking over shells in the insufficient light. "Ahh, the damn coal boxes are falling again, b'ys." By necessity and long practice, they had become expert in the various sounds of the German artillery. It was the long-range howitzers that unnerved them most. They destroyed bunkers and dugouts in a puff of sooty black smoke. Another landed nearby with a huge crump, its explosive force converted to low vibrations that traveled out for a surprising distance through the chalky earth.

"May be walking the barrage towards us," said Ned, not hiding his apprehension, shared in nervous silence by the others. Ned lit a new cigarette from the glowing butt of the one he had not yet finished, keeping his unsteady hand hidden in the shadows. The bullet-picking went on, a little quicker and less exacting.

They listened for the next rounds, relieved when the deep basso explosions moved away, down the trench line. "Not today," said Geordie. "Some other poor bastards." The barrage returned to the whooshing of outgoing British shells, punctuated from time to time by return fire from smaller German whizz-bangs.

SHREE-bang-BOOM… SHREE-bang-BOOM…

Jack pulled back his tunic cuff to check his wristwatch in the lantern light. In their subterranean existence, it was too easy to lose track of time. He squinted at the watch face in the gloom, then scrubbed his hands over his cheeks and eyes, rubbing out the lethargy from hours of sitting. "We'll head up after sunset. There'll be a good half-hour of twilight for having a look at Fritz's parapet. We might even get some shooting."

Ned sat up and said, "Mind if I come along, boys?"

"I don't want a crowd moving about the trenches with this iron foundry dropping on us," Jack said. The Yank slumped back against the smudgy wall and into the shadows. Jack sensed his dejection and tried another tack. "Hard enough keeping His Majesty here out of sight." He slapped Geordie's leg. "Haven't any idea what possessed me to make him my spotter. He's better suited to being spotted."

"Because you're wise beyond your tender years, seeing how I provide excellent protection for your wee pink body."

Dull orange light flashed as the gas curtain over the shelter entrance was pushed aside, followed by scuffling on the rough-cut steps. Two shadows passed down the earthen stairs, fifteen treads in all. Then Will, followed close by Toby, materialized within the weak pool of light. They all stood when the officer entered, but Geordie and Jack could not maintain the pretense and broke into laughter. Will had a quick glance around. With no one other than the familiar American idling in the shadows, he joined in.

"Not very sincere in your respects, Oakley and King. Not a good show at all," Will said, slapping his malacca cane, a perfect mimic of a headquarter's major. He hated carrying the cane, but it was standard for officers in the trenches. Supposed to show one's disregard for danger or some such nonsense. His father's agents, Beasley & Atherton, sent the cane along to him after appropriate inquiries as to acceptable style and quality.

"What brings you down to the poor side of town?" Jack said. "Don't have enough to occupy you in your platoon?"

"Heading back down the line from battalion HQ. The communication trench was collapsed by one of the Boche's big mortars. Took a meander, thinking we'd have a chin with you sorry lot." The five settled on whatever seats they could find or improvise. The damp earthiness of the dugout made the space suffocating. Layers of cigarette smoke, greasy food and dirty men created foul strata in the close air. They could feel the fetidness on their skin.

Will unstrapped his helmet and handed it to Toby. Uncapping a flask from an inside pocket, he took a short drink and passed it. "Compliments of my father. Some advantages in returning to his good graces." It was against King's Regulations for an officer to drink with private soldiers but the Dominion troops took a relaxed view, as did the British pals' battalions. As often as not, the men had grown up or been at school with their officers.

Jack raised the flask. "Here's a health to Walter Parsons. Long may he reign." He passed the flask along to Ned Tobin, the cap jingling at the end of its fine silver chain.

"Much appreciated, Lieutenant. Fine tonic for the nerves, my old Da always said."

Whoosh, whoosh. They glanced upward, another reflex. Then, more distant, *phoom, phoom.* Outgoing friendly. Big ones.

"You'd best call me Will, now you're with these ne'er-do-wells of my youth." Then he added, awkwardness creeping into his voice, "Of course, when none of the other men are nearby." He sketched with a thumb in the palm of his opposite hand. "You can understand."

"No need to mention it," said Ned. He looked back at Will with the open candor that seemed an American's birthright, never meeting a man to whom he did not feel the equal. "And thank your father for the fine hooch." Ned passed the flask to Toby, who screwed the cap tight without taking a drink.

"What words from the top then, William?" said Geordie. "Here's hoping for more than 'sit and be shelled'."

"Not far from the mark. Continuing our barrage two more days."

"Jee-zus," said Jack, "could there be a bloody shell left in France?"

"We've fired over a million," Will said. "No good count of what the Germans have fired back. It's, well, quite awesome really."

Ned Tobin leaned into the light and said, "Still, the boys in the next section were out on patrol last night and said the wire isn't well cut. Any openings are damned narrow."

"Not a problem after two more days," Geordie said with his usual confidence, back to sorting through rifle rounds. Jack studied Will, searching for some sign of surprise at Ned's news. It was evident Will knew already.

"Will, if that's true all along the line, that would be *no bon* for us at jump off."

"*No bon* indeed," Will said, "but Geordie's right. The extra days will cut the wire. That much is certain."

Toby sat listening in the shadows, just beyond the yellow spill of light. Jack looked at his watch again. The sun was down. "Hate to drink and dash, but we have some sneaky-peaky work." Ned leaned forward, eyebrows up with a look of final appeal. Relenting, Jack said, "If you promise to keep your fool Yankee head down and stick close to Geordie, you can come." Ned smiled and gave a curt nod by way of thanks. Seemed safer somehow, moving about in the open air, so he gathered his gear with relieved alacrity. He reached under a bunk to retrieve his gas mask.

"Goddamn it all to hell!" he said, startled by a rat with oily fur scampering over his hand. He kicked at the rodent without effect as it scurried back into the deep shadows. The three gathered their rifles, Geordie slinging the bandolier of selected bullets across his chest. They slipped helmet straps under their chins and headed for the steps with handshakes and goodbyes all around.

"Keep moving and stay close to the bags, lads," Will said, a reflexive warning he had repeated to his own men a hundred times. He sat finishing a cigarette, enjoying the escape from his responsibilities for a few moments longer.

Thump-phoom. Thump-phoom.

The heavy German howitzers were walking the front trenches again. Will could see even in the weak lantern light that Toby was deathly pale. He patted the younger man's knee a few times. "You can't let yourself concentrate on the individual rounds. It'll drive you mad."

Thump-Phoom. Thump-PHOOM.

The lantern bounced from the crate and extinguished on the floor as the air filled with choking dust and their heads were pummeled by bucketsful of dirt. The cracking sounds in the darkness told them some part of the dugout had collapsed. So far, not on them. With the light of his electric torch struggling through the airborne dust, Will could see part of the roof had collapsed, blocking the steps but not the entire stairwell. A little ruddy twilight filtered through as the dust began to settle. Will shined the light around the dugout, spotting Toby. He had been knocked to the floor from the near miss and there he remained, knees pulled to his chest and head down.

"Get up now, Toby. We need to clear the stairs."

Toby raised his head and stared up from the floor, eyes wide in his chalky face. His hands clutched his knees, knuckles whitened, not yet able to stand. Will uprighted an ammunition crate and sat next to him. Toby turned his face back to the floor.

"I've been thinking, when the big push comes you ought to stay with the ten percent. I haven't sent in the list for the platoon yet." Will extracted another cigarette from the silver case. He was not altogether steady either. Digging out the stairs could wait a few minutes.

Toby's head snapped up and he began shaking it back and forth with increasing intensity. "No, no, please no! You can't do that."

"Toby, you know we have to leave a tenth in the rear to get the battalion back on its feet after the attack," Will said, trying to justify himself. "You're familiar with everyone in the platoon and the battalion staff. And you're an experienced runner, which would be useful."

Rising anger steadied his legs and Toby sprang up. His head touched the battered ceiling. Glaring with wild eyes at Will, he shouted, "Don't you think I knew what you were up to at Gallipoli? Hiding me from the fighting? And I might have helped with… with… Sandy."

Will jerked away, avoiding the accusing look on Toby's face. "You were so young then. And not much older now."

Slapping the dugout wall with his long palm, the sound dulled by the earth works behind the planks, Toby was determined to have his say. "I'm well past eighteen now. And I've been through as much and more than many of the men. Like Ned Tobin." Toby pressed his case, "I came to fight and fight I will. I'll ask for immediate reassignment if needs be."

Will sat silent. This was not a Toby he could fob off with a few words and a smile. How could he explain to the commander why his soldier servant requested reassignment on the eve of battle?

"You'll be forward with me."

Toby's excitement spread over his face and down his long body, allowed to play with the senior boys again. This was a very dangerous game though, Will knew.

"By God you'd better stick close like my shadow or I'll shoot you in the bloody leg myself."

Toby rummaged through the broken planking and jumbled pieces of kit, somehow extracting an entrenching tool from the darkness. "We better be digging ourselves out, Lieutenant. They'll be missing you in the platoon."

CHAPTER ELEVEN

Will

They were the reserves.

Not a bad draw, behind those with the dirtiest work. Maybe not so dirty this time. Barrage couldn't have left much, Will thought.

They waited in a second-line support trench. They were to follow the first wave into the German trenches. That was the plan. Will rubbed his brass whistle, cool and smooth. It felt clean and new, not muddy and gritty, tired and worn. It soothed him.

Mustn't let the men see any nerviness. Not from an officer.

The whisky helped. Walter's finest whisky, nothing being too good for his lieutenant. He had drunk more during the barrage than he cared to admit. No sleep otherwise. Two-thirds of a waterless tumbler this morning, too.

Who wouldn't have nerves with that bloody bombardment? Couldn't have left much standing on the other side.

After his outburst a few days ago, Toby seemed calm, or at least calmer.

Mustn't let him see any nerviness, most of all.

Will rubbed the whistle's cylinder with his thumb. He'd only used it in training. Different story today.

Jack and Geordie were with the first wave. All the brigade's snipers ordered forward, on the flanks, plinking machine gunners. Not that there would be any left after the barrage. So the brass hats assured them.

They'd seen wounded returning soon after the first wave went over. A few of the enemy always survived the barrage. And the morning sun gave the Germans an advantage.

Sun in our eyes, at their backs.

Still, there was a growing stream of wounded.

Keep the men's minds off counting. They've had their rum ration. Calms them right down. Some getting a little mouthy.

"Let's check rifles again. No time for dirt in the breech. Bayonets, too. We'll be needing those before this day's out, eh lads?"

Steady voice. Good. Mustn't let them hear nerviness.

Will walked along the trench tugging on webbing, slapping shoulders.

No use letting them count the wounded.

They were supposed to advance at 0840, but HQ countermanded with no further instructions. So they waited. They had felt the deep rumble of the big mine exploding under the German front line and heard their barrage lift for the first wave.

There was a ripple along the troops in the trench. Two insistent soldiers pushed toward Will. Parting the last of the men, Jack grabbed Will by the arm and pulled him around a traverse, away from his men. The next section of trench was unoccupied.

"You need to hold your men here. Tell battalion you can't attack," Jack panted out, his eyes wild. Will shook away Jack's hand on his sleeve.

Mustn't let the men see me too familiar.

"That's not possible. We're awaiting the word to advance now."

Geordie's eyes were wide, darting over Jack's shoulder. Lines of sweat streaked through the dirt covering his face. He had a crushing grip on the field glasses they used for spotting.

"The barrage didn't cut the wire. Only small breaches," Jack said. "Fritz has them ranged with Emma Gees. They're strafin' every openin' and the bodies are blockin' them up now." He was panting hard and stopped to catch his breath.

Will's legs were going rubbery. He stiffened himself with effort.

Mustn't let the men see. Nerviness.

"I thought you snipers were supposed to take care of any machine guns?"

Geordie handed over a canteen and Jack gulped hard at it. Geordie took up the report, "No place to get a shot. No-Man's Land's traversed by every kind of machine gun. Half the snipers already pipped."

"And they're poundin' our trenches with the big guns now. The parapets are collapsin' all along the line. It's a slaughterhouse, Will. The b'ys are gettin' gutted like fish," Jack said, both hands on Will's arms, trying to shake his eerie calm. "We're headin' to battalion to report this goddamned cock-up. They'll have to stop it."

Toby came around the traverse holding a paper. He did not brighten at the sight of Jack and Geordie. Will took the message and unfolded it. He read it without emotion. "Too late. You'd best come with my platoon. Whole battalion's been ordered forward. Soon as we can assemble." Will refolded the message and slid it into a pocket. He buttoned the flap.

Wouldn't want to lose orders. Slow and steady. Mustn't let the men see.

Jack looked at Geordie, who held his stare for just a moment, then nodded in agreement. "We've all come here together, my dear b'ys, and we'll fight together this day." He set his jaw in a grimacing smile as his eyes filled.

"Stay with the men on the right. You'll steady them. Corporal Mercer's got the wind up from seeing the wounded." Will looked to Jack, crushing sadness undermining his terseness. "Your stripes will steady them, Corporal Oakley. As will King. He's always the steadiest."

"Aye, Lieuten't," Jack said. He could see Will was shaky, just holding on. Jack understood his need for formality to keep himself gathered.

"Halfpenny, you're with me. I'll need you close at hand," Will said, taking a few steps back toward his platoon. He turned just before the traverse, Toby at his side. The four stood for a short, endless moment. There was no purpose in saying a word.

Then Will and Toby were gone.

Back in the center of his platoon, Will gave the commands he knew were required. Once more, he tugged on straps and belts, slapped shoulders, spoke platitudes.

"Finally out of these muddy holes, Kennedy. Fine day for a stroll through Picardy, eh?"

"Surely is that, Lieuten't. Fine a day as you could want."

Mustn't let them see. Nerviness.

"Only one way home to that wife of yours, Rideout, and that's through Jerry yonder."

"Not sure she'll have me back, sir, if'ts with a wooden leg!"

"Do your duty and maybe we'll get you a medal to go with it."

"A gong might just make up for the lack o' leg, Lieuten't. Might'n it just."

Will tugged his sleeve and glanced at his watch. Toby stayed close as they wove back. In position, there was only waiting now, each to his own thoughts. 0915 was jump off. Will removed his revolver from its holster. It creaked in the silence, new leather flexing.

Just a few minutes. Mustn't let the men see. No nerviness. Steady.

Back down the trench, Will heard a faint sound. The commander's whistle. It repeated down the line as each platoon took up the signal. Will felt the brass wrapped in his palm, smooth and warm from his skin. He blew it hard, emptying his lungs and chest, lifting himself up the trench ladder. He looked left and right. No hesitation, no cowering.

Stout lads, steady men. Not nervy.

They had 250 yards of open ground to their own front line. He could already see the battering the first trench had taken from the German heavy artillery. The battalion was all out now, two companies leading, the other two following. Long lines moving forward at a steady walk.

Then it began.

No surprise to the Germans, this wave.

The German field guns found them soon enough. Then in between the artillery explosions, Will heard a steady *pffft-pffft* from the impacts of the German's heavy machine guns. They were firing over the heads of their own men, the bullets arcing down into a killing field.

Gaps cut in their own wire last night were narrow and zig-zagging to confuse the enemy. The German gunners had spotted the openings and trained their fire there.

So many nameless men falling. Falling forward without a fuss. Some crumpled on their sides, others on their backs. Moving but no cries making it through the bombardment. Some seemed part of the churned-up earth, not moving at all.

Will saw his own men falling. Not nameless now. All names to him.

Keep them moving forward. Only hope is off this field. Mustn't let them see. Too nervy.

Stumbling over the steep edge of a fresh shell crater, Will went down on his knees, dropping his revolver. Toby caught him under an arm and jerked him back up. Will reeled in his dirty Webley by the lanyard. Nothing to fire at anyway.

Keep moving. Mustn't let the men see.

Through their first line of wire. Then the second.

Thump-PHOOM. Thump-PHOOM. The enemy's howitzers. Tall plumes of dirt and rock followed each beat.

Third wire and clots of still bodies piled around the gaps, groping at each other's bloody arms and legs. The living swerved away from the dead in horror, creeping through the openings.

Half the platoon still on their feet. Keep advancing. Get off this fucking field.

Fourth wire. The men thudding down into what was left of their front trench. At least some cover here.

Thump-PHOOM.

Can't stay. They've ranged us.

Looked to be fifteen or sixteen. Out of forty. Strung out along 100 yards of trench. Will couldn't see Geordie or Jack. They'd been on the far right. No telling.

"No proper place for Newfoundlanders, b'ys! Let's get out of this ditch and pay Fritz in kind!"

Good words, strong words.

Will thumbed the cool brass again and blew the signal to jump off.

Their own wire again. Cuts marked with white cloth and piled bodies. Other regiments' dead.

Pfft-pfft-pfft. Pfft-pfft-pfft.

The machine guns from the German front line had them. Their field guns soon followed them into No-Man's Land.

Shree-bang-BOOM.

Will and Toby made the nearest gap first. Filled with cordwood stacks of dead Worcesters or Hampshires, no telling in their jumbled filth. Green heaps of muddy wool. Husbands and sons, just this morning.

Can't have the men climbing over corpses. Make them nervy.

A German shell had cut some nearby wire a little. Will grabbed Toby's sleeve, yanking him to the break. They pulled apart the remaining strands, each with a free hand, making an opening a man could get through. Will beckoned the others with waves of his Webley. The remnants of his platoon sprinted to the new gap and started through single file. There was a new crater from a big gun just beyond. The men cleared the wire and tumbled into its cover. Will could see some of his platoon fifty yards away, making their way through the wire.

Looking behind to see if anyone remained, Will holstered his revolver and Toby shouldered his rifle.

"Alright, through you go, and get into cover with the others," Will said.

I'll be right behind.

The words never came. No one to hear.

In the stop-frame of shock, Will watched the fat shell lope through the acrid air, a black silhouette, falling slow.

Too slow to be real, surely.

There was a whoosh—all that he heard—then the big mortar's explosion deafened him with a skull-piercing ring. The explosion forced the air from his lungs, throwing him backward in a long arc. He felt terrible heat on his face and hands. Landing on the rim of a shell hole, he slid a few feet down for cover. There was a searing pain in his left cheek.

Arms work. Good. Legs, too.

He wiped his eyes with a dirty hand and could see from both. His hearing was almost gone and his cheek burned with pain, but he was alive and moving. Crabbing up the crater, he raised his head and shoulders above the rim. He could see the platoon, tossed about in twisted positions. One dragged a wounded leg, trying to help others worse off.

He looked back along the wire.

Toby not in sight. Told him to stay close.

Will crouched, wending through the churned-up chalk and stones. A rifle stock, a helmet, some darkened cloth. He wiped at his eyes again.

Strange this sleeve is so bloody. Arm wounded after all?

He flexed his arm and worked the elbow while he made his way back to the wire. His other sleeve was bloody, too.

He was spun around by a rough hand. More men coming through the wire, over the bodies. The sergeant who grabbed him mumbled, though he looked to be shouting. Will shook his head, pointed to his ear.

The sergeant leaned in close and yelled, "Where are you hit, sir?"

Will shrugged and shook his head, moving his arms to show he was not hurt.

Two soldiers ran to the sergeant's side, eyes wide. "Bloody hell! How's he even standin', Sergeant?"

"Says he's not hurt."

"Can't be. That much blood don't come from nowhere."

The sergeant looked close at Will. Left and right, up and down. His face whitened as he understood.

"Not his, lads," the sergeant said in a husky voice. "Not his." He turned away with rising nausea.

Will watched without speaking, puzzled at the sergeant's close inspection. Not able to make out the words between the three men, he followed the line of the sergeant's stare.

Then he saw, too.

He slumped to the ground, nothing left to hold him upright. He spread his arms and legs in the dirt, afraid to touch his own body, abandoned to horror at the gore that coated him. His mouth gaped wide, searching for a scream. He began to shake, as the realization seized him.

He had found Toby.

CHAPTER TWELVE

Deirdre

It was a tide at first, a rising pool of mangled arms, shattered legs, ripped chests. By early afternoon it had become a crashing wave, flooding them all at once. Their careful organization and preparations gave them the means just to poke their heads above the torrent, take a bite of breath, keep from drowning. The chaotic swarm of ambulances with exhausted drivers raced back and forth to the forward aid stations, well beyond anyone's idea of safe limits. They might save one more, with luck two or maybe three. Triage had been moved to the parking area, with the ambulances relegated to unloading along the crushed stone lane that ran up to the chateau. At least the division staff could see the results of their handiwork, should any think to glance out a window.

Deirdre had been given charge of triage—every doctor was needed for surgery, whether experienced or novice. There was too much need. "Keep these stretchers moving through!" Dee called out to the orderly sergeant who was marshaling ambulances and stretcher bearers.

"Sister, we've every hand to it already," called back the sergeant. "There's no more."

She gathered the five VADs assisting in the triage area. "Ladies, those of you who feel able, we need more hands at the stretchers. Only if you're able." With just enough hesitation to understand what was being asked of them, all five turned heel and reported for stretcher duty, some coming barely to the sergeant's shoulder.

The first of the new arrivals was a smooth-faced young man who might be mistaken in poor light for the minimum age of nineteen. He was crying out from the pain of a jagged wound across the back of one leg, stanched by a filthy field dressing. He writhed on the stretcher as Dee knelt beside him searching for bright blood from an artery. The young soldier's contortions made it impossible for her to unwrap the field dressing, so quieting him became the immediate need.

"What's your name, soldier?"

"Fuller, Sister," he managed between groans.

"And where's home for you, Fuller?" She got hold of the pin securing the bandage.

"Newfoundland, Sister. Trinity," replied the wounded man, a little calmer now. "I was one of the first in the regiment."

"We'll take fine care of you, Fuller, and see you back safe to your Trinity, God willing." She gave the lad a reassuring smile, motioning for bearers. Two of her VADs came in reply.

"There may be open beds in C Ward. Take Mr. Fuller there and ask the nurses to change his dressing and give him a quarter grain of morphia. Off with you now."

She turned her attention to the next stretcher. This soldier was unconscious and unmoving. She felt for a pulse along one wrist, then his neck. She opened one eye, then the other. With a short sigh, she caught the attention of the orderly sergeant again and nodded at the stretcher. The sergeant picked a blanket from a nearby pile and with a single practiced motion billowed it down over the immobile form. They'd move him around to the cemetery once some bearers were back from the ambulances. No good comes from leaving the dead among the living too long.

Dee moved on to the next stretcher, noting that at least four new wounded had arrived since she started with young Private Fuller. "Sergeant, find more hands for these stretchers!" she bellowed at the much put-upon man. "I don't care if you have to dragoon Field Marshal Haig himself!"

The next stretcher held a young officer, eyes rolling about and senseless. He was drenched in blood. She scanned his arms and legs and saw no torn uniform or obvious wound. Rolling him onto a shoulder, she found no gaping gash from artillery shrapnel or wide exit wound from a tumbling bullet. "Where are you wounded then, lad?" She expected no response, but asking such questions aloud helped her sense an answer.

VAD Bannerman had just entered the ambulance yard, having heard hands were needed for stretchers. Dee hailed her. "Bannerman! Fetch some water and towels over here for me." She returned her attention to the young officer, noticing he wore the same peculiar insignia as Fuller. Some sort of large deer. Another Newfoundlander.

"I brought some soap as well," said Bannerman, a little tremulous at the sight of the bloody young officer.

"Kneel on the other side and help me scrub some of this off him. I can't find a wound, other than that gash on his cheek. That didn't produce all this."

Bannerman began wiping the right side of the wounded man's head and face, then took up the towel to refold it to a clean side. She stared with undisguised shock into the dirty towel, then held it up for Dee to see the clots of brain and bone.

Both women realized then.

"Holy Mother of God! 'Tis not his a'tall?" Bannerman shook her head in unsteady reply, but did not lost her composure as the wounded man began to shake all along his body. Dee looked down at Will's wild darting eyes, his mumbling lips unable to utter a coherent sound. Two stretcher bearers arrived and she stepped aside to allow them to their work.

"Bannerman, take this man to an officer's ward and see he's well sedated. That gash on his cheek will take some stitching, but with a clean bandage it'll wait." The VAD led the stretcher bearers, their hobnailed boots crushing down the gravel pathway with loud crunches.

Dee watched for a moment as they walked away, whispered to herself, "For the love of God, what's he seen this day?"

CHAPTER THIRTEEN

Jack

The right section made it to the wire with only two men lost. From what Jack could see, they were luckier than most. But now, any attempts to crawl forward were met with the *pfft-pfft-pfft* of a machine gun on their right. The soil along the shell crater's edge popped and sprayed with each burst.

"We're not moving with that Emma Gee ranging us," said Geordie. "Not and live to speak of it."

"We could hunker down until dark, then make our way back to the support trenches?"

"No good. Those gunners have us marked. Artillery will range us soon, too." Jack looked around the big shell hole at the nine other men. "One round in here will catch us all."

"We might find a seam in their field of fire," Geordie said, calmed a little by studying their predicament. "Plenty of shell holes for us to choose after that. Maybe find one where you can pip those goddamn gunners."

"Won't get much older sitting here. Let's have a crack."

Sliding down to Mercer, Jack spoke to the rattled corporal. "King and me are going to see if we can do something about that machine gun that's got us pinned." Mercer nodded, nervous and needy, not knowing what was expected of him in Jack's absence. A German shell hit fifty yards away, showering them with dirt.

Jack motioned to Geordie and they made their way back to the battered trench. Staying low, they stopped after a hundred yards behind two white cloth strips that marked a pre-cut gap in the wire. They went back out through the wire and zigzagged forward from hole to hole. At the fourth, Jack spotted a little motion through a narrow break in the Germans' sandbags.

They dared not use field glasses. The morning sun would reflect from the lenses. It took a few long moments to spot the movement again. Breathing with a controlled rhythm, Jack targeted the rectangular opening along his rifle's iron sights. He would not lose them again.

Like huntin' seals. They'll come back up.

One helmeted head moved through the opening, too fast. The machine gun burped three times. They were still strafing Mercer and the others.

Must be a nervy young crew. No way Mercer showed a hair above that hole.

Jack spotted a grey figure turn to the opening and bend over, reloading or bringing up a new belt of ammunition. He breathed in, let out half, and squeezed the trigger with gentle sureness. The Ross barked and the grey back slumped down and out of sight. The machine gun fired again at the wrong hole. Jack cycled the bolt on his rifle, the smoking brass rolling down the slope beside him. He could hear Geordie breathing hard and anxious behind him.

Shoulders appeared in the opening again. Jack sighted and squeezed, just as the German ducked from sight.

Patient as you please. Like huntin' seals.

The machine gun fired again. Dirt flew just to Jack's left. The Germans had them.

One last shot. Sure there's time.

A bare-headed German popped into view again. He turned in profile, with a handset to his ear. Jack pulled back his rifle and slid down to Geordie. "They've called in our location. I saw one on a field phone," he said in hurried bursts while wrapping the breech of his Ross. "We best be scampering, toot-sweet."

Shree-bang-BOOM.

"Shite, their whizz-bangs have us!" shouted Geordie, sliding on his backside and hands down the shell hole.

Shree-bang-BOOM. Shree-bang-BOOM.

Jack stood to sling his rifle, adjusting the strap across his chest.

Phumph.

Geordie watched a fat black shadow fly up from the German trenches. It hung motionless like a big sausage at the top of its lazy arc, then began its plummet. As it fell, Geordie watched it grow bigger and bigger.

"Mortar! Cover!"

Jack did not see the shell before it burst on the slope above him.

Jesus, but I'm tired all of a sudden. Can't seem to lift a leg.

Geordie was blown flat, the blast of the large trench mortar plastering him with dirt. He coughed and spit, struggling for breath. The acrid smell of burnt gun cotton hung in the enlarged crater, burning his nose and throat. Contained by the lopsided bowl of the shell hole, the smoke from the explosion clung like ground fog, obscuring the bottom.

"Jackie! Are you hit?" Geordie slid down the crater, tumbling and rolling on his shoulder before righting himself.

Geordie's shouting for me. Need to get up.

As he tumbled downward, Geordie made out a figure half-buried by dislodged dirt. He flew across the last few yards, plopping down beside Jack. Geordie rolled him off his side, careful as his fear would allow, brushing away what dirt he could.

"Jackie, oh dear God!" He pulled the field dressings from his own pocket and wrapped one tight as he could around the bright blood spurting from a huge gash in Jack's left thigh. "Jackie, stay with me, darlin' b'y! Stay with me now!" The bandage could not cover all the ragged wound, so Geordie wrapped the second bandage over the first, already soaked in blood. He patted Jack's outer pockets to locate his bandages. The cloth packet was covered in blood, but the contents were intact. He bit through the waterproof inner packet and wrapped one bandage around a second oozing gash in Jack's right thigh.

Why is he fussin' about so? And he's bleedin' from his arm, too.

"That's it, Jackie. That's a good lad. Look at me now, look at me." Jack's eyes were open wide, but the left was blinking away blood running from dirty lacerations along that side of his face.

Can barely see him through this…what?

"Oh, that's bad, Jackie, that's bad." Geordie pressed down on the soaked bandages wrapping Jack's left thigh. He took the bandolier from across his chest and stripped off the ammunition pouches, wrapping the broad leather belt above the wound and cinching down as hard as he could. The bleeding slowed.

One sleeve of Jack's tunic was in bloody tatters, too. "Oh holy Jesus, look what they've done to you, Jackie! Your poor arm, too."

Wish he'd not fuss so. Just the wind knocked out of me. Jesus, that hurts my arm.

Using the last of their field dressings, Geordie wrapped Jack's lower arm carefully and pinned the bandage. There was nothing left for the nasty gashes on the side of his face, but those seemed to be clotting on their own. Geordie laid down in the dirt next to Jack's head. He spoke in fragments and bits of sentences, trying to calm himself as much as reassure Jack.

"Oh, we've got ourselves…"

What's he babblin' on about?

"Too close to the Bosche lines…"

Lord, my leg does hurt.

"On our own 'til dark…"

His arm is bleedin' fierce. Needs to bandage that.

Jack spoke but Geordie didn't react, continuing his rambling monologue. He tightened his throat in what felt like a shout.

"Your arm's bad."

Geordie's head snapped up and he leaned down close to Jack's face. "Jackie, you're speakin'!" He turned his head so his ear was near to Jack's mouth. "What's that you said?"

"You should see to that arm, b'y," Jack said with another great effort.

"My arm?" Geordie said, smiling wide, his friend conscious and knowing him still. "My arm's the least of our problems, Jackie." Geordie lifted his right arm and looked it over from fingers to shoulder. When he tried to lift his left, he saw the sleeve was soaked in dark purple.

"Shite, you're right, b'y," Geordie said, concerned with the amount of blood already out of his wound. He'd be no use to either of them if he fainted dead away. Jack gave a small nod to acknowledge he should help himself now.

Strange it took him so long to notice that.

Unbuttoning his tunic with his right hand, Geordie ripped the tail of his grey-back shirt up to the buttons at mid-chest, then bit a notch in the cloth to divide it. He felt a throbbing pain in his stiffening arm as he tore. Wrapping the makeshift bandage around his wound, he tied the ragged ends with some difficulty, pulling the knot tight with his teeth. He folded another square of the sweat-stained flannel into a pad, wiped the blood out of Jack's eye, and placed the cloth against the gashes in his face. He wrapped a long strip around Jack's head to hold it.

"Makes you no more handsome," Geordie said with a weak smile of encouragement.

Damn, but I'm thirsty.

Jack again forced out what he thought a scream, whispering, " Any water?"

"Of course, Jackie, you must be thirsty," Geordie said, reaching to pull the canteen around to his front, unsnapping the web strap. "You've no belly wound, so have as much as you like."

Able to speak with more ease after a few dribbles, Jack said, "We're here 'til dark." There were no stretcher parties coming forward in daylight. They both knew it.

Geordie watched Jack throughout the afternoon, startling whenever his breath caught or he moaned in his delirium. From time to time, Jack came around and spoke a few raspy words. Geordie gave him more water and encouragement. The time passed with excruciating slowness, punctuated by random whizz-bang shells, bursts of machine gun fire, and solitary pops from a sniper's rifle. With the lowering sun shrouding their hole in chill shadows, Geordie decided when next Jack woke he would move him up the slope to await the stretcher parties.

With a soft moan, Jack stirred and licked his lips. Geordie bent low over him and said, "Time to move up, Jackie. It's not going to be a walk in the meadow for you." Jack nodded, eyes wide to the darkening sky and set with a determined look. Digging his heels into the loose dirt, Jack's head between his spread legs, Geordie inched his way up the slope. Jack grimaced as they moved but the only sounds he made were low grunts and a few soft yelps as they scraped upward.

Near the top, Geordie fell back flat in the dirt, drenched from exertion and his lungs burning. After resting a few moments, he crawled around to face Jack. "This should do us fine."

Choked with pain, Jack croaked, "Some water?" He was disoriented by his thirst and his unfocused pain from the excruciating move. As Geordie fished for his canteen, Jack stretched his right arm toward the orange and purple clouds in the fading light.

Just like the sunsets behind the lighthouse…

As Geordie turned back with the canteen, there was a single sharp crack. Jack cried out with fresh pain, shoving his hand under his wounded left arm. He rolled his head back and forth, face contorted with the effort to stifle his screams.

"Oh Christ!" Geordie cried as he hugged Jack to the dirt. He rolled to his side and eased Jack's right arm toward him, prompting another round of moans. There was a clean bullet hole right through the palm of Jack's hand, with an ugly exit wound out the back. Not much bleeding though. Pulling out the last of the dirty flannel, Geordie halved it and wrapped a long strip around Jack's hand. He took the last remaining piece and carefully slid it between the two sopping field dressings on Jack's left thigh.

"Jackie, we've been out here near eleven hours. It's almost dark, so we can move about if we've a mind." Jack stared back without answering, in agony from the pain of his wounds, old and new.

"You've lost a lot of blood, sweet b'y."

Jack was calmer now, Geordie's determined voice giving him a focus. He blinked his eyes hard in agreement. It was cooling off fast now with a sliver of moon visible low on the horizon. Jack had begun to shake a little.

"There's no telling when a stretcher party might get this far forward. We can't risk the wait." Looking close into Jack's eyes, the tears in his own invisible in the feeble twilight, Geordie said, "I'll not have you die out here."

He hefted Jack onto his shoulder, wrapping his good arm around his friend's shredded legs. Geordie's knees nearly failed as he pressed up with his load. A tortured moan came from Jack, his face buried in the back of Geordie's tunic, as they set off at a steady pace toward their own lines.

CHAPTER FOURTEEN

Deirdre

Wounded and dying came to them in a steady parade of horrors, but they managed somehow in the dark with paraffin lanterns and the acetylene headlamps of the ambulances. Stretchers in, stretchers out—most to surgery and the wards, too many behind the old chateau. There had been a short lull as day dragged toward evening, before the darkness allowed stretcher parties to move forward into No-Man's Land. This had freed ambulances to take some wounded to the medical trains that would transport them to the port towns with big base hospitals. Not that there were enough trains this day.

The whole staff was numbed by the enormity of suffering that had passed through their hands since morning. Dee took ten minutes to gulp coffee and a few biscuits, sitting on a supply crate below a lantern hanging on a post, stealing a few moments off her feet. Dr. Macintosh came outside and, on his way back from the jakes, stopped for a coffee, too. He saw Dee on her crate in a wan pool of light. He was haggard and pale, yet still carried his accustomed calm and determined look. Their uniforms were festooned with random dabs and splatters of blood, black against the doctor's khaki shirt and crimson against Dee's white apron.

"You look a fright, Major," Dee said, offering one of her biscuits.

He took one and chewed between sips. "Ta. With all due respect, you're no spring blossom yourself, Sister Brannigan." He smiled into his mug.

They sat in silence, gazing absently down the long line of buildings, most of them wards for the wounded, a few set aside for other uses. They had been slap-dashed out of green lumber, gobbling up the terraced parterres. All that remained as telltales of the chateau's gardens were a few pea gravel paths and a lichen-encrusted fountain with a leering satyr that once spouted water, now sitting behind an incinerator for bloody bandages and amputated limbs. Below the hospital buildings, set into a broad lawn that stretched down to a stream lined by sorrowful willows, the new cemetery grew apace.

"There'll be more soon with the dark," Dee said, looking over to the near-empty parking area, just a few stretchers with lifeless forms under blankets awaiting the exhausted orderlies for their final trip around the back. "Any new arrivals will've been lying out all day."

"Aye, that they will," said the doctor. "That will mean more amputations. And more gas gangrene in the days to come." They both feared the gangrene. With every form of microbe lurking in soil churned up by the relentless bombardment, gas gangrene could take hold even in vigorous patients that looked set to make a good recovery. Once the stench of infection set in, the gas gangrene could spirit away a young soldier in three days, a single day, even a dozen hours.

The next wave of ambulances arrived. Dee nodded to the doctor, rose and walked toward the arriving stretchers. Macintosh gulped down the remainder of his coffee and headed back to one of the surgical buildings.

The VADs assigned to triage huddled around the parking area with lanterns as Dee approached the first wounded man arriving from the ambulances. Two orderlies carried the stretcher, accompanied by a large man, his left arm in a makeshift sling. As they set the stretcher down, she knelt beside the silhouetted form and motioned for a VAD to bring her lantern nearer. The paraffin flame spilled over the unconscious man, his face almost entirely obscured by dirty makeshift bandaging, and illuminated the larger soldier kneeling at the side of the stretcher.

"He's wounded all over, Sister, the worst being his left leg. He's a shrapnel wound in his right leg and a nasty one in his left forearm, too," Geordie said, drawling out his tired words.

Dee glanced at the thick, soaked bandages around Jack's left thigh and the broad leather strap lashed above the wound. "How long has that tourniquet been round the leg?"

"Since minutes after he was wounded. What time is it now?"

One of the VADs bent into the light to read a small gold watch pinned to her apron bib. "It's gone half eleven."

Geordie wrinkled his face as he struggled through his crippling fatigue to do the simple math. "He must have been wounded about half nine this mornin', so that'd be fourteen hours, I suppose."

"Did the bleeding ever stop altogether?"

"No. That concerned me greatly."

"Forget your concern, now you've got your mate here alive, soldier," Dee said. "We might just have a chance at saving this leg."

Geordie didn't understand much, other than her positive tone. "His left arm is tore up bad, Sister, but his right hand had a bullet go through clean. Maybe three or four hours ago."

Dee's head snapped up. "This man was wounded as he lay out there? In No-Man's Land?"

"Yes, Sister. Fritz finds great sport in sniping the wounded. You'd think he'd figure out we're more a burden alive and bleedin' than dead and gone."

"Alright, let's get him to the surgical ward right away." Dee motioned to the orderlies and a VAD. "They'll need to attend to the left leg, no telling what will happen when that belt is removed. The arm can probably wait, once it's been cleaned and packed with a fresh dressing." As the stretcher was raised, she crossed to help Geordie to his feet. Turning her chin over her shoulder to the VAD, she said, "Get Dr. Macintosh to look at that right hand. He's the best hand surgeon we have. Might save some movement, if we're lucky."

Geordie was leaning hard against Dee, who stumbled a little under his weight. She motioned with her head to the orderly sergeant, who dashed over to help. "Let's get you a bed, soldier, or at least a chair. Someone needs to look at that arm of yours," she said, steering him toward the line of low wooden buildings.

"I'll not leave Jackie 'til he's safe, Sister, not 'til I know he's safe."

A VAD exited the surgical building, looked about in the darkness, then made her way over to Dee. "Sister Brannigan?" called out Bannerman as she strode across the gravel pathway.

"Yes, over here. And give us a hand, so the sergeant can get back to the ambulances."

The VAD took the load from the much larger sergeant with a grunt. "Dr. Macintosh asked me to fetch you to surgery. He said the nurses are overwhelmed and you're needed there more than here."

Dee knew the Major would not have sent for her if it was not a desperate situation. "Who's to take over triage then?"

Bannerman hitched Geordie's arm tighter over her shoulders and said, "I'm to relieve you, Sister, according to Dr. Macintosh." Dee heard a quaver of uncertain fear in the young woman's voice. This was an unconscionable burden to put on the poor girl. But these were unconscionable times.

"You've been assisting all over today, Bannerman, and you're as steady as they come. You can do this, and do it well."

The VAD straightened up under the weight of the wounded soldier and said, "I'll do my level best, Sister."

"No one can ask more than that, Bannerman. Now let's get this poor lad to a bed."

As Dee and the little VAD limped on with their slumping patient between them, they heard the big soldier let out a quiet sob with each slow step.

GREAT BRITISH OFFENSIVE
ATTACK ON A 20 MILE FRONT

GERMAN TRENCHES OCCUPIED
MANY PRISONERS TAKEN

OUR CASUALTIES NOT HEAVY
OFFICIAL STATEMENT

The following telegraphic report has been received from British Headquarters in France at 11:55 a.m. to-day (Saturday): —

Attacks were launched on the north of the River Somme this morning at 7:30 in conjunction with the French.

British troops have broken through into the German forward system of defences on a front of sixteen miles. Fighting continues.

The French attack on our immediate right is proceeding equally satisfactorily.

On the remainder of the British front raiding parties again succeeded in penetrating enemy defences on many points, inflicting loss on the enemy and taking some prisoners.

(From the Press Association's Special Correspondent.)
British Headquarters, France, Saturday, 9:30 a.m.

At about half-past seven this morning, a vigorous attack was launched by the British Army. The front now extends over about 20 miles, north of the Somme. The assault was preceded by a terrific bombardment lasting about an hour and a half. It is too early yet to give anything but the barest particulars, as the fighting is developing in intensity, but the British troops have already occupied the German front line. Many prisoners have already fallen into our hands and as far as can be ascertained our casualties have not been heavy.

CHAPTER FIFTEEN

Deirdre

The Big Push ground on into its sixth week. There was no end in sight to what was now known as the Somme Offensive. The wounded came in surges, like the fighting, but never stopped. When the generals were not planning grand frontal assaults, there were still casualties from the day-to-day trench raiding and sniping or from the morning and evening hate, reciprocal barrages that made life miserable for both sides. The barrages kept the heads ward full.

Dee had been much in demand since the beginning and drove herself hard. When Dr. Macintosh found her sleeping on a table in the coffee room and was unable to rouse her, he assigned her as senior nurse to the heads ward, thinking the calmer environment might rejuvenate her. She had been on the ward for two weeks, but took up other duties during surges of activity. That could not be helped. Dr. Macintosh kept a close eye on her, however, and would not allow her to get as fagged out as she had during those first weeks of the offensive. The infrequent times she managed to drop off to sleep, she was shocked back to wakefulness within minutes by formless images she could never identify but nonetheless filled her with terror. Although she would not admit it to herself or anyone, her work on the heads ward had begun taking its toll, too.

They had found the best way to calm the head patients when they became delirious was to play along with their hallucinations. Once they felt validated in their fears and anxieties, most of the patients would settle. The patient in Bed 12, for example, believed the middle of the ward was his fruit orchard. If left to this fantasy, he was content to watch over his trees until he tired. Then the patient in Bed 5, closer to the orchard than Bed 12, provided night watch to ensure no naughty boys stole Bed 12's lovely fruit while he slept. Dee was able to speak of the orchard with all sincerity, which was very reassuring to the men. But the orchard, together with all the other fantasies of catching rats or dousing fires, began to wear on her.

In particular, the patient in Bed 24 counted ceaselessly in a low voice, out of sequence, throughout the day and most of the night. Always more or less downward, always starting at ninety-nine. "Ninety-nine, ninety-eight, ninety-five, ninety-seven, ninety-nine, ninety three…" Although not conscious of Ninety-Nine's counting most of the time, Dee was always attuned to any changes. If he managed to count down in correct order for more than five or six digits, she noticed. If he stopped counting for more than a moment, her attention went to him. The result was a constant edginess, an inability to quiet her mind, which only aggravated her trouble sleeping. Coupled with this was the sad fact that precious few of these head cases survived more than a week or two. Any who did were destined for a lifetime in an asylum.

There had not been a serious incident of violence for some days, but there was always that threat. Such incidents often arrived without warning, the staff unable to foresee most of the outbursts. This night, the ward was quiet, having calmed to the usual level of occasional groans that indicated most patients were in some level of stupor. All except for Ninety-Nine, who kept up his idiosyncratic counting. Dee sat exhausted at a small table near the end of the ward, gazing along the darkened line of beds in half-attentive grogginess.

"Ninety-nine, ninety-seven, *hic*, ninety-*hic*-nine, *hic*…"

She dashed down the ward. Ninety-Nine lay under his bedclothes, unmoving. His entire head was bandaged, but for his eyes and mouth. She lifted a hand and felt for a pulse. It was there, albeit weak and thready. As she placed his hand back, he sat bolt upright and began bellowing, "Ninety-nine! Ninety-nine! Ninety-nine!" He grabbed Dee's forearm and pulled it hard across the bed, then swung his other arm back, hitting her across the bridge of her nose. She sprawled across his legs and he began thrashing wildly, trying to throw off the unknown weight. He rolled hard and fell off the bed, still clamped to Dee's arm. The weight of his fall jerked her to the floor next to him. Falling heavily onto her hip and shoulder, she lost her breath as a crippling pain shot through her. Getting to her knees, she pulled Ninety-Nine's arm up over her shoulder. The delusional man twisted and squirmed to get free just as she heaved to raise him back to the bed. A white-hot shock of pain radiated out from her lower back, intense and electric, nearly taking her consciousness. She willed herself to stay upright. Ninety-Nine flopped back on his bed, a trickle of blood running across the bandages around his mouth.

He had stopped counting.

Moving with excruciating care, she managed to lift his legs back onto the bed. Even the weight of one limb was painful for her to bear. She shuffled with difficulty to the end of the bed where his head lolled half over the edge. He wasn't long for this world, but she would not let him go like this, not on her ward. She slid an arm under his shoulders and placed her other hand under his bandaged head. Blinking away tears and gritting her teeth to keep from crying out, she gave another heave, aiming to return the dying man's head to his pillow. As she lifted, her hand sank into the back of his bandaged skull. While she was pondering how odd that seemed, a huge dagger of renewed pain stabbed up along her spine and down both legs. She grimaced and clenched her fists. Unable to sustain the lift, she dropped the unconscious man on his side. As he rolled away from her, a large wad of bandaging stayed in her fingers. The mass of bandages had constituted the back half of his head, the rest having been blown away by some atrocious weapon. Holding the bandages in her hand, she began to giggle as Ninety-Nine's breathing ceased.

All this time, and Ninety-Nine had no head. At least the parts that hadn't to do with counting.

Crumpling under the pain that pulsed from her back and hip, she slid to the floor in a heap, laughter and sobs mixing. With no notion how long she had been on the floor, Dee felt herself being rolled over by strong hands. She looked up, eyes not focusing well through the pain, into the face of Dr. Macintosh.

"Deirdre lass! Deirdre! Are you hurt?"

She grabbed his arm and began pulling herself up, but the pain in her back flattened her again. "I've thrown my back getting this patient back in his bed." She wiped at her tears and her hand came back bloody. "He got the best of the argument."

Alerted by the doctor's urgent voice, a VAD ran to his side, shocked to see the indomitable Sister Brannigan in a heap on the wood planking of the floor. "Nurse, get an orderly and fetch a third-grain of morphia," Macintosh said while the VAD stood gaping. "Off with you now. Do as I've asked."

The doctor held Dee's head in the crook of his elbow, keeping it off the floor while he waited for assistance to get her to a bed. He had heard her wild laughter and sobs. It's what brought him to this corner of the ward during his evening rounds.

"Have we worn you right down to the nub, lass?"

18th of September, 1916
Chapelheath, Shropshire

Dear Mother and Father,

I hope you will forgive my dictating this to a nurse (a lovely young lady from Leeds) but I still have a little trouble seeing due to the wound to my face. By now you will have read of what transpired on the 1st of July. I wish I could claim a stunning success for the Regiment, there having been such horrible casualties, but the most I can say is we acquitted ourselves bravely and honourably. And we gave the Germans as much as we got. You will have heard we lost Toby. There is really nothing more to say, other than to assure his mother he never faltered and died as bravely as the rest. I shall miss him greatly. Both Jack and Geordie were wounded, Jack getting the worst of it. Geordie is already back to duty, assigned to division transport. Jack is at a hospital here in Blighty, too.

As for me, I am on the mend. The wound to my face is healing. My leg, on the other hand, is proving slow to improve, so there is really no telling when I shall be back to the battalion. I get round well enough with the fine walking stick Mssrs. Beasley & Atherton procured on my behalf. My thanks to Mother for arranging an invitation to visit Reverend and Mrs. Harper in Somerset. I shall write them with my thanks, but defer my visit until such time as the doctors tell me I am fit for travel. It will be soon, I am sure.

We have certainly seen much in these past two years. I had never thought when this began I would see two of my dearest friends buried, Sandy under the miserable rocks of Suvla and now poor Toby in the mud of France. And the other three of us wounded. Nine of ten in the battalion casualties, so no surprise. How did this all come about? Seems a fair question.

Well, I have nattered on long enough. Please give Cordelia my congratulations on the birth of her son and my best wishes to Victoria and her children. Hug Gussie for me as well. The house must seem very quiet to her now.

> *With my dearest regards and best wishes,*
> *I remain, as ever,*
> *Your son William*

Dr. Macintosh insisted Dee take a full week's bedrest for her back to heal. The ruptured disc was very painful, but a week away from duties with regular meals did much to mend her. Macintosh had prescribed morphia tablets for the pain, which had also resulted in her first decent sleep since the 1st of July, although decent was a relative term. The drug made her unconscious, but as its effects wore off, the terrible images would creep back. She had begun taking a second dose to get her through the rest of the night. Because she was a senior nurse and the hospital a chaotic place even in the slowest times, no one noticed how often she was refilling her tablets.

After ten days, Major Macintosh had allowed her to return to duty and she had assigned herself, with the senior matron's permission, to the moribund ward. Dr. Macintosh concurred, knowing the chance of a violent encounter with one of these dying patients was very remote. The patients were kept free from pain with liberal injections of morphia. As Macintosh had acknowledged early on, there was not much use worrying whether these men died from their terrible wounds or the drugs that kept them free from pain. What no one had reckoned was what the effect might be on the nurses and VADs who had to watch these men die, day in and day out. There was great mercy on this ward, but also great hopelessness and, inevitably, despair.

As attuned as Dee had been since her earliest training days to the smallest cues from patients, she could tell with some reliability when patients would die, often to within the hour. This had first been pointed out to her by a Catholic chaplain, routinely called to administer Last Rites. But was it a blessing, as the priest called it? The poor men were past noticing. With the clarity of her thinking lessened by the lingering daytime effects of the morphia, she began to wonder—and then almost convince herself—that she had somehow caused their deaths rather than just foreseen them.

She chastised herself for her wandering imagination, but the seed was planted and continued to twine in and out of her thoughts, day upon day. The worst was at night, lying in bed and waiting for the morphia to carry her off. She lost all control of her thoughts then. The images of the dying men she had left on the ward—she knew which would be gone when she returned—jumbled in her mind with the shadowy figures that had haunted her for over three months. They would often writhe and twist around fleeting visions of her own father. She knew she had to wait them out, suffer them for just a little while until the morphia took her away to a thoughtless oblivion. In the past few weeks, she had begun taking half-doses of morphia to get through her days on the ward as well. So much suffering and dying, how else could anyone be expected to tolerate it, she had convinced herself.

In late October, the Somme Offensive still grinding on to its inevitable stalemate, Dr. Macintosh came to the moribund ward on his usual rounds before retiring. Dee was still on duty and it had been a bad day, with four men passing within a few hours of each other.

She knew others would slip away overnight and this troubled her more than it should have. She had taken a full dose of morphia and was looking forward to slipping between the clean sheets of her bed and floating away in just a few minutes when her shift ended.

Major Macintosh strode down the ward, glancing at each unconscious man, noting a few involuntary movements but nothing more. As he approached the table where Dee sat, she rose to greet him. Noticing she wavered while rising, Macintosh became concerned she was overextending herself again. He placed a hand under her elbow and said, "Please, Sister Brannigan, sit yourself down. You're overtired and there's no reason to rise on my account." He helped her to the slat-backed chair.

Looking up at the doctor, Dee's face was illuminated by the small goose-neck lamp on the edge of the table. It was in this light that Dr. Macintosh noticed her eyes. He had always been struck by the deep green of them, set off by her fair skin and thick reddish-brown hair, always a few strands out of place. Now he saw something very different. Her eyes, tired as she was, were shining under the stark light and appeared almost china blue. As she blinked languidly up at him, the doctor realized with growing sadness just how this fine, strong woman had soldiered on through her painful injuries and crushing workload.

"Deirdre lass, what have we done to you?" he said with painful resignation. "Have we used you all up?"

Forcing herself to attentiveness, she said, "Sure, I don't know what you're speaking of Major. I'm fit as a fiddle now." Her words were precise but slower than usual.

Glancing down at the pocket of her pinafore, he spotted the small brown bottle. "Let me see what you have there in that pocket, Deirdre. And I'll take no excuses. Hand it to me now."

Thick, hot tears formed in her eyes as she reached into her pocket and offered up the cylindrical glass bottle, meek as a child caught in some petty transgression. Holding the translucent brown bottle up to the lamplight and giving it a slight shake, Dr. Macintosh saw the small white pills clearly. "How long, Deirdre?"

"It's... it's for my back, you see," she stammered out. "You gave them to me when... when that patient in the heads ward attacked me."

Macintosh was neither angry nor disappointed, but rather filled with unalloyed concern for this woman he had come to hold dear over the months they had labored together in the face of such ceaseless suffering. "Your back was healed long ago, Deirdre." He gently shook the bottle before her eyes. "These are for some pain much deeper." He fell to one knee beside her, his face awash in the light now. She looked down at him, his salt-and-pepper hair reminding her so of her father's. She let her tears fall upon the table top.

"I'll get you free of this place, lass. You've given all you can here," he said, wiping her cheeks with his clean white handkerchief.

CHAPTER SIXTEEN

Will

Chapelheath was a decent enough place, Will thought, converted from a country house lent to the war effort by some patriotic member of the minor nobility. His mother would know of Sir So-and-So and the house's pedigree, if he cared enough to write her and ask.

As soon as his filthy uniform had been cut away, his body washed, and the laceration on his face cleaned and stitched, he had been transferred by train to a base hospital on the French coast, then by ship back to England. He was unaware of all this activity and movement, having been labeled 'Not Yet Diagnosed' and heavily sedated throughout. This succession of hospital wards registered in his memory as little more than fuzzy glimpses until he began emerging from his drugged delirium somewhere in England. He had finally been diagnosed as "shell shocked" at one hospital or another, that being the current term for all sorts of derangements induced by the quotidian horrors of trench warfare.

Some medical experts believed shell shock a result of neurasthenia, physical damage to the nervous system from the concussive effects of the prolonged bombardments. A few at Craiglockhart Hospital in Edinburgh, trained before the war in the theories of Freud and Jung, were having a little success treating shell shock as a psychological disorder. Chapelheath's resident physicians were unconvinced by any such innovative thinking. Treatment at their hospital was based on the time-honored Victorian proposition that a gentleman should not be mollycoddled, but rather must be returned to his normal state of self-discipline and uprightness through a predictable regimen and strong suasion. They had faltered through moral weakness, understandable for a gentleman in such horrendous circumstances, but it was weakness just the same. This needed to be corrected sternly and quickly—but not with the military discipline and courts-martial reserved for shell-shocked private soldiers, presumed to be cowards and malingerers.

Placed under the care of Lieutenant Colonel (Dr.) Harcourt, a man absolutely certain of his seat upon the moral high ground, Will was subjected to the full force of Chapelheath's discipline-and-domination approach. On this particular mid-October day, Will sat before a large mahogany desk in what was, outside of wartime, the baronet's rather sparse library. He let his eyes float around the room with a perfected look of tedium. Whenever Will's eyes passed over the doctor, the little man glared back through his pince-nez as if he were smelling spoilt milk.

In his pre-war civilian practice, Dr. Harcourt had specialized in the treatment of married women suffering from hysteria. Most of his patients had been referred or dragged to him by their proper middle-class husbands. Wealthier men managed to keep their troublesome wives better hidden in the spas of France and Germany before the war, Bath or Brighton for the duration. These officer shell-shock patients, however, were not hysterical women. Harcourt had determined that they needed sterner handling, so away with the laudanum and cocaine and snake oils of his civilian practice.

"I see you are still walking with a stick, Lieutenant Parsons," observed the doctor. "Why do you find that necessary?" He had prescribed a course of faradization, the application of electric shocks, to Will's trembling extremities. "I see from your file that the treatments have arrested the tremors in your leg, have they not?"

Running his thumb over the brass head of the walking stick, cold and reassuring, Will replied, "Yes, well, that's true. But there is still a pronounced weakness and I wouldn't want to fall and injure some other part of me."

The balding doctor looked from the case notes to Will and back again with a noncommittal, "Yes, quite." Rising from his seat, Harcourt came around the desk and stood beside Will. "Could you turn to face me, Lieutenant?"

Will moved his chair around, facing the diminutive doctor.

"Now stand and hold both your arms out towards me, palms down, please," said the doctor, direct and businesslike. "I see you still have some noticeable trembling in both arms?"

"Yes, it has diminished but not gone away entirely. I'm still not able to write legibly."

Making some notes in the folder before him, the doctor said, "We shall continue the faradization then, and increase the frequency. That should break the tremors."

Sitting down and taking out a cigarette, Will fought the shaking in his right hand as he tried to hold his lighter to the cigarette end. He was beginning to despair that it would ever go away. Returning to his seat behind the protection of the capacious desk, Harcourt asked, "And your sleeping, has that improved at all?"

Now there was a subject of great interest, thought Will.

"Still a little insomnia, I'm afraid." He took another shaky drag of the cigarette, then flicked it into a large Venetian glass ashtray on the edge of the doctor's desk.

"That is not what the night nursing staff reports, Lieutenant. Quite the contrary," said the doctor with a note of self-satisfaction in catching Will in a tiny lie. "They report you are awakened, on average, two to three times by extreme night terrors."

Exhaling smoke through his nostrils, Will turned his head to the window. He fingered the short gold-braid wound stripe just added to the left sleeve of his tunic, noting at the same time that the beech trees, planted by one of the owner's ancestors in a precise rank right along this side of the house, had gone coppery without his noticing.

Quite lovely in autumn. Nothing like that at home.

"Not sure how I would know, Doctor, as I'm asleep at the time," said Will, returning with peevish reluctance to the conversation.

The doctor would have none of this facetiousness from a junior officer. He leaned forward in his chair and squared himself to his full unimpressive height, attempting to look foreboding. "I am prescribing additional road walking, Lieutenant Parsons, to fatigue you during the day," he said, scribbling with great scratching purpose in the folder again. "This languid lounging and louche attitude exacerbates your physical and moral decay, young man." He rose again and walked around the desk.

"Not under my care, Lieutenant," he said, shaking a stubby finger in Will's direction, not daring to close the distance too much. "Most decidedly, not under my care. My task is to return you to the fight with dispatch. And I intend to do just that." The little medical officer strode to the door and opened it with what might resemble determination. "Good day, Lieutenant Parsons. We shall discuss your lack of insight into your condition and lackadaisical approach to your cure at our next meeting. Of that you may be sure."

Will stubbed out his cigarette, rose and limped out of the library-*cum*-surgery leaning on his ebony and brass walking stick.

Quite fashionable sensibilities, that Beasley & Atherton. Fine stick, this.

Making his way down the long central hallway with its age-polished parquet floor and faded wall coverings, the triple clicking of his heels and cane sounded back off the high ceiling. He opened a French door, filigreed wrought iron over the glass, and stepped out onto the south terrace. It was a peerless day, clear and bright, the incomparable light saturating all the colors of the dying season. He sat on a stone bench near the edge of the terrace and lit another cigarette, inhaling the clean autumn air along with tart smoke. As he exhaled, he again studied the long line of carefully placed beeches. He felt his chest release a little of the tension that accumulated during every appointment with Dr. Harcourt.

Good thing they don't know the whisky it takes to keep those terrors to three or four a night.

CHAPTER SEVENTEEN

Jack

The one redeeming aspect of wretched London winters is they give way to London springs. And glorious things those are, with riotous blooming everywhere from the smallest front gardens to the grand London airs of Hyde and Regent's Park. What was left unbuilt on Wandsworth Common joined in the blooming, too. The stunning effect on the morale of the wounded men filling the 3rd London General Hospital, a girls' school requisitioned by the War Department and abutting the Common, was a marvelous thing to behold as well.

Corporal Jack Oakley had wended his helpless way through the medical evacuation system to a bed at the very end of a ward in one of the wooden buildings thrown up on the school grounds after the existing structures proved wholly inadequate to the demand generated by the Somme and a dozen smaller operations. Jack endured the boredom of his convalescent's life by storytelling, much as he would have done through a long and dark Newfoundland winter. His stories started out as short jokes to the men in the beds nearest, just to cheer them a little. They had soon grown into the long hearthside tales he had heard since infancy, becoming a regular event for those who could drag up chairs or strain to listen from their beds. The senior ward nurse had noticed these stories were as much benefit to the storyteller as the listeners, so she encouraged Jack. Many of the staff stayed past the end of their duty day if there was a tale underway, too.

Still, it was the effect had by Corporal Oakley's quiet voice on whomever was nearest him that astonished Sister Brannigan. She realized early on that the bed next to Jack was the place to put the most despondent patients, those who had given up hope or slipped into a silent and sullen depression. It was a heartbreak to her that most of these were the youngest of the wounded. To multiply this effect, she had Jack moved one bed over, allowing for a wounded man on each side. He had at first complained, but soon seemed to understand what she was about and settled easily into his new routine of cheering whichever neighbor was awake.

When making her rounds of the ward—twice each hour, even in quiet times—Deirdre found herself more often than not ending at Corporal Oakley's bed. He had begun to coax out her story as well, something she had found excruciating even in letters to her mother and sister Molly. Perhaps especially in those letters. She had been healthier since ending up here, her transfer arranged by Dr. Macintosh through an old medical schoolmate. Dr. Buchanan, on loan from the University College Hospital across the Thames, was as good a surgeon and almost as fine a gentleman as Major Macintosh.

Jack's condition had stabilized months ago and it was obvious early on he would never return to his battalion or any other active service. His mangled left arm was, like his legs, chewed by shrapnel and studded with dirt and stones. In his early weeks at the hospital, this wound had been opened and reopened to deal with all manner of problems, including early signs of gangrene from the soil embedded in the tissue. His leg wounds had, rather surprisingly, escaped infection, but the meaty flesh of the thighs was much less delicate than a forearm. The trouble with his legs was the awful amount of scar tissue. Some surgeries had been necessary to cut away the hardened and puckered skin to allow his left knee to move freely. Although carrying long and ugly scars, Jack's legs were as good as they would ever be. He limped heavily on his left leg and, with both hands immobilized, he could not grasp a crutch or cane.

The hospital's surgeons had given up hope of returning any function to Jack's left hand. There was too much damage to the arm. His right hand was another matter. Bullets, producing a cleaner wound than shrapnel, had saved the hand from infection. But the human hand is a complex machine and the path of a bullet could sever tendons and shatter small bones in atrocious ways. He had suffered through four surgeries to clean out fragments and reset broken bones that had not healed properly. His hand had been hidden in copious bandages and plaster casts as a result. A few days before, Dee and a VAD, watched by the specialist who had performed the last hand surgery, removed the latest cast and the stitches from the surgical incision. The doctor had prescribed massage of the limb, as well as hot wraps.

"Well now, let's have a peek at that hand, Corporal," Dee said, pushing up the jacket sleeve of Jack's blue hospital uniform. She commenced massaging from the elbow downward, concentrating on the hand with its stigmata of red scar tissue. She then began to work each finger to its full range of motion. She watched his face as she worked. Whenever a nurse did anything to assist him—feeding or urinating or bathing—he turned away. The bathing was hardest for most of the men, so vulnerable in their nakedness, but Jack seemed to have such a particular pained look. Not physical, although there had been plenty of that along the way. After weeks of studying him, Dee knew it was rather his deep humiliation from his helplessness. This was a man accustomed to taking care of himself, she sensed, and his neediness was eating away at him. This did not bode well for Jack's recovery, she knew to a certainty. She had struggled to find ways to help him move past this ordeal, but so far he seemed to find a little escape only while spinning one of his yarns of the fisheries or the forests of home. She placed much hope in his getting mobility back in his right hand. They had discussed these feelings of helplessness, Dee having approached the subject a few times after sharing something personal about herself. From time to time, he opened the door just a crack.

"You mustn't look so down at the mouth, Corporal. We might just have some luck with this last surgery," she said as she continued to work his fingers. "And it's alright to accept a bit of help from a nurse. 'Tis our job, after all, fussing about and helping."

Jack stared down the line of beds, silent and detached.

"And you wouldn't want to put such fine ladies as me out on the street to beg our bread, would you?"

"I don't like my prospects, Sister, battered and banged up as I am now." He stole a look at her, then reddened and looked away again.

"You'll have a long and fine life, Corporal Oakley, with your gift for the gab. Sure, couldn't you talk the paint off the wall, if you'd a mind." She hoped a friendly insult might stir him.

"I'll live that long life alone," he said with a despondent flatness that made her wince.

"So there are no women in that Newfoundland of yours then? Although I wonder why any woman would want to live at the edge o' the Earth, had she any choice in the matter."

"None who'd choose to live with a man who'd give her no children," Jack said with such resignation she feared his heart might break in his chest.

"What in the name of all the blessed saints gave you that idea, Corporal Jonathon Oakley?" Her exasperation with this lovely pigheaded man grew louder now.

Jack flushed crimson and spoke with his chin down, almost into his shirt. "You've seen the scars on my legs. They're a true horror."

"Get on with yourself! There'll be many a man much worse returning home before this nonsense is ended. And many of those with no legs or arms a'tall, mind you." Kneading his palm around the fresh incision, she added, "With so many good men dead and gone, there won't be many a woman particular about a few scars."

She could see he wished to continue, but his chin sunk deeper and the fiery blush of embarrassment intensified. "Now out with it man, and tell me what's truly eatin' you so." Far from shaming him, she wanted to learn what had him suffering in silence to such a painful extent. It all came spilling out once he started, in a halting flow of words.

"It's just that… since I was wounded near…ten months gone now. There's been no… movement or… or… feeling," he motioned with his head to his waist, "down there… you know."

This was no small matter to a man not yet twenty-three, Dee knew, and she needed an appropriate way to deal with it. She had heard him often speak with such warm affection of his younger siblings and cousins. Indeed, many of his stories featured them or his family's house or his grandfather's ship. His parents seem to have set a fine example for him. From a young age, he had wanted a family of his own, so this was a heavy burden indeed.

"The doctors don't see any reason why that should be so, Corporal, and you know that yourself, even if you won't believe it." She did not sound quite as confident as she intended. All the medical staff knew the knock-on effects of such terrible wounds were oftentimes strange and inexplicable. "There was no direct injury and no possibility now of nerve damage, since those nasty leg wounds were below... that area."

Jack heard the words, but was unconsoled. He raised his head and with pleading anguish said, "But near ten months, Sister? It might as well be ten years." He was near frantic. She had pushed too far and sought a way out of the emotional hole they had dug together.

"Well then, we'll just see to one thing at a time." She pulled down the sleeve of his hospital jacket and added, "We'll start with this hand of yours, shall we then?" She patted the back of his right hand. "Let me punch up those pillows so you can have a good chin with Williams and Donoghue here." She motioned with her head to the men in the adjoining beds while she set to work. Dee leaned over Jack and placed his right arm under her left, holding it there so she could tuck the sheets tight along that side of his bed, oblivious that his wounded hand was resting along her hip.

With a jolt, she felt his fingers tighten, just the tiniest bit, on her backside.

"Sweet Jayzus! Can you do that again?" she blurted without thinking.

His mouth and eyes screwed up in concentration. She felt a little harder squeeze. Jack's face was all astonishment as she laid his arm back atop the bedclothes. Standing to smooth her apron, she bought time to settle herself before braving a look at him. The surprised joy that infused them both was hard to hide.

"Well now," she said, breaking the excited silence, "we'll have to find you an india rubber ball to practice with." She arched an eyebrow and pursed her lips for effect. "That might be a more fitting exercise for that new hand of yours, Corporal." She moved beside his head and punched up the pillows a last time, bending down to whisper, "And perhaps if you work very hard, you might try that hand on a fine bosom like mine one day."

Standing, she gave a nod of encouragement with a wide smile, a little naughty at the edges. He gave her back the smallest wink and a tiny curl of a smile. She gasped at the familiarity of it.

CHAPTER EIGHTEEN

Will

Lieutenant Colonel Harcourt peered through his pince-nez with superlative pleasure as he pushed the War Office order across his desk. Taking up the paper with little enthusiasm and less surprise, Will glanced at the salient details and folded it into a pocket. The doctor, growing disappointment overlaying his smoldering irritation, watched as Will removed a cigarette from his silver case and lit it with his exquisite brass and silver inlay trench lighter. He craved the satisfaction of some protest or complaint from Lieutenant Parsons. Or rather Captain Parsons, for whatever inscrutable reason the War Office had found to justify promoting him. But they had also assigned him to a Welsh regiment effective immediately, ridding Lieutenant Colonel Harcourt at last of this troublesome young officer. Will took a languid drag on his cigarette while ignoring the doctor altogether, tapping his stick against the leg of his chair.

"I would suggest you either dispense with that pretentious walking stick, Captain Parsons, or at least replace it with a malacca cane," Harcourt burst out, unable to sustain the silence any further. "I suppose every officer needs a stick for authority, but you certainly do not need it for walking." Will exhaled a cloud of smoke, rubbing the brass head of his stick with his thumb, then tapping it against his heel.

"I suppose you think it too soon to return you to the front lines, Parsons?" the diminutive doctor asked rhetorically, since he would not be receiving a reply. "Well, you will be pleased to hear I have certified you available for unrestricted duties." The big Venetian glass ashtray sat in its accustomed place, positioned there by the owner of the house and not moved since except to empty it. Will flicked his cigarette at it.

"The faradization treatments to your leg and arms have been completely successful, as far as we are concerned." Harcourt opened Will's treatment folder and leaned forward in a feeble attempt at looming. "And can we not agree your actual injury was rather superficial?" Flipping back through the fastened papers, he read the notations from the Casualty Clearing Station where they had stitched Will's wound. "Facial laceration, left mid-cheek to jawline. Removed 1.5 inch bone fragment, origin unknown…"

Reeling from the blood rushing down toward his stomach, Will steadied his head by placing a hand to his chin. The cigarette dangled, limp and untouched, from his other hand.

"…closed laceration with 22 x 6-0 silk sutures to minimize scarring." Closing the folder, Harcourt looked across the desk again. Even a man of much less cunning would have noted the sudden change. "Is anything the matter, Captain Parsons?" asked the doctor, with perfect disingenuous concern.

Will reached forward to stub out his cigarette, unsuccessful in concealing the shaking of his hand. "Not really, Doctor. It's only… I hadn't known exactly what caused… this gouge in my face until now." He leaned back and steadied the shaking by grasping an arm of his chair. "Thank you for sharing that with me."

Harcourt was not convinced by this play at nonchalance and proceeded to twist the knife, this likely his last opportunity. "You were not alone when you were injured, yes? Wasn't your batman with you?"

Will felt sweat beading beneath the collar of his shirt, but resisted fidgeting with it, striving to appear calm before this supercilious little man. Their long-running joust was coming to an end and Will was determined to depart with at least a draw.

"As you were not otherwise wounded, Captain, would it not seem logical that you were injured by a bone fragment from your soldier servant?" the doctor posited with unctuous self-satisfaction. "Would you not concur, Captain?"

Will glared at the pretentious little shite, this comic-opera officer, with a well-trimmed flame of hatred. "Private Tobias Halfpenny was a dear friend of my youth. He served with distinction in that circus at Gallipoli and with equal dedication in France. He died next to me on the first day of the Somme, having just turned nineteen."

Will rose and stepped toward the door, then turned to Harcourt with a withering look of complete disdain. "That poor lad lived a fuller life in his few years than you'll ever know, regardless how long you take slouching to your coward's grave." Turning back to the door through Harcourt's shouts, Will turned the polished brass knob and pulled it.

"Out of my office, you insolent... such insubordination... better to let the Germans sort you... hope you never see England again!"

Will leaned harder on his walking stick and limped down the familiar hallway toward the French doors. He slid through them and out onto the equally familiar terrace, stark and cold in the filtered winter sunlight. He sat on his accustomed bench and lit yet another cigarette, giving rein to the tremor in his hands, needing both to steady the lighter. He raised the fingers of his right hand, the cigarette between the first and second knuckles, to the scar on his left cheek and grazed them down its crooked length.

His cheek twitched once, then again.

He looked along the beeches, standing in their row with military precision but stripped of their leaves this deep into winter, and raised the cigarette again to his lips. He glanced down at his wet fingertips as he exhaled.

BRIGADE OPERATION ORDER No. 74   *Copy No.* **12**

16th April, 1917

Ref: Trench Maps 1/20,000 and
        SAINT-MARTIN-DES-CHAMPS and BELMARAIS Sheets

1. *The 1/8th (Glamorgan) Battalion will provide a diversionary attack on the enemy's first line of defences at zero hour minus 30 minutes on 29th April.*

2. *INFORMATION:* *The attack will be made in conjunction with and in support of French operations to the south. Exact coordinates of enemy first line allocated to the battalion will be notified NLT 19th April.*

3. *OBJECTIVES:* *(a) The attack will be prosecuted with the utmost vigour to give appearance to the enemy that the larger operation to the south extends well north, causing him to commit additional troops and artillery.*

(b) If battalion secures portions of the enemy's first line, minimum consolidation will take place. Battalion is to hold in place until withdrawal may be safely made after dark.

4. *SILENCE:* *Absolute silence will be maintained when moving into position. It is most essential that the assembly movement be concealed from the enemy, otherwise a heavy barrage will have to be traversed.*

5. *ARTILLERY:* *During the night, artillery will continue to fire according to ordinary night firing programme. 35 minutes before zero, all guns will fire as rapidly as possible for five minutes and then lift to the enemy's second line trenches. The absolute necessity of the infantry following immediately on the lifting of the barrage cannot be too strongly impressed on all ranks.*

Direct liaison with artillery and aviation authorised.

6. *ZERO HOUR:* *Zero hour is 5:30 a.m., 29th April, 1917.*
7. *REPORTS:* *Reports will be sent to Brigade HQ at VERGER REDOUBT.*

C. C. Folkes
Brigade Major

CHAPTER NINETEEN

Jack

He found simple things rewarding now. With his right hand growing strong and flexible, he could light a cigarette and feed himself, although he still needed assistance cutting meat. With the last of the bandages removed from his face and one good hand to shave himself, he could no longer avoid mirrors. The scarring was not as horrible as he had feared, but it was bad enough. With a cane, he could use the toilet alone. His ability to walk unaccompanied widened his world within the hospital. Everyone loved to hear a story, especially soldiers who had passed long hours of boredom and fear distracting each other with lies and exaggerations of sporting and sexual exploits. Wherever Jack toddled about on his cane, he was sure to draw a crowd.

Sister Brannigan was making her rounds, murmuring instructions to the VADs and dispensing cheerful encouragement to the men. She approached Jack's unoccupied bed, noting that he was sitting in a chair and talking with the soldier in the next bed. The man was in and out of consciousness, but Jack knew from his own experience that he could hear and remember some of what was said.

"Corporal Oakley, can't you leave poor Evans be, lost to the world as he is?" Dee said, not meaning a word. She checked the unconscious man's bandages while conversing. "And how is it you never exhaust your stock of tall tales?"

"Ahh, I hail from a long line of storytellers. I heard tales by the hundreds, perhaps the thousands, at fireside and aboard ship since before I was even old enough to understand. And we Newfoundlanders are a mostly Irish race, which may go a long ways to explaining it, too."

"So 'tis a *seanchaí* you are, is't? Mam often speaks of how she misses the long nights round the hearth whenever a *seanchaí* visited their village. He'd stay for days telling stories that lasted all the night through and more." The mention of her mother brought a twinge that she brushed away with a few deliberate blinks. She had not been back to Dublin since the war began, excusing herself in letters by claiming the demands of the hospital were too great. "We don't get many of the traveling storytellers in Dublin. Great liars and braggarts in the pubs are the best we Dubs can usually muster. Now let me see that hand."

"What say you, Sister? Fancy a trot round Wandsworth Town this fine day?" Jack said, intending this for a tease and a little flirting.

Much to his surprise, Dee thought for a long moment, gave a curt nod, and replied, "Indeed 'tis, Corporal Oakley." She glanced about the placid ward. "I'm owed a half-day off. Truth be told, a great many half-days am I owed."

Half an hour later, they were strolling down the Earlsfield Road, albeit rather slowly. Dee was in her nurse's uniform with a short shoulder cape covering most of her apron bib. Jack limped from the scarred skin tugging at his knees but he neither noticed much nor cared greatly.

"Tell me of Dublin then, Sister, and your coming up there." A few medical vehicles passed, delivering or fetching patients. They received several severe scowls from VAD drivers at the sight of a nurse on the streets, unchaperoned, with a patient.

"'Tis a grand place, Dublin, full of odd folk and hustle-bustle. Music near everywhere, so it seems some days," she said, thoughts running back to the only place she had known before the war. "And we Dubs are insufferable proud of the place. The River Liffey's a stinkin' ditch as she runs through the town, but our poets have heaped so much praise upon her you'd think she were the very River Nile."

Jack studied her as she spoke so freely, disarmed as she was by the warm day and thoughts running to home. She was a handsome woman, but not delicate by anyone's reckoning. And whatever time of the day or night, some bit of her wild hair was flying away from beneath her cap.

"So what of your Newfoundland then, Corporal Oakley? What sort of place is that?" She had noted him studying her. While not altogether unwelcome, she thought it best to divert his attention, hard as he was staring.

"It's a difficult land oftentimes, especially in winter, but she's rich in many ways. Out on the Banks, the fish are so thick you can walk across their backs and never wet your boots."

"What kind of fish?" asked Dee, innocent enough.

"Bah, my dear maid, fish is fish," he said with smiling outrage, "but you Europeans might call 'em cod, if you must." Jack picked up the line of his story again. "My family, like most others, make their livelihood from the fish. My Grandpa, God rest him, was as fine a fisher as ever there was and he had a way of makin' up a full hold on every voyage, regardless of sea or weather." Jack paused, remembering his grandfather with obvious fondness. "He started as a fisher, then captained others' ships, 'til finally putting enough aside to buy his own schooner when my father and uncle were just small ones. He named her after them, the *Ricky Todd*, my father getting pride of place."

"It sounds a hard life."

"Only for them that aren't raised to it, I suppose. Pa and Uncle Todd were borne and bred to such a life. When they joined Grandpa, the family found success and added ships 'til today we put to sea four schooners and a coastal boat, as well as havin' our own premises ashore."

Dee listened close to him as he spun out his family's tale, thoughts far across the ocean. She watched his profile, the cheek with the scars, as he spoke. *Still a solid man, a sound man, despite all he had been through. Handsome enough, too.* His eye sagged from the pull of scars beneath it, with his left cheek down to the jawline a switchback of ropey lines, fading to pink in places. But it was his eyes—such window-glass eyes, as if they went right down inside him—that drew her to him. This man, she knew, would be an abysmal liar, should he so much as try. It was how despairing those eyes became at random moments that tugged at her heart.

"So I'm stepping out with the heir to a shipping fortune, am I?" She broke off her gaze before he became uncomfortable. This was not a vain man.

"Ahh, my dear Sister Brannigan, Ma has been tryin' to make silk purses out of we Oakley sow's ears for some time," Jack said, smiling at the thought of his mother. "She sent me to the finest Anglican school in all of Newfoundland to make a gentleman of me. You'll have to judge for yourself how successful she was." He had slipped back into his school speech, now that he'd returned from home and family to Dee and London. "Grandpa used to tease her mercilessly, telling her she'd toil the rest of her days scouring the fish stink off an Oakley."

"And you have four brothers and sisters, like me?"

"That I do. Three brothers and a single put-upon sister. Although truth be known, we spoil Nell fiercely, sweet maid that she is."

After some comfortable quiet between them, Dee decided to broach a more dangerous topic. "The doctors say there's nothing to stop you from fathering your own children, Jack," she said, declarative as she could manage. She steeled for an angry retort that, much to her surprise, never came.

"You know, you've never called me by my given name before," Jack said.

"Aye, I'm well aware. And you mustn't let it be known, as I won't be repeating it on the ward before the others, Jack Oakley." She flipped the flaps of her short cape back over her shoulders—shameful on the street!—it having grown suddenly warmer.

"You best be calling me Deirdre, or Dee if you've a mind."

"I prefer Deirdre, if it's all the same, my sweet maid, it being such a lovely name," Jack said, barely able to contain his pleasure at so much sudden familiarity after the long months on the ward.

"Don't be sweet-maiding me, just because I gave you my name."

"It's just our way. We're always 'my darlin' and 'my sweetness' and 'my love,' one to another. Odd to people from away, I suppose."

"'Tis too much like the Irish for your own good, you Newfoundlanders are, so full of the flattering words and tall tales.

Might not be an altogether strange place to one like me." She pulled her cape back around her shoulders and gave out a loud sigh, signaling it was time to turn back. "Well, they'll be wondering what's become of us if we don't return soon, pleasant as this stroll has been."

They stood on the pavement, neither wanting to return just yet. Jack reached over to her and tucked a wild lock of fly-away hair behind her ear. "Must be a breeze coming up off the Thames," he said. "Be a shame if it brought rain to spoil our beautiful day."

She had lowered her eyes as he brushed the hair back. She looked up and he gazed into her face, his window eyes shining with aching and longing. She met his look without wavering, a rush of warmth blooming in her chest.

There was little to be done when contagion took hold among the staff, particularly one populated with volunteers without the resilience of experienced nurses. Such was the case in September at the 3rd London General. At the first signs of illness, Dee hustled her VADs and junior nurses off to their beds. It was not a particularly dangerous flu, but it laid up those stricken for ten or twelve days before they were fit to return to their duties. As a result, the ward was working extraordinarily short-handed.

Deirdre was sharing bathing duties with a mousy young woman from Cheshire who had been at the hospital only a few weeks. She was sure it was only a matter of hours before this poor waif would succumb, too. Dee was nearly done with the twelve men on her side of the ward while the young volunteer was only on her third patient.

"There now, we've washed all we can round those bandages, Sergeant Wainwright. You're ready for the grand opera in Covent Garden, clean and proper as you please." She gave the wounded man a fond pat on the back of his hand and went on to the last patient.

Moving the cloth screen around the bed, Dee refilled the wash basin in the sink at the end of the ward and returned to the bedside. "Now, if you can stop relying on that cane so much, Corporal Oakley, the doctor might see his way to trusting you to shower yourself." She recognized immediately he was in a dark place, not rising to her gentle challenge. She had seen this often enough to know his thoughts were on an uncertain future. These melancholies were becoming more frequent as his inevitable return home loomed, undetermined but certain.

"Now then, let's get you polished up, shall we?" She adopted the same bustling manner she took with all the other patients. As she unbuttoned and removed his shirt, he kept his head turned, his stare fixed on the empty bed next to his. The miasma of humiliation hung thick about him, all the worse that it was Deirdre bathing him. Drying his torso and arms, she folded the bedclothes back over his chest. She took a step down the bed, folded up the blanket, and removed his pajama trousers and underwear. As she soaped along his legs, blotting the sponge gently against his scarred thighs, she saw his penis stiffen, growing toward his stomach.

Now that's something indeed, she thought.

She looked up at Jack, but his head was still turned with determination. His face flushed crimson with anxiety and embarrassment.

'Tis time for this to end, here and now.

She set the sponge back in the basin. Reaching upward, she wrapped soapy fingers around his penis and, with a slow and gentle motion, stroked it. Jack's head stayed turned to the wall, his eyes screwed shut as if in pain. With her other hand, Dee placed her palm under his cheek and turned his head to face her. When his confused eyes met hers, she placed a finger over his lips. She began moving her hand again, never breaking her gaze. As his legs and stomach tensed, she moved a little faster, pushing him to deeper and deeper breathing. In a very short time, his body jerked with a spasm while he bit back a groan that emerged as hard exhalations through flaring nostrils. As he settled back into the pillows, Dee was disarmed by the tears running down his cheeks. She scurried to clean up with the sponge and towel, pulled a clean pair of pajamas over his legs, and dashed down the ward to the storage closet near the entrance.

Breathing hard from her exertions and tumbling emotions, she tried to gather herself before a VAD or someone worse found her. She fumbled for the chain on the single lightbulb and pulled. The swaying light made bottles and cartons pulse in and out of the shadows, seeming to move along the walls. She grabbed the edge of a wooden shelf to steady herself.

"Jesus, Mary, and Joseph, what have you done now, Deirdre Brannigan?" she said aloud, panting the words. Straightening herself, she squared her shoulders, smoothed her apron, and tucked a few stray hairs back under her cap.

Well, if 'twere a sin, venal or mortal, 'twas the kindest sin I've ever committed. She brought her hand to her mouth to cover a nervous laugh. Feeling steadier now, she reached for the doorknob.

CHAPTER TWENTY

Will

Lieutenant Ned Tobin stretched his legs against the firewall of the three-ton lorry driven by Corporal Geordie King of the Transport Service. Both dangled cigarettes from their mouths, bouncing in time with every rut Geordie failed to avoid. And there was copious mud. The distinguishing feature of the Western Front was the universality of mud. Soldiers developed a keen ability to distinguish various types and textures, much like Eskimos and snow. Sometimes the mud could save them, absorbing blasts from artillery rounds. It was, however, more often an enemy.

"I'd have thought the roads would dry out come spring," said Ned. "Goddamned stuff gets in everything."

"No, the Turk flies in Mesopolonica got *in* everything, including your ears and arse. Your garden-variety Frenchy mud gets *on* everything."

Ned had been tasked by the Machine Gun School to visit as many companies as he could in this sector, checking the wear on equipment and the tactics adopted by the crews. He had added Will Parson's 1/8th Glamorgans to his itinerary. Geordie's unit was located just outside Amiens, so Ned requested him by name from a quiescent transport captain. He knew this was his last chance to catch up with the boys from his old platoon. Since the U.S. entered the war a few weeks ago, he was in contact with the American military attaché in Paris. The U.S. forces were starting near zero for officers with battlefield experience. The French and British were more than willing to release American volunteers, overjoyed in their bloodlet exhaustion that the Yanks were at last coming. Now he was awaiting orders for the States. As a windfall, he was to be promoted to major, having only recently begun answering with any reliability to "Lieutenant." Still, it was not easy leaving the men with whom he had passed through the Somme.

Geordie slowed to a crawl, then hit the squeaky brakes at a road intersection, sticking his head out from under the truck's canopy. He hailed a gendarme *adjoint* directing traffic.

"*N'arrêtez pas ici!*" shouted the corporal at Geordie, continuing with a flurry of rapid and profane French, accompanied by appropriately Gallic hand gestures.

Geordie turned to Ned, who could not see the Frenchman from the passenger side. "Lieutenant Tobin, it appears this gendarme is angry. And he's speaking faster than my school French can follow." Ned leaned forward across Geordie's chest and called out the window. The gendarme saw his officer's rank and came to a desultory position of attention.

"*Pardonnez-moi, lieutenant. Vous ne pouvez pas arrêter ici.*"

"He's still angry, just politer," Ned said to Geordie. Then to the gendarme, "*Nous sommes à la recherché du le régiment d'infanterie galloise, les huitième de la première Glamorgans.*"

The gendarme looked noncommittal, less from ignorance than annoyance. "*Je crois qu'ils sont sur la route, lieutenant,*" the Frenchman said, scratching his stubbly cheek. "*A quelques kilomètres d'ici,*" he added, looping the thumb of his other hand through the shoulder strap of his rifle and shifting his weight from one muddy foot to the other. "*De toute façon il y a une sentinelle anglaise au prochain carrefour.*"

"*Merci, adjoint,*" Ned replied as the Frenchman threw up a bored salute and returned to his makeshift sentry box. "He says the Glamorgans are up the road a piece, then fobbed us off on the British sentries at the next crossroad."

Geordie looked over at Ned with an incredulous smile. "Why Edmund Tobin, where did you get the Louis Quatorze? Last time we drank together, you could scarcely get wine from that poor serving girl."

"Is that right? Hmmm. I don't recall," said Ned with exaggerated nonchalance, glancing over an area map.

"Neddie, your French was a bloody nightmare."

Folding the chart, Ned shoved it back in his map case. "Well, Geordie, there's a lovely *lycée* teacher lives near the Machine Gun School in Amiens." He extracted a pack of Navy Cuts from his pocket and offered one to Geordie. "Seems she was widowed when her husband got himself killed back in '14 at Charleroi," Ned continued, leaning over to light Geordie's cigarette, then his own. He exhaled a long stream of blue smoke and said, "May be true what they say."

Geordie looked over at Ned, cigarette dangling, and took the bait. "And what is it they say, Lieutenant Ned?"

Taking another draw on his cigarette for effect, he said, "The best way to learn a new language is…horizontally."

After a beat, Geordie threw his head back and let go a belly laugh. "Ahh, *cherchez la femme*, is it?"

Ned slouched in his seat with a wry smile and thoroughly enjoyed the remainder of his cigarette. At the next crossroad, they pulled up to the promised British sentry post and Geordie asked after the Glamorgans.

"Right. Three-quarters a mile up this 'ere road 'n yer'll sees a village," said the military policeman, a short and thickset Cockney who resembled a green fireplug. "Well, more's a pile of bricks each side the road." The corporal spat prodigiously into the mud. "Then yer'll finds 'n entrance to a comms trench be'ind wha's left of the churchyard. That'll take yer right along t' Glamorgan's HQ."

Geordie popped him an outsized salute and said, "Thanks, mate. That'll save us much wading through this muck."

"Don't be salutin' me. I'm not a bleedin' officer," said the corporal with a gapped smile. He hawked again for emphasis. "I works for a livin'. Errr, beggin' the left'nts pardon." He half-saluted Ned by way of apology.

Ned chuckled and returned the salute, "No offense taken, Corporal. Just traded in my own stripes a few months back."

The corporal pulled a puzzled look and said, "By way of yer manner of speakin' suh, would I be wrong in takin' ye for a Yank, suh?"

"Boston born and bred, Corporal."

The soldier came to proper attention and threw up a much smarter salute. "It'll be a sight for sore eyes when yer mates come marchin' over, suh. A sight indeed, suh, 'cept for them bleedin' Bosche, tha' is."

Ned pointed up the road, signaling to Geordie to head on. "Indeed it will, Corporal."

They had little trouble locating the piles of rubble and parked in the churchyard full of toppled headstones and blasted graves. The entrance to the communications trench was properly duck boarded and well revetted with new sandbags. Yanking up hard on the hand brake, Geordie jumped down from his driver's seat. "Shall we go scare up our good Captain Parsons then?"

The two men made their way through the trench's meanders and traverses, all designed to make things harder for the Germans, asking a few soldiers along the way to confirm the location of the battalion HQ. In less than fifteen minutes, they were outside a dugout which looked suspiciously new and well-kept for this long-established sector of trenches. Geordie stuck his head into the doorway and said in a stage whisper, "We have top secret business with Captain Parsons and must see him, toot-sweet!"

A muffled voice within said, "What the devil is…" as Will emerged into the daylight. He immediately broke into a surprised grin and shook his head. "Well, what ill wind blew you two onto these lovely shores?" He offered his hand to Ned and, with a quick look around, offered it again to Geordie with a hearty grasp. "It is surprisingly fine to see the both of you, even back in the trenches. You'd better come down. Jerry is due to show us a bit of hate, as is his habit about this time." They followed Will down the steps into the HQ. Will said to the soldiers sitting at two rough wooden tables attending to their staff duties, "Why don't you men go find yourselves some tea? I'd like to speak privately with the Lieutenant and his man here."

"Very good, sir," said a sergeant-major, motioning to the others to follow him out. When the three stood, Ned and Geordie towered over them.

After the sergeant-major and the others cleared the dugout, Ned said, "Will, is this a command dugout or a damn faerie hole?"

"Those are some tiny men there, Captain Will," added Geordie.

"Yes, well, the 8th Glamorgans are a bantam battalion. Not one over five foot three. Supposed to be a minimum height of four foot ten, but I have my suspicions about a few of the tinier lads."

"I thought they were assigned to mining and trenching?" said Geordie.

"No longer, seeing as how Field Marshal Haig used up most of his full-sized alternatives. They've a lot of fight in them."

"They'd have to. Doesn't appear to be much else," Geordie said with a disbelieving smile.

"You remember how Pilmore used to ride you about all the Kings in the old regiment, Geordie? All that George the First nonsense?" Will asked.

"Oh, I well recall the good sergeant-major's consternation," said Geordie, a touch less jovial at the reminder of Pilmore and Sandy.

"Odd thing is, in these bloody Welsh battalions, it's much worse. I have fifty-two Evanses, ninety-six Williamses, and an even one hundred and twenty Thomases. It's enough to drive one mad really." Both Geordie and Ned noted how he sounded much more English than when last they had seen him on the Somme. But he always had a little English undercurrent in his manner of speaking. From his mother, they supposed.

"You're looking well after your long vacation in Blighty," Geordie said, changing the subject. "And you have some shiny new quarters here as well."

Will looked about the dugout for no apparent reason. He rubbed the fading scar on his left cheek. "Yes, well, it is all new. Seems Fritz ranged our previous dugout last time we were forward. Dropped a barrage right on it."

"Good Lord," said Ned. "How many?"

"That's just the problem," Will said, his cheek twitching once, twice. "Wiped out the whole battalion command staff in one go. I was on the line checking observation posts. So with just three months in rank, it seems I'm now the senior captain," Will said with strained amusement. "All we have are lieutenants actually. Not nearly enough of those."

Will walked across the room to a bunk with a straw mattress and retrieved a bottle and three glasses from a shelf above the bed. He poured healthy amounts in each with a shaky hand and placed two on the table in the center of the room. "Gentlemen, please." He motioned with his own glass, then gulped down his whisky in one go. Before Geordie and Ned got their glasses to their lips, he was pouring himself another.

"Cheers," he said, downing the second glass. This seemed to calm the trembling, but Geordie noticed the tick in his cheek continued. "My fine gentlemen, you have the honour of drinking with the acting battalion commander." Both visitors were speechless. Will was a good junior officer, but command of a battalion was beyond what anyone should expect of him.

"By the way, we're to jump the bags near the end of the month," Will said almost as an afterthought. "Of course, all very hush-hush. It's a diversionary attack. The French will have the main show farther south." Will poured a third glass and offered refills with a wave of the bottle's neck. Both Ned and Geordie shook their heads. "So I am to lead my men against the German wire and machine guns in a Mummers' parade for the benefit of our dear French allies." He threw back the third glass, now looking very well collected.

There was nothing Ned or Geordie could say. The battalion had drawn the short straw, as was the way of things in this war. Both were sure nothing they said would make much difference. Ned broke the awkward silence. "Here on official business, inspection tour of machine gun sections and emplacements. I managed to get your battalion on my list and scared up our Corporal King here as my driver. Never pass up a chance to abuse a *carte blanche*."

Will rose and buttoned his tunic. "Well, no time like the present, I suppose." He buckled his Sam Browne and picked up a malacca cane lying on the bunk.

"You care to join us, Geordie?" Ned said.

"Much as I enjoy a good machine gunning, think I'll laze about the HQ while you subject yourselves to enemy fire."

With that, Will and Ned made their way up the dugout stairs, Will leaning on his cane with each alternate step. Geordie followed a minute later, settling himself on a brown-smudged bench just outside the dugout where it appeared the soldier servants sat to polish officers' boots. None of the Welshmen had returned yet. The sun had broken out while they were underground and Geordie leaned back, his head against the sandbag wall. He looked out over the parapet and could just see the tops of some skeletal trees along the sandbagged horizon. A few incoming artillery rounds thumped somewhere along the trenches.

Look like the winter birches back home. Not that these will ever leaf again.

He closed his eyes and let the sunshine warm his face, luxuriating in the warmth and dryness. The lightest breeze wound down through the trench.

Someone mowing hay? Smells like the fields round St. John's of a summer's day.

A content smile settled over his face as he breathed in the fresh grass smell. He sighed with thoughts of home, far away from this wretched place. Suddenly his breath caught hard, throat constricting as he tried to cough away the burning in his chest. Penetrating through his daydream, he heard the clack-clack of a warning rattle. He remembered taking off his webbing to make the driving more comfortable, stowing it behind the seat. Where it was now.

With his gas mask.

All Saints' Rectory
The Triangle
Wrington, Somerset-shire
27th of September, 1917

My Dear William,

What a pleasure it was to have you with us here at our humble abode. You do so favor your dear mother, Fidelia, who was much like a sister to me as a child. It brought tears to my eyes each time you sat across from me. Ah, the wings of time! I have written your mother and father, letting them know how well we found you. That you were able to join us on your leave from France was a great joy, although I might say to one of us in particular. Sophia has related the contents of the letter you posted her from Dover and she has informed me of her great desire to accept your offer of marriage.

I understand the exigencies of wartime make observation of the old traditions difficult, but I do wish you had discussed this with me, as is the custom, while you were with us. However, perhaps you required the train journey to the Channel to solidify your feelings and desires? No matter. I hold your mother in such high esteem that I will forgive such a minor transgression in her beloved son.

My wife and I wholeheartedly approve this engagement and look forward to joining our two families. We will wait a few weeks to write your parents to discuss arrangements, allowing you time to inform them first. All that remains for you, my dear boy, is to return safely to us. We pray that God keeps you in His care each and every day.

> With my warmest regards to you, my dear boy,
> I am, may I be so bold to say, your loving father,
> The Reverend Edwin Harper

CHAPTER TWENTY-ONE

Deirdre

With ten days of enforced inactivity (enough to drive a decent woman mad by the seventh day), Dee was allowed to return to her duties after her inevitable bout with influenza. She looked forward to seeing Jack, although she knew she was growing overfond of him, something nurses from their earliest days in training are cautioned against. She could not ignore her growing affection for this good and decent man. Only one other like him she had known in her two and twenty years.

Since bathing him, she hadn't seen Jack. When she left the ward that day in search of some tea to settle herself, she began to feel flushed and unsteady in the staff cafeteria. The watchful Matron diagnosed influenza at a glance and packed her off to her sickbed. Now as she passed the Matron's Office just inside the hospital's main entrance, Dee stopped to report herself back. Matron was at her desk, reviewing personnel reports and shift schedules.

"Matron, I don't mean to disturb you, but I wanted to let you know I'm back to full duties today," she said. "Fit as a fiddle."

The older nurse looked up from her papers and greeted Dee with a maternal smile, odd coming from a woman who had never had time for children of her own. "It's a relief to see one of my best nurses sound again. I mean that not as idle flattery, something quite alien to me, Deirdre. You truly have a gift for this work. But I'd venture to say you've heard that from others before me, yes?"

Uncomfortable with compliments, Dee waved away the question and said, "No more than all the others here who've left lives more interesting than mine to help these poor brave men, Matron."

The older woman looked at Dee with searching eyes, not quite sure what to make of this indomitable young woman, so full of care and kindness yet striving a little too hard at everything she undertook. She wondered what this remarkable girl was running from or toward. Now she was only going to add to Dee's troubles, of that she was certain. Rising from her desk, the Matron came around and motioned for Dee to sit on the faded mohair sofa along the far wall of her office. Settling into a bentwood arm chair, she began. "Before you return to the ward, there is a patient I should like to discuss with you, Deirdre."

"Of course, Matron. I hope there weren't too many difficulties while I was away sick," Dee said, no idea where the conversation was headed.

"It's about Corporal Oakley, I'm afraid," the Matron said, studying Dee's reaction.

Her heart in her mouth, struggling to keep up some pretense of professional detachment, Dee said, "He was proceeding well in his therapy. I hope he hasn't taken a turn."

Noting her fight to appear calm, the Matron said, "No, nothing like that I'm happy to say." Dee's breath came in gulps of relief. "Would I be correct in saying that you've grown rather fond of Corporal Oakley, Deirdre?" They were merely keeping up appearances now, they both knew, but continued the charade out of probity.

"I suppose any nurse would become a bit… *partial* to a patient who has been on the ward as long as Corporal Oakley's been on mine, Matron."

"I only allowed you to take occasional walks with the Corporal because I knew you to be a young woman of good sense and dedication, Deirdre. Not like so many of the VADs and an unfortunate number of the sisters." The Matron was looking closely at Dee now, not unkindly, but scrutinizing her nonetheless.

"And great good those airings did for Corporal Oakley, too, Matron," Dee hurried to interject, trying to show some professional basis for her heartfelt desire to be in Jack's company off hospital grounds. Matron was having none of it and finally cut through the obfuscation.

"Deirdre, it is understandable that your affections fell to this man. The Corporal was a tonic to the entire hospital and so well regarded by much of the staff." Dee hung her head, staring into her lap, working her hands, confused. "Before you return to the ward, you should know that Corporal Oakley has been invalided out of the service and departed for home six days ago."

There was a strange rushing sound in Dee's ears. She felt her face go pale and her hands cold. Breathing deep and slow, she forced away the faintness creeping over her. She concentrated on the sonorous ticking of the wood-cased pendulum clock on the wall above Matron's desk.

Tock. Tock.

Once when she came looking for Matron, there was a hospital porter standing on a ladder, winding the clock with a big butterfly-shaped key.

Tock. Tock.

She wondered how often the clock needed winding, since she had never seen it stopped. It kept perfect time. Like a clock in a railway station.

Tock. Tock.

Dee focused on the Matron's face and asked, "Did he leave a letter or a message?" She knew the answer already.

CHAPTER TWENTY-TWO

Will

Geordie had so far kept down four meals without complaint. He sat in a canvas deck chair in his greatcoat and uniform hat, enjoying the sparse winter sunshine that squeaked through the low clouds from time to time. It was made quite cold on deck by the wind coming over the bow, but he was shielded behind the second-class lounge and facing aft. Between his Newfoundland blood and three years in French mud and rain, he did not much notice the chill. Closing his eyes, he began to float off into the pleasant half-awake indolence common among travelers at sea with no land in sight. He heard a vague sound of heels on the teakwood deck as he drifted. A shadow fell over his closed eyelids and he opened one and squinted the other to see if it was anyone worth noticing.

"Ehh, just you then is it, Major Will?" he said to the looming silhouette. Geordie hitched his coat tighter and didn't make the slightest move to rise.

"Suppose it's too late to have you disciplined for lack of respect, Sergeant King?" Will took out his silver cigarette case, the long-ago gift from his sisters that now bore a patina of scratches and indentations. He offered one to Geordie, who waved it away. Will hooked his cane over his forearm, cupped his hands around his scarred trench lighter, and gave several hard flicks before managing to light his cigarette. Will settled into the deck chair next to Geordie's and exhaled a long stream of smoke.

"So home at last."

"Home at last," echoed Geordie. "That picture is almost faded away in my mind. Seems a century." He felt the cold now, wrapping his arms around his chest. Both men gazed out along the ship's wake, watching it separate at mirror angles as the ship plowed westward through the steel-grey winter sea. They were too far out for gulls now. Capricious black smoke from the ship's funnels dipped with the wind toward the wake before dissolving out over the water.

Will was back in the uniform of the now-Royal Newfoundland Regiment, having been returned like a deposit bottle by His Majesty's Forces to his home unit for demobilization. Probably best to be back with the old regiment when he landed in St. John's anyway, Will had thought at the time.

"Good of you to come slumming in Second Class with the working men," Geordie said. "Wasn't sure I'd see you before landfall."

"Not much they can bloody well do now, one would hope," Will said, still sounding every inch the proper English gentleman. Geordie smiled at his poshness and wondered how much would wear off once they were home. Perhaps none, with an English mother and, soon enough, an English wife. "Certainly the company's better down here," Will added.

Geordie shifted in his seat as Will stubbed his cigarette in an ashtray on a side table, the sparky ashes flying off in the wind. Not wanting this to be the signal for Will's departure, Geordie asked, "So how exactly did you get that medal then? I've heard some wild stories."

Smoothing the front of his overcoat just over where the purple-and-white ribbon of his Military Cross lay beneath, Will squinted a moment in thought before answering. "It was for that diversionary attack we launched just after you were gassed in our trenches."

"That much I know," said Geordie, "but rumors I heard in hospital from some of your Welsh lads was that it was a close-run thing whether the brigade commander would decorate or court-martial you."

Will turned and smiled, patting Geordie's knee with old affection. "As it has always been with such foolhardy acts." He took the moment to examine his big friend, his smile fading. Geordie's eyes were sunken, his face thinner, his shoulders narrower. To Will's eyes, he seemed to take up less space in the world.

"You did seem none too keen on that attack," Geordie said, moving Will along in the tale of his medal.

"We were both at the Somme on the First of July," Will said, his voice brittle and cold like rime with this particular memory. "We saw how many men we left on that fucking field." Geordie raised an eyebrow at Will's casual profanity.

"We were and we did, William."

"It seems I was unwilling to lead several hundred more to needless deaths," Will said. "And since I was in temporary command of 742 fine Welsh miners, I determined our time before battle could best be spent digging."

"I did appreciate your pygmies carrying me back to the field hospital after my brush with Fritz's phosgene," Geordie interjected, then gave an involuntary cough with his mention of the gas.

"Took nearly a platoon of them, like Gulliver in Lilliput," Will quipped, then continued. "So the sergeant-major and I decided if they were to be digging, they might just as well be digging forward as downward."

"There was no possibility you could get a mine under those German lines, not in the time you had. Where did you imagine you were going to get the mountain of explosives you'd need to blow the German trench anyway?"

"Ahh, Geordie old boy, there's the rub. We had the men digging observation posts, so HQ believed. And bloody long OP trenches we dug, right up to the German wire."

The picture began pulling into focus for Geordie. "Why William, you are a dodgy bugger!" he said, pleased as punch. "But how did you keep all this diggy-diggy hidden from the Bosche and your own brass hats?"

"Through the abundant plenitude of the pater's whisky," Will said, taking out another cigarette. "It took several cases of the bloody stuff, too. Hope dear Papa wasn't checking our agent's accounts too closely." Will lit another cigarette and continued. "Made a few visits to the local artillery spotters and the commander of a Seaforths battalion with whom we were swapping trench duty." He paused and smoked, thinking back with amusement. "Only the good Lord will ever know how much whisky it took to bribe a kiltie colonel and his entire battalion staff. The jocks are born with hollow legs for the stuff."

"So we dug at night and by day covered the work with planking and dirt," Will continued. "Our well-liquored mates in the artillery lobbed enough shells through the night to keep Fritz on edge and in his dugouts."

Geordie was entranced, sitting forward in his deckchair.

"The night before the attack, our artillery spotting officer agreed to hold off on the preparatory barrage if we still had patrols out," Will said. "So I had two messengers standing just round the traverse from his dugout…"

"Why would you position messengers at someone else's dugout?"

"…and with borrowed watches," Will continued through the interruption. "One with a message saying we still had patrols out, to be delivered five minutes before the barrage was scheduled to start. The second carried a message for delivery five minutes before we were scheduled to jump off, saying all patrols were back in."

Geordie, rather puzzled, interrupted again, "Why would you give up two-thirds of the duration of your own barrage?"

"Because the patrols we reported out were actually the entire bloody battalion," said Will, very chuffed with himself at the sight of Geordie's shocked reaction.

"You jammy bastard, William Parsons!"

"Yes, Geordie, I had my wee miners just yards from Fritz," said Will, "so we had little need of a barrage, other than to scare the Bosche to their dugouts. Before the operation, all I had the lads practice was cutting wire as fast as they could and carrying round bloody great sacks of Mills bombs."

"You had them damn close to your own barrage, that far forward."

"That's true," said Will, some sadness tinging his voice. "The sergeant-major and I decided it was worth the risk. They were in communications trenches, so protected from anything but a direct hit from friendly fire." Will paused and studied the ship's wake again, his hand to his cheek and a finger of his glove running down the scar. "We did lose a few men to our barrage."

"How many casualties, all told?" Geordie asked.

"Fourteen killed. Nine to our barrage and five to the few Germans who made it up from their bunkers. Another two dozen wounded. None captured or missing."

"That's the total? In the whole damned assault?" Geordie exclaimed, completely incredulous. "That's scarce five percent."

"Yes, worked better than we deserved, I suppose. So well we sat waiting for the barrage to move to the second line of German trenches and managed to catch them in those dugouts, too. We had to use captured German grenades by then, since we were out of our own Mills bombs."

Geordie sat staring with unalloyed admiration at this boyhood friend, a picture of nonchalance in his deck chair. "B'God, b'y, that was a fine piece of soldiering. Why wasn't it in all the papers?"

"That's the curious thing," Will said. "When a field phone operator caught up with me, which took some time since he had to splice extra wire to even reach us, the brigade commander was not altogether pleased we'd advanced beyond the first trench. His words were, 'You weren't suppose to *take* the Germans' trench, you were only to *annoy* them.' Quite surprising, really, when one thinks about it."

"So no reserves sent up to consolidate the position?"

"To the contrary. I was ordered to retreat to the first trench, hold until dark, then give it back to the Germans. And to report to brigade upon my return." Will turned in his seat to half-face Geordie. "As to publicity, we couldn't have the home front thinking it possible to take German positions without the accustomed slaughter, could we?"

"How was the brigade commander when you reported?"

"Similar to a wet hen. Angrier than I thought possible. Apoplectic, really. Said I'd flouted orders and was a disgrace to the Regiment. Mentioned a general court-martial amongst a noteworthy string of rather profane oaths."

"He accused me of not being a gentleman and a sportsman," Will said, drawing on his cigarette. "As to that allegation, I pleaded guilty as charged." They sat quietly, Geordie turning several times to shake his head and chuckle. Will kept silent, having spun out the whole of his tale. After a few minutes, Geordie spoke up.

"Wouldn't your brigadier have had to recommend you for the MC? Give up his plan to have you brought up on charges?"

"It seems Field Marshall Haig's opinion differed somewhat," Will said, "realizing that the court-martial of a half-English officer from one of the loyal dominions would generate unwanted interest, at home and abroad. He therefore directed I be promoted to the permanent rank of major and decorated. The Military Cross seemed the appropriate honour, since it could be approved by him in France." Will exhaled another tight stream of blue smoke through pursed lips and watched it dance away. "And ours is not to question why, dear Geordie," he said with a rueful smile.

"Well, you'll be quite the hero back home regardless of the provenance of that medal, Major Parsons," Geordie said, adopting the proper form of address at the sight of a clutch of sergeants ambling down the deck near them. "Pity you're promised to that Miss Harper already, since a medal and that fetching saber scar would turn quite a few pretty heads in St. John's."

"What Sandy wouldn't have given for a fashionable wound and a gong to go with it, eh?" Will said.

"Poor Alexander," said Geordie. "He deserved better than to die in that shitty trench in Jolly-Polly, didn't he?"

"Indeed he did," said Will. "And laid beside Sergeant-Major Pilmore, out of all the dead we left in that blasted place."

Having grown sentimental since the fighting ended, Geordie knew better than to continue this maudlin discussion, so he turned the conversation. "What of your future, William,"—the group of sergeants had moved down the deck—"besides your looming nuptials?"

Will tapped his cane on the teak a few times and tightened his jaw. "The *paterfamilias* is somewhat surprised I managed to survive the war and now has great plans for capitalizing on my ill-gotten rank and reputation. I shall be joining the Parsons Premises, as Director of the Division of Something or Other."

"Your mother will make quite a show of your wedding."

"Of that you may be sure, Geordie," said Will without enthusiasm.

"Let's hope I can wrangle invitations for you and Jack. Perhaps near the back."

"Your father would hardly miss a chance to make an impression, now would he?" Geordie said, sensing Will's sourness. "The important thing is that Sophia is a fine girl from a good English family, just like your Ma."

"That she is," Will said, perking a bit. "She really is quite lovely and decent. I'm lucky to have her, when all is said and done."

They sat without speaking, each to his own thoughts now, as the sea slipped away behind them, pushing them homeward.

CHAPTER TWENTY-THREE

Deirdre

The Liberties was much the same after four years without her. The hubbub endured with a few more motors, a few less horses. The morning calls of street vendors, some now veterans with empty sleeves or trouser legs, was unchanged. They were joined as before by the rush and jostle of porters pushing crates and kegs of beer at reckless speed along the pavement, often spilling onto the road to dodge autos and wagons alike. She had not returned to work at St. Vincent's, although Sister Mary Evangeline paid a call to ask her in person. Quite an honor for such a senior member of the Sisters of Charity to visit a publican's flat. She had sobbed with deep fondness at the sight of the old nun, the lines of her face etched deeper and, Dee imagined, the hair under her wimple grown greyer, too. But she had said she was not ready to return and Sister Mary Evangeline accepted this, not without a look of concern, and blessed Dee, kissing her cheek before leaving.

"Francis is seein' to opening below, so we have the morning to ourselves, just we ladies, Deirdre," said Eda, putting the kettle back on the stove. "We've not had a good talk, just the two of us together, since you came back." Eda had aged, her hair gone half to silver and the crow's feet at the corners of her eyes constant rather than reserved for laughter. She was still a handsome woman and Francis grumbled that a few men came around the pub for more than the drink over the last year or more. Frank was convinced it was the income of a pub owner they were after, not willing to admit his mother might be a catch in some other ways. Settling down at the table with two mugs, Eda turned to her daughter, with a breathy, "Well now…"

Dee ran her hand along the surface of the familiar, worn-shiny table that had made the short trip from the house around the corner on New Street. Although Eda had let the old place furnished, she could not part with this piece of furniture around which so much of her and Daniel's married life had taken place, adding another chair or a longer bench as each child arrived. The smooth feel of the burnished wood affected Dee with equal measures of homey comfort and lingering sadness, like seeing a long-stored picture of a dead grandparent.

The terrible loss of her father had come rushing back when she returned from London a fortnight ago. Work and more work had kept her guilt and remorse at bay while she was with Queen Alexandra's Imperial Military Nursing Service. Such a grand name for a gaggle of tired and frightened young women. She had prolonged her departure from the 3rd London General as long as she could, fearing what her demobilization might bring. Finally, Matron had, in what she thought an act of kindness, directed her discharge and saw her onto the train for Holyhead and home.

So here she was, back in the bosom of a family much reduced by the absence of the father and the bitterness of the eldest son. Molly was fifteen now, as if that were possible in Dee's reckoning. Sean would turn seventeen next month. He had become a handful for Mam since the rising in '16 and a source of daily worry and grief, so much was he gone from home now that he had left school. And sweet little Brendan—'Danny' as Mam insisted on calling him now—was gone nine years old, and him little more than a toddling babe when Dee left for the war.

Of course, this new place was not her home. The flat above the pub was comfortable enough, but smaller than the old house. Sharing a bedroom with Molly and Mam, she and her sister slept together in the double bed while Mam took the smaller bed that stretched under the window. As a result of the closeness of these sleeping arrangements, Dee had started taking larger doses of the morphia tablets she got from Cahill's, the chemist shop up the street. Old Mrs. Cahill never seemed to notice how often she was coming back to buy tablets and the increased dosage had for the most part allowed her to keep her nightmares and terrors hidden from her mother and sister.

There was always commotion when the pub was open, with Mam dashing up and down the stairs until well past the closing bell. As each evening wore on, Frank become less useful as he commenced to drinking with his friends and any other veterans who shambled in searching for a free drink from whomever would stand them. He was not able to make the stairs more than a few times a day on his crutches, even with the new leg from the Government. He was less able toward the end of an evening, banging his way upstairs in his drunkenness. When Dee complained about Frank's drinking, Eda dismissed her with, "Sure isn't it the good man's weakness, and him havin' gave so much and all."

Dee helped in the pub when she could, but Mam much preferred she look after the flat and the younger children. Since Dee had little desire to hear endless tales of the Great War, as it was now called by all and sundry, keeping house and minding Molly and Danny suited her fine. The least she could do was try to give the smaller ones a little normality in their young lives. Mam wouldn't let Molly work downstairs after suppertime, much as it might ease her burden, believing her daughter too young and innocent to hear the talk of men well into their pints and drams. The language had been softened by the presence of decent women in the pub, the war having changed that custom, too, but the men's tongues still turned rough in the hour before the closing bell. Deirdre was sure Mam kept Molly away because she had grown to such a beauty.

This brought to mind a safe subject for discussion and Dee set down the mug she had been blowing and sipping. "'Tis still a right shock to my mind, seeing what a beauty our sweet Molly has become."

"Hasn't she just, dear. Sure, hasn't she just," said Eda. "She's as fine a scholar as you were, too. The Mercy Sisters have the high hopes for her, just as they did for yourself. They even mentioned university for her, God be praised."

"It's a new Ireland, if the politicians are to be believed, with opportunities for women all round," Dee said with a hint of sarcasm. "Course, 'tis hard to tell which politicians will be in charge next week, let alone when Molly is of an age for the university."

"*Ach stórin*, let's pray to all the holy saints and martyrs that whoever our future government, they manage it without shootin' and burnin' half Dublin City to the ground again," Eda said, crossing herself. Dee had heard from Sister Mary Evangeline of the chaos during those few days, with St. Vincent's treating all manner of wounded. She couldn't imagine the charity hospital having to cope with gun shots and shrapnel, like some battalion first aid station in France.

As if reading her thoughts, Eda turned the subject to St. Vincent's. "Deirdre, I wonder if it mightn't be the proper time for you to return to your nursing at the hospital now. You've such a God-given gift for the healing, 'twould be a sin to waste it." Eda patted her daughter's hand with such fondness and pride that Dee hesitated to disappoint her.

"Mam, I spent the past four years trying to heal men blasted and gassed and shot up so bad you'd not believe they could still draw breath," Dee said, her voice tightening. "So many broken bodies, so many we couldn't save, so many with the life drained out of them even if they did survive."

Her mother leaned across the table and took both Dee's hands in her own. Eda's face shone with such pity and love that Dee's shell crumbled. As silent tears ran down her cheeks, her mother squeezed Dee's hands again and again, as if wringing the weeping from her. Her mother saw right down into her heart and she could no longer fight the pent-up strain of four long years of guilt and regret. Her shoulders slumping, hands limp in her mother's grasp, Dee's chin sank toward the table, unable to bear the tenderness and pity of her mother's gaze. She began to sob, meek as a mewing kitten at first, then building into huge gasps and gulps of air. Eda rose from her chair and moved around to Dee, cradling her daughter's lolling head against her waist, hands smoothing the thick hair.

"Oh, my sweet girl, *mo chailín milis*, what have they done to you? Have they taken your very heart? Have they left you with nothin' at all?" Eda's tears flowed now, too, taking what pain she could from her daughter. As they remained locked together, Eda began to keen. Not the wailing of the old Donegal funerals, but keening none the less. She rocked back and forth, Dee's head against her stomach, the soft moans reverberating through her body and into her daughter's. After a few moments, Dee began to moan too, the full anguish of her broken heart pouring out in such a torrent she feared she would never be able to stop. As her mother swayed back and forth, their wails came in time with the rocking and Dee's tears flowed hard and steady.

Eda began to interrupt her own moans with soft chanting, again from the old customs of her youthful home. "Oh, Daniel Brannigan, when will we see one like you among us again?" Dee's sobs grew louder with her mother's words. "Why did you leave us so soon, our Daniel? How can our hearts bear the loss of your kind face and good heart?" Eda's tears dropped on her daughter's hair as they rocked, her keening growing louder until she could no longer bear to speak.

"How could I have hurt you so? How could my last word's have been such bitterness?" Dee took up the chant now, speaking aloud what she had buried so deep for so long. "How can I go on without your forgiveness, such a wretched daughter am I?"

Eda rejoined with Dee, their wailing filling the rooms of the flat in which Daniel had never set a foot. Finally, their keening began to subside and Eda slid down onto the bench, her arm around her daughter's shoulders, their heads propped one against the other. Sobbing gave way to sniffling as they dabbed at their blotchy faces and reddened eyes.

Eda whispered in the kindest voice Dee could ever recall hearing, "He wouldn't want you to beg his forgiveness, Deirdre. He loved you far too much for that." Dee's breath hitched with another sob, but Eda squeezed it away, pressing her daughter close to her chest. Dee breathed slow and deep to steady herself. "He was too good a man for that, as you well know," Eda continued. "And you were the very light of his life, Deirdre. You must never forget that simple and plain fact."

"Aye, Mam, I'll not forget, long as I draw breath." She paused, not sure she could keep that promise. She went on now, resolved to have nothing left unsaid between them. "Oh Mam, I met a man every bit as good as Da, and he slipped away from me. Without a word he went, home across the sea," she said in nearly a lament again. "He broke my very heart, Mam, clean in two."

"A good man he may be, Deirdre, but a good man can be a foolish man as well," said Eda. "And this may be just such a man."

They sat together, the sounds below of people carrying on with their ordinary lives a comfort to them, while Eda agonized over how her daughter might escape the terrible burden she had taken upon herself. With a flash of clarity, like some holy saint's vision, she saw the answer plain as day. Calm as you please, she said, "Deirdre, you must leave this place. It's no good for you now and I fear you'll not find your way out of this terrible sadness if you remain."

"Mam, I'm just home these few weeks. Why would you have me gone so soon?" Dee said, feeling the daggers of rejection.

"I'll miss you as if I've cut off my good right arm, sweet girl, of that you can be sure. But you must go, for your own sake. I'll telegraph to your Auntie Nola in Halifax to see if she'll have you with her in Canada."

And with that, Deirdre knew she would leave Dublin behind.

CHAPTER TWENTY-FOUR

Jack

Five years on, the old juniper still leaned away from the sou'westers, alone in the midst of the broad flat marsh running back behind the lighthouse. The four stood along the edge of the wetland, one billowing smoke. "She's still standing then, Uncle? She's a joy to see again," Jack said, his right hand on his uncle's shoulder to steady himself on the uneven ground. Uncle Johnny did not turn to his nephew, concerned he might betray a look of unwelcome pity. He stood puffing in quiet thought, pondering the old tree.

"Maybe we'll forego the footrace this year, Jack?" suggested Will with an uncertain glance.

"Absolutely not," protested Geordie. "This was to be the year I finally beat Jackie to that damn tree." He gave Jack a hard pat, small payback for all the preceding lopsided competitions. Jack looked down at the wiry sedge coming up around his feet. Will and Geordie hesitated, fearing they had perhaps probed too deep with reminders of happier days on this very spot.

Without looking up, Jack murmured,"You hated the race to the juniper because you always fell into a pool or got a boot sucked under." He glanced at Geordie with an accusing half-smile.

Relieved by this jab, Geordie said, "Least I had a go at beating you. Not like William here. Might just as well have crawled, he went so slow and careful."

"He couldn't abide getting his kit dirty," said Jack. "And no batman now to clean his boots and brush up his trousers, has our Major Will."

"Especially hard on him, after impersonating the proper English officer," Geordie added.

Will, undeterred by the jibes, leaned on his old brown malacca, its smooth crook worn to his hand. "Perhaps we're too old for the footrace?" Will suggested. Geordie nodded his agreement.

Jack crunched some sedge with his toe, then looked out again at the lone juniper. "Perhaps so."

Uncle Johnny tap-tap-tapped his pipe against the heel of his boot, then rooted about in the bowl with a yellowed bone pick, removing the last bits of sticky resin. "We best be gettin' back to the house, b'ys. Rosie'll have dinner on the table soon enough." He never carried a watch. Never owned one, as far as Jack new, but Johnny Barlow always knew the time of day to the minute.

Within a few days of returning, Geordie had cajoled them into making this visit to the lighthouse. They had arrived by coastal steamer, a few days before the letter informing the Barlows of their intentions. With the wild excitement of the children and Aunt Rosie's unruffled addition of three plates on the table, any fears of a cold welcome danced away like water beading off a hot griddle.

Midday dinner at the lighthouse was the featured meal and the time when Aunt Rosie shone brightest, master of her domain that centered, night and day, on her kitchen. She was a skilled cook in all the ways that mattered and was accustomed to feeding a large crew. Three more mouths mattered little, although Geordie had always been a cause for concern. As they finished the fish and potatoes and pies, Aunt Rosie gave an elbow to Geordie as she cleared away, helped by Prudy, now grown a foot and full of confidence.

"You scarce ate a morsel, Geordie, compared to what you used to gobble at each and every meal," Rosie said, her doting smile disguising genuine concern. "'Twas a day I could scarce keep up with your stomach, my sweet b'y," she said, a hand on his arm. Geordie looked over his shoulder, patting her hand, and smiled up at her. She saw, close as she was now, how hollow his eyes and cheeks had become, the creases well etched in his forehead and around the corners of his mouth. Last night, the whole house had heard his wheezing and coughing from the assistant keeper's room.

"Aunt Rosie, the army food was so mighty bad I near went off eating altogether," he said. "In Gallipoli, it was more flies than food by the time you got the fork to your mouth."

Prudy wrinkled her face and let out a young girl's "Ewwwww!"

"No matter. I've a fortnight to fatten you." She gave his tawny hair a rough muss before stacking dirty plates in the wooden tub that served for washing up. "We'll have your appetite sharp as a blade in no time."

Uncle Johnny rose and extracted his pipe from a front trouser pocket, making his way around the table for the door. As he passed Jack, seated at a side bench with his cousins, he grasped his shoulder. "I'm for a pipe after that fine meal, so why don't you join me and have a cigarette." Geordie and Will knew he wanted private time with his nephew and namesake, so they asked for second cups of coffee, poking and tickling the nearest Barlow child.

Jack struggled up from the table, his legs stiff whenever he sat for long. He swung them out one at a time from behind the bench, steadying with his right hand for a moment, then walked to the door with the limp that came from their battered condition. Johnny held the door. The two walked down the grassy slope to the shore, where they had often studied waves and clouds and wind. Johnny packed his pipe and struck a lucifer along his trouser leg. Jack took a red pack of Cravens from a pocket under his baggy jumper and shook one out. He tugged it with his lips and then rummaged for his lighter. Uncle Johnny struck another match for him. Hiding his embarrassment at this rescue from his fumbling, Jack said, "It's become a fair ordeal to get a smoke going with just the one hand." He held the good right one to his mouth and took a drag.

Uncle Johnny stood upwind of his own blue cloud, listening to Jack as he spoke of his limitations. He looked back out to sea and pointed with his pipe stem, as he always did when starting an important topic. "Last time you lads were here, there was that queer berg down at the mouth of the bay."

"I recollect her well, Uncle. Very queer for August she was."

Johnny motioned with a long sweep of the horizon, Jack's eyes following. As they had seen on their way up, there was an extraordinary amount of ice all along the coast and out to the horizon line. Hundreds, maybe a thousand bergs, large and small, visible out to sea. The coastal steamer set a double watch each night to ensure they steered clear, despite the bright waxing moon.

"Even with a sea filled with ice, there's many a way through," said Johnny. "We don't stop fishing or hauling or moving passengers. Not in Newfoundland."

"That's a truth, Uncle, least not those in our family."

"Every vessel finds her way, depending on her size and her sail and the skill of her crew," Johnny said, pausing to exhale another billow. He squinted out to sea, sighed through his nose, and moved the pipe from one side to the other. Jack stayed silent.

"Last time, there were the five of youse, all our good and sweet b'ys," Johnny said, deliberate and slow, his voice revealing little of the deep emotion he felt at the memory.

"And the war took two of us entire," Jack said, "and a few more by bits."

"Alexander and Toby were fine lads who'd have grown to fine men, had they been given the very chance. And we'll hold them close in our hearts as long as we have days." Jack swallowed hard, fearing he would shame himself before his uncle if this went much further.

"But you and Will and Geordie came back to us, my dearest b'y."

Jack dropped his cigarette onto the rocky soil, rubbing it out with the toe of his boot. He pulled his left arm against his chest to hide the hand which had contracted over time into a tight curl. Johnny watched from the corner of his eye as Jack performed this ritual with his disabled arm. He'd already noted it several times since they arrived.

"Jackie b'y, you must find a new course," Johnny said, his eyes intense with affection and concern. "It won't be what you'd planned, that's certain, but you have your life still, no matter your trials and troubles." He turned and put both hands on Jack's arms, giving him a gentle shake. "That's far, far more than poor Toby and Sandy, mind you."

He turned Jack with an arm about his shoulders, their backs to the sea, and pointed with his pipe to the gnarled old tree up in the bog. "Yon juniper was just a sapling when I was a b'y. We were surprised to see her punch up through the peat. Never thought she'd endure. You see how she twists and curls and leans back into the wind? That's how she grew and that's how she thrives."

Jack struggled with the obvious lesson in his uncle's words, mumbling, "I'm no tree, Uncle."

"But you're an Oakley, and you have the root of an oak, sunk deep within your family and all those who care for you," Uncle Johnny said. "You need to stop shunning their help in pulling you up from this deep place you've fallen." Uncle Johnny released Jack and turned back seaward. "I've had letters from your dear mother, pouring out her grief at the state you've been in since comin' back."

Jack backed away from his uncle, putting a little distance between them. "Geordie and Will have said much the same to me."

After sucking a few times on his spent pipe, Johnny slid it back in his pocket. He crossed his arms and shook his head at the ground. "Jackie, you can see Geordie's a sick man, not half the strappin' lad we sent off to the fight. He may not be able to help himself, let alone you. And that'll be a hard thing, being used as he is to looking after the lot of you."

"There's always Will. He's my oldest friend."

Johnny crossed the few feet between them, close to Jack. "There's a powerful pain in young Will. He's been torn harder and deeper than any of you."

Jack was startled by this. Hadn't Will come out of the war promoted, decorated and respected? Strange Uncle Johnny seemed so afraid for him.

"But you must help yourself, Jackie. You need to find your new course and you need to do so right soon." The keeper turned back toward the lighthouse, leaving his nephew in the wind rising off the sea.

CHAPTER TWENTY-FIVE

Will

Delia arranged the fresh flowers from her back garden in a slender cut-glass vase on a side table. She stepped back from time to time to assess the balance of her arrangement and crept a little closer to the conversation between her husband and son. Walter Parsons sat in one of the Empire armchairs. He never much cared for the furnishings in this room, but they had to buy in a rush after the old house burned, along with most of the city, twenty-five years ago. The canny furniture makers of Boston and Philadelphia had emptied their warehouses at obscene prices, so they were forced to settle on furnishings that were acceptable rather than preferable. Although he was itching for a cigar, he remained in the sitting room with Delia out of a fleeting and grudging sense of obligation.

"I can at least be thankful we shall have decent blooms to greet the Harpers," Delia said, finally satisfied with her work. "I shall be overjoyed to see dear Edwin again. It must be more than thirty years." Sophia and her parents would be arriving in a fortnight.

"He has missed you, Mother," Will assured her, not knowing whether he had or not. He fingered the curve of his malacca to keep his hands away from his cigarette case, since mother only allowed the men in the family to smoke in Walter's library. Unless there were guests, of course.

"I do wish you would find a new walking stick, William. That one looks as if you bought it for sixpence off the pier at Brighton," his mother said.

Will fidgeted with the cane. He sighed without a sound and, languid as a sloth, answered his mother, "It served me well in France, *mater*, and I expect it will suffice for St. John's."

"At least promise you will use that lovely walking stick Beasley & Atherton procured for you on your wedding day."

Will reversed the cross of his legs. "I may have to do without for the ceremony and just limp along on Sophia's arm."

"William," his mother scolded, "you will do no such thing."

"Since Father insists I marry in uniform, I can't have her on my left arm because of the sword. Sadly, the Germans chose the wrong leg."

Walter sniffed at the sarcasm. Slouching back in his chair, he said, "You will marry in uniform and with medals, as a war hero."

Will's hand drifted to the scar on his cheek. "Not much of a hero, really. Others did more."

Delia broke in, chastising them both. "Walter, do stop slouching. You know how that distresses me." Turning to her son, "And William, will you please stop calling attention to that horrid scar. Thank God it has faded since your return."

Grasping for a change of subject, Will asked, "The plans for the wedding are progressing, Mother?" Delia blinked a single time in surprise. Will had never asked after any of the preparations.

"Everything is proceeding most satisfactorily. We shall have a few minor matters to resolve once Sophia and her mother arrive."

Walter rose from his chair, no longer able to resist the call of his humidor. "Since the discussion has turned to wedding plans, I shall take this opportunity to retire." Before his wife could protest, he was gone.

Turning to face her son, Delia examined him like some exotic object. Since his return, she had felt him more a stranger than her child, supposing this was only to be expected after his experiences in the war. Still, it distressed her, at least as much as anything could. "William, are you looking forward to commence your married life with Sophia?" She paused for a reply, signaling this was not a rhetorical query.

Not looking forward to anything really. Nothing at all…

Will recrossed his legs again and squeezed his cane. Delia noticed the whitening of his knuckles. He hesitated, giving her a twitch of concern. Sensing he had waited a little too long, Will said, "Of course, Mother. Sophia is a lovely girl and most devoted to me."

She knew he was lying but did not know why. "I do not understand all that you saw in France, William. Certainly you have not chosen to share anything with me," she said. "But you must find a way to avoid bringing it to your marriage. Sophia and the children you will have, God willing, deserve the best from you."

Deserve the best from me?

Will could think of nothing in reply. He wondered if he ever would. Instead, he said, "If you'll excuse me, Mother, I have some business matters to discuss with Father." Will limped down the hall to his father's library and went directly to the sideboard. He helped himself to a large brandy with a dollop of soda, then swallowed half the tumbler's contents.

"Bit early in the day, isn't it?"

Will took a second long drink, draining the glass. He stared back at his father with unblinking disdain.

"It wasn't in France."

CHAPTER TWENTY-SIX

Deirdre

Aunt Nola and her husband Arthur worked hard to keep a fine public house and had achieved some prosperity as a result. People came for Nola's good Irish kitchen. And for their bootleg whisky. At Donovan's, their particular method of operation was to sell (legal) 2.5% beer at a shocking price, then pour a shot of (illegal) whisky from under the counter to accompany it. Uncle Arthur had thereby convinced himself he was not *selling* hard liquor. Regardless of its origins or justifications, this had become an established tradition at Donovan's. Much to Deirdre's surprise, she discovered shortly after her arrival that Nova Scotia had been dry since the war and she and Uncle Arthur had laughed more than once over the ludicrous thought of such a prohibition in Ireland. Dee soon fell into a comfortable routine in Halifax, with an aunt and uncle who loved and appreciated her with understandable self-interest, given her help in running their business at very modest wages. As the months progressed, she had taken on bookkeeping and ordering, including the off-the-books portion.

On a showery day in May, she was seeing off the last of the lunchtime stragglers when the door swung open and a well-dressed man just a few years her senior entered, brushing rain from his homburg and shaking his sleeves. Welcoming him from beside the beer pumps, Dee said, "Sure, no man should be caught without an umbrella in Halifax, spring, summer, winter or autumn."

"The bigger fool am I," replied the customer. "Too late for a bite?"

"For anything hot, but I can scare you up a ploughman's with a bit of soda bread. Would that suit?" The American settled in against the bar, smiling his thanks and nodding. "What will you have by way of a drink then?" Dee asked. "We've all manner of sodas, phosphates, as well as what you Yanks call the low-point beer." She nodded to the hand pumps. There were plenty of Americans in and out of Halifax and she had learned early on to note the accent.

The American smiled and said, "In these trying days, I suppose the best an honest man can expect is a weak beer."

She pumped the beer into a straight pint glass, setting it in front of him. The foam lapped over the edge and trailed down the side as the head shrank up from the settling beer. "That'll be one dollar and fifty cents, if you please."

The American let out a choking laugh of surprise. "That's quite a price for a ten-cent beer."

"Well, you bein' an honest man, accept a gift from the proprietor," she said, placing a small glass next to the pint and producing a bottle from below the bar. She poured whisky into the glass.

"Please convey my sincerest thanks to the proprietor." He raised the smaller glass to look over the whisky, placing his nose over the rim for a long sniff. "Not your average rot gut."

With showy indignation, Dee replied, "I should say not, sir! No self-respecting Irish pub would serve such a thing." Turning with a tiny wink, she disappeared through a door behind the bar, leaving the American alone. She returned after a few minutes with a plate piled with cheese, cold meat, pickles and boiled eggs, as well as a stack of sliced bread and butter. Placing the heaping plate in front of him, she said, "Now get that in you, and I'll draw another beer to wash it down."

After eating in silence for a few minutes, the American was ready for a conversation. "Curious you pegged me as a Yankee so quick. Back home in Boston, my family thinks I sound like a far northerner, having spent half the war with the Newfoundlanders."

Finding this much more interesting than the usual bar patter, Dee eased forward against the polished wooden rail. "You were with the Newfoundland Regiment in the war then?"

"That I was, until America joined the fight. Pained me to leave the boys." He looked her over again. "Quite apparent you're Irish." She nodded—he had her full attention now. "Any of your ones in the war?"

Dee shifted, scolding herself for still recoiling at thoughts of her father. "Aye, my Da was a sergeant-major in the Dublin Fusiliers. We lost him at Suvla Bay, God rest his soul."

The American took a long sip of the weak beer and then downed the whisky in one. "Gallipoli was a waste of good men. Someone should pay for contriving that slaughter."

"And my brother lost a leg there as well, poor man, and he's had a difficult time of it since. He finds what peace he can in the drink." She sensed a sadness pass through the American while she spoke, though his face remained almost impassive. "And I was nursing for most of the war, in France and in London."

He looked across the bar with such a knowing and sad smile it tugged her heart. He held her eyes for a long moment, longer than would be polite under any other circumstances. Neither of them minded. Dee broke the spell of their shared remembrance. "So what brings you to Nova Scotia then?"

"On my way to St. John's, hoping to find a few of the old regiment." He raised the whisky glass, just a few shimmers of amber left in the bottom. "Have a business proposition for them." He tipped the glass toward her and gave a showy wink.

"Ahh," she said, "so many thirsty Yanks down your way, is't? I'd have thought there'd be plenty of business opportunities down there already."

"Not as many as you'd think. Not for my particular clientele."

Dee startled herself by reaching a decision then and there, sure as she could be of the rightness of it. Just as her mother had been so right in packing her off to Halifax, where she had put a little distance between herself and at least some of her troubles. But there were still a few needed tending, one in particular.

"So when will you be sailing for Newfoundland?"

"Day after tomorrow on the *Rosalind*, coming up from New York."

"Would you fancy the company of a proper Irishwoman on your journey?" The American looked up in surprise and whistled a little breath between his teeth. Appraising her again in a new light, he paused for a long moment. The woman staring back with such an air of unwavering confidence made up his mind for him. His face spread into a broad smile.

"I might like that very much. Do you mind me asking why you feel the sudden need?"

"You've new business with some of the regiment?" she said, arching an eyebrow. "Well, I've a good deal of old and unfinished business with one of that selfsame lot."

"I suppose we ought to introduce ourselves," she said, reaching a hand across the bar with self-assurance. "Deirdre Brannigan of Dublin City, late of Halifax."

He shook her offered hand with a firm grip. "Ned Tobin of Boston, and your servant, Miss Brannigan."

The *Rosalind* slipped past the Narrows and into the compact harbor through the last threads of morning fog. Tended and tied off at the steamship docks, the passengers made hurried farewells to shipboard acquaintances and disembarked with the usual excitement, tinged with relief, of a completed sea voyage. It required a single inquiry to a passerby of remarkable friendliness to locate the Oakley's business, a neat whitewashed two-story warehouse fronting on the water. A placard along the waterside, the lettering large enough to read from a ship in the harbor, read "Oakley Premises" in red letters outlined in gold paint and black pinstripes. Smaller versions adorned each landward face of the building.

"And here we be," she said, slipping a hand through Ned's elbow and gesturing to the sign. "There must be a public entrance somewhere here about." They turned right on Water Street, the last road before the quays, and found a solid wooden door with the business's name lettered on it. Dee opened the door onto a bustling front office, with several clerks, both men and women, working at small desks arranged in a row on the other side of a well-polished counter. Behind was a partition wall interrupted by a few doors with names stenciled in black on the frosted glass, the first two labeled "R. Oakley" and "T. Oakley." Dee smiled to herself, remembering Jack's tales of his father and uncle, the eponymous sons of his grandfather's schooner, the *Ricky Todd*. A young woman rose from her desk near the counter to greet them. Before she could ask after their business, Dee spoke up.

"I am Miss Deirdre Brannigan and my companion is Mr. Ned Tobin, a veteran of the Royal Newfoundland Regiment. We're both acquaintances of Mr. Jack…Mr. Jonathon Oakley and arrived from Halifax just this very morning with the intended purpose of seeing him."

The young clerk fidgeted with an uncertain smile, looking them over with a puzzled and nervous expression. "I'm afraid Mr. Jack isn't in, nor is he likely to be today." Seeing Dee's disappointment, she added in an attempt to be helpful, "But his father, Mr. Rick, is in. Perhaps you'd like to speak with him?"

Dee looked to Ned who replied with a shrug and a nod, turning his hat brim in his hands. "That would be much appreciated, if it wouldn't be an imposition."

The clerk relaxed a little and motioned to sit on the bench behind them. "I'll just see if he's available then, shall I?" She made her way through the desks and rapped on Rick Oakley's office door. They heard a muffled reply, followed by a turn of the brass knob as the clerk stuck her head behind the doorframe. The higher and still somewhat anxious voice of the young woman alternated for a few moments with a relaxed and affable voice from within the office. Although the conversation was unintelligible to Dee and Ned, it reached some sort of conclusion after a few exchanges. The clerk pushed open the door and the proprietor passed into the outer office.

Dee gave out an audible gasp, causing Ned to turn to her. "Saint's preserve us, he has the very eyes of his son," she whispered, not taking her gaze from the approaching man. Ned gave her arm an encouraging squeeze, having heard much of the tale of she and Jack during their sea crossing.

Rick Oakley made his way from behind the counter and through a slatted swinging half-door, smiling warmly at his visitors. He extended a hand to Ned and said, "I'm Rick Oakley, Jack's father. Let me say any friend of my Jackie is more than welcome here and at my hearth as well."

"Ned Tobin, Mr. Oakley, and a pleasure it is to meet the father of that rascal Jack," he said with an exaggerated expression, gripping Rick's palm and pumping it, a hand on his forearm for good measure.

"Fine it is to meet you, my b'y, and you better be callin' me Rick, lest people round here think me puttin' on airs." Releasing Ned's hand, Rick turned to Dee, saying in a softer voice, "And you're Deirdre then?" She offered her hand and he took it in his rougher one with surprising gentleness. He looked at her, his eyes gleaming with emotion and Dee knew he was aware what she had been—maybe still was—to his son. She squeezed his fingers in her gloved hand. That was all that passed between them for the moment, all that was needed.

"I couldn't be more honoured were I to meet the King himself, Mr. Oakley."

"No, my sweet maid, the honour is mine," he said, producing a pang in her with his easy manner, so familiar to her already. "You'll come to my office so we can have a proper talk then?" They followed into a sparse room, taking the two offered chairs facing his desk. Rick asked one of the clerks to bring coffee, then settled himself into his own seat.

"I don't much like haulin' people into this office," Rick said, motioning around the room. "I'd as soon work from the warehouse or the deck of one of the schooners, but Jackie's mother tells me I'm a proper businessman now and must have my name on a door somewheres or other." Rick shook his head in smiling abandon to his wife's gentle tyranny, adding, "My father and grandfather must be spinning in their graves each and every day."

The coffee arrived and Dee did the pouring. She was anxious to get to the matter at hand. "We're here to see Jack, Mr. Oakley, and hope you can tell us where we can find him," she said.

Rick was conspicuous in his avoidance of her imploring look, smoothing the wooden arms of his chair and exhaling through pursed lips. His hesitation was telling and his guests grew concerned at this taciturn tack in the conversation. After a very long silence, Rick's face brightened with a new resolve. "You being old friends from the war, and I sense mighty fond of our Jackie, I'll be free with you," he said. "Jackie's not in such a good way."

Dee placed a hand on the edge of the desk and glanced over her shoulder at Ned, who wore an obvious expression of surprise. "Then 'tis all the more reason I... we need to see him this very day," she said.

Rick gave her a searching look, weighing what would be best for his troubled son. Dee saw the weather-lined face and thick eyebrows working through his conflicting considerations. After another lengthy pause, Rick continued. "He doesn't work here, you see. Refuses to do so."

"Where does he work?" Ned asked.

"At one of the other premises, hired as a bookkeeper for their warehouse. I'll tell you now, it's as a favor to me the owner keeps him on. And you're not like to find him there this time of the day."

"Mr. Oakley, can you please help us find him?" Dee said, her rising anxiety coming out as pleading.

"I'll ring round to the haulage company and have Jack's mate, Geordie King, give you a hand in finding our poor b'y," Rick said. "Best that I not be seen tracking him down."

Dee was near frantic, so resigned was the man's voice. "Aye, that might be best. If you would ring round for this friend of Jack's?"

Ned slapped his leg and said grinning, "Geordie King? Why that lunker owes me considerable drinks from France and I mean to collect." After instructions to another clerk, the three sat in Rick's office awaiting Geordie's arrival, making uneasy small talk as they conspired to avoid any more discussion of Jack.

"The King's garage is right near," Rick said after ten minutes or more. "I can't see what's taking Geordie so long to leg it over." As if conjured by this statement, the door flew open and the room was made conspicuously smaller by the entry of Geordie King.

Ned flew from his chair and grabbed for Geordie's hand, pumping it as if bringing up water. Geordie let go of Ned's grip and wrapped him in a tight bear hug, then pushed him back to have good look. "Well, would you look at the fine toff from down the Boston way? Neddie b'y, you're a true sight."

Ned noticed with some alarm the toll the war had taken on Geordie, noting his lined face and the scattered threads of dull grey in his hair.

"This is Deirdre, Geordie," Ned said by way of introduction. "She was nursing at the division's Casualty Clearing Station on the first of July." Turning to the woman he had barely noticed upon entering, Geordie halted with a start, his surprise matched by Dee's.

"Sister Brannigan! Why I'll be damned outright!"

"You're the big soldier wouldn't leave his friend 'til we got him on the evacuation train," she said. "I remember you right well. Whatever became of that friend of yours, so grievous wounded? I never got a good look at him, his face all swathed as it was."

Geordie looked with confusion from Ned to Dee to Rick, then stuttered out, "Why… why that… was Jack."

"Thanks be to God he had you as a friend, Geordie King. I doubt he'd have made it through without you." Dee regretted this almost as the words left her mouth, seeing the ashen look of Rick Oakley. Jack had not shared everything with his father, so it seemed. "I nursed him for months at the 3rd London General Hospital, after I was transferred to England."

Geordie, unable to suppress his look of stunned surprise at that revelation, turned to the door and shooed them through. "Well, we best go find our Jackie then." The last one out, Geordie turned and gave a knowing glance back to Rick.

"I believe I know where we might find him."

CHAPTER TWENTY-SEVEN

Jack

The streetcar rattled and squealed its way up the hilly street to Military Road. After a short ride, they alighted at Rawlin's Cross. Walking a few doors down, they stopped at a small store with a plate-glass window framing a marble-and-steel soda fountain. The sign above read, "THE BLUE PUTTEE."

"It being near noontime, I'd wager our Jackie will be here," Geordie said.

"An ice cream parlor?" Ned said. "Not the Jack Oakley I knew in France."

"But it's the finest ice cream in all St. John's," Geordie said with a mischievous look well known to Ned from the war. Swinging open the door, Geordie said, "Good day, Peter," to the man polishing the countertop, his neat white-shirted appearance highlighted by a black patch over one eye.

"Geordie, sweet lad, what brings you in here midday?" the proprietor asked.

"Just touring a couple of friends round the finer sights of St. John's," quipped Geordie. With a quiet voice, almost an aside, he added, "Is he in?"

"Where else would he be?" said Peter with a shrug.

Geordie led them to an unmarked door at the rear. As they stepped through, eyes straining to adjust to the gloom, Dee realized the shop only occupied about a third of the building. In the large windowless back room, several men stood along a wooden bar, while four sat at a table playing cards. The room smelled of the familiar pub blend of smoke and old beer. Newfoundland had succumbed to the prohibition craze, too, she recalled.

Walking along the bar, Geordie slapped several backs, calling each patron by name and trading friendly insults. When he reached the end, he sidled up to a man half-turned to the rear of the room. Even from behind, she recognized Jack. The two spoke for some time as Ned and Dee waited, awkward and uneasy, near the front of the barroom. Finally, Geordie returned and said, "Alright now, let's have the joyful reunion, shall we?"

Jack had moved to a table at the very back. He had not yet looked up from the large dark rum sitting before him.

"Well then, aren't we a sorry gathering of the Old Boys," Geordie said, "and Old Girls, if you'll excuse my saying so, Sister Brannigan."

At the mention of the name, Jack looked up from the table.

"Hello, Deirdre."

Working hard to appear casual, his eyes, as they always would, betrayed him. She could see a confusion of anguish and elation swirling behind them. She wondered how she appeared to him, hard as she was holding onto her tears. He seemed to her, above all else, exhausted. He had been drinking, that much was clear, but was not drunk. That it was not yet noon was disturbing, but she had seen enough of that at her mother's pub and at Donovan's. The scars along the left side of his face had faded since she last saw him in London. His left eye still drooped a little. There was no cane in sight, so she assumed his leg had improved enough to do without. She could see he was hiding his ruined left hand under the table.

"And hello yourself, Jack Oakley," she replied, smiling through her own awkwardness. "You look none the worse for these two years gone and more since last we met in London."

At the mention of London, the discomfort was now all his. He stared down at the glass-ringed tabletop and said, "I left without a word, I know. I've not forgiven myself for that, Deirdre."

With Geordie and Ned at her elbows, this was not the time to delve into her hurt and disappointment. She shunted the matter aside with, "Well, aren't we all together here now? No use trying to unring the bell, is there?"

Ned threw them a lifeline in their awkwardness, shifting the conversation. "It's a fine thing seeing you in St. John's, Jack. I suffered through enough tales of this godforsaken place, I feel quite at home." He nodded at the glass before Jack and said, "Miss the army rum ration, do you?"

Twisting his glass but not raising it, Jack shrugged. "A fisher's drink as well, Ned. Why don't you all sit down?" Deirdre studied this exchange with great interest. The indifference Jack showed to the glass before him told her he was not a slave to the drink, as she had feared when first she saw him. He was, she realized with much relief, simply bored.

"Jack, I made the journey north from Boston with a business proposition," Ned said. "I enjoyed some lengthy chats with Deirdre during our crossing. She's gained much experience at her aunt and uncle's fine establishment in Halifax these last many months."

"You were in Nova Scotia, Deirdre?" Jack said, his surprise evident, not knowing what to make of this news.

"Aye, working in my Aunt Nola's pub. Which brings us back to Ned's point."

The American leaned forward on his elbows, champing to talk business. "Jack, there's much opportunity to be found from the Prohibition in the States," he said, direct to the point. "With the lads back from the fight and itching for a drink, there's good money to be made in supplying their need. I'm told there's no better source of good Canadian and Scottish and Jamaican stuff than your own dear Newfoundland."

Looking into the swirls of dark liquid, Jack inched his glass away, sloshing the rum a little as he did so. It laced down the side in translucent caramel ribbons, puddling around the glass on the tabletop. Waiting to judge the effect of his words, Ned took out a green pack of Lucky Strikes, tapped a few out and offered them to the men. Geordie and Jack waved him away. Lighting one, Ned leaned back in his chair to allow Jack's rumination to continue uninterrupted. He had seen Jack like this plenty of times during the war, puzzling over hard problems with much higher stakes.

"And you're here now, I'm guessing Ned b'y, because you've no present means of getting said liquor down to the Boston states?"

"You'd be right, Jack. And Deirdre has reminded me in some detail of your access to shipping," Ned said, at the critical juncture now.

"I'll not have my father and uncle involved in something like this," Jack said with irrefutable finality.

"But you were raised above and below decks, Jack, you told me and all the others many times in London," Dee said. "And aren't there ships aplenty to be had here?"

The mention of London knotted Jack's stomach again. He inched the glass a little farther away. "I can't fish with just the one arm." The flatness in his voice and the pain of this admission made Geordie and Dee wince in sympathy. It passed without Ned's notice.

Geordie, seeing a fine opportunity about to go begging, said, "Ahh, but Jackie, can you skipper a schooner with the one good arm and a few trusted stalwarts? Like Admiral Nelson, eh b'y? Particularly if the intent is… not to fish?" Geordie's raised brows and wide impish eyes dared Jack to contradict his rhetorical questions.

All three around the table witnessed the transformation creep through Jack. He shoved away the rum glass with the back of his crippled hand and leaned in over the table. Wiping his good hand across his mouth, he looked at each of them, one at a time, with an earnest expression. They knew he had the bit now. His mind was racing over all the problems and possibilities, clearing out the lingering cobwebs of alcohol.

"That's true enough, Geordie, very true," Jack said, excitement building over the huddled group like a thunderhead. With his eyes darting from one to the other, Jack's mouth spread in a wide and wonderful smile. "And the *Ricky Todd* is done with fishing, Pa thinks her too old to compete with the newer ships."

Geordie and Dee looked at each other with delight and excitement.

"Isn't that your granddad's ship, Jack?" Ned asked, scratching deep into memories of their endless talks in the trenches and *estaminets*.

Geordie jumped in, cutting off Jack, "That it is, Ned, and our lovely Jackie knows that venerable maid like a second skin."

"I'd need you to crew, Geordie," Jack said. "And to keep your meals down at sea. Wouldn't your father miss you at the haulage company?"

Geordie doodled with a finger on the table and said, "For all of a day or a week. Plenty of the lads back from the war looking for honest wages still. And he has my brothers besides." Reaching across the table to slap the back of his hand against Jack's chest, he added, "I'll not miss this grand adventure, Jackie. Who knows, we might even make a few dollars, too."

Ned took their focus on details for a tacit acceptance. Dee was overflowing, watching the man she had nursed and loved in London coming back to life before her very eyes. The realization pounded in her chest, surging through her, shortening her breath. It also brought her to a decision she had hoped since Halifax would somehow be allowed her.

"We'll need at least two, maybe three more men to crew her," Jack continued, "with me not able to haul sheet nor halyard with the one hand."

Ned shifted, knowing what he was about to disclose might not go down well, recalling how clannish the Newfoundlanders could be. "Our investors will provide one man to accompany each voyage," he said, attempting to toss out this condition as a bit of nothing. Jack and Geordie looked across the table at each other with real concern. The first serious cloud had appeared on the horizon of their enterprise. After a long pause, Geordie gave a shrug and Jack turned to Ned with a determined look.

"You, Ned Tobin, will be responsible for ensuring this man can pull his weight," he said, leaving no doubt this was a serious matter. "He needs to be either a man with time at sea or at least one with the sense to follow commands and learn quick."

Relieved this condition had not scotched the project, Ned said, "I know the very man they've in mind, Jack. I served with him in France after leaving our regiment." Hesitating with the memory, each one at the table understanding, Ned added in a quiet voice, "He won the *Croix de Guerre*."

Geordie slapped Ned on the back and said, "Why he's near one of the lads already then, isn't he, Neddie?"

To clear the air from this moment of uneasiness, Ned thought it a good idea to mention some of the arrangements already made. "Our investors offer us generous terms for our services, I can assure you. We'll be running into the smaller ports along the New England coast. Bar Harbor, Rockland, Kennebunkport and the like. The established syndicates already stitched up all the ports nearer to New York and Philadelphia, far south as Baltimore."

Jack smiled around the table again, brimming with excitement at this new and purposeful challenge. "Now what might the bad news be, Ned?"

"Not much really, as long as we stay clear of the syndicates. They're an unfriendly crowd. The Coast Guard has patrols along the coast, but they're concentrating on big ships unloading near the three-mile limit."

Geordie leaned in again, a mischievous grin slipping across his broad face. "If you truly think you can pry the *Ricky Todd* away from your father, sentimental as he is, we might just get her a little speed below decks."

"You mean give her an engine, Geordie?" Jack asked.

"Perhaps two? She'd seem a simple coasting schooner under sail, but able to outrun most of the Yanks' Coast Guard."

Ned slapped both his hands on the table and said, "Well, it seems we've a deal then, gentlemen?" Geordie and Jack gave firm nods, each shaking Ned's hand in turn.

Dee had held back from the business discussion. The deal now done, she said, "Geordie and Ned, to the bar with yourselves for a drink in celebration." Seeing she was not to be gainsaid, the two men rose as one. Dee added, eyes locked on Jack's, "Corporal Oakley and I have some matters yet to be discussed." Jack's excitement with the new venture drained away, sure this was to be the reckoning for his inexcusable departure. Scraping her chair on the plank floor as she turned to put her back to the barroom and her face to Jack, Dee resettled herself and raised her chin to him.

"Now you'll listen to me, Jack," she began. "We parted poorly, given your scurrying away in the night like you did, but that's water under the bridge, well and truly."

This was not what he had anticipated hearing and it knocked him off kilter. He began the apology he assumed was still expected, stammering, "Deirdre my dear, dear maid. If I… I…could take back what I did… "

"Hush yourself, Jack Oakley," she interrupted.

"I couldn't bear the guilt… of… of saddling you with a man… so ruined… for the rest of your days. I couldn't bear the… the selfishness… in giving you such a burden." His eyes were huge with doubt and fear at what he had just admitted but he did not look away from her. She saw in his agonized appearance just how much he had punished himself these last years. There was neither the bitterness nor the will left in her to add to it. Of much greater importance, she knew without any lingering doubts that she still loved this man greatly—and that he had never stopped loving her.

She gave his right hand a gentle stroke or two, then said in a quieter voice, "I've said that's water under the bridge, Jack. You hurt me deeply, right enough, but we're here now, the two of us, and it's an entire new day." His head drooped toward the table as he sought, without much success, to hide the relieved and overjoyed tears swelling in his eyes. She placed her hand over his with such incredible lightness every nerve of his arm vibrated with her touch.

"And I have a stake in this adventure, too," she said. This took him by surprise and she was pleased with the effect. "I've acquaintances in Halifax familiar with the Nova Scotia end of this business. They've agreed to supply us Canadian whisky, as well as what they can spare from elsewhere. Like here, they may not be allowed to drink it, but they can surely sell it for export."

"Well, I'd not have thought we'd end up business partners, Deirdre," Jack said, much uplifted and a little bemused at this turn of events. Dee did not return his smile and her intensity silenced him.

"But there will be two conditions, Mr. Oakley, or I'll tell our man Ned here that none of you are to be trusted and we'll move this whole shebang back to Halifax City. A place where I'm well known and highly regarded."

He had not the slightest doubt this was true. "And what might these conditions be?" Jack asked, a little shaky in anticipation of her answer.

Sweeping up the glass from the edge of the table, she brandished it under his nose and said, "You're to give up the drink, starting this very day. I've seen too many a good man destroyed by the *craythur* and I'll not have you added to that sad tally." Jack hesitated, having grown comfortable with the rituals of his daily visits to the bar. She saw his reluctance and added, "You're only drinking out of boredom anyways, Jack, and well we both know it."

He looked away embarrassed, then forced his gaze back to hers. He would not abandon this conversation—nor her—ever again. And she was right about the boredom.

"Trouble is you get yourself into the habit. Drink is a powerful seducer and a cruel mistress in the end," she said. "I've seen it too many times to let you go the same way." He knew he would not regret accepting this condition and nodded his agreement.

"And what of your second condition?"

"That you marry me, Jack Oakley, and as soon as we can make it so."

CHAPTER TWENTY-EIGHT

Jack

They had first taken up residence with Jack's family. A bedroom had been freed by Nell's marriage the year before, and the teenage Dickie, who had claimed it, was not happy to find himself back under the third-floor eaves with his two younger brothers. Although Dee felt awkward descending upon Jack's family, unknown as she was to them, it was the only practical solution after their whirlwind marriage. In no time at all, however, any uneasiness burned off like dew under the warmth of the Oakley's immediate affection for her. Viola in particular was pleased to have another woman in the house again. The two had grown very fond of one another, particularly when Viola saw the rapid changes Dee had wrought in her dear boy.

When they came down to breakfast each morning, Dee and Jack were greeted by sniggers from all but the puzzled Charlie, who was not yet twelve. To the others around the table, the noises coming up through the floor and down the hallway from their back bedroom, evening and morning, made the presence of newlyweds quite obvious. Jack and Dee had ceased feeling embarrassed soon after realizing they were the source of the tittering. At first, they made half-hearted attempts to quiet their lovemaking, but that proved harder than they had imagined.

The extent to which they gave themselves over to long-pent lustiness came as a mutual and happy surprise. Jack's injuries, in particular his scarred thighs, rendered difficult what their limited experience told them was the proper man-atop positioning for sex. Instead, after much fumbling and giggling, they discovered that other positions, worked out through delightful trial and error, were effective and rather more exciting. Jack in particular loved having Dee on top, allowing his eyes to explore the remarkable woman who had chosen him. The washing away of his three years' longing and regret by her unbridled love sometimes made him turn away to hide welling tears from her. But mostly he was like an excited boy, exploring her body with his eyes and hand and mouth.

As she straddled him, her unruly auburn hair fell in long loose curls over her shoulders, sometimes covering one or the other of her ivory-pale breasts. He had taken to studying the designs of blue-green veins pulsing here and there, interrupted by a half-dozen beauty marks. He traced them, drawing his own secret puzzles, with the tips of his right fingers, sometimes startled by her sharp inhalation if he brushed the pink of a nipple. This close study of her face and skin helped him not finish too soon, something he had discovered was much appreciated by Deirdre. Since he feared being unable to perform for so long, he often rushed, propelled by some lingering anxieties. Dee loved the feel of him inside her and had given herself over to the pure joy of it, moving faster and faster against him regardless of position, crying out through deep shudders and great gulps of breath, collapsing beside him in a haze of heat and sweat and tousled hair. They had even managed to finish together a few times. But for Jack, who could climax at will, so hungry was he for his new wife, giving Deirdre such obvious pleasure was most important to him. He would spend the rest of his life making up for his past sins against her and he thought this the most pleasant penance ever devised.

For the first time since returning to Newfoundland, he slept like a child, so content was he most every night. He imagined Deirdre was also, but she usually rose from their bed, shaking out small white pills from a brown bottle and swallowing them with water poured from a milk-glass pitcher she kept filled on the chest of drawers. She still suffered from a back injury during the war, she told him, but it mostly bothered her at night and he wasn't to fret over it. He had taken her at her word—she was a nurse, after all. He also thrilled at watching her walk across the room without a stitch on, the late-lingering twilight of a northern summer glowing off her pale skin. Some days she had taken the pills during the daytime, too. No matter, he thought, her being healthy as a horse in every other way.

So it was with lightness in both heart and step that Mr. & Mrs. Oakley ambled down from their own new home on Prescott Street, en route to the Parsons Premises. Dee had not yet met Will, although she had heard so many tales of his and Jack's exploits she felt she already knew him. "I've not seen him since his son was born in April," Jack said, "although I sent round a gift for the lad."

As they approached the premises, Dee spotted a slender and well-dressed man turning the corner toward them. He walked with a very slight limp, helped by a cane that appeared to her more affectation than necessity. He seemed distracted, looking about the street at everything and nothing at the same time.

"Will, we were just here to see you!" Jack called out.

The man's head spun to follow Jack's voice, confused as to the origin for a moment. Spotting them, he broke into an easy smile. "Why I haven't seen you since word of your hasty marriage spread all over the town," he said, walking up to them and removing his hat. Will nodded to Dee and she noticed the scar on his cheek.

"I'm Deirdre Brannigan," she said, then seeing Jack's exaggerated look of hurt, corrected herself. "That would be Deirdre Oakley. And you, I might venture to guess, are Major William Parsons?"

"At your service, Mrs. Oakley," Will said, giving her hand one gentle shake before releasing it. He smelled a little of cologne and whisky. She had a brief flash of familiarity but having seen so many men like him during the war, she let it fade without another thought.

Jack slapped Will on the shoulder with his good hand and, full of animation, said, "And you're a father now? That I should live so long as to see that. And you the first of us all."

The side of Will's face twitched, the scar reddening a bit, Dee noticed. Will touched his cheek to still the tic and said, "Surprised me too, since Sophia and I weren't married ten months when the little beggar arrived. I'd rather thought it would be longer."

"The *paterfamilias* must be right proud, with a new namesake to continue the legacy?"

"Yes, I suppose he would be, having insisted we name the unlucky little man Walter," said Will. "But I've managed to anger him sufficiently by calling the boy Terry. Just to avoid confusion, don't you know?"

"He'll think you a proper Bolshevik, rebelling like that," Jack said. Will gave a weak chuckle.

Looking to change the subject from his father, Will sized up Jack and said, "Why you look quite presentable. Marriage must agree with you." He added, with a less playful tone, "And a good deal better than last time I saw you."

"Aye, that's certain," Jack said, with a rueful smile that stood in good stead for an apology between such old friends. "But this lovely maid has rescued me from the brink of disaster." Dee's smile masked how aware she was of that statement's truth.

Jack made a move toward the door and motioned Will to follow. "Now that we've dispensed with the small talk, Major Parsons, my dear wife and I have a small business matter to discuss with you, if you've a moment for such trifles?"

"Of course," Will said, as the three made their way into the bustle of clerks and typists that comprised the offices of The Parsons Premises (Ltd). They trundled up the side staircase to the second-floor Exports Office. As they approached the clerks' desks in the outer area, a petite young woman leapt to her feet and ran to Jack, throwing her arms around his neck. What she might have lacked in native beauty was more than compensated for by an outsized personality.

"Where have you been hiding yourself, Jack Oakley?" Gussie said as she released him. "And after you promised you'd marry me when you came back! I haven't seen you since you were in that crush at Will and Sophie's wedding last year."

"Miss Augusta Parsons, may I present my wife of forty-three days, Mrs. Deirdre Oakley of Dublin," Jack said with much flair.

"So this is the lovely lass I beat for your heart is't, Jack?" Deirdre said, extending a hand and a warm smile to Will's youngest sister. "Why, she must have been all of fifteen when you marched off to war then?"

"And a rare beauty she was even then, Mrs. Oakley, so I'd be careful how you treat your new husband," Jack said, giving Gussie another squeeze and kissing the top of her neatly brushed hair.

"You and I shall be the best of friends, Deirdre," the guileless Gussie said. "I know all his darkest secrets and shall share them as required."

"And with that, let's to the business at hand," said Jack, moving them to Will's office. After settling in appropriate places, Jack said, "We're engaged in a small business venture with my old friend and yours, Neddie Tobin."

This drew a surprised look from Will. "I haven't heard that name since the Americans joined the war and he left the Machine Gun School."

"Neither had I until he turned up, Deirdre in tow, from Halifax in May," said Jack.

Will looked completely puzzled. "You and Deirdre had no plans to marry until she arrived with Tobin in May?"

"The 17th of May, to be exact," Dee interjected. "But we had known each other quite well in London during the war."

Jack sought to retrieve the discussion. "There will be all manner of time to discuss our strange and wonderful history, once you and Sophia are receiving guests again." They were interrupted by a sharp knock on the door. Gussie, not feeling in the least that she required her brother's permission, breezed into the office with a bundle of papers.

"I am sorry to interrupt," she said, "but I need Will's attention for just a few moments. Time, tide and commerce wait for no man." Flouncing around the desk to her brother's elbow, Gussie spread a portfolio before him. "William, you need to endorse these dock receipts for two cargoes of salt fish that arrived yesterday." She placed another folder beside the first and continued, "We also need you to countersign the export license for the shipment of spirits to Jamaica from our bond warehouse stocks." She stood watching as her brother stared down at the papers, listless trails of smoke hovering above his head from his last cigarette.

"William," she said with impatience and more than a little annoyance, "you must see to these matters as they are presented to you. We cannot have ships lingering in port." Gussie had run the office during the last year of the war, her father unable to keep male staff from joining the regiment or running off to the merchant fleet.

Much to her parents' chagrin, she had refused to leave after the war ended. Walter had placed Will in charge of the office to keep an eye on his sister as much as any other reason. That was not how things had turned out.

"I will also need the quarterly account reconciliations for the board meeting this afternoon. You've had them since last Thursday."

Fishing into a side drawer, Will produced a stack of files and began leafing through them. He extracted one near the bottom and handed it to his sister. "Is this what you're looking for?" he said, confused by the stack before him.

She opened the file and closed it again in one motion, holding it at her waist. "Will, have you even looked at these figures? You haven't initialed anything."

Will's face reddened as she scolded him before his oldest friend. "I was certain I'd finished that." He flipped through the folders in the stack again. "Almost certain."

"Never mind. I'll have Kinsella look them over," she said, examining her brother with care. "I trust his work, so if you heed my advice, just initial whatever he hands you back." Gussie opened the door and called across the front office, "Mr. Kinsella, would you come for a moment, please."

A young man of about Gussie's age entered the office, pushing a shocking amount of curly red hair back from his forward. "Yes, Miss Parsons, Mr. William?"

She handed the quarterly reports to him and, her briskness hiding the small falsehood, said, "Mr. William would like a second review of the quarterly accounts and feels it would be excellent experience for you." The younger man looked very pleased and took the reports with alacrity.

"And could you get to them immediately? Mr. William would like them back before lunch." With a nervous nod, the ruddy clerk turned and fled to the safety of his own small desk. Gussie sighed, then leaned over her brother and kissed his head. "We'll sort this, William." Turning to Dee and Jack, she said, "More of an interruption than I'd planned. So sorry." She flashed them a smile, then slid out the door, closing it behind her.

Will looked across the desk and, shaking off his sister's chastisement, smiled anew at his guests.

"So to business," Dee said, relieving Will's discomfort.

"To business," Will echoed, liking her forthrightness very much, so unlike his Sophia.

"I've convinced Pa to sell me the *Ricky Todd* for use as a coastal trader," Jack said.

"She's a fishing schooner, Jack, and an old one at that, much as you love her," Will said, already wondering what kind of business proposal this was to be.

"That she is, and humble as can be," Jack continued. "Which is why we have her in the old Jenkins dry dock where Geordie is fitting her with twin gasoline engines."

"Why in God's name would he waste his time and your money doing that?"

"To cut the time to the New England coast," Jack said.

"Where they have plenty of their own ships in the coasting trade already," Will said.

Dee shifted forward in her seat. "But they don't have good whisky, with all their madness over the Prohibition. And those towns so full of thirsty men."

"Where it's just as illegal to sell whisky as it is here," Will said with what he thought was finality.

"But here it's not illegal to *buy* Canadian whisky and export it, Will b'y," Jack said.

"So you intend to become a rumrunner?"

"That I do," said Jack. "And Ned Tobin is to handle the American end of things, with some lads from his old Yank regiment."

"How will you crew her? You can't sail her singlehanded and, although your wife may be intrepid, she strikes me as a city girl without much time before the mast."

"Geordie will crew, as well as Deirdre's brother, Sean, who just arrived from Ireland. Ned's partners in America are sending a man up from New York."

"So what is it you need from me then?"

"A corner of your bonded warehouse and licenses, you being an established exporter of all manner of things."

"And it's nothing exactly illegal we'll be asking of you," Dee said. "For how are you to know upon what shores the wild winds might blow the old *Ricky Todd* once she leaves this port?" She lilted this out, punctuated with the sweetest innocent smile. Will grinned at the brass of this woman, despite himself, then turned to the window. He smoked the last of a cigarette in silence, staring out over the harbor. Dee and Jack stayed quiet, knowing Will was struggling with their request. Finally, he spun in his heavy swivel chair, stubbed the cigarette in an ashtray at the corner of his desk and looked back to Jack and Dee.

"I'll need to bring Gussie in on this, since she prepares most of the export licenses. She'd cut off her arm for you, Jack, so I wouldn't think there will be any problem there. And the *pater* won't question anything that pays."

Will rose, signaling the meeting was at an end. "When will you need the first license?"

"We'll have the *Ricky Todd* ready to sail end of September."

CHAPTER TWENTY-NINE

Deirdre

7th of June, 1920
The Coombe

My dearest Deirdre,

    I stood holding your telegram in the middle of the pub, crying and laughing so that the customers thought me gone mad. To hear my own dear girl had been married was the last thing I'd thought when the Post Office boy handed me the telegram. May the Lord bless you and your dear Jack and may the Blessed Virgin shower you with peace and happiness.

    Your brothers and sister were as surprised as me and each sends their congratulations and best wishes, too. Our sweet Molly was all teary over the thought she wasn't with you on your wedding day, so kind a heart has she. And we're all waiting on the tenterhooks to hear more by letter, praying one is already on the seas to us. Deirdre, I want you to take to your heart what I write here now. Your father is smiling down upon you this day, so pleased would he have been at the news of your wedding. My wish to you, and it would be his were he here, is that you and your Jack find the love and the friendship we found during the years the Lord saw fit to give us.

Now, let me wipe the tears from off my cheeks and attend to the other important business at hand. As soon as I received your telegram, I determined we must send your brother Sean to you. I could have burdened your Aunt Nola again with another mouth to feed, but now that you're in St. John's and with your dear Jack, I'm putting him on the next steamer headed that way. I'm sorry my dear, but there's a great need for this hard decision.

Things have gotten so much the worse since the end of the war, what with the shooting and the burning and the bombing all through the countryside. I'm afraid our Sean, young as he is, got himself all tangled up with the Sinn Feiners. He's been up to God knows what and is in grave danger from the Brits, of that I'm sure. They've flooded the country with Englishmen back from the war who don't have better prospects than to take their pay for abusing the people here. Your brothers are fighting and arguing whenever Sean is home, so angry is Francis at what he sees as treason to the memory of all who died in the trenches and on the beaches. They're like to kill each other if I don't do something. It breaks my heart to see your brothers all torn to bits as they are. I've never missed your father more than I do this very day, Deirdre. So with that by way of explaining, I pray you'll forgive me for imposing this burden on you, newly wed as you are. And to your own dear Jack, I'm sending my deepest affections along with an apology for upending your lives like this.

I love you with every nook and cranny of my mother's heart, Deirdre, and pray that one day I may hold you in my arms again and shower the tears and the kisses upon your own lovely head.

> *All the blessings of the Holy Family be upon you both,*
> *Your own dear Mam*

"Mind you leave the door unlatched, Jack!" Dee shouted down the hall from the dining room in reply to the shuffle and scrape of more arriving guests. "I'll not have you locking our spirits out in the cold!" She dashed back and forth to the warm kitchen, more than the usual amount of hair struggling out from her braid, fetching pitchers and platters of food for the New Year's dinner at the house on Prescott Street.

"And that includes my own dear departed ones, with the fond hope they'll find me here at the edge of the world, Deirdre my dear."

Setting down a huge bowl of boiled potatoes, Dee flew to the new arrival and threw her arms about him, planting a loud kiss on his cheek. "Leave it to the likes o' you, Ned Tobin, to arrive just as the food is headed to table," she said, turning to heft the bowl again. "But thanks be to God we've another Irishman in the house, these Newfoundland heathens not knowing the first thing regarding a proper New Year's celebration."

"It's a wonder they've avoided all manner of misfortune," Ned said, patting her back with awkward hesitation until she released him. Balancing the bowl under her left arm, she grabbed a basket with a split loaf of crusty bread protruding and motioned with her head for Ned to follow. He was still a little startled from her overenthusiastic welcome, but trailed her dutifully into the dining room. Once through to the others, Dee held the basket out to her younger brother. "Time to beat the walls, Sean, before we sit down to eat." All heads but one snapped up with amused smiles at what this might possibly mean. Sean shrugged and rose, extracting a half-loaf and slapping the wall with desultory strokes. His sister whacked the opposite wall with much greater enthusiasm.

"'Tis a silly superstition, Deirdre, and well you know't," said Sean, embarrassed before his crew mates.

"'Twas good enough for your mother and your mother's mother, and you've never wanted for bread in your life, Sean Brannigan," Dee scolded, brandishing her battered loaf at him.

Jack elbowed Geordie and said, "You'd not believe what she's been about, starting with cleaning the house 'til the very wood screamed. She's been like a madwoman."

"Best not to question her ways, Jackie, strange as they may be," Geordie replied. "There's no telling what level of mischief this one could conjure if she'd a mind."

Jack rose and crossed the room to Dee, offering his good arm to take the bowl off her hip. "Let me help with that great pile of potatoes, Deirdre, complaining as you've been about your back today."

She waved him away with a stern shake of her head. "Don't be daft, Jack Oakley, with just your one good arm." She turned away, missing the look of hurt that flashed across his face.

"It's just that you've had to take your pills twice already today," he said as she brushed past in her manic rush to get dinner on the table. Plopping the bowl of potatoes near the center and at the very end of her reach, Dee startled with a realization that she had forgotten something important.

"Oh my goodness!" she said, spinning to face Ned. "What direction was the wind blowing when you arrived?" This would be a strange question, even to Ned's big Irish family.

Sean shook his head, exasperated. "Deirdre, I reckon that only counts if you're in Donegal."

"Nonsense," she said, dismissing him with the back of her hand, her eyes a little wild as she turned her attention back to the American. Ned thought for a moment and replied, "In my face walking up the hill, so blowing down toward the harbor."

"Saints be praised, 'tis a westerly then," she said with genuine relief. "Good fortune to us this year. And with Chester the first to arrive, 'tis a fine year ahead for this household, right enough." With this pronouncement of her deep satisfaction with the state of things for the New Year, she sat herself down in the vacant chair at the end of the table, the one nearest the kitchen.

Ned Tobin chuckled and turned to Chester Dawkins, who had been crewing on the *Ricky Todd* as the representative of the New York partners since its first voyage almost a year and a half ago. "So you were the first foot then, Chester? That should mean good fortune indeed." Chester and his sister, Lena, were often confused by some of the strange ideas of the partners, particularly Deirdre with her Irish ways. Still, she had proven a generous woman who welcomed them with open arms and heart. She was a good friend to Lena, two kindred strangers in this far-away place.

Taking up the explanation herself, Dee said, "The first foot across the threshold on the New Year is a great and powerful omen for the coming twelve months. 'Tis held by many," she paused and gave a shushing stare in reply to Sean's audible scoffing, "including *most* of my own dear family, that if the first foot is a tall and dark and handsome man, good luck will follow all the year long." She patted the table with both palms to emphasize her point, adding, "And you're nothin' if not a fine fetching man, Chester Dawkins."

Chester was relaxed with Dee's attention, as he always was. Like his sister, he had developed a true fondness for her. "Don't know about handsome, but you'd have a hard time finding anyone darker in St. John's," he said, a disarming smile escaping across his comely brown face. His dark eyes gave his sister a sideways glance and Lena let out a burst of laughter into her napkin.

Landing in a small city devoid of colored people had been a shock for these New Yorkers, imagining the worst possibilities during their first few weeks. Just as Chester had with the French during the war, however, they realized early on that Newfoundlanders were not Americans. These islanders lived in blessed ignorance of the thousand ways, large and small, white Americans had found to keep down Negroes. Sure, there were some stares on the street, much less frequent now than before, but they were looks of curiosity, not glares of suspicion. They had settled into a decent life, quite comfortable now with Chester's share of the earnings from the voyages. He had at first approached his work on the schooner with reticence, but he was smart and could haul line, so at the end of a few months under Jack, he had grown into a passable journeyman sailor. And the venture was going very well.

Ned Tobin walked around the table filling the short glasses set before each person except Jack, including the ladies, with some good malt whisky. He was always happy to partake of the best of their own merchandise. Finishing the pour, he stood behind his own chair and raised his glass. "Let me offer the first toast, with a hope the coming year will be as prosperous for us as the last proved to be."

"Oh, that would be grand!" cried Dee, above the calls of "here, here" from all around the table. "And that it be safe and healthy for us all as well."

Jack smiled across at Dee, still with the eyes of a man a little incredulous of his undeserved luck. "With all your superstitions satisfied, dear wife, how can we not be safe and healthy and prosperous?"

"And mind you leave out the back door this day," she said to all their guests, adding a final inscrutable custom in reply to her husband's affectionate taunting. Sean heaved another put-upon sigh at his sister, then stood to make his own toast.

Clearing his throat with great intent, he waited for the table to fall silent. "I lift my glass to the year nineteen hundred and twenty-two, the year that will see at long last an independent Ireland," he said, his young eyes bright with pride. "Long may she stand as a beacon of freedom to small nations, having thrown off the English yoke after these many centuries."

"Here! Here!" seconded Ned, springing out of his chair, eyes shining with near as much emotion as Sean's. Dee was a little surprised by Ned's exuberance, but the Irish in America were a peculiar lot, what with their sentimentality for the Old Sod, even those who had never set a foot ashore there. But Ned had worked his grandfather's farm in Tipperary after the war, until the fighting in Ireland had driven him back home. Not as caught up as Sean and Ned, she was nonetheless pleased that this should mark an end to the fear and violence of the past four years and more.

The others rose and raised their glasses in respect. "To Ireland then," said Jack, raising his water glass, the toast echoed by those all around the table. They settled down again with a hubbub of sliding chairs and scuffing feet.

Ned thought it the proper time to conduct a little business. "As we all know, our operations have been running smoothly of late, save for the few small challenges."

"Like those drunk bastards you hired droppin' six cases of Bushmill's off the dockside at Jonesport?" interrupted Sean.

"Or those sheriff's deputies turning up in Booth Bay?" added Chester.

Ned went on, "As I said, save for a few small challenges," persevering despite Chester and Sean's groans, "that were easily cured by a friendly donation to the deputies. And our American customers can't seem to get enough of our fine wares."

Jack leaned forward and, knowing Ned Tobin's self-interested mind all too well, cautioned him, "We'll not add additional voyages, Ned, and the *Ricky Todd* can't be overloaded and keep up speed and maneuver, even with Geordie's engines."

Chester crossed his arms, considering what had just been said. "Demand is high for our premium liquor, but trading at a reasonable volume through the small Maine ports has kept us below the notice of the big syndicates." Then he added, specifically to Ned, "That will continue to keep us safe. If we don't get greedy."

The hard stares exchanged by Chester and Ned had soured the atmosphere in the dining room, so Jack broke in to clear the air. "Bah, we'd need a second schooner and crew to carry any more than a few extra cases, and I'm not much interested in that. Doubles all the costs and the risks."

Ned turned his attention from Chester, who had relaxed back into his chair, and downed the last of his whisky. "Perhaps it's for the best we stay the course then," he said. "Why tinker with something that's not broken, eh?"

6th of April, 1922
St. John's

Dearest Mam,

I didn't think it possible for Sean to become even more aggravating, but he's found a way. By the time you read this, Lord only knows where he'll be. Perhaps sitting in your own front parlor. You know he's been working with my Jack in our sea trading business, and he's been a good member of the crew. Jack says he's a regular sailor now, which is much to be said for a boy who only went to sea in the muddy puddles of the Liberties before landing here in Newfoundland. I'm sorry to write this, Mam, but on their last voyage they put into Salem down in Massachusetts and our Sean took it in his head to jump ship. They searched the port and asked round in the pubs, but found neither hide nor hair of him. Needing to keep to schedule, they left on the next tide. Our partner, Ned Tobin, asked round the port in Boston and heard some say they'd seen a lad of Sean's type taking passage on a steamer bound for Queenstown. If that be true, he'll be back in Ireland.

Mam, he was full of talk about the Treaty and the Free State, with a bellyful of fire and spitting angry as he was. If the fighting were to start up again, there's no telling where he'll end up. You put him in my care, Mam, and I've failed you. But he's a grown man now and has to make a man's decisions, wrong headed as he might be. I only hope he doesn't find himself shot or hung. This family's known enough grief.

Jack and me are getting on as fine as two people could and I love him to the bottom of my heart. We'd like to start filling the house with children, but we've had no luck there yet. Soon enough.

I miss you every hour of the day, Mam, and hope we'll see each other again someday. The ocean's not as wide as it once was, with the fast steam ships criss-crossing every week and more. Give a kiss to Molly and Danny for me, and a hug to yourself as well.

Your loving daughter,
Deirdre

CHAPTER THIRTY

Will

The preternatural calm that always followed in the wake of Fidelia Parsons permeated the sitting room of Will and Sophia's house at No. 7 Church Hill. She had come to see her grandson and to check on her daughter-in-law, now heavily pregnant with her second child. Young Walter—Delia of course did not call him Terry—was beside her on a rose-satin upholstered settee, balancing a tea cake on his napkin while chewing at another he had stuffed in his mouth all at once. Delia poked with delicacy and futility at the copious crumbs tumbling from the corners of the boy's mouth. As the two women sipped their tea, the front door opened and Will soon appeared at the sitting room doors. He carried the malacca cane Delia so detested on his forearm, his hat in the same hand. It was not yet four o'clock.

"William dear, I did not expect to see you today," said Delia, "but here you are. What a pleasant surprise." Will walked across to his wife and kissed her cheek, then crossed to his mother and did the same. Both women were surprised by his early return from work.

"I've been struggling with this blasted headache since morning," he said, handing his hat to the maid who had followed him into the room. She dropped a half-curtsy and disappeared.

"Please mind your language, William," Delia said, unperturbed as a frozen pond. "Little pitchers have big ears," she said, motioning with a single raised eyebrow to the small boy gobbling cakes next to her.

"Besides, Gussie and Kinsella can handle things just as well in my absence," Will said in reply to his mother's fastidiousness.

Delia turned her languid gaze on him and said, "I should appreciate it if you would rely less on your sister Augusta. I do not approve of her penchant for a… *commercial* life that is utterly inappropriate for a young woman from a good family."

Sophia squirmed about in search of some relief in the only chair she could still abide. "Granny, surely the war changed ideas about what is proper activity for a young lady?"

"Perhaps, Sophia dear, but if so, it is all to the worse," Delia said with gentle certainty, rising to leave. She patted her grandson on the head, not at all interrupting his concentration on the second tea cake. Crossing to Sophia, she kissed her cheeks and said, "I'll take my leave, so William may rest his aching head and you, my dear, may rest whatever you can manage."

Will kissed a proffered cheek as his mother floated by him. With an ethereal smile, she disappeared down the hall, followed by the maid with her hat and parasol.

Sophia heard the smooth slide of a glass stopper, followed by several gurgles. She tensed as Will replaced the decanter and made his way back to the settee, stretching out his legs as he lounged against the camelback.

"I thought you had a headache, William," the tension throughout her swollen body increasing as Will gulped the large brandy. She glared with deliberate obviousness at the glass in his hand.

"Helps settle my nerves, dear." He drained the glass with a second gulp and rose to refill it.

"It helps you sleep as well, so you claim." She was determined to push, having remained silent far too long. "And steadies you for meetings with your father. And settles your stomach after meals."

Will returned with his second brandy, the glass feeling heavier to him now.

"And it seems to help you… even *allow* you… to be… intimate with me," she rasped in a whisper through her angry embarrassment.

The boy chewed on, not taking notice of his father. Will gathered the crumb-filled napkin in the lad's lap and shooed him out the door.

"Go find Mary in the kitchen and ask her to give you something to drink," Will said. The boy trotted out of the room and down the hall toward the rear of the house. Will turned to Sophia, his testiness showing in the jerkiness of his movements. "You're in no condition for such prattle, Sophia, so I'll not dignify your observations with an answer."

"I am fully aware of what I am saying, William," she said, "so do not patronize me. I am your wife and the mother of your child. I deserve to be acknowledged." Her cheeks were now blotches of angry red, all the more vivid against her porcelain-white skin. This was new, seeing his wife so confrontational. He stood in silence, puzzling over what he might say to put a stop to this unpleasant discussion. Sophia was not ready for an end, not yet.

"You are a cipher to your own son, William, because you are absent from his life," she said, angry and frustrated tears now welling hot in her wide dark eyes. "Even when you are physically here, you are absent." She nodded to the brandy glass. "Were you like this before the war, I wonder?" she exclaimed. "Your sister says you were a treasure when she was younger."

She doesn't have any idea where she's casting about, Will thought. *Not the slightest idea. And she can't possibly know the first thing about the war.* He took another long drink, turning his back to her probing eyes.

"Do not turn away from me, William!" she cried out, her voice choking in her throat. "I saw how you first came to us in England, fragile as a sparrow. And they sent you back to that wretched fighting anyway." Struggling to her feet, she placed both her hands on his arms and forced him to face her. He shook off her touch and staggered back a step, his hand rising to his cheek, touching the pink scar.

"What did they do to you?" She reached for him again, backing him another step or two. "How can I help if you won't explain?"

Will's eyes darted across his wife's face and then all around the room, searching for a means of escape. He emptied the second brandy and reached to set the glass on a side table. Missing the edge, the crystal crashed and sprayed shards across the floor.

The jagged sound refocused him. "There is no way for you to understand what we went through."

She reached for him again and he rounded the settee, putting the heavy couch between them. "There are so many. So many gone. First Sandy. Then all the rest on the Somme." He touched the scar again. "All gone. Or maimed like Jack." His thoughts began to float away again, but he caught himself and turned for the door.

"I'll ask Mary to clean this up."

CHAPTER THIRTY-ONE

Jack

She had begun to worry. A half-day was not unusual, with the fogs and squalls that troubled the coast from New England to Nova Scotia. The *Ricky Todd* had been late before, so no cause for fretting, she told herself. A few tablets helped settle her nerves, so she busied herself with sweeping and dusting, not able to justify the expense of a maid, despite Jack encouraging her to hire one. She had already made her way through the entire house and was just beginning a needless second circuit when the door burst open and Jack hollered down the hall to her.

Whenever they returned, the crew was in the habit of gathering at Jack and Deirdre's to discuss the voyage and hear any news that may have come while they were at sea. This time was no exception, so they all sat down to a meal of thick pea soup and a cold joint from the larder. Subsisting at sea on salt fish, hard bread, and tinned beans, the men devoured their food without a word. After supper, Jack was in the kitchen washing up the dishes, a task for which his paralyzed left hand proved a little useful. Oblivious to the rising color in Dee's cheeks, Geordie spun out the derring-do of their near escape from the Coast Guard this voyage, thinking it a very grand adventure. It had been, however, a close-run thing, the Coasties lobbing a few dozen small-caliber shells into their wake, getting perilously close when one of the schooner's engines failed.

Finally, she could hold her tongue no longer. "You damned eejits were like to get yourselves killed out there! And you sit here thinking 'twas all a lovely lark with the lads!" Geordie deflated from her burning anger so she redirected it at her husband, just returned from the kitchen in time to hear the end of her rebuke. "And you're the greatest eejit of all, Jack Oakley," she said, jabbing a finger at his chest. "Why in God's name would you carry on in American waters as if nothing in the world had happened, with a righteous angry Coast Guard captain prowling for you?"

"He'd no way of knowing when or where we'd emerge from that blessed, holy fog bank we made for, my dear wife," Jack countered with a self-satisfied grin, hoping that would end the matter.

"Don't they carry the wireless now on those American ships?" she persisted. "You had not the least idea how many other patrols might've been about, now did you?" She rounded on Geordie again, one hand to her hip and one pointing an accusing finger in his smitten face. "A small-calibre gun indeed, Geordie King. With the three of you sitting atop three hundred gallons of petrol! In a wooden ship!"

Chester rallied now, saying to Dee, "All's well that ends well though, Deirdre. We'll know better the next time, right Jack?"

Jack nodded to Chester and said, "That we will, Mr. Dawkins. We'll turn tail for northern waters at the first sign of trouble." He gave Chester a wink and smiled back at Dee, all innocence and contrition.

Dee slapped the side of Jack's head. He laughed as he rubbed his hair, but she was not to be placated. She gave Chester, lounging back with a whisky, his due portion of her wrath now. "And you, Chester Dawkins, I'd have given more credit to a university educated man for having at least a thimbleful of good sense," she said, taking a swat at his shoulder before turning away and setting herself with unabated indignation on the sofa next to Geordie.

Geordie patted Dee's knee and rose from the couch, uncomfortable to be so near her fury. "As Chester said, sweet Deirdre, all's well that ends well and we're home safe and sound." He went to the pegs near the door and slipped on his jacket and soft cap. "We've another five or six days until our next sailing, so you've time to chastise your husband to your heart's content, Mrs. Oakley," Geordie said, not helping Jack's situation at all. "Come along, Chester my lad, and let's leave the happy couple to their bliss."

Chester, who had thrown back his whisky and donned his coat already, turned to Dee and said, "Thank you for the supper, Deirdre, and forgive me for upsetting you. I'll keep an eye on them next trip, I promise." With that, the two of them were out the door, Dee watching their heads bob by the bay of the front windows as they strolled off down the street. She sat staring out after them, letting her anger cool. When she turned back to Jack, it was apparent she was still quite troubled.

"It was a close call, Deirdre, to be sure, but the very purpose of putting the new engines in the *Ricky Todd* were why we escaped. The only reason it was so close-run was we lost an engine and had no time for repairs."

She did not reply. He saw the fear in her from the set of her shoulders, the fidgeting of her hands, the worried lines of her face. He could think of nothing more that might soothe her, so he sat in silence, studying the arm of his chair, then his trouser leg, anything other than her. After long, slow minutes, Dee let out a sigh and patted the sofa cushion beside her. When Jack joined her, she took his right hand in both hers and locked eyes with determination.

"I want that to be the last of it, Jack."

This was not what he expected from her, invested in the venture as she had been since the beginning. She had shown herself an able businesswoman, as organized and detailed as any three men, finding a rewarding purpose in the work.

"We've plenty of money now, Jack, with our double share, as do Geordie and Chester. There's naught to be gained from courting such danger any further."

"You're not thinking clear, Deirdre. It was one brush with the Coasties is all, not enough to make you lose your nerve, surely?"

She pulled his hand into her lap and clung to it so hard he winced. She bowed her head over their joined hands, her closed eyes squeezed tight. He could see she was working to control herself, to make him understand. "Jack, you must believe what I'm about to say to you," she said, her face pleading for his agreement.

"Of course, I'll believe anything you say, Deirdre. You must know that."

She steeled herself again and continued, speaking each word as if it carried the heaviest weight. "I've never felt anything so strong in all my days as I do this. There's disaster afoot."

Jack knew how much stock she put in her mother's intuitions, but he only indulged her in what he thought was a lot of superstitious nonsense. But this was different. "We owe it to our partners, to Ned in particular, to give them notice of such a change in our agreement," he said in a businesslike way that grated on her. "And we've goods in bond here and in Halifax we need to clear out."

She could see there was no way he would abandon the work today, this moment. Still filled with the terror of some unknown catastrophe, she saw nothing but to compromise. "You'll agree we don't need another penny then? You've paid your father and uncle a fair price for the *Ricky Todd* and we've nearly $100,000 in banks here and in Halifax and Boston. That's enough for us to start again, any way we want."

Jack removed his hand from between hers and stood, walking toward the window and looking after Geordie and Chester, although they were long out of sight. "It's not just about the money, Deirdre."

She leapt to her feet and flew to the window, throwing her arms around him and looking up into his face. "Don't you think I know that, Jack? I know right well this is what brought you back to me." He stiffened in her arms as she went on, "But we can make whatever life we want now, and you can find a purpose there, too."

She rested her head against his chest, tears soaking into his already salt-stained shirt as he held her with his good right arm. "Alright," he said, putting his hand under her chin and raising her face to his. He kissed her with such tenderness she could barely breath from it. "Just a few more trips to clear out what's left. It'll give us time to square things with Ned. Two or three more voyages, no more than that."

They skated between the bergs once out of St. John's, watching the ice peter out as they headed down the coast and over to Saint Pierre to load French liqueurs and good wines. They had kept these purchases small since Italians from Chicago had begun turning up at the warehouses and along the quay. Then they crossed the Cabot Strait and headed southeast along the Nova Scotia coast to Halifax, finishing their cargo with Caribbean rum and whiskies from Britain, shipped up through Bermuda. Although these extra port calls added time, their customers paid premium prices for the fine product they brought for the nightclubs and jazz speakeasies. The foulness of the bootleg gin produced in the States had sparked a craze for new concoctions to mask the wretched taste. This in turn spiked demand among club owners for any and every sort of flavored liquor for their bartenders.

"I believe I'll miss these bold adventures," Geordie said as Jack emerged from below to relieve him at the wheel. His wistful declaration was followed by a bout of hard hacking from the chest cold that had come aboard with him. He pulled big slow breaths to settle his lungs.

"You'd best get below for some rest, b'y," Jack said, "pale as you look."

"It's nothing the fresh sea air won't help," Geordie said, sloughing off Jack's concern. "I've had bouts of bad chest since my fateful meeting with the lovely German phosgene. I'm little the worse for it, aren't I now?" Chester, lounging against the edge of the main hatch amidship, rose when he heard the coughing and had made his way aft.

Scanning the state of the ship, as was his habit whenever coming on deck, Jack saw nothing amiss. The engines were running at half speed, the sails trimmed to give every appearance of a well-crewed old schooner plying the East Coast trade or just in from the Banks. There was a touch of late May warmth taking the chilly edge off the wind. With fair weather clouds above and light seas below, Jack relaxed and hailed Chester. "We didn't mean to disturb your ruminating."

"I gave up all deep thinking when I fell in with low company," he replied in his usual deadpan, not giving an inch in the banter. Jack and Geordie shared pleased glances, relieved the American that Ned foisted upon them turned out to be such a good man. They had embraced him as one of their own. Geordie gave the helm to Jack, he and Chester now either side of the companionway, facing aft.

"So how's your sister getting on lately, Chester?" Jack asked, making conversation. "Deirdre's so fond of her, you know, which is a comfort with us at sea so much of the time."

Geordie perked up, adding, "And a fine woman she is, your Lena."

Chester gave Geordie a suspicious glance, then answered Jack, "She's still glad to be shed of New York and she's made the house here her own." He looked out over the dark blue water sliding by and, not turning back, said, "I was grateful to Ned for the chance to bring her up with me. She had a hard time while I was away, with our father passing and the war dragging on."

"I can't imagine a woman as strong and straight as your sister having a hard time with much of anything," said Geordie. Chester shot him another suspicious look, well aware of the fancy Geordie had taken to Lena of late.

"Then you don't know how hard life can be in New York City for some kinds of people," Chester said.

They ploughed on for the rest of the morning and into the afternoon, throwing down a little cold bacon and hard bread for lunch, washed down with pot after pot of strong black coffee boiled up on the small cookstove in the forward berth. In the late afternoon, Jack gathered them at the wheelhouse. "We're near to having Penobscot Bay abeam, so we'll come about and head straight to the coast and skirt our way round the Fox Islands. We'll slip nice and easy into Rockland round dusk."

"Chester, why don't you go forward to keep a watch for anything surprising," Jack directed. "We want to keep well clear of those rocks off Vinalhaven."

"Right, Jack," Chester said, obscured by the jib as he made his way around the capstan and anchor chains to the bow.

Geordie disappeared below to check the engines, reappearing a few minutes later at the companionway hatch and pausing on the ladder as he was racked by another fit of hard coughing. "Get's a bit close down there," he said, offering a feeble explanation. Jack saw that he looked worse than in the morning.

"Once we get to port, I want you in a bunk and not helping unload cargo," Jack said. "You hear me well, b'y?" Geordie pulled himself up the ladder, ready to protest his fitness.

Pffft. Pffft. Pffft. Pfft.

Both men dropped to the deck, reflex memory knocking them from their feet. They turned their heads side to side, parsing the sound.

Pffft. Pffft. Pffft. Pfft. Pfft.

Splinters jumped in quick succession from the starboard rail and the deckhouse wall, ending with a ping off the brass of a stern winch. "I'll be buggered! That's long-range Emma Gee fire!" Geordie shouted. "When did they get those?"

"Get below and give us all you can from those engines," Jack said, urging Geordie on with his head. "Then get yourself forward and find Chester!" Geordie bellied his way to the ladder and threw himself down, landing below on his shoulder with a pained grunt. Jack came to his knees, keeping below the line of the deckhouse for cover, and pulled hard on the wheel to put the gunfire off their stern as the engines roared to full speed.

Another strafe dug into the schooner, spattering off the mast, rending sailcloth and rigging. After it stopped, Jack hazarded a look over the rail and saw the sun coming around the ship with the harried turn. Geordie emerged from below and made his way forward in a crouch, running from cover to cover. Jack squinted hard into the reddening ball of the setting sun. He could make out the silhouetted low outline of a Coast Guard patrol ship, turning away toward the south. Jack followed along the line of the ship's new course and spotted a big cargo steamer rounding the head at the southernmost of the Fox Islands. It was a busy day for the Coast Guard. Having warned off the smaller schooner, they were now in pursuit of bigger fish. Jack stood up to his full height, leaning for strength against the wheelhouse as he returned the rudder amidship, their narrow escape sapping the strength from him. Looking up the deck, he could just see a pair of legs under the line of the foremast's boom, moving aft toward him. He ducked down to get a clearer look, just as the untrimmed sail caught the wind and pushed the boom aside.

Geordie staggered, ashen pale, carrying the full weight of a limp and lifeless body in his arms.

They slipped back into St. John's after dark with all sails furled. The channel lights and the street lamps along the waterfront allowed them to creep in through the dark without attracting much attention. A few warehousemen working late emerged as they neared the Parsons Quay and helped them tie up. Jack shouted that they had an injured man and needed a wagon alongside. One of the dockers disappeared behind the warehouse, returning with a delivery wagon pulled by a pair of mismatched tired horses.

Geordie lifted the bound-up sailcloth that contained Chester's body, dead more than twenty-four hours, and made for the gangway the dockers had positioned. His progress was painful and deliberate as he chose each exhausted step with care. The dockers and the driver stood shuffling their feet, their attention bouncing between the canvas bundle and each other. Jack came down the gangway, hurrying to catch up. The men on the quay knew Jack well, as they did his father and uncle. He huddled them around the side of the wagon and said in a low voice, "We had a man grievous injured this voyage and we weren't able to save him. His family will be pained at this turn of bad luck, so I'd take it as a great favor if you'd not set tongues wagging."

The men all muttered their agreement and shook Jack's hand, giving their condolences to the master of an unlucky vessel. Geordie laid Chester with care on the open bed of the wagon and hoisted himself next to the body as Jack climbed with effort onto the bench seat by the driver. He murmured the address of Chester and Lena's house and the horses tensed against their harness as the wagon creaked away. They reached the clapboard house too quickly, given their sad burden. Geordie jumped down and hefted Chester's body in his arms once again. Jack overpaid the driver and asked him to return with Deirdre as soon as he could.

Going before Geordie up the few steps to the front door, Jack knocked twice, then pushed the door open without waiting for Lena to answer. Light from the kitchen spilled down the entry hallway, reflecting off a large brass-framed beveled mirror on the side wall, throwing soft patterns right up to the door. Lena stood at the end of the hallway drying her hands on her apron, outlined by the kitchen lights burning behind her. She saw Jack in the doorway and hurried to him. As she made her way down the hall, Jack moved aside and opened the door wider, right up against the wall. As Geordie stepped in with his burden, Lena stopped, her eyes darting from each of the men to the sailcloth bundle, lashed all around with rope.

She knew so very quickly. All the men saw was her silhouetted figure pull up short for a moment, her shoulders slumping just enough to be noticed. She did not cry out or fall to her knees. Rather, she continued a slow deliberate walk over the remaining distance and stood silent before Geordie. They could see her face now, calm and strangely curious, as she reached her hand out and stroked the canvas. It seemed to them she was ensuring it was what she feared it to be. She drew a long, quiet breath and pressed her lips together. Looking up to Geordie, she said, quiet and steady, "You'd better take him upstairs and lay him on his bed. He'll need attending."

She turned to the wall and pressed a mother-of-pearl button in the switch plate. With a disconcerting metallic pop, an overhead bulb illuminated the stairs. Geordie labored up the steps, stopping every few treads, his legs heavy as granite. Lena went to the sitting room, reaching her hand behind the door jam, and Jack heard another pop as the room filled with the weak light of a single bulb. He took her by the elbow, easing her toward an upholstered chair next to the cold fireplace. She did not sit. He took another chair, a gooseneck floor lamp arching over its back where Chester sat reading most nights he was home. Lena glanced over at Jack, seated in her brother's accustomed place.

"Why did he die, Jack?"

He was puzzled and hesitated, not knowing how to respond.

"I asked you why my brother died, Jack Oakley," she said again, anger rising in her voice.

"We ran into a new Coast Guard patrol ship off Maine, coming at us right out of the sun. They had a machine gun."

Lena walked over to Jack, just inches now from where he sat on the forward edge of her brother's comfortable chair. She pulled her arm back above her shoulder, holding her hand flat, and swung down hard, catching Jack with a loud smack across his scarred left cheek. He did not dare grab his smarting face.

"I didn't ask you how my brother died," she said with a bitter snarl. "I asked you why he had to die. On your ship."

Jack could not stand up without pushing her away, so he sat silent, grasping for words he knew would be the wrong ones. A hand came from behind her and encircled her waist. She collapsed against Geordie, who pulled her gently back to her chair as she began to sob and choke in her grief. As they moved away, Jack saw Deirdre standing in the doorway of the sitting room, staring at him in shocked disbelief. She hurried over to Lena.

"She needs to be in bed by the looks of her, Geordie," Dee said. "I'll care for her now." As Geordie turned to thank Dee, she saw how deathly pale and grey he was. "Sweet Jaysus, Geordie!" she cried out, as he crumpled to the floor in a dead faint. Jack jumped to help, rolling Geordie onto his back.

"Take Lena upstairs, Deirdre. I'll see to Geordie."

By the time Dee had settled Lena, assuring the stricken woman she would look after the household this sad night, Jack had brought Geordie back around with a cold towel from the kitchen, managing to sprawl him across the mohair sofa. Jack fed him sips of brandy, but he still looked so weak and ill.

Deirdre sat in Lena's chair, stricken by the awful events. "Jack, what in the name of God happened? It was to be your last voyage."

He could not stand the indicting look from her, so he searched for some escape, rising and walking to the front window as if addressing the street rather than his wife and old friend. "We all knew there was danger in this, Chester as well as any of us. It's a sad day to be sure, but one we all knew might come." He sat back down next to Geordie on the sofa in a show of false confidence. Geordie moaned from the coldness of Jack's words, lacking the strength to protest any other way. Jack braced for his wife's anger, certain it was flaming high. It never came.

She crossed the room and knelt before him, taking his good hand in one of hers, patting Geordie's knee as well. "Jack, you convinced yourself this was about clearing the warehouses and making right with Ned," she said, "but I know it was never about the money for you, right from the very start."

He studied random reflections in the divided-light windowpane while he swallowed a hard lump.

"I thought it would bring you back from the war, finally and for good," she said, leaning over and forcing him to look at her. "But it took you back to the danger and the thrill. God forgive me, I pushed you right back into it, sure as I'm kneeling here now." He could avoid her no longer. Tears streamed down his cheeks, his made-up bluster crumbling under the weight of her pity.

"A good man had to die for that," she said, quiet but determined, as Geordie let out another low groan, ending with a single choked sob. She rose from the floor and smoothed her skirt. "I kept the driver, not knowing what I'd find here. I'll send him round to fetch Dr. Chesley and notify the undertaker." Jack nodded in agreement. It was all in her hands now anyway.

"Rob Chesley was with the regiment. He'll handle this without a fuss," she said. "And Geordie surely needs attention." She patted Geordie's arm as she passed him, pausing to rub her palm along his sleeve a few times. He was soaked in sweat, his skin dank and lifeless as clay.

"We need to see to Chester and care for Lena now."

CHAPTER THIRTY-TWO

Deirdre

It was near half past eight in the morning when the doctor finished with Geordie. Hearing his long strides and brisk footsteps down the stairs, Deirdre came out from the kitchen to see him to the door. Since she was an experienced nurse, he always spoke with her before leaving the house each morning and evening.

"He seems past the point of crisis now. Lord only knows how, sick as he was."

"Geordie's a strong lad," she said, handing the doctor his hat.

"He's not anymore, Deirdre," he said, looking down at her with earnestness. "He'll need a long time to recover from this, assuming he ever does. He's not out of danger yet. And his lungs were already compromised from that gassing in the war."

"Well, Lena's not left his side since Monday," Dee said. "And it's given her something to take her away from the grief."

Settling his hat on his head, Dr. Chesley gave Dee a tight smile. "I'll be back tonight. Give my condolences to Miss Dawkins after the burial, if you would." The doctor was out the door when he turned back, his hand in his jacket pocket. "I nearly forgot your tablets, Deirdre." He produced a small brown bottle with a black bakelite cap. "If your back is worsening, you may want to let me have a look at it."

Sliding the bottle into the pocket of her long black cardigan with a little glance over her shoulder, she motioned for the doctor to step outside. "'Tis just the last few days have taken a toll on me, I fear," she said, adding a tired smile.

"We seem to be refilling this rather more often of late, Deirdre. You need to be careful, you know."

"That I will, Doctor, of course." She gave him another disarming smile. "Thank you for your concern." With that, he was down the street and she back into the house. Dee looked through the crack left between the doors of the sitting room. Chester lay before the curtained windows, Jack and his parents the only mourners with the body. Jack had again sat up through the night, his parents arriving just before eight this morning. He looked haggard and worn, his shoulders bent forward.

She stepped softly up the stairs and back to the small rear bedroom, pushing the door open with her fingertips. Geordie was propped up in the small iron bed, groggy-eyed but lucid. Lena was feeding him beef broth from a small porcelain bowl.

"You'll be needing to ready yourself for the graveyard, Lena. The Oakleys have arrived and more are sure to be right behind them." Lena continued feeding the broth as if Dee had not said a word. Geordie gave Dee a crooked smile and blinked away the fuzziness from his vision. He turned his head to Lena and, ensuring she was looking back at him, gave her a few weak nods and moved his lips, saying something that was all but soundless to Dee. Lena set the bowl on the nightstand and smoothed her hand over Geordie's unkempt hair.

"Alright," she said, "but I'll be back up as soon as we say goodbye to Chester."

"Jack's sister Nellie is coming to sit with you, Geordie," Dee said, "so Lena can see to her duties with the mourners."

Lena rose and repeated to Geordie, "I'll be back as soon as we return." She floated by Dee without a word, disappearing behind the door of her bedroom.

Dee sat next to Geordie on the edge of the narrow bed, not knowing how Lena managed to balance there for hours on end.

"She's a diligent nurse, Geordie." He nodded in agreement and whispered something Dee could not make out. She leaned in close and he repeated his words.

"She's doing... too... much."

She smiled down at him, remembering when she first encountered this big man with the outsized heart. "She brings to mind a muddy fool of a soldier who'd not leave another's side, these seven years gone now." Wiping her cheek with the back of her hand, she said smiling, "And I'm forever grateful for your pig-headed stubbornness, knowing what might have become of my Jack without you." She held his hand above the bedclothes and they sat smiling, eyes moist with shared and sad memories of the bloody, bloody war.

The rest of the day flickered on like a jerky cinema picture. The undertaker and all his assistants arrived before nine and hovered in the corners. More mourners arrived and the house was filled by the time the undertaker nodded toward the carriages and automobiles lining the street. The horse-drawn hearse gleamed, glossy with black paint and spotless glass, waiting right before the house. At another discreet sign from the undertaker, Lena, with Jack and Dee on either side, approached Chester's coffin to have her last view. Having avoided this room the last two days, she had not been close to her brother's prepared body. With sad composure, she took note of the fine suit he wore and the cool stillness of his face and hands. With the undertaker shuffling his feet, she reached forward and brushed his cheek with her black-gloved hand, then turned and walked with even steps out the front door. Dee and Jack followed in silence, the undertaker signaling an assistant to close the doors while they secured the coffin lid.

There was no church funeral planned for Chester. Rick Oakley begged a favor from the new curate at their parish to say the graveside rite from the Book of Common Prayer over the poor man's bones. That would have to suffice. It was a clear and bright day, a blustery wind up the hillside blowing them toward the cemetery. The ritual was over in ten minutes and they headed back for condolences and the food and drink. Good to her word, Lena disappeared upstairs as soon as they returned, leaving Dee, with her mother-in-law's assistance, facilitating as short a stay as would be polite for the mourners. Before one o'clock, the house was silent, the sitting room draperies drawn open, and the displaced furniture back in place.

With only Viola left in the kitchen clearing up and scrubbing down, Dee sat in Lena's chair, looking over at her desolate husband seated in Chester's. He had withdrawn to wherever he would go at the London hospital when the burden of his wounds became too great. A coldness ran up her spine and out through her veins, chilling her very fingertips, as she realized how affected he was by Chester's death. She was inches from losing him to drink or despair or whatever could pull him down again.

"Jack?" He turned and looked at her with wide eyes that asked nothing, allowing her to plumb the depths of his fear and guilt. "Jack, you'll not do this to me again," she said, not a drop of threat in her voice. "You can't, not this time. I'm your wife, and you'll not abandon me to grief or guilt or however else you may choose to punish yourself."

"I'll never leave you, Deirdre, never again. I've promised you that much."

"But that doesn't mean your spirit won't leave me, and I'll not lose that either."

He sat brooding for some time, not able to look up for fear of breaking one or both their hearts. With the drapes open, the afternoon sun flooded the room, the clear spring light spilling across the floor and halfway up Jack's legs. He reached into the sunshine with his good hand and spread his fingers in the warmth. He turned to his wife, whom he loved more than his own life, and said, "I know I must find a way out of this, but I need your help. Maybe more than I needed it in London."

She slid from her chair and knelt next to him, taking both his good right hand and his curled and useless left in hers. She kissed both and laid her head in his lap. She resolved not to let him see any more tears. He needed strength from her now, not sorrow. Sitting back on her heels, she slapped her thighs through her black crepe skirt, giving off an air of crisp efficiency. She knew presenting a problem to be solved pulled him back once and might do so again. "I've given some thought to our next enterprise, Jack."

"I've no doubt you have, Deirdre," he said, attentive to her words but lacking any enthusiasm.

"We've two choices," she said, holding up fingers to tick off the list. "First, we live off the great pile of money we've made off those dear thirsty Yanks until we've spent it all on the high living." Jack gave her the soft chuckle she was hoping for. "Or two, we can start our own legitimate business, one that might get by without winking at a law no one wants to obey anyway. We have our own warehouse, owned free and clear, and we have the *Ricky Todd*," she said, toting their assets. "And we've seen that the holds of the Parsons' ships and others sail with vacant space, enough for small cargo."

Jack wasn't sure where she was headed, but knew she had more to say. "What are you after then?"

"We learned how much money can be made from small cargoes of high value, liquor being just such," she said. "There are other small things of value to consider as well." She rummaged in a stack of newspapers next to Chester's chair, pulling out a thick book with a green cover and a frontispiece with a steamer belching smoke at dockside. Across the front, in yellow block letters, read *1922 Sears, Roebuck Catalogue - Thriftbook of a Nation.* "Lena got this in the post from someone in New York." She handed it to Jack, who leafed through it with concentration.

"Lord, Deirdre, they sell houses in here. That's hardly a small thing."

"Bah, that's just for show, I'm certain," she said, flipping over several pages. "But look at everything else in here. The Americans are crazy about anything new and shiny."

"I'm not seeing your plan, Deirdre."

She grabbed the catalogue, laying it in her lap and slapping it with her palms. "These big American companies aren't going to give a fig about Newfoundland and Nova Scotia and Prince Edward Island, least not for some years, but there's people here wanting these selfsame things now." He was nodding with the realization that there might be something here after all. "We take our fine pile of money and use some to purchase goods in Canada or America or Ireland or England, ship them back here in Parsons' or others' holds for next to nothin' and store them in our own warehouse."

"And what do we do then? There are plenty of stores in St. John's selling such things already."

"Not with their own schooner," she said, with a precocious smile spreading below her cocked eyebrows. "Nor a fine captain who knows every outport from north to south."

"We'll need a bigger crew," Jack said, turning over the possibilities.

"That should be a mite easier, don't you think, without the chance of seeing the inside of an American prison?"

"Won't be the same kind of money we're accustomed to making, Deirdre."

She hauled herself to her feet and stood staring out the window, seeing again in her mind's eye Chester's coffin as it moved out the door into the sunlight that morning.

"No, it will not," she said. "Nor as deadly."

LETTERS PATENT

By virtue of the powers vested in me under the Corporations Act, I do by these letters patent issue a charter to the applicants named below, constituting them a corporation without share capital under the name:

Brannigan & Oakley Ltd

Subject to all terms and conditions of the same Corporations Act.
Applicants:
> *Jonathon C. Oakley*
> *Deirdre M. Oakley (née Brannigan)*

Dated: 12th day of June, 1923

> *Arthur Barnes*
> *Minister*

Per:
> *D. S. Nagel*
> *Director*

CHAPTER THIRTY-THREE

Deirdre

No matter what your family—rich or poor, town folk or baymen—when the fish started landing and the flakes were readied for the season, every child in Newfoundland wanted to be at the shore to watch the day's catch being split and salted. The flakes were filled with the earliest cod of the season, pulled from the fish pounds where they had been curing, now drying in the breeze and whatever sun was to be had. Every inch of the quays and beaches, it seemed, were tiled with flattened fish. Children were welcomed down at the stages and among the flakes, expected to help with small tasks when old enough. So much of life and prosperity in Newfoundland rested on the fishery that every hand was turned to clean, salt, dry, sort, pack, press and ship their most valuable export. Young Terry Parsons, just turned four, was as fascinated as any child.

Although his grandparents disapproved of his mingling with all sorts at the waterside, he begged his parents with such pleading insistence that they made a regular habit of strolling the quays while salt fish was being made. Will and Sophia thought it a healthy diversion for their son, expending some of his boundless energy somewhere other than within the four walls of their house. Terry was ecstatic, bounding along the narrow walkways that wended through the fields of salt fish, most on the wooden racks of the flakes, some spread on the ground when the flakes were filled. He had learned last year to be very careful not to step on any fish, so he made his way as if avoiding sidewalk cracks to spare his mother's back.

As they passed the Murray quay, Terry spotted old Bobby Merrill standing in a covered stage at the water's edge. Bobby had started working for Walter Parson's father as a teenage boy and had been with the company ever since, over fifty years now. He had known both Walter and Will as curious boys of four, too. When he spotted little Terry picking his way toward him, he plunged his hands, slimy with blood and entrails, into the wooden dipping tub at the end of the fish table. He nodded to one of the younger men, who stepped up without a word, took out his splitting knife, and continued pulling the long spinal sound-bones as the splitter slid the headless cod down the table to him. Another man then tossed them into a fish box for transport across a gangway bridge to the salting shed.

Terry loved Bobby with all the intensity a four-year-old could muster for an old man of mysterious powers. Whenever Terry visited his father and grandfather at their premises, Bobby was up to something he found of the keenest interest. Bobby always had time to heft Terry onto his shoulder, spin him about one or two times, and explain in words a boy could understand what he was doing that day. Terry had already learned—and quickly forgotten—how to press the dried fish in barrels and weigh cargo leaving the warehouse. But nothing could possibly be more fascinating than fish splitting, at least for today.

Bobby hailed little Terry, wiping his hands on the back of his dirty trousers. "What's tha' we have here, this fine day? Could't be young Master Parsons hisself?"

"It's me, Mr. Bobby! It's me!" squealed the boy, running headlong into the old man's long leather apron. Bobby bent down and threw one sinewy arm behind the boy's legs and swept him up onto his shoulder. His forearms, bare below his rolled-up sleeves, were brown and leathery from years of work in the sun and weather.

"Spin me! Spin me!"

Bobby gave a few quick turns, stiff from bending over the fish table since early morning, then plopped the boy down on his feet.

Will and Sophia had caught up with their precocious son and laughed together at the boy's delight. "He always seems to find you, wherever you might be, Mr. Merrill," Sophia said with a smile of genuine pleasure at the old man who was so fond of her boy.

"And he always finds a way to interfere with whatever you're doing, too," Will added, patting Bobby's shoulder with easy familiarity. The two men exchanged smiles, much unspoken between them in just these few seconds of recognition. Sophia was moved almost to tears by her husband's simple affection for this loyal old man he had known all his life.

"As you did as well, Mr. Will, before y'ever went off to the fightin' and were lucky enough to meet this lovely young maid," Bobby said, raising a spiky white eyebrow and giving a wink to Sophia, who blushed at the innocent flirting. "And you loved to watch when we were makin' fish, just like this sweet b'y here," Bobby said, patting the side of the boy's head. He was pressed against Bobby's leg, oblivious to the smell indelible in the old apron.

Terry watched spellbound as Bobby returned to his work. Bones and fins and entrails slid through openings in the table overhanging the edge of the stage, plopping into the water below for other fish and gulls to pick. The livers went through another opening into a bucket, saved for rendering into oil at the premises's train house. Bobby always put some heads aside for anyone with a mind to retrieve the fleshy tongues for frying up at home.

Two people stood waving from beyond the mosaic of drying fish. Will squinted against the harsh reflection off the whitewashed walls of the Parsons Premises. "That's Jack and Deirdre now," he said, pointing to the two figures distinct against the stark white building. "Come along, Terry. We have to join mummy and daddy's friends now."

Terry clung again to Bobby's leg and shook his head with determination. "I want to stay here with Mr. Bobby and help make fish."

Sophia placed a gloved hand gently on the boy's head, easing him away from the old waterman's side. "Come Terry, you know we came to meet Mr. and Mrs. Oakley today." He slipped under his mother's hand and reattached himself to Bobby's leg.

"Ahh, I don't mind if the b'y wants to stay while youse have a palaver with young Oakley and his misses," Bobby said. "It bein' such a pet day, 'twould be shameful for the b'y not to have a good airin' down here by the water."

Will was awful at denying his son anything and said to his wife, "We can walk about the quay just round here with Jack and Dee. Terry will be fine with Bobby, as long as he stays out of the way."

Bobby set down his knife and scooped up the small boy again, setting him down atop a pile of fish boxes stair-stacked back from the table. "That's a fine spot for you to watch all the goings-on from, Master Terry," Bobby said, more to the parents than the child. Turning to Sophia, he added, "He'll be well out o' the way on them boxes thar, misses. Naught to worry y'self now."

"Alright then," Sophia said, turning to the boy. "You may stay if you promise you will mind Mr. Merrill and stay well out of his way." She looked at the boy with contrived seriousness and repeated, "You must promise."

"I promise, Mummy."

They picked their way between the splayed fish drying in the sun, Sophia holding her skirt with one hand to keep from displacing the careful array. When they reached Dee and Jack, there was more room for walking right alongside the buildings. Sophia felt warmth radiating from the sun-heated walls of the warehouse as they approached.

"We saw your nurse up on Water Street with young Lizzie all bundled in her pram," Dee said to Sophia. "She's a lovely wee colleen, such a sweet face."

Sophia took Dee's hands and kissed her cheek. Dee returned the kindness with a little awkwardness, having still not accustomed herself to such genteel greetings. "Thank you, Deirdre," Sophia said, pulling back from her. "That is so very kind of you to say. She is a treasure to us, such a little darling."

Will saw a look of uneasiness pass over Jack and steered the subject from children to business. "From all reports, the new enterprise is thriving?"

"That it is, William, that it is," Jack said, "all thanks to my darling wife."

"Perhaps not quite as lucrative as your prior endeavour?" Will asked, a little archly.

"Perhaps not," Dee said, "but a mite easier on the nerves, you can be sure of that."

"Well, Father was very disappointed when I lost the export licensing business with you. I'm rather glad to see you shed of that particular line of work. Although there are plenty of others ready to take your place." The four walked together along the warehouses, thankful for the fair weather.

Young Terry loved watching fish making, but perched atop the boxes, he began to fidget as any young boy would. Bobby kept one eye on him, content as long as the boy stayed among the boxes. One of the younger men was falling behind, slowing the others working the table. Bobby told the man hauling fish boxes to take his position and he stepped down the table to assist the struggling man with his splitting.

"You're usin' too much effort sawin' away with that half-dull knife, b'y," he said. "Here, mine's just sharpened. Let me have yars and I'll put it to the stone." Bobby turned his back to fetch the whetstone, so he missed Terry making his way down from the stacked boxes. The boy then climbed an upended tub onto a four-quintal barrel that sat right behind the man who had taken Bobby's place. The younger man was just sliding his knife under the soundbone of a big split cod when Terry slipped on the slimy barrel, landing flat on the end of the table. He let out a sharp, piercing yelp as he hit the wooden planks.

The cry startled the young fish maker, who spun without thinking toward the source of the unexpected sound. The splitting knife flashed as he turned, slashing its way across Terry's leg. It sliced clean through his dark blue plus-fours and deep into the white flesh of his small thigh. The boy let go a terrible agonizing scream. All motion on the stage hung suspended at the horrifying sound while dark wetness soaked the boy's leg. His face whitened as the blood flowed from his tiny body.

Bobby leapt toward the stricken child, bellowing as he did, "Sweet Jaysus, what's been done to the b'y?" The young assistant stood staring at the lad's leg, then at the knife still in his hand, shaking with shock and fear. Bobby shouldered him away. He pressed a big hand across the huge laceration in the boy's leg and yelled for a cloth. The man who had been splitting fish took his knife and cut the sleeve from his striped cotton shirt and rushed it to Bobby. "Give me that jacket hangin' there, too!" The old man wrapped the sleeve around the cut, then folded the jacket and pressed hard against the bandage as the boy was reduced by shock to pitiful whimpering.

Along the warehouses, the four friends heard the terrible scream. Only one knew exactly what the sound signified. Sophia spun away from her husband and stumbled roughshod through the drying fish, screaming "Terry! Terry!" as she flew toward the stage. Dee, more from instinct than conscious thought, kept close behind. Will dropped his cane and followed, with Jack limping at his heels. The women reached the fish table first and saw Terry splayed out, his blood running across the wood planking and mixing with that of the fish. Sophia threw her arms around the boy, cradling his head against her chest.

Dee saw how much blood the boy had already lost and yelled out, "I need a stout belt from one of you men!" Bobby pulled the wide leather belt from his own trousers and handed it over to Dee. She slid it under the boy's thigh, as high above the slice as she could, threaded it through the buckle, and cinched down hard. Terry let out another scream, not as loud as the first but all the more heartrending to those near at hand. Will and Jack looked on helpless as Dee worked on the boy, his mother cradling him.

"Sophie, you have to put his head lower to keep the blood flowing there," Dee urged. Turning to the men, she shouted, "Where's the nearest doctor's surgery? He'll not make the trip to the hospital."

Jack leapt at doing something useful and said, "Rob Chesley's is just round the corner on Water Street."

"Let's get the lad there now!" Dee cried out. Will began to move toward his stricken son, but Bobby Merrill had already swept the boy up in his arms. Dee ran alongside holding up the mutilated leg. Will put an arm around Sophia as she collapsed in sobbing misery onto the fish table. With Jack on her left, the two men hurried her along behind Deirdre and Bobby.

They burst through the door of Dr. Chesley's office, shocking a pair of patients in the waiting area and calling for help. The doctor opened the door from his examination room, revealing an old bent man sitting on the table with his shirt off.

"What in the name of…" he said, interrupted by the sight of the young boy and the copious amount of blood across Dee's beige waist jacket and white blouse.

"Bring him in here," Chesley directed. "Mr. Hartley, I'll need you to dress and return tomorrow," he said as he lifted the man off the table by an armpit.

Bobby laid the stricken boy down, limp as a rag, on the leather examination table. The doctor pulled away the wadded-up jacket and, taking a pair of surgical scissors from off the counter, cut away the shirt-sleeve bandage. The belt tourniquet had slowed the blood flow to an ooze. "Deirdre, I need your assistance," said Chesley, pushing Bobby back toward the open door. The poor stricken man looked every one of his many years. He slumped into a chair in the corner of the waiting room as Jack and Will came through the door with Sophia.

Revived now and focused on her son's welfare, she broke away from her husband and flew into the examining room. "My boy, my sweet boy! Terry!"

Dr. Chesley looked up once, distracted, and yelled, "William, get your wife out of here! We're trying to save your son!"

At those words, Sophia lost what was left of her color but kept her feet and her composure. "Of course, of course. Please help him, Doctor." Chesley gave one terse nod then motioned with his head to Will, who led his wife back to the waiting room.

"Deirdre, there's a surgical kit in the drawer behind me." She retrieved it and handed the doctor a clamp, a second in her hand at the ready. She grabbed a bundle of several large gauzes from a glass-doored cabinet and swabbed as the doctor located the hemorrhaging blood vessels. After several tense minutes, the doctor looked up and said with some relief. "We need to clean this up, close the laceration, and get him warmed. He should get through this, so long as the wound doesn't go septic."

Jack stood in the doorway, watching Dee as she assisted. She moved with assurance but with a faraway look on her face. He closed the door and joined the others. After almost an hour, Dr. Chesley emerged from the examination room door, his shirt soaked through with perspiration and blood. He had removed his tie and collar, bloody sleeves rolled well above the elbows. Removing his wire-rimmed glasses, he swabbed his face with a crumpled handkerchief. "We gave him a little morphia for the pain and he's sleeping now. We have to watch for infection, but he has a good chance of recovery."

Sophia grabbed the doctor's hand and held it against her chest. "Thank you, Doctor, thank you for saving my son." She pressed his hand against her cheek and let her relieved tears run onto it. The doctor extracted his hand and patted Sophia's shoulder.

"He's a young and healthy boy, that's what saved him, Mrs. Parsons. And it will go far to help heal him. Children are very resilient."

With a wave of guarded relief flooding the room, Jack wondered where his wife might be. He stepped past the exhausted doctor and stuck his head into the examining room. Little Terry was asleep on the table, his chest rising and falling in a steady rhythm. When he stepped in the room, he found his wife sitting on a stool in the corner. At the sight, his heart sank to his knees. With nothing more to do for the boy, she sat with her palms up in her lap, staring at the blood-soaked front of her clothing.

"Sweet Lord, Deirdre!" Jack said in a raspy whisper, not wanting to wake the sleeping boy. She raised her head and opened her mouth but no words emerged. He pulled her close to his waist, an arm around her head, and rocked her. She buried her face into his side, her muffled cries flowing into the wool of his coat.

CHAPTER THIRTY-FOUR

Will

It was a relieved and very shaken gathering in Dr. Chesley's waiting room. Will and Jack had carried Dee upstairs, laying her on a tufted couch in the doctor's jumbled sitting room. There amongst the shelves of books and lingering tobacco smells, the doctor had injected her with a bromide sedative, dropping her into a stuporous sleep. Sophia emerged from the examination room. Her skin was almost translucent with exhaustion, a few streaks of blood on her sleeve and a single narrow smear across her cheek. "Terry is sleeping quite easily," she said. "I must look in on Deirdre." She turned without waiting for objections and disappeared down the hallway toward the stairs. Will stood and removed his silver cigarette case from the jacket slung over an empty chair and offered one to each of the men. He then sat and gazed back at the closed examination room door while he smoked.

This uneasy quiet vanished when the street door flew open and Walter Parsons strode through it, followed with less drama by his wife. "What in God's name has happened to my grandson?" Walter bellowed before the door had closed behind them. "We stopped at your house only to be met by your hysterical nursemaid. It was all we could do to get her to say where you were to be found."

Will rose to face his father and said, "There was a terrible accident down at the stages while the men were making fish."

Dr. Chesley stood beside Will and said, "The boy is out of immediate danger, but he has lost a significant amount of blood and is very ill."

"Praise be to God!" exhaled Delia, the ever-present calm slipping aside with worry for her grandson. "I feared we would arrive to the worst of news. Our dear, dear boy!" Sophia had heard the commotion from upstairs and reentered the waiting room. Her mother-in-law hastened to her and took her hands, kissing her cheeks with fondness and reassurance. "My dear Sophia, how you must be suffering with worry."

"Better, now that Terry is safe," Sophia said, "for the present at least. But we must pray for his complete recovery, mustn't we?"

"Indeed, for only He can protect our dear boy now," Delia said. "We shall pray most fervently morning and evening for our Saviour's healing grace." Delia had returned to her accustomed serenity.

Walter noticed Bobby sitting slumped and dejected. He turned on the old man with flashing anger. "What in hell are you doing here, Merrill?" he snapped, startling the stricken man. "Why are you not at the premises?"

Sophia stepped beside Bobby and placed a small hand on the old man's rounded shoulder. "Mr. Merrill may well have saved Terry," her voice catching at her son's nearness to death just a few hours ago. "He carried our boy here in his own arms."

"I left off lookin' o'er the b'y for such a short moment, Mr. Walter," Bobby said, his self-blame pitiful to hear, the old voice thick with emotion. "Master Terry slipped off a barrel he was climbin' and spooked young Tom while he was pullin' sound bones. 'Twas his knife cut the lad so bad when he spun about, startled at all the clatter."

Walter's face was afire with rage as he spat at Bobby. "Take yourself out of here, Merrill, this instant. I shall deal with you and your negligence in this matter later." The old man rose and began to gather his apron off the floor. "I would not expect any future with Parsons," Walter added as the man opened the door.

Bobby turned and, with more sadness than surprise, said, "I reckoned as much, Mr. Walter." The old man bobbed his head to

Will and Sophia, saying in parting, "'Tis a sad day for that sweet b'y and for that I'm most grievous sorry, Mr. Will and Miss Sophia. I'll be prayin' as well for the dear b'y, youse can be sure." With that, the old man moved off, pale as a ghost, down the street.

Walter now rounded on his son, his ire undiminished by old Bobby's departure. "What kind of damned fool did I raise, William? How could you leave a boy of four in the care of that broken old man?"

"We had just stepped a few yards away, chatting with Jack and Deirdre..."

"I should have known," Walter interrupted, shooting a scornful look at Jack, "your old friend would be involved in this debacle. Those shabby Oakleys are an irresponsible lot, one foot just out of some wretched outport." Turning back to Will, he added, "That silly wife of his is none better from what I've seen. Bold as brass and no shame in her. Shanty Irish, all she is."

Sophia shook herself free from Delia. She interrupted Walter's tirade with cold determination. "Your grandson and namesake would not be alive had it not been for that brave woman and Mr. Merrill. And you will treat them both with gratitude and respect in my presence."

Unaffected by Sophia's hard words, Walter dismissed her with a sneer and a scoffing snort. He rounded again on Will, his blazing anger unbanked. "This is how you allow your wife to address your father? Do you have no control over your own household?" Will worked his mouth in search of some words to stop his father. "Of course you don't," Walter said, withering his son with his dismissive scorn.

"Father, the important thing is Terry's well being..." Will said, grasping at something conciliatory to say.

"You will call him young Walter when I am in the room, not that insulting nickname!" Walter spit the words at his son's lowered head. Will could not look up to argue, drained from shock and worry.

Dr. Chesley, watching in horror as Will shrunk from his father's tirade, attempted to intervene. "See here, Parsons, there's no reason to attack anyone in these difficult circumstances."

"Your work, as far as I am concerned, is done here, Chesley, so please limit yourself to sending me your bill for the boy's treatment," Walter fired back. "I would not expect a man without a family to understand the first thing about what I'm saying." Walter huffed in disgust and turned to his wife. "This is what your overindulgence has brought upon us, Delia. He's come up as weak as you intended all along. Now we reap all that you've sown."

"Walter!" she gasped out, unable to say anything more in her mortification.

"You shame yourself and you shame me, William. I had hopes for you, great hopes, but you have been a shambles since you returned from the war. Other men fought, too, most of them better men than you. They've managed to take up useful lives again." Walter pointed at the examination room door. "You nearly killed your own son with your weakness and your self-pity and your drunkenness." He ended with a dismissive backhand and a grunt of disgust.

As Walter turned back to Delia, his face was stung with a sharp, loud slap. He reached up to soothe his smarting cheek as Sophia closed on him again. "Get out of here this instant! Get out!"

Delia grabbed her husband's arm, jerking him toward the door. "I am feeling suddenly quite ill, Walter. We must leave at once." She looked over her shoulder at her daughter-in-law with a pathetic pleading glance, then bustled her dazed husband out the door.

Will collapsed back into a chair, drained and dejected. Sophia sat next to him and pressed his hand against her cheek. They sat huddled in this wretched tableau until Sophia finally said, "I must get back to Terry now."

CHAPTER THIRTY-FIVE

Deirdre

Terry had fought off a minor infection that had troubled his parents much more than him. He was on the mend and his squirminess with his enforced lying in was a very good sign for his recovery. Sophia had not left his side for the first ten days while the slightest residue of fever remained. Since then, she had allowed her mother-in-law to take her place for a few hours at a time so she could see to the household. After Sophia's confrontation with Walter, an uneasy distance lingered between the two Englishwomen. Regardless, the boy was glue enough to hold them together, mother and grandmother.

Late on Thursday morning, Delia arrived to relieve her daughter-in-law for a few hours again. Sophia rose to greet her at the door of the bedroom where Terry was convalescing, kissing her cheeks and attempting a heartfelt smile. Little Terry fidgeted in bed, sitting up against several pillows while marching painted toy soldiers over the topography of the wedding-ring quilt wrinkled up around him.

"Granny!" he squealed when he saw Delia floating to his bedside, calm and unperturbed. She bent at her waist and kissed the top of the boy's head, then cupped his cheek in her palm, confirming for herself there was no fever. "I'm fighting with my soldiers, just like Daddy did," he said in excited innocence.

Sophia joined Delia at bedside and said to her son, "Terry dear, I must be off for just a short while. Granny will sit with you and perhaps read some stories. Nurse will bring up your lunch soon, then she and Granny will move you back to your own bed near all your toys in the nursery."

"Alright, Mummy," he said, much more concerned with a flanking movement of his small army around a pillow sham.

Sophia said to Delia, "I am off to visit Deirdre Oakley, which I should have done days ago. Her husband says she's not been well since the day Terry was hurt."

"I'm not hurt anymore, Mummy," Terry said with petulant indignation, then carried on with his military maneuvers.

"That may well be, young man, but you will not climb out of bed until Dr. Chesley has said you may," his grandmother said. "Now say goodbye to your mother."

"Goodbye, Mummy," said the boy with a perfunctory glance.

Sophia gathered her small hat and light coat at the door, pulling on her summer gloves. She covered the few blocks to Jack and Dee's in less than ten minutes. Reaching their house, she pulled the bell once. After a short wait, Jack opened the door and greeted her with a very tired smile. "Now Sophie, what a pleasant surprise," he said, motioning her inside. "Let me take your coat."

"I am so very sorry it has taken me this long to call on Deirdre, after she did so much for our dear boy. It is horrible to think what might have happened had she not been there."

Jack nodded with sympathy and said, "She was a fine nurse in her day, that I know well. And she was pleased she could help your sweet b'y that terrible day, Sophie."

She smiled, Jack and Dee being the only people in St. John's—England as well—who called her Sophie. Her parents disapproved of foreshortened names and her own siblings, when no adults were present and they were feeling daring, called her Fifi. Will had taken his cue from her parents while they were courting, such as it was, in England during the war.

"Now, if I may see Deirdre."

Jack, shifting from foot to foot, looked from his visitor to the stairway. Sophia discerned his discomfort and wondered at the source of both his obvious exhaustion and present trepidation. "She might not be awake at the moment," he said with little conviction.

"Well then, I shall just pop my head in her room and have a look. Regardless, I must at least see her asleep and leave my card." With this, she swept past Jack, who knew a protest was useless, and made her way up the stairs. She paused at the landing and, turning back to Jack, motioned to the door of the front bedroom with a raised eyebrow. She heard Jack sigh as he nodded.

She pushed open the unlatched door and slipped into the room, the dim illumination filtering through the closed shades. Letting her eyes adjust, she walked over to the bed where Dee lay on her side, her back to the door. The sound of Jack and Sophia's footsteps made her start. "Who's that then? Is anyone there?" she said, turning on her back and raising herself on unsteady elbows. As she turned her face to them, Sophia gasped. Her eyes were sunken dark circles and unnaturally wide in the gloom. Dee struggled to focus on her visitor. "Jack, who's there with you?" she said, anxious and unsettled.

Jack leaned over her and said, "It's Sophia come to pay a visit, Deirdre."

Her thick hair hung untied all about her, unbrushed for some time. Her nightgown hung off one shoulder, nearly exposing her breast. Her face showed no immediate sign of recognition, even after Jack's words.

"Sophia Parsons, Deirdre. You know her well enough," Jack said. "Will's wife."

Dee's eyes grew wider still. "The mother of that poor, poor boy?" She gathered her nightgown about her throat as she struggled to sit up. Jack reached to place some pillows behind her. Sophia came to his assistance as he fumbled about with one hand. "That poor boy, that poor, poor boy," Dee repeated, floating away from them again.

"Yes, yes our little Terry," Sophia said, "whom you saved, Deirdre. And I have come to thank you with all my heart."

"That poor, poor boy," she said again, looking down at her arms and nightgown. She fell silent, raising her hands with palms up, examining them with intensity and growing alarm. She looked up at

Jack now, showing him her upturned hands. Sophia saw tears flowing down her cheeks as her shoulders began to shake.

"My medicine, Jackie," Dee said, "Give me my medicine now."

He glanced over at Sophia, ashamed, before turning to the bedside table. He poured half a glass of water, then pinched in what seemed far too many drops of liquid from a stoppered bottle. Sophia watched the slow process, all done with Jack's one good hand. He gave the glass to Dee, who drank it greedily, wiping the back of her hand across her mouth as she sank back into the pillows. "That poor, poor boy," Dee repeated. Sophia and Jack watched her slide from them, her eyes fluttering, slow and languid, as the hefty dose of laudanum carried her away. Jack signaled toward the door with a pleading look. Sophia moved away from the bed and padded soft as she could down the stairs and into the sitting room. He closed the doors and turned toward her with sad anticipation of what he knew was coming.

"For the love of God, how long has she been like this?" Sophia asked, searching Jack's face in disbelief.

He studied the Persian carpet, his paralyzed left arm across his chest, the hand snug under his right arm. Finally, he raised his head and Sophia's chest constricted as she saw the deepness of the despair in his tormented, tired eyes. "Since we brought her home from Rob Chesley's surgery."

"How much morphia is she taking?"

Jack paused, knowing he had to tell their secret now. Through his crushing guilt, however, he could feel a swell of relief as he opened his mouth to speak. "Far too much, but it's what's needed to calm her now." Then with a painful pause that spoke much to Sophia, he went on. "She's been taking morphia, one kind or another, since France. Said it was for an injury to her back and I've no doubt that's true. I never gave it a thought, her being such a fine nurse—that I know well firsthand, as you do now, too. But lookin' back over it, she's been takin' more and more since we married. She was a little strange or moody some days, but I thought she was missin' home or some such thing."

"Why didn't you do something, Jack? I mean once you suspected it was too much?"

He pulled the back of his hand across his upper lip, wiping under his nose, then glanced down at Sophia with tears coursing down both cheeks, those on the left meandering around the scars. "I'd hurt her so when I left without so much as a word in London, then she came and found me here to give me a second chance. I was so filled with a fear she'd just up and go away one day. Afraid I didn't really deserve her after all."

Understanding now a little of what had come before and led up to the deplorable condition in which she had found Dee, Sophia took Jack's good hand and held it tight under her chin. The depths of his despair were confirmed for her by his hanging head, the poor man unable to say more. She put her hand below Jack's chin and lifted his face. He glanced down at her with the most pitiful look of relief at having someone share in the long secret. Sophia let out a deep sigh as she looked into his face, so devastated with worry. She consoled him with a kind smile and said, "Well, we must help her then, mustn't we?"

Well past midnight, a nodding Sophia was startled awake by a soft touch to her arm. She awoke to Lena standing over her with a small kerosene lamp, motioning to the door. Outside the room, the two women stood in a pool of yellow light at the end of the dark hall. Sophia just came up to Lena's chin. "Jack came looking for Geordie after he brought Dee home," Lena said. Her caramel skin glowed golden in the muted light, the long glossy ringlets of her hair shimmering as her head moved in time with her words. Sophia thought her like a vision.

"He will need his friends now more than ever I fear," Sophia replied. "Will says Geordie was always the reliable and strong one."

Lena moved the lamp to her other hand and leaned down close before continuing. "Jack told us about the morphine, not that I didn't have suspicions before. Geordie pledged to keep Jack away until she's through the worst. He'd be more hindrance than help, so I came to assist with what's to come."

"You know what to expect then?"

Lena nodded her head. "My father was a doctor in New York City. There was a frequent problem with morphine among his patients. I saw quite a lot, Mrs. Parsons."

Relieved to near rejoicing that Lena could shoulder some of this burden, she squeezed the woman's hand. "You had better call me Sophia. Or Sophie, as Deirdre insists." Lena stood in silence, assessing with keen interest this small pale woman before her. She gave a slight smile in conditional acceptance of the proffered friendship.

"There is a daybed in the room, which I found adequate for a few hour's sleep while my boy was recovering," Sophia offered. "There is also a small bedroom just above the landing. It has a full bed."

Lena straightened to her full height, the loose black curls of her unpinned hair falling past her shoulders. She smiled and said, "It will have to be tight sleeping for the next days then, since we won't be leaving Deirdre long enough to lie ourselves down anywhere else, Sophie." Their muffled conversation was interrupted by a low moan, both women turning like terriers to judge their patient's wakefulness. Lena held the lamp out to her side and led them back to the bedroom. Dee had settled again, but her jagged respirations filled the quiet room with unnerving breathy sounds.

At dawn, Sophia was asleep on the daybed while Lena dozed in a wing chair that Will had carried upstairs when Terry was convalescing. Dee had begun to toss her head with halting groans, still not fully conscious. Sophia awoke and joined Lena by the bedside, taking up her place in a spindle-back chair at the opposite side. Lena turned on the small electric lamp on the nightstand and in its harsher light, she could see a thin film of sweat forming along the sleeping woman's forehead. She went to the dry sink near the window overlooking the back garden and, wetting and wringing a small linen hand towel in the basin, she crossed back to the bed and laid it across Dee's forehead. The sleeping woman sighed two or three times, then seemed to settle.

The two women took turns throughout the early morning bathing Dee's face and head, but her agitation continued to grow. Finally, just before ten, she began waking by inches, trying to make sense of her unexpected surroundings. "Why on earth did you drag me here, Sophie? Is this your house?"

Sophia and Lena exchanged concerned looks, not sure which should speak first. Lena took the lead, determined to hide nothing. "Deirdre, we know of your troubles with morphine," she said, sure and steady, no judgment in her voice. "You would hardly be the first." Fully awake now, Dee's eyes cast about the room, panicked by Lena's flat assertion of her addiction. She gave a pleading stare to Sophia—surely Sophie!—hoping for rescue. Sophia nodded in sad agreement, overflowing with pity for her son's savior.

"Sophie found you in a wretched state, with your husband near insane not knowing what to do," Lena continued. "But you know what has to be done."

"But 'tis for my back, you know! Since the war, I've had the worst time with my back!" she whined, pleading her shabby and timeworn excuses. "It was always given me by a physician, Dr. Chesley and others."

Lena took Dee's clammy hand in her own. "Jack says you were getting it from every doctor in town and the druggists, too. He said there were tablets and powders and laudanum, some patent medicines he wasn't sure about. You've enough experience to know what's happened here."

Sophia, tears brimming, took Dee's other hand in both of hers. "We shall not leave your side, Deirdre. We shall stay with you throughout whatever is ahead."

With her arms spread to each side, too weak to resist even the gentle grips of her friends, Dee stared up at the smooth plastered ceiling. "You've no idea what you're asking!" she wailed through ferocious tears and sobs, her shoulders rising from the pillows. "I've tried! You've not a notion what you're doing to me! I can't sleep without it, not a wink." Sophia smoothed Dee's thick wet hair back from her forehead, struck cold by the terror in her friend's eyes.

"Whatever we're asking, it's not more than you can bear," Lena said. "And we'll bear what we can with you. But you need to do this for yourself and for your Jack."

Every fiber tensed with fear of what she faced, Dee collapsed back into the bed, sobbing beyond any consolation. Lena cradled her head and dabbed her face with the damp cloth, while Sophia held her hand and hummed softly. Her nightdress was soon soaked, hair hanging in stringy ringlets across the pillow, and her face was slathered with tears and mucus. She continued to choke out protests, terrified of what she knew was coming.

For Lena and Sophia, the next few days were a blur of short naps, inadequate meals, and visits from Dr. Chesley. Sophia made a few short trips to the nursery, staying just long enough to hug her children and give directions to their nurse.

These same days were torture for Dee. In the early afternoon of the first day, she was ripped from her restless sleep by stabbing cramps that doubled her over, screaming in pain, into a fetal curl. The cramps progressed all that day, constant and fierce throughout the night. Sophia kept forcing her to drink water and weak tea, but Dee shook her away after only a sip. Even those few drops were too much. By the next dawn, the cramps came accompanied by horrible diarrhea, running like water from her, and powerful vomiting that soon produced nothing but bile. The awful nightmares that had plagued her since France returned with a vengeance. Without the drugs to buffer them, her night terrors came in new weird and twisted forms. The dark parade of shadowy shapes she knew to be the men she had not been able to save pressed close in their gory spectacle. No matter how many or how awful they were, she knew her father was among them, calling to her from the horrible mass of twisted and maimed bodies. She could never quite reach him, no matter how she strained and stretched. Crying out to him in desperation over and over, she awoke to her own screams resounding off the walls and ceiling.

Sophia and Lena shouldered their responsibilities without complaint, strenuous and distressing as they were. Dee was vaguely aware of being tossed and turned several times a day as they pulled off soiled nightdresses, rolled her to change sheets, and bathed her clean. Sophia had warned the maid, who complained about the filthy laundry, that this was not to be a subject of gossip within the neighborhood. Sophia knew she was asking much of the girl and resolved to find some way to make it up to her. Later, not now. In brief snippets of conversation with Will, Sophia noted how tired he looked, smelling of liquor most of the time. He had been stopping to see Jack to offer what news he could. She could see this was taking a toll and he would need attending soon. That would have to be later, too.

Imperceptible at first, the cramps and vomiting slowed while the periods of sleep stretched longer. By Thursday afternoon, the worst of the crisis was past but Dee was very pale and weak. Sophia redoubled her efforts to get liquids and a little solid food into her. Although she could still take only small amounts, what she did swallow stayed down.

When Dr. Chesley arrived late in the afternoon for his regular evening visit, Dee was sleeping. He sat and watched her for several minutes, then felt her forehead and pulse. He motioned to the women, who joined him across the room near the door. "The worst is past and for that we can be very thankful," he said. "Does she sleep easily yet?"

The two exhausted women both shook their heads. Sophia said, "Not for very long, Doctor. She was terrified she could not sleep without the morphia when this all started."

"She's fighting some powerful demons, Dr. Chesley," Lena said, "much like Chester did from time to time." She looked down and smoothed the front of her skirt to hide the hurt she still felt at the very mention of her brother's name.

Dr. Chesley blanched a little, although the women failed to notice in their fatigue.

All three startled at a loud scream. Dee jerked up in bed, arms outstretched and eyes wide, not fully awake. The doctor hurried to her bedside and eased her back against the pillows. "You're alright, Deirdre, nothing to fear."

She turned toward the sound and focused on the doctor's face, panting heavily. As she settled back, she gave the doctor a weak smile. "'Tis only you, Dr. Chesley."

He patted the back of her hand. "Yes, it's only me." Then turning to Sophia and Lena, "Why don't you ladies step outside for a turn. It's a fine warm evening and you look in need of a good airing."

"Perhaps just the back garden," Sophia said, "such a fright we both must look, we wouldn't want to distress the neighbors." Lena smiled and placed an arm around Sophia's petite frame, pulling her close to her side as they made their way down the stairs and out into the sunshine.

Dr. Chesley pulled the spindle-back chair close to the bed. He paused and looked at Deirdre with intensity but hesitated to speak, weighing his words. She wondered what caused his usual confidence to wane. "You best just be out with it, Doctor," she said, "you and I having precious few secrets now, after all."

He leaned forward, his elbows on the side of the bed, and said, "Deirdre, you didn't need the morphia for your back, did you?"

She picked at the rumpled quilt with the fingers of both hands. "At first I did, when a heads patient at the Casualty Clearing Station in France knocked me to the floor. He threw out my back and I was in a bad way. 'Twas the only way I could continue working."

"But that should have healed in a few weeks, surely?"

"Aye, it did," she said, overcoming her hesitation and resolved to reveal all her secrets. "But it helped me sleep as well. And I was getting precious little of that as the fighting ground on." The doctor sat back in his chair, purposely studying the ceiling, and dragged a hand down along his mouth and chin. To Dee's astonishment, he looked a little vulnerable at that moment.

"The ladies tell me you've had terrible nightmares, perhaps hallucinations? Are they of your time in the war?" This sounded less a forensic question, more one of genuine personal interest.

"Aye, all the time. Strange and terrifying shadows and shapes, all moving toward me, like they're begging for help. I know it's the men we lost or sent home maimed, although I can never see their faces." She paused to gather herself. With a visible effort, forcing out her words, she murmured, "I always know my father is among them."

"You lost him at Suvla, didn't you?" he said. Dee replied with a jerky nod. "What a terrible business, Gallipoli was…" he said, trailing off into his own memories of the wretched flies and wrenching disease, windswept graves scratched into the rocky hillsides. Dr. Chesley took her hand and held it while looking at her, direct and deep. She could see his face clouding as he swallowed hard. They sat like this for what seemed minutes, perhaps it was only seconds. The doctor blinked several times to clear his vision and squeezed her hand with affection. Then he spoke almost in a whisper, but Dee heard him well enough.

"At least you don't have to see their faces, as I do."

Her expression opened with comprehension and she raised her head from the pillow, attending close as he continued in the same near-whisper. "Since so many came from here, I see their faces on the street. Brothers and fathers, cousins I suppose. Most of the time it's my imagination, I know. Less often now. For that I should be grateful." He smoothed the side of his hair and rested his hand on the back of his neck for a long moment. "I stay awake when they... the nightmares... when they come on, staring out the window at the deserted street below my rooms, smoking until daybreak."

Now her turn to comfort, she pulled his hand toward her and held it tight, smiling in sad fellowship with this man who had done so much then and did still more now. "Sure didn't I see so many poor souls with the shell shock in France, but they were beyond our help, so we shipped them on as fast as we could," she said, thinking back over those terrible months on the Somme. "Are there so many... of us?" She was relieved he did not bristle at the first-person plural.

"No telling really," he answered, back to his brisk doctor's voice. "Some who went through absolute horror, even many times over, seem unaffected. Others who were never near the trenches but might have been shelled a few times suffer hugely. Officers, noncommissioned, private soldiers—seems to make little difference. And all manifested in different ways."

"What of Jack then? He'd so much suffering and seems to have come through well enough. He sleeps like an innocent."

"Your Jack is a remarkable man, Deirdre. But he's been running hard from the war, too. You've seen the results."

"That I have. Poor Lena and Geordie likewise."

"Now Geordie King is something else again," he said. "If anyone seems less affected emotionally by the war than that man, I have yet to meet him. Every time I sent him back to hospital sick or wounded, he returned to the fighting before any of us thought it possible. He does suffer physically now, to be sure." They had both witnessed the deterioration in Geordie after his terrible struggle with pneumonia. He was on his feet and back to work with his father now, but was still very thin and haggard.

"And what of the man downstairs?" Deirdre said, glancing at the floorboards.

"Ahh, William Parsons," said the doctor. "He's a puzzle of a different sort."

"Aye, that he is, Doctor. And I fear he has demons would put all mine to shame. And not only from France, I'd wager."

Dr. Chesley smiled and nodded as he rose, not willing to say more, even to the wife of Will's oldest friend. "Well, shall I retrieve the ladies then? They must think we're plotting some mischief, long as we've been in here without them."

The late sun was spilling through the southwest window, creeping over the hardwood. Dee had asked for the curtains to be left open so the sun could warm her. She watched, her mind wandering, the bright swath of light creeping toward the bed. As Lena and Sophia returned to the room with Dr. Chesley, all three jumped at a sharp cry of pain. Dee grabbed her abdomen with both forearms and rolled to her side. They hurried to her bedside.

"Jesus, Mary, and Joseph! I thought the cramping was passed?" Dee cried out.

"It should be, Deirdre," the doctor replied, his face pinched with new concern. She was gripped by a second spasm but forced it back between gritted teeth with a low groan. "Let me palpate your abdomen, Deirdre," he said. Lena and Sophia folded back the bedclothes so the doctor could examine her. They gasped in unison at the blossom of dark red spreading across her nightdress from high between her legs.

"Get some towels and a basin of water," the doctor said to Lena, rolling his sleeves. He eased up the hem of her nightdress, revealing a larger puddle of blood soaking down into the sheets. "Has she had any vaginal bleeding these last several days?"

"Yes, yes she did," Sophia said. "In the midst of, well, all the rest we just assumed it was her monthly coming on."

Dee continued to cramp and bleed, punctuated by short bouts of fitful sleep, for the rest of the evening and into the next morning. At some point, in all the flow of blood and clots, she passed the tiny fetus, not quite the size of a cherry, that had been struggling to survive inside her these last few months.

CHAPTER THIRTY-SIX

Will

Jack fiddled with a jar of Dundee marmalade, working at the sticky lid with his good hand. Dee set down the coffee pot she carried and eased the jar from her husband. "For the love o' God, Jack Oakley, you'd think asking for help opening the marmalade wouldn't be too demeaning for you," she said, placing the jar down over his shoulder, then throwing both arms around his neck and kissing him with a loud smack on the scars of his left cheek. He thanked her with a broad smile and a pat on the hip as she broke away and headed back to the stove.

She let slip a contented sigh. They were enjoying a somewhat later than usual breakfast. With nothing scheduled at the quays until afternoon, they had taken the opportunity to linger in bed and indulge in some sweaty and rigorous lovemaking, something that had improved over the past few months, to both their surprise and delight.

"Do you think we should have a telephone put in here, Deirdre?"

Back in her chair, she said, "It might've been a comfort to me, back in your buccaneering days, but I can't say as I see much point now."

"We're owners of a proper business that's enjoying substantial success," he said with bluster. "It might save running up and and down the hill to the warehouse for every little thing. We've already one in the offices, after all."

She thought on this while chewing toast and marmalade. "Perhaps you're right. Let's see how much the telephone company wants to extort before taking a decision."

Ending her use of morphia had not solved the problem of her night terrors, of course, but Jack was attentive to her and awoke at the first signs of disturbance. Sometimes that meant holding her until she stopped shaking, other times discussing whatever she could remember. Oftentimes, he just listened while she talked of her father. The sharpness of her guilt regarding him, Jack noticed, had begun to dull a little. He had written to his mother-in-law, Eda, and her detailed and loving replies helped him understand a little of his wife's extraordinary grief.

The coffee was growing cold, so Jack took his turn making a fresh pot. As he stood at the stove, they heard a terse ring as someone jerked their doorbell. Before he could reach the front, the bell rang again. When Jack opened the door, a flushed and anxious young man with a mop of gaudy red hair protruding at unruly angles stood in the doorway. Jack recognized him, although he could not peg the name. "You're one of the clerks from Parsons, aren't you?"

The winded man panted out, "Yes sir, David Kinsella. I work in Mr. Will's office."

"Well, what brings you puffing and wheezing to my door, David Kinsella?" Jack said with an amicable smile.

"Miss Parsons asked me to fetch you to the premises as fast as you can come, if you please," David said with growing agitation. "And Miss Parsons says you might want to bring Mrs. Oakley as well."

Jack could see this was serious, since Gussie was not a woman prone to panic at trifles. "Wait here and we'll be right with you."

"I can't do that, Mr. Oakley," the younger man said, "Miss Parsons said I should go on to King Transport and fetch Mr. King as well."

Jack regarded this odd messenger with growing concern. He could see there was indeed no time to waste. "Get along then, Kinsella, and we'll make our way to the premises ourselves." Jack grabbed his coat and Deirdre's as well, striding down the hall to the kitchen. He grabbed her arm and lifted her from her chair, waving her coat, now draped over his stiff left arm, and hustled her toward the door.

"What do you think you're doing, manhandling me so, Jack Oakley? Is the bloomin' house afire?"

"We need to get down to Will's office," he said, brooking no dissent. "Something has happened. Gussie's sent for us."

"Sweet Mother of God," Dee said, shoving her arms through the sleeves of her coat and following Jack out the door, slamming it behind. The downhill walk to the waterfront was a quick one and they reached the Parsons Premises in just a few minutes. They burst through the office door and flew behind the counter, leaving the clerks and secretaries bewildered as they rushed up the stairs to Will's offices. What they found there was startling and troubling in equal measure.

Two young female assistants were cowering in the corner nearest the door, clinging to each other, afraid to move. Gussie stood outside Will's closed door, holding herself with both arms, shock and fear contorting her face. They could not make out what the shouting voice from within was saying, but Jack knew it was Will's. He rushed toward the door but Gussie shoved an arm across it, shaking her head with a wild look. "Jack, you can't go in," she said, trying with little success to keep her panicked voice low. "It's past that now. We need to call the Constabulary."

Jack pulled her arm away, but she clung to his shoulder. She was terrified, that much was obvious. Going up on tiptoe, she hissed into Jack's ear, "I don't think he slept a wink. And he's been drinking, I don't know how long or how much. Possibly all night."

"He's my oldest friend, Gussie," Jack murmured, trying to reassure her. "I'll be going in there regardless." She stepped away and nodded in nervous jerks, holding her hands over her mouth to somehow keep the fear from escaping. Jack turned the knob and stepped through the doorway while Dee slid an arm around Gussie to steady them both.

Will was in his shirtsleeves, hair uncombed and tousled, pacing between his desk and the window overlooking the harbor. At the sound of the door closing, he turned to challenge the intruder. With a glance at his crazed eyes, Jack pulled up short. Will saw him and took a long pull from the silver flask he had carried in France. This was worse than Jack had imagined.

Will was gesturing around the room with the hand that held the whisky flask, sometimes following it with his head, other times not, giving the appearance of a disjointed marionette. Drops of whisky spurted out of the narrow neck of the flask. "Come to see the disgraced scion of the great and noble House of Parsons, Oakley, my boy?" Will shouted. "Not worth the clothes I'm standing in, don't you agree, Jackie?" He spread his arms out wide so Jack could inspect him. Will took another long pull at the flask and flung it, empty now, against the shelves behind his desk. Jack watched it carom off the books and clatter to the polished wood floor, bouncing with high-pitched pings. When he turned back to Will, he saw the shiny blue-black of a Webley revolver in his hand where the flask had been just seconds before. The frayed khaki lanyard, still attached to the grip from the war, dangled loose along Will's leg and danced about each time he swung his arm.

"Oh, Jesus no, Will." There was no fear in his voice, just sadness and pity. "What are you doing with that?" He extended his arm and motioned to Will to hand it to him. Will shook off Jack's beckoning and raised the gun closer to his face, studying the barrel and frame, as if seeing it for the first time.

"It gives me great comfort, don't you know, old man," every bit the English sportsman, even in his whisky haze. He ran his left hand over the metal, rubbing the barrel between his thumb and fingers. He closed his eyes and smiled at the smooth and cool feel of the metal, the faint smell of gun oil. Jack took a step forward, then a second, while Will's eyes were closed. He extended his hand again, motioning with his fingers and nodding to Will, who stared back with a puzzled expression. Will spun and staggered back to the window, waving the gun toward the harbor. He pointed the barrel to the east, toward the open Atlantic.

"I was a bloody hero, over there," he said, pointing again and again with the gun barrel. "I was Major William Parsons, MC, of His Majesty's Newfoundlanders or Glamorgans or some-stupid-royal-fools jumping off to the slaughter."

Jack put his arm down. "I know, Will, I know well what you suffered and what I suffered and what Deirdre suffered and… too many others." Will looked back at Jack now, his face twisted in pain or anger or guilt—Jack could not tell, perhaps all three. Tears were running down his face as he gestured around the room with the pistol again. Jack could see the shiny rims of the big brass cartridges inside the black cylinder as Will swung his arm in slow arcs.

"Ahh, but yours was enough for your father, my dear Jack, more than enough!" Will stared with an odd fondness at the Webley in his hand. "But my suffering was not near good enough for Walter Parsons, having through a terrible lack of decency managed to survive the war so I could embarrass him back here."

There was nothing Jack could do but let the heartbreaking scene play out. If Will needed to shoot someone, Jack hoped he would turn the weapon on him, since Will had two children. Jack could feel anxious sweat soaking through the back of his shirt under his coat. Will staggered behind his desk and flopped down in the big chair, the pistol, still in his hand, resting on the green blotter. He looked a thousand miles away.

"We left poor Sandy in a shite grave on that fucking beach, Jack," he choked out. "And Toby…" He reached with his left hand to his cheek and lightly touched the scar.

Jack saw an opening. "Will, what happened to Toby?" Will's head snapped up, his face wide-eyed, almost unrecognizable. Then he faded again, out across the water. There was a quiet creak from the door, which neither Jack nor Will noticed.

"He wanted to jump the bags that first day on the Somme, wouldn't be left back with the ten percent that time." He stroked the scar with unbearable lightness. "We found a break in the wire and were holding it open for the men to get through, he and I." Will stopped stroking the scar now, his headed cocked to one side. "Then everything went topsy-turvy… And he was gone." Will looked down at his waistcoat and shirt, dropped the Webley on the desktop, and began to wipe at his clothing. He began lightly, like petting a cat, then harder and faster at his sleeves and shirt front. As he rubbed, his body began to shake. He looked up to Jack with wild pleading. "Get it off! Please God, get it off!"

There was a loud sob from behind and Jack turned to see Deirdre and Gussie in the doorway, the younger woman crying into an already soaked handkerchief. Dee had a look of astonishment Jack had never seen before. She walked forward, not taking her eyes from Will. Jack eased the gun from off the desk and slid it into the waistband of his trousers at the small of his back. Dee came to the desk and turned

Will in the swivel chair until he faced her, still shaking and rubbing at this clothing. She knelt on the floor and took his hands, one at a time, into hers. She looked up at him with such compassion Jack could scarcely bear to watch her.

But she knew now. Will was the only other one in the room who might know, too. "It was you at the Casualty Clearing Station, wasn't it? I remember you now." Will stared back, eyes pleading for help. He wrenched his hands from Dee's grasp and began rubbing furiously again. "You were covered in blood and... and... all manner of..." Her voice caught, daring no more detail, for both their sakes. "That was Toby, wasn't it, Will?"

He stopped rubbing but began to shake all the harder, barely able to keep upright in the chair. Jack came from the other side and steadied him with an arm on his shoulders as Deirdre said, "That's what happened to Toby, isn't it?" Will's mouth gaped, trying to let out a cry to relieve himself of his terrible burden.

There was a bustling in the outer office and Geordie stepped through the open door. He took in the scene in one sweeping, shocked glance, then turned to Kinsella. "David, b'y, first get those two hysterical girls out of here. Then get yourself up to Church Hill and fetch Mrs. Parsons here as fast as those bandy legs will carry you." He shook the young clerk by the shoulders and clapped his cheek. "You hear me, lad? Now get on with it." David bundled the two secretaries down the stairs.

Dee leaned over Will's lap and looked straight up at him, forcing him to meet her gaze. "You don't need that cane either, do you? I cut your uniform off myself and cleaned you up." He began making small jerky nods, his eyes shockingly blank. "That gash in your cheek was all there was, wasn't it?" Will kept nodding.

She looked up to Jack and said, "How long was he in hospital in England?" Jack hesitated, not able to pull up a ready answer.

Geordie said from behind her, "Nearly eight months."

"Eight months? For a cheek we stitched in France?" she blurted out in astonishment.

Jack turned to study Will, a pitiable heap in the chair. He could scarce find words after these sad revelations and whispered in a hoarse voice, "Oh sweet Jesus, Will..."

Dee glanced back to Geordie, who wiped tears with the back of his big bony hand as he said, "Why did they send you back, William? To the Glamorgans? How did you stand it?"

"You gave all you could and then some, Will," Jack whispered, holding the side of his stricken friend's head under his chin as his own tears ran onto Will's disheveled hair. "And our poor Sandy and sweet Toby would have asked no more from you."

Deirdre understood, too. She rose and stepped away, leaving him to his oldest friend and his devoted sister, who had rushed to take Dee's place on the floor at her brother's feet. Dee knew he bore terrible scars none could see, all the more painful for it. She walked, unsteady on her legs, across the room. Facing out the window to the harbor, she squeezed away a spasm of shivering, her arms wrapped tight around her. The room fell quiet, the only sounds for the next ten minutes or more soft groans from Will and sniffs from Gussie.

"Goddamn those stupid old men and their bloody, bloody war," Deirdre muttered at the windowpanes, just as Sophia rushed through the door.

CHAPTER THIRTY-SEVEN

Will

"Sophie girl, you're a fright," Dee said, kissing her friend's cheeks and studying the gaunt eyes that rendered Sophia's skin all the paler by contrast. "But I can well understand why you might be." She patted the small woman's cheek with her hand, then pushed a few stray hairs, most uncharacteristic for Sophia, behind an ear and kissed her cheek again. Jack gave Sophia's hand a squeeze and held it in his own for a moment while they exchanged careworn looks. Dee had been here many times since her days recovering in the bedroom upstairs, having grown very close to Sophia through the trying events of the last months. Often she came with Lena, other times alone.

"How's our Will then?" Jack said.

"He's up, but still in his dressing gown. Dr. Chesley has been to see him again this morning." She motioned down the hall. "He's in the dining room, having a coffee. He insisted on coming down, although I urged him to rest as the doctor advised."

Sophia led them down the hallway and through the sitting room, sliding open the pocket doors that led to the dining room. Will sat at the far end of the long cherrywood table, his chair pushed back at an angle to the rectangular top. He wore a heavy, burgundy-colored robe, his legs crossed, displaying striped green silk pajamas beneath. An untouched cup of coffee grew cold before him and there was a half-filled ashtray at his elbow. He was passing vacant glances over the morning's newspaper, not lingering to read anything in particular, a cigarette between the fingers of his right hand. Although his hair was carefully combed and brilliantined, there was a strange vacancy about him.

"Bit of a mess, yesterday, I'm afraid," he said, all nerviness and self-conscious glances.

Jack made his way, direct as an arrow, right up to Will. "There's no more to be said of that between us." He squeezed Will's arm through the lined sleeve and felt a flinch. "No more at all to be said," Jack repeated. "Do you understand me, William?"

Will gave a passing smile that looked little more than a tic, but it was enough to satisfy Jack. He retreated to a chair at Will's right.

"I'll have some fresh coffee sent in, shall I?" Sophia said and, not waiting for a reply, passed through a swinging door to the kitchen pantry.

Dee settled herself into the chair at Will's left and smiled across the corner of the table, struggling to purge any look of pity. "Aye, what's done is done, so let's only consider today and all the days yet to come." She sat erect, her back not touching the chair, and placed her folded hands in her lap for emphasis.

Will replaced the cigarette he had just stubbed out with a freshly lit one and gave a little wider smile to Deirdre. Then, addressing the tabletop in a murmur, he said, "I may need some assistance in determining just what today and tomorrow might bring, I'm afraid."

Sophia returned carrying a tray of fresh coffee and additional cups, not wanting the maid in the room just now. She poured, well aware how each of her guests took theirs, then handed around the cups to Dee and Jack before settling behind one of her own.

"That would be why we've come this morning," Dee said, "having stayed up half the night considering your... let's just say, your situation." She had Will's full attention, even more so Sophia's. Jack sat bemused over his coffee, satisfied to let his indefatigable wife carry the conversation. As Dee was about to continue, they were startled by the unmistakeable basso timbre of Walter Parsons' voice, arguing against the less resonant alto of his wife.

"You cannot barge into a home like this, Walter. Not even your own son's," Delia said with indignant insistence. "Especially not your own son's."

"I don't see why not, since it was my money paid for it." Walter stomped his way down the hall.

There was a rapid shuffling, followed by the timorous voice of their young maid, "Mr. Parsons… I don't know…it's just that… Mr. Will's not yet dressed… and I don't know that Miss Sophia's receivin'…"

"Take our coats and stand aside," Walter snapped. He entered the sitting room and called out, "William! Where the devil are you?"

Delia continued to protest his boorish behavior. "Walter, you are not hailing the fleet!"

As the four sat at the dining table in various degrees of surprise, heads cocked to the sound of the angry voice, both doors flew open with a loud scrape and in strode Walter. A sneer crossed his face as soon as he saw them, particularly his son still in his night clothes.

"What a lovely party this is!" he spat at them, "and I should have known your friends would already be here to give you sympathy."

Delia rushed to her daughter-in-law and in an attempt at a whisper heard by all, said, "Sophia, where are the children? They mustn't hear."

"At the Government House grounds with the nurse," she replied, calming the older woman. Walter arranged himself before the unlit fireplace, one fist to his hip, posed like a Regency portrait and ready to declaim to the room. The sneer never left his face as he glared at his son. The current cigarette betrayed a slight shaking in Will's hand as he avoided the eyes of his glowering father.

"You have gone too far, William. It was one thing for me to suffer private humiliation at your abominable weakness and failure of character. But to humiliate yourself and your family before half the town? Before clerks and typists within the walls of my own establishment?" Walter's face radiated heat from his roiling anger. "Is there no bottom to the depths of your shame?"

Sophia made to stand, but was thrown back by a hateful look from Walter. "And I shall not hear a word from you this time, young woman, nor will you lay your, your… feminine hand upon me again," he threatened, shaking a finger at her frightened face. Walter continued with icy deliberation, "William, you will not set foot within the Parsons Premises again. You are not to be trusted with important business matters, now that the entire staff is aware of your inexcusable callowness."

Will, still not looking at his father, spoke to the wall in a quiet and even voice. "Perhaps that would be for the best," he said, fishing with his fingers for a shred of tobacco. Sophia lost what little color was left in her and clutched her mouth. The silent room was thick with threat and fear.

"Do you have nothing to say for yourself, William?" Walter bellowed, somewhat disappointed at the lack of impact his words appeared to have on his son. Dee stroked Will's arm, his head still turned to the wall, then offered a calming look to Sophia. She placed both her hands on the table top and pushed herself up, her expression shifting to one of flashing anger. It was apparent in an instant to Walter Parsons this was a woman, unlike his wife and daughters, wholly unafraid of him. It unnerved him just enough for her to notice as she bore down.

"In all my days, I've never met a greater fool nor a bigger blowhard than you, Walter Parsons," she said, not raising her voice, adding to the menace. "Nor a more ungrateful wretch of a man."

Walter blew and puffed in shock and anger, shouting back, "I do not have to stand here and be insulted by such a... a woman as this. A drug addict at that!"

"Aye, that I was. And I hope I'm well cured now, saints be praised," she said, glancing at Sophia. "But there'll never be a cure for what ails you." Delia sank into a chair, sobbing in horror at the unspooling scene, her seamless calm evaporated into the thick air.

"You've no right to judge your son, not knowing what he went through and survived to come back to you and yours," Dee said, slicing Walter with her razor-sharp scorn. "And how ungrateful you are, compared to all those, myself among them, who carry the grief for ones we lost in your bloody war!" Approaching close, pointing a finger in the tall man's face, she added, "There's none here could begin to fathom the depth of shame you should be carrying, you wretched wicked man."

Jack rose and took his wife by the arm, an electric pulse coming off her tensed body, and set her back in a chair. He then turned to

Walter, who stood fuming in livid silence. "I believe it'd be best if you were leaving, Mr. Parsons. There's nothing left for you here." Delia's sobs cut the tense silence as the two men stared each other down. Walter was the first to break, already rattled by Deirdre's onslaught.

Grabbing his wife's wrist with a rough jerk, Walter pulled her from her chair. "You'll have nothing from me, not a penny, William! We came here to take your poor children away, so they could be brought up in a decent home, but I'll now have nothing to do with them either." Delia was in hysterics as he continued jerking her toward the door, farther and farther from the lives of her beloved grandchildren. Her husband took no notice of her agony.

Jack stepped toward Walter, close in now, and silenced him with the cold eye of an old sniper. "You'll leave now, without another word, Walter Parsons. You've done your worst and we'll hear no more of you."

With that they were gone.

Dee hurried around the table to Sophia, comforting her with an encouraging smile. "Quiet yourself, my sweet Sophie, 'til you hear why we've come." Lost in her shock and fear, Sophia clutched her friend's arm. Dee looked to Jack to continue with their purpose.

Jack struggled to shake off his encounter with Walter, a sham martinet of a father he had disliked since he was old enough to pass judgment on a man's character. He drew long deep breaths for a few moments, knowing his oldest and dearest friend was suffering in silence, waiting for Jack to come for him, as he always had at eight and at twelve and at fifteen. He walked over to Will, crouching down so he could see his face and judge his condition. He took the cigarette from Will's hand and extinguished it. With that, Will looked at him with an expression of shocking calm. "William, I need to know that you're truly hearing me. I need you to come back to me."

Will nodded his head, locking reluctant eyes with Jack's. There was comfort there, old comfort and trust, just as he had found when his father terrified him as a boy.

"Walter's gone and won't be coming back," Jack said, encouraged by the signs of Will's engagement. "You're safe with me and Deirdre and your own dear Sophie, just the four of us."

"Yes, yes, I suppose I am," Will said, looking to his left at the two women, side by side. "You've stood by me, Sophia, haven't you?" he said, with an acuteness in his voice that acknowledged her five years' heartache. With a rush of relief, Sophia lunged across the table and grabbed her husband's hand. She smiled through wide and hopeful eyes, nodding for him to continue with Jack.

"Will, there's no use carrying your burden alone anymore. You've a good and strong wife and two of the loveliest children ever put on this Earth."

"And I've seen what loyal friends you have, William Parsons, my good man being first among them," Deirdre interrupted. "I count myself among them now as well."

Sophia wrapped both her arms around Dee's waist and said, "Oh, Deirdre, of course you are. And all the dearer to me for it!"

"But Will, you must see you can't dwell in your father's shadow any longer. He'll poison all that's good in you," Jack said, "as he has long tried to do." Will studied the floor, nodding agreement with a painful awareness that wracked his whole body.

Deirdre came back around the table, seating herself next to Jack so she could speak straight to Will and Sophia. "You know our business… our new business… has done remarkable well this first year and more. Better than we'd any right to expect." Without waiting for a reply, she continued. "We've been buying products through wholesalers, but they're not able to guarantee regular supply of what we need. And they mark up their prices however they please."

Will stopped her to ask, "Sophia and I have been ecstatic at your success, Deirdre, but what has this to do with us?"

She took a deep breath. "Well, we've determined the best way to ensure the future profits of Brannigan & Oakley is to establish our own agents in the USA and in Britain. And we would be most grateful, William Parsons, if you would accept the first such position, as our London agent."

Sophia gasped, not able to contain her excitement at the thought of returning to her family and friends in England. "Oh William, can you imagine such a wonderful thing?" She grasped his hands over the tabletop. "We could be happy there, surely?" Will grew a little in his chair, seeing a way through his long-draining hopelessness in this chance at a new start.

"But there will be three conditions," Dee said, now casting earnest eyes on Will. "First, as I required of your friend Jack Oakley before I'd condescend to marry him, you must quit the drink." Sophia squeezed Will's hands and urged him with her eyes, while Dee added, "It didn't cause all your troubles, William, but the liquor has kept you from finding any way through them."

Will nodded at his wife with a hesitant smile then, turning to Dee, said, "I've used it as a crutch since the war, I realize that. God knows how much I drank in the trenches with my Welsh lads." Reaching a tentative resolution, he said, "Yes, it would be for the best. I expect it will be bloody hard though and I can't promise I won't falter."

Leaning in to slap his friend's shoulder, Jack said, "Easy as pie, once you've developed a taste for tea and malted milks. You'll see." Dee put up a hand to hush her husband's joking encouragement before it derailed the seriousness of the discussion. She also knew how hard keeping this promise would be for Will, so deep into the drink was he, after this moment of hope had passed.

"Second, you'll need to confront what's weighed upon you in such a frightful way since the war," she said, "and starting tonight. These last months, Geordie's been gathering some of the lads of a Wednesday evening up at The Blue Puttee. I've even dragged our man Jack here a few times, along with myself."

Will made to object, but Dee cut him off before he could say a word. "Now you can hush yourself and hear me out, Will Parsons. It started as just a lot of telling lies and reminiscing about the war, but some of the lads started in to talking of their troubles with too little sleep and too much drink and too quick a temper and all manner of other difficulties. Geordie says it's appearing to help many of them quite a lot, just sharing with some others who are suffering in their own ways, too. Geordie thinks it's so important to the fellas that he's made an offer to buy The Blue Puttee, if you please, to make sure the meetings continue."

Jack nodded in agreement with his wife and said, "We spoke with Rob Chesley last night as well. He's read a good deal about some of the success they've had treating shell shock in Britain. He says they made some progress up in Scotland during the war and there's been a good deal more since." Sophia, radiant with hope, squeezed Will's hands in hers, smiling and nodding as Jack continued, "The good doctor says he'll write a few of his acquaintances in England and make enquiries as to who might help once you get to London."

Will, his eyes locked on Sophia's, did not turn from his adoring and long-suffering wife when he answered, "I should appreciate his help very much, Jack."

Silence hung. Dee cleared her throat for the final condition. Not even Jack knew what this was to be.

"The third and final condition, William Parsons, is that you're not to return to St. John's as long as your father draws breath this side of the sod."

White Star Line
Ticketing Office
84, State Street, Boston

16th of March, 1924

Dear Mr. William Parsons,

Please find enclosed herein tickets for first-class one-way passage, five persons (inclusive of two children) in two adjoining cabins, Boston to Liverpool (via Cobh/Queenstown), aboard R.M.S. Celtic, *departing on Sunday, the 26th of July 1924.*

Departure will be from the White Star Line berth on the east side of Commonwealth Pier No. 5, in South Boston. Sailing will be promptly at 4:30 pm, with all visitors to be ashore not later than 3:45 pm.

We note that our liability for baggage is strictly limited, but that passengers may provide for separate insurance as they deem fit.

I remain, kindly at your service,
T. M. Lawrence
Director, Boston Offices

CHAPTER THIRTY-EIGHT

Will

They both held true to their word. Will did not set foot in the Parsons Premises again, his work in the exports section taken over by his eminently better qualified sister, Gussie, assisted by a diligent David Kinsella. Although Will had been unaware of it, David had long noted his difficulties with concentration and, having revealed this to Gussie, worked with her to cover any resulting shortfalls in management.

Will passed a month's holiday with Sophia and the children up the coast in Trinity at a lovely cottage provided by Sandy Hiscock's grandmother who owned a thriving supply business in the old fishing port. Sandy's family was of course very interested in the events of his military service and death in Gallipoli, the telling of which seemed less a burden to Will than Sophia had feared. The open and warm hospitality extended by the Hiscock clan, true baymen and women running back for generations, welcomed Will and his family from their first day. The tears they shed together worked as a tonic on them all.

There was much preparation to be done for establishing the American and British offices, so Will began work at Brannigan & Oakley as soon as they returned from Trinity. Dee had insisted on this, mumbling about "idle hands are the Devil's workshop" and other more ominous bits of Irish wisdom, most of which were indecipherable to Jack. They had also decided to keep their plans secret from all in St. John's, first and foremost for pragmatic purposes. They had no desire to spook their current suppliers until they had provided for alternative sources. They also did not want to give Walter, spiteful to the core, any opportunity to meddle with their plans for expansion.

With Will on the company payroll, Sophia's anxiety over their immediate future faded and she set about overseeing the thousand preparations needed for their move to England. Her parents were ecstatic at the news of her imminent return, with their unmet grandchildren in tow, and burdened the postal packets with letter after letter containing advice and offers of assistance. They had of course been cautioned to keep all matters private, especially within the clerical circles in England to which Will's mother maintained many family and social connections.

Poor Delia had, after a few month's absence, come to Sophia with an olive branch, desperate to see her grandchildren. Terry, long recovered from his horrible accident, flew to his grandmother's arms with a loud squeal once Sophia consented. It tore at her heart when sweet little Lizzie showed not the slightest recognition, wailing and squirming away as Delia made to gather her in her arms.

Walter carried on his usual routine, unaware in his arrogance and self-righteousness of all that was proceeding behind his back. He made his usual rounds of endless committee meetings and boozy club evenings with no regard whatever for his own wife's suffering. Having grandchildren from their older daughters, Walter could not see why any woman would be stricken with grief over the loss of two from their tainted wretch of a son.

By Christmastide, however, it was becoming more difficult to maintain the secrecy around Will and Sophia's upcoming departure, St. John's being a town that reveled in other's business. With her husband's concurrence, Sophia had resolved to tell Delia after the New Year. Although only a few blocks away, the Parsons' driver had delivered Delia curbside to Will and Sophia's home on Church Hill due to the January snowfall that had continued unabated for a full day. Sophia was upstairs in the nursery when she heard her mother-in-law arrive and Delia was still brushing snow from the hem of her skirt when she bustled down the stairs to greet her. Sophia had asked the nurse to keep the children occupied, giving her the opportunity to break the news to Delia undisturbed.

"In all my years in Newfoundland, I have never become accustomed to the vast amount of snow, I'm afraid," Delia said, breathy and red-faced from the cold. "Shall I go up to see the children?"

"I thought we would have tea in the sitting room first, if you would like," Sophia said. "There is a matter I've been wanting to discuss with you for some time."

Delia followed into the adjoining room and settled herself on the edge of a sofa, calm descending over her like a drawn window shade. The two women spoke of the children until the tray arrived. Sophia poured and they attended to their tea in comfortable silence for a few minutes, Delia appreciating the warmth, Sophia the time to collect her thoughts.

"Mother dear, I hope not to shock you with what I am about to say," Sophia said. Although still unruffled, Delia was fully attentive. "As you know, William has been working at Brannigan & Oakley since the break with his father." Delia acknowledged this by setting her teacup and saucer on the side table, a twinge of discomfort wrinkling the corners of her mouth at this reminder. Sophia knew there was substantial emotion beneath the placid features of her mother-in-law. She also knew she was about to add to her pain as she continued. "Well, the true purpose of Will agreeing to join the firm has been to establish an agent's office in London," Sophia said, mustering a businesslike facade for the coming denouement. "We are to depart for England in July. Permanently."

This unexpected news tested the very limits of Delia's long-cultivated coolness, sending her thoughts tumbling off in a jumble. Her face, however, betrayed only the smallest reaction in a series of syncopated blinks. She sat in silence as she collected herself. Picking up her cup and saucer again and, finding it an effective shield against the rush of muddled thoughts, she sipped with care. "Why my dear, you must be overjoyed at the prospect of returning to our beloved England," Delia said with complete sincerity, alighting upon the least distressing aspect of this revelation.

Sophia was not surprised by Delia's unshakeable passivity, but rather was a little bemused as she studied the expert deportment of this parsonage-raised and young-ladies'-boarding-school-trained woman, steadfast to the very soles of her feet.

"Perhaps we can go up to the children now?" Delia suggested, rising before Sophia could disagree. She was fleeing to the refuge of the nursery, that much was clear.

"Of course. They will be ecstatic to see their dear Granny. However, I must ask that you not inform your husband of this for the time being. Although William has little affection for his father now, as you are only too aware, he feels honour-bound to inform him of our future plans himself."

"Of course, my dear," Delia replied, relieved not to have to face alone what was sure to be Walter's livid reaction. With that business concluded, the two women made their way in silence to the nursery at the top of the house.

More than a week passed before Will made any mention of confronting his father with the news. Delia had visited twice since being informed herself and, now past her initial surprise, had spoken at length with Sophia of plans for the upcoming departure. Sophia had, after ten days, prodded Will on the matter. As a result, they made their way through the slush and mud of melting snow on an unseasonably warm and slate grey afternoon toward Will's childhood home. The two wives had made arrangements to ensure Walter was both at home and aware of his sons's impending visit. They had made some other arrangements, too.

Will and Sophia entered the front parlor of his parent's home, led by Delia who had greeted them at the door. Walter stood in his accustomed posing place before the mantel, the fire having just been stirred and stoked to a bright blaze. He beamed with confidence in his belief that Will was coming to beg forgiveness and plead to be readmitted to the business.

"Sit down and say your peace, William," he snapped, even before the ladies had settled themselves. "I've little time or patience for your usual foolishness."

"I would prefer to wait for Gussie," Will said. "I've asked her to join us."

With great annoyance, Walter said, "Why would Augusta need to join us? Or are you unable to speak for yourself? That would not in the least surprise me." He looped a thumb into a waistcoat pocket and rocked with determined petulance upon his heels, thinking this an excellent demonstration of his impatience.

Just a few moments later, Gussie appeared from the hallway and greeted her brother and sister-in-law before sitting on the smaller of the two sofas. Will had chosen a chair across from his father. He was immaculate in a navy worsted suit, double breasted with cuffed trousers, and a soft-collar shirt with a smartly knotted red silk tie. His hair was smooth and as glossy as his shoes. He was relaxed and confident, with none of the haggard and confused look of the last few years. Walter was, of course, oblivious to this, seeing only the son he was confident of once again dominating. Will cleared his throat and sat forward in his chair before beginning.

"Father, I felt it only proper that you hear what I am about to say directly from me. Sophia has already informed Mother, who has, I am sure with the greatest reluctance, not shared it with you at our specific request." Walter cast an angry glare at Delia, somewhat stunned at her disloyalty in not coming to him immediately. No surprise, he thought, since she was always too soft on the boy.

"Out with your news then, William, I haven't all evening to waste here."

Will glanced around the room, in full knowledge that everyone else was well informed. Everyone but Walter. "From the first, my joining Jack and Deirdre's enterprise was with a specific purpose in mind," he said.

"You mean Brannigan & Oakley?" Walter sneered, interrupting, "Such insufferable pretension from those two. And with their ill-gotten money."

"Which they amply shared with our bonded warehouse, in case you've forgotten," Will replied. "But no matter now, their latest undertaking being fully legitimate and, I am pleased to say, very successful."

"They're little better than one of those American mail-order houses," Walter muttered, well aware of the company's early success, as it was the talk of the business community.

"And highly profitable regardless," Will continued, "which has necessitated establishment of company agents. And I am to be that agent in London, commencing the first of August."

Walter was, for one of the few times in his life, dumbstruck.

"We depart for Boston the middle of July, and from there on the White Star's *Celtic* to Liverpool on the 26th."

Regaining his composure, Walter said, "And how long is this little holiday of yours in England to last before you return to St. John's?"

Will now caught and held his father's condescending stare, returning it with unalloyed pleasure as he said, "Why, we're to remain permanently, Father. I assumed you understood that."

Walter blew out his cheeks dismissively and said, "You've no idea how much it will cost to maintain a proper household in London with servants so expensive there since the war. And good luck finding a decent nurse for the children on whatever pittance your friends are allowing you."

"I believe you underestimate just how successful Brannigan & Oakley has become," Will said with a self-satisfied smile he knew would only stoke his father's rage.

From the sofa, Delia now spoke in her usual unruffled manner. "They needn't be concerned about finding a proper nurse, Walter. I shall be accompanying them to England to assist with the children's upbringing." Her calmness rendered this stunning revelation as mundane as an invitation to tea.

Walter exploded, turning on his wife and sputtering, "What in God's name are you on about, Fidelia?"

The gracious woman to whom he had been married for more than thirty years raised a hand to needlessly smooth her immaculate silvering hair, patted her daughter-in-law's hand, then turned her attention back to her blustering husband. "Walter, I have borne witness to your ill treatment of William and your disregard of his sisters for many, many years now. I have tried without success to lessen your horrid behavior. I shall bear it no longer."

Eyes bulging in a crimson face, Walter spoke from deep within his chest, rumbling, "You cannot possibly be suggesting a divorce? You are the daughter of a Church of England bishop and I am a man of importance here."

Her serenity undisturbed, Delia made the slightest dismissive wave and said, "Why of course not. You may visit me in England any time you like, but you will need to find a hotel or perhaps reciprocal accommodation at a London club." With a lovely small smile, she continued, "You will get on splendidly, Walter. I have little doubt of that. You can dine at your club or with business associates, freed from maintaining further pretenses of domesticity."

She arched one eyebrow just a touch, then continued, "And as to your other needs, this should make your arrangements so much the easier. Are you still keeping that mousy seamstress in her little flat over on the Forest Road?" Walter sensed he should protest for the sake of appearances before his children. Delia read his thoughts and waved away any words he might consider saying. Then with elegant finality, she said, "You will of course provide me a generous monthly allowance."

Walter raged about the parlor, exploring the perimeter with his pacing, all stops and starts in his confusion. He paused behind his daughter, putting a hand on her shoulder over the back of the small sofa where she had perched. "Well then, Augusta will manage the household," he said, "so you will not be missed in the least."

Not even bothering to turn to her father, Gussie said, "Not past June, I'm afraid, Father."

"Is this entire afternoon to be taken up with riddles at my expense? What are you saying, Augusta?" With an arm-waving expulsion of self-pity, Walter sat his heavy frame into an unoccupied armchair.

"I've agreed to marry David Kinsella, in June," Gussie said. Walter glanced at the faces around the room and knew he was again the last to know.

"Kinsella? Isn't he one of our clerks?" He was choking with rage and disbelief. "And he's Irish? And Catholic?"

Gussie smiled at this recognition of her fiancé and said, "Why yes he is, and a very fine clerk at that. I've of course agreed to raise our children in the Catholic church, it being of such importance to David's parents."

"And when was he to seek my permission?" Walter demanded.

"Oh, I told David not to bother with that, since you were sure to fly off at him and show him the door. I'm far beyond an age where I need your permission to marry, after all."

Walter sat bolt upright, rallying himself for a final foray. "You will not marry a clerk in my employ, Augusta. I will not allow it!"

Gussie replied, "I have no intention of continuing to run your export office once I'm married, Father, so it would seem to me you could solve your dilemma by promoting David to director. Of course, Jack and Deirdre have already offered David a place at their premises once Will departs, so no matter. Either way, I suppose." Gussie grinned at her dear brother, a clear signal to her father that she was done discussing the matter.

As they all were.

Mrs. Fidelia Parsons
announces the marriage of her daughter
Augusta Catherine
to
Mr. David P. Kinsella
on Saturday, June the sixth
Nineteen hundred and twenty-six

In the Catholic Cathedral of Saint John the Baptist
Saint John's

THE EVENING TELEGRAM
17th of May 1926

Weddings

Dawkins - King

On Friday last, Miss Lena Dawkins, daughter of the late Dr. & the late Mrs. Clarence Dawkins of New York City, was married to Mr. George A. King, of 81 Flower Hill, St. John's, son of Mr. & the late Mrs. Harold King. The wedding was a quiet one, held before a commissioner at City Hall, with a few intimate friends and the groom's immediate family in attendance. They intend a wedding trip up the coast with close friends in early June. They will reside in the bride's home at 68 Lime Street.

CHAPTER THIRTY-NINE

Deirdre

The old tree was gone, a few sharp spikes left poking through the peat where it had sheared off in a fierce storm a few years back. Deirdre struggled to spot the ragged stump until Jack placed his arm over her shoulder and pointed so she could sight along it. "There 'tis, I have it now," she said, excited to find something of which her husband had spoken with such fondness all the way up the coast.

"I still can't seem to make it out," Sophia admitted, straining on tiptoes to gain a few more inches of sight over the marshland. Will wrapped his arms low under her backside and lifted her up. She gave a squeal. "William, I say, really!" she said in insincere chastisement, not struggling in the least. He walked her over beside Dee so she could sight along Jack's arm, too. "Oh there, I do see it now," she said. "I thought it would be much closer."

"And you forced your friends to race through that muck and mire, just so you could lord it over them, Jack Oakley?" Dee said to her grinning husband, pulling down his extended arm.

"That he did, Deirdre, year in and year out," Will answered for his friend, pressing his face against his wife's bosom. Sophia gave him a quick slap on the back, then pulled herself more snuggly against him.

With the wind blowing back toward the lighthouse, they had not heard Geordie and Lena approaching over the crunchy seagrass and were startled by a sudden voice. "And I left more than a few boots out there, sucked into that mud."

Lena held her arm loosely through his, smiling broadly as the others turned to greet them. She held a hand to the scarf tying up the black ringlets of her hair, threatening to fly off in the breeze. "This must've been a wondrous place for boys," Lena said. "It's beyond my imagination, growing up a city girl."

The three men exchanged telling looks and nods, indecipherable to their wives, but conveying volumes of their shared memories of carefree summers and lost friends. The women allowed them to linger, disturbed only by the steady beat of waves and the rush of salt breeze off the water.

Their serenity was broken by a quiet, high voice from behind. "Cousin Jack, Cousin Dee, Ma says to fetch Pa and come up. Supper'll be on the table in no more than a quarter of an hour, she says to tell you all."

Jack turned and gave a long sigh, still not accustomed to the young woman his sweet Prudy had grown to become, nearly sixteen now. She was solid and steady, like her mother, but had never lost her wide cornflower eyes with the faraway look to them. Pity he could no longer swing her up, light as a feather, onto his shoulder.

"I believe Mr. Barlow was heading down to the shore when we were coming up," Geordie said. "Or we could just search for the Indian smoke signals."

"Too windy today for the smoke signals," said Prudy, without the slightest hint she was joking.

Together, they ambled down the rough grass and small wildflowers toward the steep sea cliffs where they could just make out the figure of a man gazing out to sea. Prudy split off to help her mother lay the supper. When they joined Uncle Johnny, it seemed to be all the reason he needed to refill his pipe. The men filled their lungs with the fulsome tobacco smoke, the smell of simpler times, as Johnny clouded them over with his puffing.

He was studying the *Ricky Todd*, bobbing at anchor in the bay below. With the help of Bobby Merrill, their new warehouse foreman, Jack had outfitted the old schooner with some makeshift accommodations, knocking together double bunks and dragging in mattresses. Will and Sophia had left their children at home with Delia, so the journey up the coast had been a relaxing cruise. They had only started the engines for docking and departing, otherwise coming up the entire way under sail. Deirdre and Lena and Sophia had insisted on joining the crew in borrowed trousers and fisher caps, lending their hands to the sails and at the wheel, too. Sophia in particular loved the feeling of freedom and honest fatigue out on the sea.

"She rides well at anchor," said Uncle Johnny. "She's a fine old girl, your granddad's schooner."

"That she is, Uncle," Jack said. They all joined in looking out to sea now, the steel-blue surface dotted by just a few bergs.

"Not so much ice this spring, Mr. Barlow," Will said. "Not like in years past."

Uncle Johnny let go a few thick plumes before answering. "No, not so much as you'd expect, right 'nough, Will'am."

Dee slid an arm through the crook of Uncle Johnny's elbow and hugged her face to his shoulder. "'Tis beyond kindness for you and Aunt Rosie to put up with us, Uncle Johnny, with all your work and family."

"How else would we have met our Jackie's own dear wife then, my sweet maid?" he said, surrounding her with his arm. Johnny gave her a squeeze and said, "How many months gone are you then?"

Dee, like every woman before her, placed a protecting hand on her belly without a thought, and said, "This particular Oakley ought to be here in late October, so the doctor tells me."

Johnny looked over at his nephew, who beamed back at him. He let go another cloud of smoke, a sure sign of satisfaction. "That's a fine time for a baby, Deirdre. A fine time."

They turned to the sea a last time, knowing they should return for supper or face Aunt Rosie's gentle chastisement at their tardiness. Uncle Johnny tapped his pipe against the heel of his hand, the cold ash flying off on the wind.

"No, not so much ice this year," he said. "With a little care, 'twill make for clear sailing, right enough."

HISTORICAL NOTE

I've long been fascinated by the period in and surrounding the First World War, so when deciding on a time in which to set a novel, I found myself irresistibly drawn to the Great War and its aftermath. Initially, I thought of basing the main characters in one of the Pals Battalions of Kitchener's New Army but in searching for one that fit my narrative needs, I stumbled upon the Newfoundland Regiment. I was attracted to the strong sense of place represented by Newfoundland, at the time a remote land on the edge of the British Empire, and how it contrasted starkly with the mud and noise and violence of the Western Front. Since the population of Newfoundland & Labrador was less than 250,000 at the time, everyone knew someone in the Regiment. The Newfoundland Regiment, therefore, is a real unit that fought in the War. However, I purposefully never placed Will, Jack and their pals in a specific company of the Regiment, nor do I refer to any officer above platoon-level by name. This allowed me great flexibility in putting them where I needed them to be for narrative purposes, although the Regiment did fight at Gallipoli and on the first day of the Somme. None of the characters were based on specific persons, although for authenticity I pulled most surnames from the regimental roster or St. John's city directories. And there were indeed many soldiers named King in the Regiment (42 by my count), which gave me the idea for Sergeant-Major Pilmore's great consternation. The Newfoundlanders did wear blue puttees for a short time— one of the ferries that currently runs between Nova Scotia and Newfoundland is named the *MV Blue Puttees* in commemoration. There was a real "The Blue Puttee" ice cream parlor on the street car line at Rawlins' Cross in the 1920s, although its back-end speakeasy was entirely my invention. The Newfoundlanders did have higher quality uniforms than the English Tommies and were paid much better, hence the epithet, "five-bob fuckers" we hear in the *estaminet* scene. They also started the war with Canadian Ross rifles, later turning them in for the less finicky British Lee-Enfields. And the Ross was indeed a better sniping rifle.

There were actual "bantam battalions" comprised of short men, like my fictitious 8th/1st Glamorgans. The Newfoundland Regiment was part of the 29th Division, with their garnet triangle patch, and they did have a Lancaster regiment as a sister unit, albeit in a different brigade. There were *estaminets* all through the Allied rear areas, where a soldier could always get cheap wine and an omelet.

Much to my surprise as a typical U.S. citizen woefully ignorant of Canadian history, Newfoundland has only been part of Canada since 1949. It had, like the Canadian provinces (except Quebec) its own law from 1915 to 1924, allowing the sale of only 2% alcohol beer. Nova Scotia had a similar law from 1918 to 1930. Prohibition was not just a U.S. phenomenon. Rumrunning was a regular feature of life in the Canadian maritime provinces and Newfoundland, given that the *production* and *transshipment* of whisky was never prohibited, coupled with the insatiable thirst of their neighbors to the south. The dominance of organized crime syndicates in this trade is true, it being reported in a few sources that Al Capone himself made at least one trip to the French islands of Saint Pierre and Miquelon, just to the south of Newfoundland.

The details surrounding Sean Brannigan's hasty departure from Ireland are plausible, since young men and teenage boys of his age were involved in running supplies, ammunition and messages to and from the Easter rebels in 1916. (We'll hear more of Sean's involvement in the Irish War of Independence and Civil War elsewhere in this trilogy, particularly the last volume.) That the brewery cooperage where Daniel and Frank Brannigan worked resembles a large and famous real-world brewery in Dublin should be no surprise. I learned most of what I know about brewery barrel making from a wonderful exhibit at the Guinness Storehouse in St. James Gate. That a foreman and apprentice would live in The Liberties district of Dublin is also reasonable and the streets mentioned in the book are real. There was a hospital run by the Vincentian Sisters of Charity on St. Stephen's Green, although Sister Mary Evangeline is my own invention. Having taught for some years at a Vincentian university's law school, St. John's in New York City, I couldn't resist adopting the religious order for my characters.

Women of all social classes participated in the various medical services during the War, including the Red Cross, which sponsored the women who joined the Volunteer Aid Detachments, as well as Queen Alexandra's Imperial Military Nursing Service, my character Deirdre's branch. These brave women underwent unimaginable hardships and experienced indescribable horrors, shouldering the burden of putting back together the millions of men torn apart, both physically and mentally, by the sundry instrumentalities of modern warfare. I'm very pleased I was able to tell a little of their story through the experiences of Deirdre Brannigan.

It's rather astounding that so many men were saved, given the horrendous violence and deplorable conditions they faced in the trenches. That all five of the pals in my book were either killed or wounded is not merely plausible, it's quite likely—the Newfoundland Regiment suffered over 90% casualties on the 1st of July 1916. Geordie was not an unusual example of a survivor who was, in turn, felled by disease, wounded in battle and gassed in the trenches. The American Expeditionary Force, for example, lost almost as many men to the Spanish influenza epidemic in 1918 as to enemy fire.

Before U.S. entry into the War, Americans volunteered with the Canadians, the British, the French and the Newfoundlanders—Ned Tobin of Boston was therefore based on fact, although he's fictitious (with my maternal grandmother's last name). You'll see him again as a main character in the second volume of the trilogy after he transfers to the U.S. Army in 1917 and experiences a very unique war thereafter. (We'll also discover the alluring *lycée* teacher from whom he learned his excellent French.)

There are over 90 lighthouses in Newfoundland & Labrador. Until the lights were automated in the decades after World War II, each had its own keeper. At several lights, families handed down keeper duties between fathers and sons or uncles and nephews for decades. The Barlows would not have been unique in that regard. Although the lighthouse in my book is fictitious and its location never quite specified (other than being somewhere north of Bonavista and south of Lewisporte), it is based on the beautifully preserved lighthouse and museum at Bonavista. You can see a set of signal flags and a Lloyds book there, as well as a collection of glass chimneys and a wooden pail of jeweler's rouge. I also saw plenty of icebergs from the Bonavista lighthouse in May. It would indeed be unusual, but not unheard of, to see an iceberg along the Newfoundland coast in August. And icebergs do ground themselves, founder and capsize.

The Church Lads' Brigade was a men and boys' paramilitary organization much like the Boy Scouts. It's still in existence today with an active membership. The CLB Armoury sits on Harvey Road in St. John's, uphill from the harbor and the old train station.

Cod fishing was the economic engine of Newfoundland for nearly 500 years. In a sad example of a tragedy of the commons, the United States and Canada were unable to agree on effective management to prevent overfishing, resulting in a total collapse of the Grand Banks fishery in 1992 to 1% of its historic biomass level. This threw 40,000 Newfoundlanders out of work, devastated the outports and forever altered the traditional culture of Newfoundland. (As of the publication of this novel, there is cautious optimism regarding recovery of the codfish stocks, now exceeding 10% of their historic levels.) Fishing and fish making were activities of the utmost importance in early 20th-century Newfoundland and I sought to reflect this in my book. Admittedly, it would have been unlikely to have found widespread fish making along the waterfront in St. John's, a city which by the 1920s was well urbanized, but locating that scene on the quays there fit my narrative quite well. That little Terry Parsons could be injured down on the fish stages is not completely a flight of fancy. Jack's grandfather's schooner, the *Ricky Todd*, is based on detailed models of two cod schooners, *The Blue Nose* and the *Lloyd Jack*, as well as photographs in various collections, and belowdecks on the description of the *We're Here* in Rudyard Kipling's marvelous tale of sea adventure, *Captains Courageous.* Onshore establishments that supplied the fishing fleet, stored and shipped salt fish, and conducted general mercantile activities were (and are) called "premises" in Newfoundland. You can stay at a premises converted into a hotel, the Murray Premises (mentioned in the book), in St. John's or visit the historic Ryan Premises in Bonavista. That the fishery was the ultimate source of the prosperity of both the Parsons and the Oakley families is therefore quite possible. Many fishers (the more common term in Newfoundland at the time, rather than 'fishermen') kept wooden structures, known as rooms, along the shore to process their cod catch. This is the genesis of the name of the excellent Newfoundland & Labrador provincial museum and archives, The Rooms, in St. John's.

I included a variety of written communications in the book for two reasons. First, these letters, telegrams, and other written missives were a very efficient device for moving the narrative along. I have, after all, packed what could easily have been a 600-page novel into less than 300 pages. Second, reading these forms of handwritten and slowly delivered messages plays a role in imparting a sense of the time in which these events occurred. People were accustomed to waiting for news, even of crucial events, though the waiting could be excruciating. Imagine the families awaiting casualty lists from the first day of the Somme, which did not start arriving in England for two or three weeks.

I couldn't resist booking passage for Will and his family on the White Star Line, the steamer company that sank the *Titanic* off the coast of Newfoundland, lest we forget. The *R.M.S. Celtic* was a real White Star liner that did sometimes sail from Boston. The White Star berth was at Commonwealth Pier No. 5 and the *Celtic* would often dock at Cobh, the Irish town (then known as Queenstown) that was the *Titanic's* final port of call.

Finally, a few words on the injuries of the main characters. World War I was the first large-scale conflict that saw a multi-tiered and reasonably efficient system for getting the wounded off the battlefield and into some kind of medical treatment facility. Reliable anesthesia and early methods of disinfection, although there were no antibiotics, were also major innovations. That Jack Oakley could survive multiple serious wounds to his legs, arm, face and hand is therefore not improbable. Deirdre's addiction to morphia was all too common at that time, given the loose regulation of distribution and use of narcotics. Contemporary sources recount the widespread abuse of opium in pill, liquid (laudanum) and injectable forms. I was startled by how normally many addicted persons were able to function on a day-to-day basis, very much like Deirdre Brannigan. It is, of course, not shocking to find war veterans self-medicating with drugs or, as with Will Parsons, alcohol. Although it was not fully understood at the time, the effects of repeated exposure to horrible deaths, sustained artillery barrages, and unrelenting fear and stress in the trenches led many men to succumb to what was colloquially called "shell shock." (Post-traumatic stress disorder or PTSD was not formally recognized as a psychiatric disorder until the 3rd edition of the *Diagnostic and Statistical Manual* was published in 1980, five years after the end of the Vietnam War.) In the First World War, there was a marked divide in the way officers and enlisted men who suffered from shell shock were treated. Officers were given the benefit of the doubt, gentlemen temporarily exhausted by the fighting. Enlisted private soldiers were treated much more harshly, the assumption being that they were shirkers or, more ominously, cowards. Had Will Parsons remained a corporal, his treatment would have been much worse. In the end, I was astounded that these men could endure, sometimes for years, the inhuman deprivation and danger that characterized life on the Western Front. They are a testament to the boundless resiliency of the human spirit.

ACKNOWLEDGEMENTS

No book of this length incorporating so much historical context and geographical range could have come about without assistance from many generous people. I cannot possibly name everyone who helped me along the way, some of them unknowingly. For example, one of my best discussions about St. John's was with a gentleman recently released from prison and living in a halfway house—a converted big Queen Anne mansion that served as the model for the home of Walter and Delia Parsons. That said, some people and institutions warrant special mention.

The Imperial War Museum in London should be the first stop for anyone writing about the First World War. Their newly refurbished and expanded exhibits are a unique and invaluable resource. The Royal Newfoundland Regiment Museum in St. John's is a small jewel that provided me with enormous insight into the Regiment that features so prominently in the first half of my book. In particular, the (volunteer) director, Frank Gogos—an author himself and the grandson of a RNFLD Regiment soldier—was very generous with his time and expertise, allowing my wife and me to explore the exhibits before the new museum was even opened to the public. The Rooms, the Newfoundland & Labrador provincial museum and archives, is another gem. Although their World War I exhibit was not yet open when I visited, their regular exhibits were of inestimable value in regard to life in Newfoundland and in St. John's, providing me with the nuances and texture of everyday life around the time the novel was set. In addition, the archives let me rummage through their old St. John's city directories and microfilm collection to get a feel for commercial and residential life in the city around 1920. (This is where I discovered the actual "The Blue Puttee" ice cream parlor.) Likewise, the St. John's City Museum, located in the old railroad station, is another beautiful place, filled with artifacts and interpretive displays about the city and surrounding area.

On my visit to the Bonavista Lighthouse, a beautifully preserved light with a small museum, Amanda Abbott gave a remarkable tour (we were the only ones in the light at the time) and Brenda Taylor answered any questions Amanda couldn't, as well as chatting to me about Newfoundland generally.

Derek White allowed us to nose around the small museum and archives at the Church Lads' Brigade Armoury in St. John's, a building that makes a cameo appearance in my book. Thanks also to the CLB archivist, Adrian Heffernan, for painstakingly reproducing the organization's archive files after a catastrophic fire in 1992. I hope they'll both be pleased that my five pals were all members in good standing of the CLB.

One of my favorite characters, the iceberg in Chapter 2, is thanks to a fantastic tour I took with Twillingate Adventure Tours. Our guide, Kim Young, gave me more than enough information on the composition and behavior of icebergs and the berg in the book is based on a beautiful one we saw that very day. Kim also gave a marvelous tutorial on Newfounese dialects, of which a few bits made it into the book.

The economic lifeblood of Newfoundland was, for centuries, the fishery and there is no greater expert on cod fishing and fish making than Captain Dave Boyd, owner and manager of the Prime Berth Fishery & Heritage Centre in Twillingate. He generously allowed us free rein of his collections after hours, while he was out on a boat tour. (Only in Newfoundland would you find that kind of trust.) The *Ricky Todd* schooner is based in part on a beautifully detailed model of the famously fast schooner, *The Blue Nose,* in his collection.

Many people read all or part of various drafts of this book, starting with my always-first reader, my wife, who read several subsequent iterations well beyond the first draft and served as the final copy editor. Two dear friends, Pam Kanner and my cousin Susan Schwartz, read early chapters and gave me invaluable notes. Two of my children are great readers and were willing to be brutally honest with their author father—my daughter Lindsay Driemeyer and my son, Evan Walker. My wife assembled a marvelous group of beta readers, a "virtual book club," composed of four avid readers: in Virginia, Mish Kara, Teri Collins, and Denyse Doerries; and in Scotland, a dear old friend, Kathy Phillips, who also edited my French, called me out on my British slang, provided Sergeant-Major Pilmore's phrase "lucky little sausage," and set me straight on the behavior of beech trees during autumn.

In the end, however, this book would not have been possible without the support of my wife, publicist, talent manager, marketing director and chief financial officer, Kathy. This book is dedicated to her because I wouldn't have undertaken scribbling the first word without her unwavering love and encouragement.

ABOUT THE AUTHOR

JEFFREY K. WALKER is a Midwesterner, born in what was once the Glass Container Capital of the World. A retired military officer, he served in Bosnia and Afghanistan, planned the Kosovo air campaign and ran a State Department program in Baghdad. He's been shelled, rocketed and sniped by various groups, all with bad aim. He's lived in ten states and three foreign countries, managing to get degrees from Harvard and Georgetown along the way. An attorney and professor, he taught legal history at Georgetown, law of war at William & Mary and criminal and international law while an assistant dean at St. John's. He's been a contributor on NPR and a speaker at federal judicial conferences. He dotes on his wife, with whom he lives in Virginia, and his children, who are spread across the United States. Jeffrey has never been beaten at Whack-a-Mole.

Connect with him on Twitter at @jkwalkerAuthor, on his Facebook fan page at www.facebook.com/jeffreykwalker or on his website at jeffreykwalker.com.

SUGGESTED FURTHER READING

General background: Although meant to be a work of literary criticism, Paul Fussell's *The Great War and Modern Memory* (Oxford University Press, 1975) remains perhaps the best intellectual and cultural history of the impact of the First World War yet written. The poems, novels and memoirs of the War poets and the "Lost Generation" writers, including Siegfried Sassoon, Rupert Brooke, Robert Graves, Ford Madox Ford, Ernest Hemingway, Erich Maria Remarque, and Wilfred Owen gave me the foundation for developing this story. If my characters ring at all true, it is largely due to these writers who inspired me.

Soldier's Life in the First World War: John Keegan's books, especially *The Face of Battle* (Viking, 1976), are the place to start researching any war story, in my opinion. That one of the three battles he details in *The Face of Battle* happens to be the Somme was just a bonus. Two of my best sources came from the gift shop at the Imperial War Museum in London. The most downright fun to read—and one of the more useful books for a fiction writer working in this period—is Martin Pegler's collection, *Soldiers' Songs and Slang of the Great War*

(Osprey, 2014). It includes contemporary cartoons from Punch as well as uncensored song lyrics, demonstrating that the 'F-bomb' is certainly not a new invention. Much made it into *None of Us the Same* from this delightful source. Although not a book *per se*, I bought a "Collection of Reproduced Memorabilia" from the First World War that was created by a company from Edinburgh, The Memorabilia Pack Company (www.mempackcompany.com), where you can also find packs from other periods and events for £7. These artifacts allowed me physically to handle things like a Red Cross entertainment program, a soldier's pay book, or a leave railway ticket.

Memoirs: These are by far the best way to put yourself in the minds of actual participants in the War. Anne Powell's *Women in the War Zone* (History Press, 2009) collects extracts from letters, diaries and memoirs of women who served as nurses, Volunteer Aid Detachment volunteers, ambulance drivers, and doctors. In particular, one of the excerpts from the memoir of Lesley Smith, *Four Years Out of Life* (Phillip Allan, 1931) so moved me that it provided much of my scenario for Deirdre's injury, including patient Ninety-Nine. Sydney Frost's recently published memoir, *A Blue Puttee at War* (ed. Edward Roberts, Flanker Press, 2014) is a must-read if writing about the Royal Newfoundland Regiment in particular, but also soldiers and junior officers in general. He served, like Will, as both a private soldier and an officer.

Royal Newfoundland and Other Regiments: C.W.L. Nicholson's definitive history of the Royal Newfoundland Regiment, *The Fighting Newfoundlander* (1964, McGill-Queens reprint, 2016) is the essential source for times, dates, locations and battles for the Regiment. Frank Gogos' lavishly illustrated guide to the Royal Newfoundland Regiment's battlefields, *The Royal Newfoundland Regiment in the Great War* (Flanker Press, 2015), gave me an invaluable sense of place for the trenches and battles. (I owe Frank for much more than his excellent book, as stated in the Acknowledgements.) Herbert W. McBride's *A Rifleman Went To War* (Albion Press, 2015 Kindle Edition) provided material for Jack's work as a sniper, although it was a stultifying read. He was, like Ned Tobin, an American who volunteered with the Canadians, then transferred to the American forces after the U.S. entry. Max Plowman's *A Subaltern on the Somme* (1928, Kindle edition 2013) was a good source for experiencing the War from the trenches. So was Bernard Adams' *Nothing of Importance: Eight Months at the Front with a Welsh Battalion* (1917, Kindle edition 2015), with the added advantage of being a very fresh account, written while the War was still raging. This source helped inform Will's assignment to the fictitious 1/8th Glamorgans. The near-iconic book by Martin Middlebrook, *The First Day on the Somme* (Allen Lane, 1971) was invaluable to bringing a level of gritty realism to my chapters set on the 1st of July 1916. It would, of course, be hard to tell a more compelling fictional story than the facts of that terrifying and profoundly sad day.

Newfoundland Dialect: The Newfoundland dialect—or more accurately, *dialects*—of English is a challenge to other English speakers. There are several good websites, but my primary source for Newfounese slang and word choice was Nellie Stowbridge's *The Newfoundland Tongue* (Flanker Press, 2008). I also raided her extensive bibliography for other Newfoundland material.

Other Sources: I relied upon scores of websites, on-line articles, photos, maps, and drawings, far too numerous to mention here. Let me just say, 'thanks Google'…

COMING SOON!
Book Two of the *Sweet Wine of Youth* Trilogy

TRULY ARE THE FREE

How did Boston-born Ned Tobin finish the War after leaving his comrades in the Newfoundland Regiment to join the American forces in 1917? What was the connection between Ned and Chester Dawkins, the African-American rumrunner who won the Croix de Guerre? And who was that alluring lycée teacher, Adèle Chéreaux, from whom Ned learned his excellent French? In *Truly Are the Free*, learn the fuller stories of the more intriguing supporting characters from *None of Us the Same* and meet some surprising new ones. Witness Ned Tobin's challenges after he's assigned as a white officer to an American "colored" regiment and returns with them to France, reuniting with the high school teacher who fell for him before he returned to the U.S. Share the extraordinary lengths to which Lena Dawkins goes as she struggles to keep the only home she and her brother have ever known. *Truly Are the Free* will take you from the muddy trenches of the Western Front to the teeming streets of Harlem in the Roaring '20s, from the deceptively quiet countryside of Ireland in the throes of a fight for independence to an artist's studio in avant-garde Paris. Coming Fall 2017.

Stay in touch!
Sign-up here to receive early notice of book releases:
jeffreykwalker.com

43778532R00171

Made in the USA
Middletown, DE
18 May 2017